Lifelong romance :
Zealand. Writing f[...]
endings and the en[...]
follow her at jchar[...]
Instagram.com/jch[...]

New York Times and USA TODAY bestselling author
Cathryn Fox is a wife, mom, sister, daughter, aunt and
friend. She loves dogs, sunny weather, anything chocolate
(she never says no to a brownie), pizza and red wine.
Cathryn lives in beautiful Nova Scotia with her husband,
who is convinced he can turn her into a mixed martial
arts fan. When not writing, Cathryn can be found Skyping
with her son, who lives in Seattle (could he have moved
any farther away?), shopping with her daughter in the city,
watching a big action flick with her husband, or hanging
out and laughing with friends.

If you liked *Bad Business* and *Under His Obsession*
why not try

Take Me by Caitlin Crews
Dirty Work by Regina Kyle

Discover more at millsandboon.co.uk

BAD BUSINESS

JC HARROWAY

UNDER HIS
OBSESSION

CATHRYN FOX

MILLS & BOON

First Published in Great Britain 2020
by Mills & Boon, an imprint of HarperCollins*Publishers*
1 London Bridge Street, London, SE1 9GF

Bad Business © 2020 JC Harroway

Under His Obsession © 2020 Cathryn Fox

ISBN: 978-0-263-27756-2

MIX
Paper from
responsible sources
FSC® C007454

This book is produced from independently certified FSC™ paper
to ensure responsible forest management.
For more information visit www.harpercollins.co.uk/green.

Printed and bound in Spain
by CPI, Barcelona

BAD BUSINESS

JC HARROWAY

MILLS & BOON

Katie. To meeting in NYC
and for your fabulous editorial expertise. xx

CHAPTER ONE

Grace

THERE'S A MEDICAL term for sudden, uncontrolled, simultaneous laughter and crying. But Friday night cocktails with besties is no time for sobbing over the life-changing decision I made a month ago.

I grab the jug of margarita and top up the three glasses on the table. Seeking a numbness from the doubts making my eyes burn and my voice squeaky, I raise my refilled glass, encouraging my friends Brooke and Neve to follow suit in the perfect distraction technique.

'To being single,' I say, trying not to think about the traditional wedding toasts that should have happened this weekend if I hadn't pulled the plug on my own nuptials.

'Yes, to sad singletons everywhere,' says Neve, quoting one of her favourite rom-com movies and taking a hefty swallow of the delicious drink. I too take a gulp that steals my breath, the burn of tequila drowning the rush of shame I feel about being single again by an act of deliberate self-sabotage.

'At least we're not desperate singletons,' adds Brooke, glancing around the bar and catching numerous eyes, male *and* female. She would protest that it's the fame thing, the unwanted lot of an international model and renowned London socialite, but in reality the gorgeous Lady Brooke Madden oozes that X-factor, drawing people in like kittens to catnip.

Neve groans, adjusting her new, trendy glasses, which are askew. 'Speak for yourself. I'm desperately desperate. It's all right for you.' She ruffles Brooke's blonde waif hairstyle affectionately. 'You're never short of offers.'

'Offers of sex have nothing to do with relationships.' Brooke bats away our friend's hand and lays a smooch on her cheek to soften the sting, leaving behind a perfect, blood-red lipstick kiss. 'I have at least four dick pics in my DMs. Besides, most of my offers want to shag a model so they can Tweet about it or steal my underwear and sell it on the dark web.'

Serious accountant Neve's eyes round before she collapses into a fit of margarita-induced giggles, which rapidly infect Brooke and me.

'And,' I say to Neve, 'you'd have your own share of dick pics if you stopped mooning over Oliver for five minutes.' I wince when my brain registers the words uttered.

'Argh! What am I doing?' I prop my elbows on the sticky table top, grainy with salt, and bury my hot face in my hands. 'I'm the last person who should give relationship advice. I throw away perfectly good fiancés like confetti.'

The familiar swirl of guilt grips my insides, churning up the margarita. I peer at my friends, seeking reassurance in their concerned expressions that I haven't made the biggest mistake of my life by cancelling my wedding at the eleventh hour.

'If it was perfectly good, you'd be shagging him in the honeymoon suite right about now, and Neve and I would be making one-night-stand mistakes with two of the dishiest ushers,' says Brooke, making an obscene hand gesture that under normal circumstances would make me laugh, but today I'm immune, panic rising up to choke me.

I groan, wishing for the numbing effect of the cocktails, which still have a lot of work to do. 'All those years spent in a relationship I threw away because it "just didn't feel right".'

I close my eyes.

Slam them open again.

I can't bear to see the hurt on Greg's face, which is etched on my mind, or my parents' disappointment as they handed me the list of deposits they lost to the caterers, the florist, the venue... I breathe through the pinch under my ribs, thinking of the pain and expense avoided if I'd been brave enough to break off my engagement sooner.

'It was more than not feeling right. Don't forget Greg was pretty lukewarm about getting married in the first place,' says Neve. 'You thought he'd only asked you because you'd been together so long and you were engaged for three years.'

'And you'd postponed the wedding twice,' adds Brooke. 'Yes, doctors are busy people, but it was starting to look like neither of you wanted to go through with it.'

I nod, ashamed it took me so long to wake up to my mediocre relationship, cruising along for at least the last two years with Greg.

'Look,' says Neve, 'there's nothing worse than feeling you're more committed to a relationship than your man. We want them crazy for us, desperate to put a ring on it…not lukewarm.'

Longing for my sister, Bryony, engulfs me, as it does every time I compare my life with what hers might have been without her health limitations. Despite her being five years younger, I could always rely on her advice, wise beyond her years, and her fearless thirst for adventure. If she'd had the chance, she'd have squeezed life dry, not settled for such self-restraint.

My friends' arms encircle me, tugging me into a comforting embrace I've enjoyed since the three of us became friends at university, but I feel like a fraud. My situation self-inflicted.

I stick a grin on my face. 'Right, come on, you

two—you're supposed to be distracting me, not indulging me to wallow.'

Neve and Brooke sit up straight wearing matching innocent expressions.

'So, the big question—' I focus on the future '—do I go to Fiji anyway…alone?' Part of me thinks going on my honeymoon alone is insane, the act of a woman desperate to prove she made the right decision, which I did. The right decision in the long run, even though it went against my deeply ingrained need to please. But I'm a capable professional. Independent. I don't need a man to visit a place on my wish list. And Fiji was *my* dream, not Greg's—in fact he'd argued we didn't really need a honeymoon given the hassle of taking annual leave from work at the same time.

'Go,' says Brooke. 'I'd offer to tag along, but I'm working in Italy that week,' she adds, refilling our glasses for the umpteenth time. The tequila begins to work its magic. I might soon struggle to remember if I even asked my friends' advice, let alone recall their sage wisdom.

I shrug, picking at a hangnail on my thumb. 'It *would* mean I could pay Greg back his share given we didn't have holiday cancellation insurance.'

'I can't come either,' says Neve, 'but Brooke's right. Go—it's your dream holiday. You deserve a break after the past few months.' She offers a sympathetic smile, referring to the patient I lost on my watch—every anaesthetist's worst nightmare. And the devastating incident had somehow acted as a catalyst for re-evaluating my life, awoken all my latent feelings over my sister's death three years ago, the outcome the realisation I was going through the motions with my fiancé.

I pull the sleeves of my sweater down over my frigid hands. There's something equally brave and terrifying about the idea of going to Fiji alone.

Neve sees the turn of my thoughts, probably in the queasy expression on my face, and says, 'They've offered you a refund if you teach the staff first aid. Think of it as work if you need convincing. Recharge your batteries in paradise and come home ready for a fresh start.'

My nod feels wooden, as if my head is a bowling ball. What does a fresh start look like? Just because I ended it, doesn't mean I won't see my fiancé at the hospital, likely every day... But one less debt equals one less shard of guilt slicing through me.

'Yeah, you haven't had a holiday for two years,' chips in Brooke, pushing hair back from my face in a gesture too tender for my bruised psyche.

'I've had exams...my promotion,' I say, defensive. 'You know my job requires unpredictably long hours...' I deflate with a sigh, because my friends are right. I have zero work-life balance. All I've known in recent years is work and study and compromise, the toll itself a kind of tribute to Bryony, who was the very reason I'd wanted to study medicine in the first place. But in the process, I neglected the one area of my life that suddenly seems so important. My relationship.

Neve nods. 'It's okay to have some you time, to plot a new direction.' Her sharp sympathetic stare slices into me. She's referring to how I haven't quite been the same since losing Mr Burgess, the professional turmoil unleashing a personal course correction with Greg as the first casualty. Not that he'd put up a huge fight, leaving me to wonder just how long our marriage would have lasted before one of us was brave enough to call it quits.

'Perhaps you're right.' As I speak the words, allow a chink to pierce my failsafe façade, seeds of possibility sprout for the first time in months...perhaps even years.

I've been surviving, not living—no way at all to honour my sister, who had so much passion for a life that was taken too soon.

'Of course we're right.' Brooke high-fives Neve as if together they're quoting the wisdom of the ancients. 'And while you're in paradise, it wouldn't hurt you to live a little, if you know what I mean?' Brooke says, waggling her eyebrows suggestively, correcting our veer into serious territory. 'There are plenty of benefits to a beach holiday.'

'Live a little?' I roll my eyes at her as she preens like a diva at her wonderful idea. 'You knit for pleasure and haven't dated in six months. Do any of us know how to let our hair down?' If I'm going down, I'm taking these two along.

Neve is the first to snigger at the severity of my tone. We crack up in unison as only the merrily inebriated can. Because all of our love lives are unmitigated disasters.

'We're all as bad as each other, aren't we?' Neve picks at the remnants of salt on the rim of her glass, sucking it from the pad of her thumb. 'I think my vagina has healed over.'

Brooke snorts, her grimace telling us she's sucked margarita into her nose. 'What about your extensive toy collection—they'll keep you patent until you abandon Oliver and give some other guy a chance.'

Neve's cheeks flame as she elbows Brooke and glances at the nearby patrons to see who might have overheard. 'I told you about those in confidence, Big Mouth.'

Brooke slings her arm around Neve's shoulders and smacks a kiss on her forehead. 'What we *all* need, is a pact.'

'We're not twelve,' I say, rolling my eyes. Most hare-brained ideas come from Brooke, who looks ice-cool and classy but has a dark and devious mind.

'No, but this is the first time we've all been single together. You met Greg at uni. Your first boyfriend. The only guy you've ever slept with,' says Brooke, one index finger levelled on me with accusation, as if never playing the field, never having a one-night regret or a string of dating disasters is some sort of crime against womanhood.

'What kind of pact?' Neve chews her lip, the accountant in her no doubt as reluctant as the anaesthetist in me to enter into any agreement with our stunning, extroverted friend.

'Nothing kinky.' Brooke laughs. 'More of a pleasure pact, a seize-the-moment kind of thing.' She rests her elbows on the table, her wince indicating she's encountered the stickiness coating the veneer. 'Grace goes to Fiji and, who knows, perhaps embarks on a passionate holiday fling that helps her to realise there are millions of penises in the world.'

'Hey, I know that—I'm a doctor, I've seen hundreds of penises.' My voice rises with indignation at the very moment the conversations around us lull. Several heads turn in our direction and we erupt into hysterical laughter.

When we sober Neve casts me a pointed look. 'Brooke does have a point, sweetie. Even I've experienced more than one penis.' She drops her voice on the last word as if she's speaking within earshot of a convention of tax lawyers.

I bristle, chugging a mouthful of margarita. 'Have you both forgotten I'll be going to a honeymoon destination, not a singles' resort? My chances of penis are non-existent.' But now I've given myself permission to embrace the idea of some me time in Fiji, a weight slides from my shoulders like the swish of gossamer.

'There's bound to be at least one cute waiter or hunky diving instructor. Improvise,' says Brooke.

I exhale the anticipatory flutters in my chest and point an accusatory finger Neve's way. 'I'll scope out available penis in Fiji if you finally confess your feelings to Oliver.' Sober I might have said the same thing—Neve has loved Oliver, her best friend outside of Brooke and me, since uni—I simply might have said it with a little more tact and sympathy.

'I'm sure he's fully aware of her feelings,' says Brooke. 'Why else would he demand she be at his beck and call?' Brooke eyes our rather shy friend with compassion and a small smile. 'But Grace is right. Perhaps it is time to tell him…'

'Oh, please, not this again,' says Neve, flashing her rarely seen irritation.

'So where is he taking you this time?' I ask.

'To his cousin's wedding… In the Maldives,' answers Brooke before Neve can open her mouth, which is pinched with defensiveness.

'Ooh. Romantic.'

'Hey,' says Neve, her neck flushed. 'Just because he needs a plus one doesn't mean anything. And without meeting you two for cocktails and occasionally accompanying Olly somewhere I'd have zero social life. Have you met my work colleagues…? Forensic accounting is hardly conducive to after-work drinks or letting your hair down.'

Brooke grins. 'Well, if you're not going to confess your lust to Oliver, I'm signing you up to my dating app so you can choose from your own collection of dick pics.'

The horror on Neve's face causes another fit of raucous laughter. Then she lifts her chin, as if accepting the challenge. 'And what about you?' She narrows her eyes at Brooke over the rim of her glass.

'Oh, no.' Brooke shakes her head, the signature pixie cut she hates but everyone else adores ruffling. 'This pact was *my* idea.'

'Yes, it was.' I level a no-nonsense finger at Brooke. 'But you just said you're off to Italy soon… I'm not the only one ripe for a holiday fling.'

Neve offers an exaggerated nod of solidarity. 'Yes—a perfect opportunity to get back in the saddle.'

Brooke lifts her chin, offering us her aristocratic profile. 'That's different. I'll be working.'

'So? Will you be taking that delicious bodyguard of yours?' I ask, my lips twitching now the tables have turned on Brooke.

Neve flicks me a knowing look. 'Yes, what's his name…? Nate? Rick?'

'Do you mean Nick?' says Brooke in a bored tone. But she can't hide the blush in her cheeks or the way her eyes light up at the mention of the big brooding bodyguard's name.

Neve and I nod. We've met the silent, intimidating Nick. We've seen the way Brooke looks at him when she thinks no one is looking.

'Anyway, he's not a bodyguard, he's a fixer stroke driver stroke personal protection expert—'

'Stroke astounding piece of man meat packing a

trouser leg full of knitting antidote.' Neve guffaws behind her hand, the quiet, serious accountant well and truly shelved for the night.

Brooke pokes out her tongue. 'I *like* knitting—it's mindful. Relaxing. I can take it when I travel. And for your information, Nick is the soul of professional detachment. I'm lucky to get a hello out of him.'

'Well, take your pick,' I say, refusing to go down alone, while a warm glow of excitement builds in my belly—I'm going to do this. Go on my holiday and embrace fun and possibility and a fresh start. Make Bryony and my friends proud. 'It's one of the dick-pic losers or an Italian fling with Nick.'

Brooke sighs an exaggerated huff, flashing her million-dollar pout. 'Fine. So it's on. A holiday fling apiece so we can avoid Neve's sad singletons' club.'

Neve shrugs and I avoid comment with a swallow of my drink.

'Okay,' says Brooke, finding her stride. 'So, to the terms of this pact.' She holds up one finger. 'Pictorial evidence of the holiday hook-up is required as proof, even if you have to take it while he's asleep or in the shower.' She adds a second finger. 'And the next cocktail night will be a full debriefing session so come expecting to share all the juicy details.'

'Cheers to that.' Neve drains the dregs from the jug of margarita, sloshing them unevenly into the three glasses.

We raise a toast, clinking our drinks together. 'To our pleasure pact,' purrs Brooke in her best Lady Madden voice.

Giggling and more drinking ensue.

CHAPTER TWO

Ryan

I POINT THE paddleboard towards the shore, my paddle slicing through the pristine clear water of the South Pacific Ocean, which covers the live coral reefs below. The early evening sun warms my back as I study the Lailai resort, my newest acquisition, from my unique vantage with a keen business eye.

Twenty secluded wood and straw bungalows, or bures as the Fijians call them, line one side of the turquoise lagoon, which is a protected marine sanctuary. The palm-fringed beach stretches in a graceful crescent to the opposite side, where a row of overwater bungalows jut out into the ocean and link to the shore via individual wooden walkways.

Currently an adults-only honeymoon destination, it's paradise. A perfect Dempsey singles' resort in the making to add to my worldwide collection.

As soon as I can dispense with the nauseating couples cluttering up the place...

I paddle away from my own over-water bungalow, the best the resort boasts, with a sigh. Why then am I forcing myself through the motions? Attempting to relax on my 'working holiday' when perhaps I should head back to London at the earliest opportunity?

I paddle harder, trying to outrun my restlessness with vigorous strokes.

The expected satisfaction at my expanding empire never arrives, my gut knotted with the looming sense of emotional upheaval I've spent my entire adult life dodging.

The frailty of the only person alive who's always cared about me: my grandmother.

I grit my teeth, telling myself that my business success ensures her comfort and the best healthcare money can buy. That's why I'm here. Business. I know from bitter experience that indulging in feelings and believing in sentiment in the past ended in decisions taken out of my control and left me alone, cold and homeless.

I stab at the water with the paddle, the break in rhythm wobbling the board under my feet. The daily check-in phone calls to the nursing home are bound to leave me edgy. Apart from the comfort of my grandmother's voice, which is increasingly frail, the calls usually reveal sobering news. But I can't think about that now; there's work to do.

Perhaps, at thirty-six, I'm bored of the lucrative singles' resorts business, my constant travelling losing its lustre. Perhaps it's time to diversify, to buy an airline or something…

Yes—that's it. I'm off-kilter for a new challenge. Nothing to do with the lure of home.

I snort, the hairs at my nape prickling to attention. Where is home? I have houses all over the world—million-dollar piles of bricks and mortar, a waste of money for the amount of time I spend in them.

In the shallows, I jump from the board, scoop it up and head on dragging feet towards the hut housing the resort's water-sports equipment. Not even the excuse of temporarily filling in for the island's paddleboard instructor, Pita, who's been called back to the main island for a family emergency, is enough of a distraction. I glance back, drawn to the endless ocean view as if I'll find solace on the horizon.

Movement catches attention. The doctor. My stare holds fast, eyes burning with curiosity.

Of course I'm interested in the resort's only solitary guest, her presence, her whole demeanour intriguing. Since she arrived forty-eight hours ago, she's kept to herself, rarely emerging from her bure before late afternoon and then only to walk along the shore looking wistful, just as she's doing now. But even wistful she's striking, stirring something in me, an attraction that makes me forget my troubles and the weird clawing restlessness. Something that makes me wonder what secrets she's pondering as she walks.

And that inquisitiveness, more than the stirring

of a sexual itch, is so rare, so enthralling I hardly recognise the feeling.

I watch her slow meander along the shoreline with growing fascination, my focus honed on her body's movements and her serene but pensive expression. She's dressed in the complimentary sarong the resort supplies to each guest on arrival and a vibrant red bikini top, her curves perfectly showcased by the revealing outfit.

No wonder I'm drawn.

The paddleboard grows heavy under my arm, but I can't move away. Why wasn't I more curious when I met with my resort manager, Taito, for a rundown of the current guest situation? Because all I was thinking was how quickly I could add my signature singles-only stamp of sexy hedonistic luxury to this idyllic resort and move on to the next acquisition, the next destination, make the next million…

Perhaps my curiosity in the doctor is professional. After all, she's here to teach my staff first aid. But why? Surely she could have found a working holiday gig somewhere less isolated. Somewhere full of singletons…

A slug of disappointment douses me as if I've been plunged into iced water instead of the warm tropical ocean—perhaps she isn't single.

The itch of attraction turns to discomfort, sliding over my skin like sunburn, which makes no sense. What do I care if she's attached? I don't even know her name.

Plenty more fish in the sea…

But I can't stop wondering if one genuine smile from this enigmatic woman, or perhaps hearing her laugh, would reset my balance. The next chance I get, I'll introduce myself to the good doctor—time to cast off this irritating fixation. I'm in the singletons business for good reason. I have no interest whatsoever in leaving the bachelor club, where I'm a lifelong member.

I catch sight of a slender leg peeking from the sarong as she walks. My groin tightens, a reminder that I've been here a week without any female company.

Hmm, perhaps a one-night stand. That would chase away the gnawing in the pit of my stomach. Help me to refocus on working through the changes to Lailai. I press my lips together, torn.

Yes, she's hitting all the right attractiveness buttons, but what are her philosophies on casual sex? She's here alone. At a honeymoon resort. That's answer enough.

I stride up the beach to the equipment hut, shaking off the moment's regret like the flick of sand from my feet. Inside I stack the paddleboard in the rack against one wall and stow the paddle. I snag my T-shirt from Pita's battered deckchair and duck outside to collect the handwritten sign advertising the recreations available on the island, which is propped against a pile of fallen coconuts.

My mouth waters, anticipating the ice-cold beer

I know is waiting for me back at my bure, but the idea of returning there alone with this strange weight dragging me down holds no appeal. I clench my jaw, fighting frustration. I'm always alone. It's never bothered me before. A shower, a bite to eat at the resort's restaurant and a chat with friendly local, Charlie, the bar manager, will shake me out of my strange mood.

'Am I too late to book a lesson for tomorrow?'

I turn towards the voice, a slug of satisfaction heating my blood at the sight of the doctor close up. I was right—she's stunning and I'm doubly intrigued, my thumping pulse proof, even as I groan in my head at the bittersweet timing.

She pushes her sunglasses from her exquisite heart-shaped face onto her head and looks up at me expectantly. For a moment, I free-fall into her eyes; they're startling, sharp, piercing, as if she instantly sees all the crappy dark places in my fucked-up soul but also open, somehow kind, as if she's about to offer the cure-all pill.

It must be a doctor thing. Perhaps she looks at everyone that way, figuring how to fix their broken parts…

But unless she can wind back the years and fix my grandmother, I have no need for her professionally.

'No, not at all,' I say with a smile that feels too wide. Too self-congratulatory. The lack of a ring on that tell-tale finger gives my libido the all-clear to get ideas.

Snapping out of the hold she's taken by catching me off guard, I stretch out my hand. 'My name's Ryan, by the way.' I train my eyes from her spectacular body, employing willpower I haven't used in a long time; she's that tempting. Rocking body, thick, glossy hair. Intelligent dark brown eyes.

Her handshake is firm and warm and too brief, because, touching her, I'm acutely aware I'm a man who hasn't had sex in a fortnight wearing only a pair of wet, clinging board shorts.

'You're Irish?' she says, pushing her long mahogany hair back over her shoulders as she gives me the kind of once-over I usually relish from a beautiful woman, because it indicates they're interested in more than introductions. 'I am, and you're English?'

'Yes.' She laughs. 'We're both a long way from home.'

I was right about her laugh—a delightful sound that swells my chest as if I'm the most hilarious comic in the world. I knew an introduction would recalibrate my mood.

'That we are.' Am I actually putting an extra lilt to the accent, trying to impress her with a touch of the charming Irish brogue? What the hell…?

Her smile curls up and she does this thing where she looks from under her lashes as if she's suppressing amusement—sexy as hell… The ends of her hair brush her freckled shoulders. I have the urge to trace those fascinating blemishes on her soft-looking sun-kissed skin until my head is full of pleasure and nothing else. Not the turmoil in me or the daily dose of worrying news from London.

'Oh,' she gasps, stepping closer. 'You've cut your foot.'

I look down to see a thin trail of blood seep from a graze on my ankle. 'It's fine—I must have caught it on the coral. It's razor sharp.'

A small pinch of concern surrounds her beautiful eyes. 'Would you like me to have a look? I have a first-aid kit in my room—I can go grab it.'

I shake my head, which feels light, spaced out, at her attention. 'It's fine.' I know it's just a professional thing—doctors are probably never off duty—but warmth spills through my veins, almost too hot to bear.

'You sure?' she asks, and I nod, as unsettled now as I am intrigued.

'If my leg starts to fall off, I'll find you,' I say. 'So, back to this lesson.'

She looks away from my foot to the chalkboard advertising the have-a-go activities available to guests. Now would be a good time to tell her I'm just filling in as instructor and expecting Pita to return tomorrow. But I stay silent. I'm a private person. My resorts often attract negative press—the last thing I need is news I've purchased Lailai leaking before the last honeymooners have departed. They won't take well to discovering their idyllic hideaway will soon be full of people looking for depraved, no-strings fun in paradise... Nor do I want the renovations disrupted by some pap sniffing out a story of Dempsey-style debauchery. The press love to paint me as a notorious commitment-phobic billionaire, a playboy of pleasure who sells sex in tropical locations, slamming my resorts as hook-up clubs. But if the shoe fits… The wealthy and single need somewhere to mingle, just like the honeymooners. So if it's legal and consensual, anything goes at a Dempsey resort.

Somehow I don't think the serious doc here would approve, and, beyond her professional credentials and the fact she rocks a bikini like a Greek goddess and rivals the sun in delivering that feel-good factor, I don't know this woman.

I grab a piece of chalk. 'A lesson for one?' I'm fishing. 'You're here alone, right?'

She bristles, her smile slipping, eyes dulling with something close to embarrassment even as she lifts her chin. 'Yes, I am. Is that a problem? Don't you do lessons for one?'

Whoa… I've touched a nerve. I'd better not probe any deeper, despite being more intrigued than ever. 'Of course we do. One-on-one it is.' Thoughts of her and I alone, every possible distraction, flash through my head, revisiting the possibility of a one-night stand. 'My favourite kind of lesson.'

I don't imagine the way her breathing speeds up or those lush lips part. Dragging my mind from all the ways I'd like to see her excited and breathless, I wipe down the board with the side of my fist, erasing today's bookings, and look up. 'What time would you like? I recommend a dawn paddle if you're an early bird—sun's up around six-thirty and the sun-rise is amazing from the water.'

'Um…' She hesitates, the small wrinkle of her nose telling me she's not a morning person but doesn't want to say so.

'Do you have a slot around nine?' She shrugs. 'You know… I'm supposed to be on holiday.'

'Supposed to be…?' Interesting… I shouldn't care that she might be struggling to embrace the island vibe. All she needs from me is a lesson in paddle-boarding. But is that all she wants…? Could we be on the same page, both looking for a temporary distrac-tion involving those shapely thighs wrapped around my waist or draped over my shoulders…?

I clear my throat. 'Of course. You probably work pretty crazy hours at the hospital—nine it is.' I shelve my curiosity at her revealing statement, desperately trying not to picture her asleep, her gorgeous, naked body relaxed…

'What name shall I write?' I ask. 'Will Doc do…?'

She flushes, perhaps embarrassed that she's for-gotten the basics of introductions. Do I make her nervous? I want to make her other things—turned on, greedy, demanding.

'Grace. Grace Metcalf.' She swishes her toes through the sand as she looks down, and I'm gifted with another flash of thigh through the opening of her sarong.

'That's a beautiful name.'

'Thanks. I'm trying to outgrow Gracie... That's what my sister used to call me when we were young...' She shrugs, all sexy awkwardness that leaves me wondering how often she flirts, because I'm getting mixed signals.

A groan echoes inside my head. Oh, Grace, Grace, Grace... Why do you have to be so exquisite? So tempting? So...unexpected?

'Have you done it before?' I write her name on the chalkboard—the laid-back, low-tech booking system on the island, where most things are done on island time—and try not to notice that she's stepped closer, so close I detect her floral scent and something purely feminine on the warm air.

'Paddleboarding?' Her cheeks darken as if we share the same dark delightful thoughts my open-ended question has unleashed.

No, fucked a stranger on a tropical island.

'Yes.' I swallow hard, tamping down the fierce surge of heat in my groin. 'Are you a beginner?'

'Oh...yes. I...mean no,' she says. 'I mean I am a beginner. I haven't done it before. But I've always wanted to try.'

I can't help my wide grin. She's enchanting—sexy as sin but a little reticent, flustered. 'Well, you're in safe hands, and you're all booked in for nine a.m.'

Shit, I'm in trouble; I had this week planned out, female-distraction-free, but that was before I met Grace. I could swap one distraction for another...

No... Walk away. Stick to paddleboarding.

But she's still here, still tracing her toes through the sand, still looking up at me with those intensely penetrating eyes, which seem to be saying things she's holding back from speaking aloud.

'Do you want to go grab a drink at the bar? I've finished for the day.' The words are out before I know what I'm doing. Curiosity, even mutual attraction, a bit of banter is one thing, but drinks with a woman who looks as if she'd run a mile from one of my debauched singles resorts and gets tongue-tied talking to a member of the opposite sex is another thing entirely. A crazy thing. A thing destined to end in trouble...

But would she run? So flirting doesn't come naturally, or she's rusty. Doesn't mean she isn't interested. I know that look on her face—she's eye-fucking me, such a contrast I'm way beyond my usual levels of fascinated, although I don't usually work this hard to unearth a woman's interest.

'I... Um...' She bites her full lower lip, her sexy eyes swooping the length of my body. My blood heats; I'm certain I've lucked out. She's going to say yes, drag me back to her bungalow and be exactly what the doctor ordered for my sexual-frustration problems.

The damp fabric of my shorts clings tighter to my eager cock.

A warm gust of wind chooses that moment to blow over the chalkboard, which I failed to jam deep enough into the sand. We reach for it together. Our hands collide, fingers brushing.

She steps back, her colour high as if I've touched her all the ways I want to, not simply accidentally brushed her hand. But that one touch is telling. Need is a roar through my head, every instinct driving my body towards hers proof that we'd be good together. But I hold my ground—Grace needs to make up her mind. Embrace the situation. Declare her interest. Take that mental leap I can see holding her back.

I secure the board, pretending I didn't notice the skittish way she snatched her hand away from mine as if I have cattle prods for fingers. It's okay if she wants to ignore our mutual attraction. It's probably for the best even though hunger settles in the pit of my stomach like a rock.

When I look up, she's no longer relaxed, her posture more rigid, arms clasped across her waist.

'I should let you finish packing up…' she says in lieu of a direct *no* to my invitation of a drink.

I shrug, hiding my disappointment, my imagination rampant to know how her letting go would multiply her potent magnetism.

'But…thanks for the offer,' she says, stepping away and putting another slice of beach between us so the earlier hollowness inside me re-expands.

Looks like I'll never know.

'No problem.' But, for the first time in my life, I regret inviting her for a drink, because I'd settle for just her company over spending the rest of the week watching and wondering from a distance. 'I just figured as we're the only two sad, lonely people here, we could get to know each other.'

Who am I trying to convince? Her or myself? I don't normally give a shit about being alone. I've been practically alone most of my life. It must be a reaction to the near constant state of worry over Grandma's health. Every time I pick up my phone, I'm almost too scared to look at the screen in case what I see changes my life in the most definitive and devastating way.

'I'm fine being here by myself,' she says, her eyes glowing bright with a hint of challenge that boosts my desire to unearth the secrets of Grace Metcalf. To see the side of her shielded behind the straight back and the stiff shoulders that she only seems to allow out to play when she smiles or laughs.

I hold up my hands in supplication. 'Hey, I didn't mean anything by that—there's nothing wrong with being single. I personally wouldn't be any other way. But a guy needs to save face after a beautiful woman turns him down.' I grin, aiming for levity.

She looks away, turning her face to the sea, a frown pinching her forehead. 'Sorry—I… Perhaps I've been too isolated since I arrived. You're probably better off without my company.'

It's only what I've just told myself, so why does it leave me cold? Why am I pushing, rather than walking away?

She seems to shake herself, new resolve glittering

in her extraordinary eyes. 'I should definitely try out the paddleboarding.'

'There's that word again—*should*. But I agree. You should. There's no feeling like it.' With clothes on. 'So, tomorrow at nine, and if you change your mind about the drink, no strings,' I add to reassure her I'm not a creep, even though my thoughts are far from friendly. 'I'm in that bure at the end there.' I point to the most luxurious of the accommodations jutting out into the lagoon and connected to the sand by a wooden walkway.

Grace raises her eyebrows, impressed. Her mouth opens and then closes again. I can practically hear her mind working—how is a lowly paddleboard instructor staying in the resort's most exclusive suite and not bunked up with the other staff? But for some reason she doesn't ask. If I were a gentleman I'd explain, but I clamp my jaw shut. We might be trapped here in paradise, but it seems we're not going to know each other, even as friends.

'See you in the morning,' I say and saunter away. My back muscles twitch with unfathomable tension. My toes scrunch the sand, each step full of resolve, as if, left to their own accord, my feet would turn tail and return to the enigmatic doctor. What the hell is wrong with me and what will it take to feel like myself again?

One last look?

I stop. Turn.

She's where I left her, staring at my retreat.

Her eyes lock with mine, widen, the only move she makes.

My restlessness returns with a vengeance. I continue towards my bure, pick up the pace. The attraction is irrelevant. Now I know the doc and I aren't going to be on intimate terms, I can refocus on work as a distraction. It's never let me down in the past.

But as I round the bungalow and catch sight of the sunset strike the water, regret clings like the salt drying on my skin. These solitary moments are the only downside to a life of determined bachelorhood. My *nothing serious* rule stops me inviting a date when I travel—wouldn't want to give the wrong impression. And, in my experience, no matter how openly I declare my stance on relationships, some women refuse to accept they can't change me, magically turn me into marriage material.

But not the guarded doc. She couldn't get away quick enough. It's a small island. The newly-weds aren't going to be very good company. It makes sense for us to get to know each other…

My dick pulses at that remembered slice of toned thigh, the curve of her breast above the cup of the shocking red bikini, the frangipani flower in that beautiful hair…

Yeah, I want to get to know her, all right.

I head to my bungalow's private pool area where there's also a Jacuzzi and an outdoor shower. There's something magical about being so close to nature, to swimming at dusk, showering outdoors, the water on my back as I watch the last rays of sun kiss the horizon.

I snort; I'll be quoting Shakespeare next. But already I calculate my investment in this place tripling.

An image of Grace naked in the pool, her hair floating in the water, her nipples breaking the surface, drags my thoughts from work… A frustrated groan breaks free. I need to get laid.

I toss my T-shirt onto a lounger and turn on the shower. I shove my shorts down my legs, kicking the fabric aside and reaching for the body wash.

I squirt out a measure, lather up and perform my washing routine on autopilot, my mind free to wander back to other business. Bad business. Grace.

She certainly eyed me like a woman interested in the contents of my shorts, despite her rejection. I can still feel her stare sliding down the length of my body, the subtle rise and fall of her chest on a tiny sigh, almost of longing, the way her spangled eyes clung to mine. Searching…

As I rinse the sand from my hair, my body energises in anticipation of the morning's lesson. Hopefully I can coax out that sexy smile of hers, that playfulness hovering behind the reserve and hesitation she seems to use as a shield.

Then I remember she'll likely be wearing another stunning bikini, those delicious feminine curves on display…

I close my eyes and grip my semi-hard cock, offering it a few lazy tugs. Tomorrow I'll determine her interest, once and for all. Figure out if her hesitation is shyness, or indifference. A shame, because we could definitely have some fun while we're both here at Lailai.

My fist grips tighter, my jerks pulling a little harder to uncoil the tension of my inconvenient attraction to my island doctor. I brace my free hand on the tiles above my head and focus on the images behind my eyelids. The evening sun strikes my back and I succumb to the presence of Grace in my head as I climb the slope towards release.

CHAPTER THREE

Grace

WHAT NOW? Do I chase after the hot stranger?

Instead, I'm frozen with indecision where he left me with a shrug of those beautifully broad and bronzed shoulders, the memory of his manly scent and the warmth of his strong fingers a call to action blaring in my head.

Why did he have to look back?

I was prepared to walk away, to stick to my decision, telling myself I imagined the way he looked at me, the heat in his playful, sea-blue eyes. Lying to myself while the taste of regret soured my tongue.

And then he looked back, and I wavered, because the expression on his face hadn't been cocky or roguish, the way it had been when he'd teased me, his smile doing things to my insides. He'd looked... lost.

No. I must have imagined it. Professional hazard; I'm always trying to fix people.

I hear Neve and Brooke's reprimand ringing in my ears.

The Pact.

I'm supposed to be making my girls proud. Not moping around feeling sorry for myself among the honeymooners and trying to forget that I was meant to be one of them.

'Shit!'

I had a perfect chance to go for a drink with a handsome work colleague, and I blew it. Easy-going Ryan with his sexy smile and his friendly banter offered the perfect antidote to being alone on an island full of in-love couples.

I scrunch my eyes closed, wincing at my knee-jerk refusal, my stupidity, my fear. I'm so rusty the offer of a drink, some mild flirtation and the touch of a hand freaks me out.

I may as well be a bloody nun.

Well, I'm not here just to hide from the consequences and wallow in guilt.

When I open my eyes again, Ryan has disappeared around the side of his bungalow taking his spectacular toned body out of sight but not out of mind. My mouth may as well be full of sand, I'm so desperate to know what's at the end of the trail of dark hair from his belly button dipping below the waistband of his shorts... How much of the visible bulge under the wet, clinging fabric is his penis? And am I brave enough to find out the answers?

Oh, God, I want to be brave enough.

I can do this, be true to myself, go forwards with courage, and demand more from life. Prioritise passion and adventure. Embrace more than work and obligation and live for all the moments Bryony couldn't have. Starting with a drink with a stranger and followed by learning to paddleboard.

With determination dragged up from my toes, I trudge across the beach after Ryan.

My reassuring self-talk slows the fight-or-flight impulses firing in my brain as I rehearse what I'll say to the sexy Irishman.

I would like that drink after all...

When you said drink, I thought you meant coffee...

I'm crap at this so can we just run through our conversation one more time...?

Or perhaps I'll be honest about my feelings. Mmm... A little holiday flirtation with a man who looks like Adonis and sounds like Aidan Turner with laryngitis. Keeping schtum and not rocking the boat hasn't worked out. My fresh start should be the complete opposite.

Hi, Ryan, sorry about my freak-out earlier, but if you still want that drink I'd love to. And if you fancy me as much as I fancy you, perhaps we could...

Could what? I've never had a one-night stand. How do we travel from strangers to shagging? I bet Ryan knows. My blood pumps harder just thinking about it. About him. About being intimate with anyone other than my ex...

Nausea and excitement battle for control of my body, but I forge ahead with renewed energy. I'll have a drink with him and see what happens. Easy. And at least I'll have something more to confess to Brooke and Neve than the books I read while working on my tan and staying hydrated.

Pathetic, Grace, real pathetic.

I step off the sand onto the wooden walkway, practically vibrating with anticipation as my bare feet pad along the sun-warmed timber.

This heady rush is the feeling I hoped to capture all those months ago when I'd woken up to my two-dimensional, mediocre relationship. This clarity is what I longed for when I experienced an epiphany after losing my patient—the fleeting fragility of life, the reminder of my beloved Bryony losing her final battle and how I most definitely wasn't living my fullest version. If Bryony had survived beyond twenty-three, if she hadn't died waiting for a heart transplant, there's no way she'd have lived such a safe and sanitised life.

She'd have trampled me out of her path to go for a drink with a man like Ryan, if she'd had the chance.

Well, I can trample. I owe it to her and myself to find that courage of conviction.

The delicate scents of frangipani and honeysuckle hit me as I skirt the side of the bure, every nerve electrified by adrenaline. I'm momentarily blinded by the horizontal rays of the setting sun, and then I round the corner and jerk to a standstill.

Suck in a gasp.

Freeze.

Ryan is naked under the outdoor shower, one hand braced on the tiles overhead, every toned muscular plane taut, his right arm bulging and flexing with a jerky rhythm that can mean only one thing.

He's masturbating.

My breath catches, wave after wave of longing coursing through my veins, burning me alive.

I should look away, tiptoe back the way I came on silent feet to avoid embarrassment, both his and mine. But it's not shame causing my heart to bang at my ribs. It's lust. Excitement.

Every inch of me incandescent. Bold. Alive.

I moisten my dry lips with the tip of my tongue, my stare raking his wet body—his thick thighs spread, his tight arse, every muscle delineated and bulging, an anatomist's dream, as his hand works between his legs—his male beauty barbaric, primal, brutal.

My unblinking eyes burn. This is wrong. I'm trespassing, invading a private moment, perving unseen in the shadows, but my feet may as well be glued to the walkway.

My throat grows tight, my mouth flooding with saliva and my aroused nipples graze against the fabric of my bikini top. I press my thighs together to ease the fierce throb that has taken up residence in my ravenous clit.

When was the last time I had sex...? The final

months of my relationship with Greg were barren, our excuses of fatigue and stress and apathy mutual.

Panic flutters in my veins as the seconds stretch. I worked myself into a frenzy with all those thoughts of one-night stands and by drooling over Ryan's sexy dimples and washboard abs, and now he's going to turn around and tell me to piss off…

I must make some sort of noise, a whimper maybe, because Ryan's head whips around and our eyes meet, his fierce with arousal, as if he expected my sudden presence, and mine dragged half closed by the most erotic sight I've ever seen, even as adrenaline spikes to every cell in my body.

My face flames at being spotted invading his privacy, as I try to battle the arousal taking control of my body. But anyone could have walked around this corner. He wanted to be caught, or perhaps he just doesn't care who sees him naked and aroused.

What now?

Don't look down.

What would passion-seeking Grace do?

The old me would run like a startled rabbit, mumbling an apology. The old me would deny her feelings, shoving them down into a sterile version acceptable for others. But no more.

I look down. I can't help myself.

He's still tugging at his cock, which is long and thick and every bit as magnificent as I'd imagined. My stare lingers, mind blank, core pulsing with need—his big hand, those warm fingers that made me shiver pleasuring himself, albeit with less brutality now he has an audience.

Was he thinking of me as he jerked off?

'Oh, my God.' I must actually say this aloud, because he chuckles, drawing my eyes back to his, which are sparking with mischief and challenge, brows arched.

'Care to join me, Doc? Or are you happy just to watch?' Gravel infects his deep voice, which curls around me, sensual fingers teasing, touching and taunting. And I want it. I want his touch on me as much as I want to watch him touching himself, the shock blinding me to reason and sense.

But join him? In broad daylight where anyone could see, not under the covers with the lights out, missionary style…?

'Perhaps you should shower inside, if you don't want to be caught.' My skin tingles, my nipples sensitive to the point of pain against my bikini top, a million feelings pounding me like the waves crashing against the reef beyond the lagoon. My body has disconnected from my overthinking mind, taking over, leaving me no choice but to stand here braced on the knife-edge of a delicious, dangerous decision.

His mouth twists, his smile slipping from cocky to downright sinful. 'Who says I mind being caught?'

Blood thunders in my ears.

Why not take him up on the offer? Be honest. Don't play it safe, always doing the right thing, the responsible, cautious, considered thing.

My whole body sags with relief as I admit that I want him and there's not a reason in the world I can't have what I want. I inch closer, drawn by forces almost too strong to resist doing something so unlike me. Unlike the old me.

But the new me? The me I came here hoping to nurture… I know what she'd do.

His hand slows, barely stroking, although he's as hard and proud as ever. 'You're free to leave if my show offends you,' he says with his trademark self-assuredness. I can tell he's expecting a repeat refusal from me by the challenging curl of his mouth.

'I'm not offended.' Turned on to the point of delirium. Sick on my wild, unexpected thoughts. So tempted to take him up on his offer, but not offended.

But I've just met him. He's clearly a man of the world and I've slept with one person in my entire life. He'll see through me, see that I'm unadventurous, a charlatan. A woman who belongs in a nice neat couple, not a 'wildly passionate one-night stand' kind of woman. A 'watching someone jerk off' kind of woman.

My thoughts turn jagged, risky, caution crumbling, letting go of all the self-imposed constraints holding me captive. I followed him not for a drink, but for what might come after.

I want the kind of passion I see in his stare—raw, hungry, undeniable.

'Good,' he says. 'Then you won't be offended to know that you're the inspiration for this.' He looks down to where his hand now caresses his erection with slow, twisting tugs that make my internal muscles clench and my entire body go up in flames. Why is that the hottest thing I've ever heard? That I've inspired his flagrantly male display. That he couldn't wait to indulge in a Grace-themed fantasy. That he's not afraid to tell me, a complete stranger, that I turn him on, when I struggled to admit to my long-term partner what I wanted.

Because I didn't know myself. I'd never allowed myself to be that honest. But now...?

I want to know what that feels like for him. I want to taste him and drive him back to that place he inhabited before I interrupted, just with my mouth. I want to be the kind of woman I imagine when he looks at me with sin and hunger in his eyes.

My feet move in his direction, while my brain screams and my pulse races so high, I'm scared of passing out before I reach the shower.

He drops his hand to his side and turns to face me, his angular face taut with arousal and his blue eyes blazing with challenge or need or something else.

Or maybe I'm hallucinating. But I'm past holding back, my body molten with the release.

Rather than dousing me in sense, the first shock of water cascading down my back inflames me higher. Ryan lifts his eyebrows, part impressed, part surprised, his expression shredding my usual caution.

He smells great, arousing—delicious shower gel, hints of sunscreen and seawater and maleness. As if magnetised, my body sways closer until I'm almost touching him, this stranger. This naked, turned-on man.

A head spin reminds me how I haven't felt this heady, euphoric and frankly terrifying rush for a very long time. But I want to live out wild erotic fantasies with this beautiful man, here where I can re-invent myself.

I want to be honest and brave.

'Kiss me,' I whisper, so profound is my desire now I've surrendered to the idea.

He reaches for my face, his palms big and directive on my heated cheeks, and then I rise up on my tiptoes, my fingers dragging at his wet hair until our mouths connect.

The first foreign, and oh-so-thrilling taste releases an involuntary moan. I collapse against the wall of muscle that is his chest, my knees soft and my body flooding with wild, wonderful and freeing endorphins.

He angles my head to the slide of his mouth, his lips soft but demanding, exploratory, his eyes fiercely connected to mine, and the spray of warm water a welcome antidote to the inferno burning me alive.

He pulls away to gruffly say my name, a groan, and then we're kissing again. This is crazy, exotic like this island. I'm sucked under by the waves of desire pounding my body. I've never kissed or been kissed this way, with such feral abandon.

My hands find his hips and I tug him out from

under the worst of the deluge until my back hits the tiles and he's a wall of naked maleness and hard muscle trapping me there.

Triumph sings through every cell. Would cautious, serious Grace kiss a naked, aroused stranger she'd interrupted masturbating in the shower? Would she hell. But I'm done with her.

I pant, my grasping hands jerky on his wet, slippery skin as I try to drag him impossibly closer. Here I am, surging against his kisses, bucking against his hips and the firm prod of his erection and practically climbing him, so desperate is my need to be consumed by whatever spell has taken hold.

When he leans back, pinning me with those piercing blue eyes of his, I almost cry aloud. I don't want this to stop.

'Condom.' His breath gusts over my lips. 'Let's go inside.'

Condom...?

My brain clamours for a solution to the problem, which feels as wispy as the steam rising from our bodies. But those few seconds are enough time for sense to return like an unwanted party-crasher.

I push at his hips, shoving him a few inches away. No, no, no. I don't want to be sucked into reality.

'I shouldn't have interrupted,' I say, lips buzzing from the delicious scrape of his stubble. But I don't want to go back to safety and caution. My fingers curl, digging into the flesh of his flanks and lower back, the only part of me bold enough to be completely honest.

Ryan braces one hand on the tiles above my head and pushes back the wet hair clinging to my forehead with his other hand, his body held inches away from mine so the only contact between us is my hands, still gripping his waist. 'Do you always do what you should, Grace?'

Yes! I do…

I'm trapped between my bold and honest leap into the unknown and mortification that he sees my failings so clearly.

'Don't you?' My voice is breathy, tinged with the ferocity of my desire. I already know the answer. I see it in his carefree body language and the rakish ease with which he's embraced the chemistry that led us here.

'Never.' His stare pierces me. 'I do what I want, when I want. That's why I invited you for a drink.' His finger traces a line down my cheek, leaving a trail of fire. 'Why I didn't stop when I turned around and saw you watching. Why I suggested you join me.' He drops his hand to his side and steps back as if releasing me to my decision.

My body clamours for the return of his touch and his incendiary kisses, even as I list what-ifs so deeply ingrained, they're part of my DNA.

'You should try it,' he says, 'now.' A shrug. 'Leave or stay, just do what you want, not what you think you should.'

This is it—my call to make.

My brain scrambles with static. What do I want? And can I be honest enough to verbalise my desires? I know what I don't want. I don't want to move, because if we go inside, I'll have time to second-guess and revisit well-worn paths of overthinking.

I sag back against the tiles; I can have what I want. I just have to say the words.

'I want to watch you finish what you started.' The words rush from the darkest corner of my mind, bringing with them a lick of shame but a flood of exhilaration. Until I spoke them I didn't know what I'd say. But they're three-dimensional, so raw and true they make me burn.

His eyes blaze. He grips his erection once more and slides his hand up and down his length with agonising slowness. I'm envious. I want to touch his beautiful cock.

'Like this?' His voice drops an octave as arousal takes him.

I nod, my breathing too thin to generate speech. Shaking off invisible shackles and acting on my desires is so foreign, it feels part of this landscape. A mirage. A fantasy that will cease to exist when I board the plane home. But I'm here in this moment. A moment I created. One I can orchestrate.

'Yes. Kiss me while you touch yourself.' I tug his hips closer and curl my hand around his neck. The minute our tongues touch, tangle, I surrender on a protracted sigh, further doubts or cold feet forgotten. I can barely stand I'm so aroused by what I've seen and what I've said and what I'm doing, caution thrown to the warm tropical breeze.

But even with a wall of determination at my back, tendrils of the old me persist. 'This is crazy... What are we doing?' I say in between the hot and frantic kisses I've demanded and which make me feel reborn.

Without breaking his pumping rhythm, Ryan rests his forehead against mine and grins. 'Well, if you don't know, Doc, I think you need to go back to med school.'

I can't help a smile. How can he make such a momentous and sexy moment light-hearted? Does it matter what we're doing? There's no one else to consider. We're just two strangers caught up in a perfectly honest moment of mutual lust.

'Do whatever you want. Ask for whatever you want,' he says, his breath warm on my lips.

I allow my stare to touch every magnificent inch of his aroused, naked body. I drag in a shuddering breath and cover his pumping hand with mine, learning the contours of his tight knuckles and how much pressure he likes in his grip. I want to know what this feels like for him. What makes his buttocks clench and his steely thighs judder against mine. While our pants of breath mingle, the heat from his body a thick cloud between us, I stroke my thumb over the crown, trace the slit at the top of the silky head, an exploratory move that drags a sexy warning growl from deep in his throat.

As if he's reached a limit, his mouth mashes to mine, blocking my delicious view. My tongue rushes to meet the bold, thrilling thrust of his, every thought unrelated to Ryan and his mounting pleasure banished from my mind. I'm tempted to slide my other hand inside my bikini bottoms and join him on the race to climax, I'm that heated and slick down there, but instead I slide my free hand between his legs and gently cup his balls. For reasons I can't explain beyond the fact that it makes every inch of me feel alive and free, I want to see and feel his moment of release. To see him complete what I interrupted, knowing he's thinking about me while he pleasures himself, and I'm part of this snatched moment.

At the last minute he tears his mouth away from mine to roar my name as he comes, hot jets spilling over the back of our combined hands. His head lolls back in glorious release as he wrings the last spasms from his orgasm in a sight so male, so primitive, my clit throbs with shocking violence before he collapses forward, his head buried in the crook of my neck, breath gusting.

I'm breathing just as hard with euphoria, the rush almost as good as if I'd come with him. And I never want this moment to end. This feeling. This freedom.

'For fuck's sake, woman. That was the best hand job ever,' he mumbles against my skin as shower after shower of elation rains down on me.

I did that. Took a leap. A risk. Made a decision based purely on instinct and impulse. But try as I may to cling to the high, my skin grows cool, goose bumps rising.

What now? Do we wash the evidence from our hands and shake on a job well done? Do we go for that drink and learn superficial things about each other? Do we say goodbye and avoid each other for the rest of the holiday?

I swallow down my questions on casual-sex etiquette, my heart galloping anew.

When Ryan looks up, vulnerability replacing the harsh arousal in his face, my instincts polarise, half of me desperate to kiss him with tenderness the way I would if I knew him beyond his first name, and the other half wishing I'd gone inside with him in the first place so that I wouldn't have to stand here horny and awkward and covered in goose bumps.

It's one thing to touch someone else, to kiss someone else, but to have a stranger touch me...? To be that intimate with a man I don't know having only ever been intimate with one person? Not that he's offering any longer, of course.

I peel my cooling body away from the heat of his. 'I should go,' I say to fill the silence.

Something like disappointment flashes in his eyes for a split second. 'Should...?'

His question slashes like a whip across my back, unleashing white-hot stings of regret. So I'm still me, then? Still hesitant and cautious. Still overthinking. So much for the new improved version...

When I look up again, Ryan's face is blank.

Almost of its own accord, my head bobs in confirmation. I need to get away. To regroup and analyse where I went wrong. To probe my instincts, which it seems can't yet be trusted for all my brave talk of sexual adventure.

Ryan appears oblivious to the cyclone of heat and chills and pressure inside me, which replaces the heady abandon and arousal of seconds ago. 'Sure.' He slides his hands from my hips and presses a brief, almost polite kiss to my mouth. 'Always do what you want, Grace.'

He steps back under the shower spray, water bouncing off his back and shoulders and cascading down his abs to his still-hard cock, his stare free of judgment, but also devoid of the addictive heat as he shakes the water from his face and slicks back his hair.

I waver back and forth a thousand times in those few tense seconds, my triumph decimated by the return of doubts. Now I've said I'm leaving, I have to follow through and he's making no move to stop me. Perhaps this is the hook-up code.

Thanks for the orgasm. Have a great evening.

With heavy limbs, I walk away from his bold nakedness and his bland expression, my mind the only fucked thing about me.

CHAPTER FOUR

Grace

THE BEACH IS quiet at this time of the morning save for the gentle lap of the sea. Propped on his elbows as he looks out to the reef in the distance, Ryan lies stretched out on the sand next to two paddleboards.

He showed up—my pulse trips over itself, the niggle of doubt that he'd stand me up evaporating. Ryan turns, his grin lit with triumph and a hint of relief similar to that now robbing every thought, every question I've had since I opened my eyes at dawn. Should I keep the lesson, or assume he'd call it off? Should I pretend last night didn't happen, or beg for a repeat? Should I stick to what I know, or take leap after leap of faith, until shaking off my reservations and being honest about what I want becomes second nature?

Ryan rises to his feet, uncurling his long limbs with natural grace, his eyes touching my bikini-clad body with heat to rival last night's too-brief touch of his hands.

'I thought you'd chicken out,' I say, something hot and drugging passing between us so I'm acutely attuned to every grain of sand on my feet and every brush of the breeze on the tiny hairs covering my skin. An awareness. An intimacy shared by two people, strangers, who've touched each other, kissed each other. Still strangers, but weirdly more because of what we did last night in the shower while the sun set.

'You thought *I'd* chicken out?' He raises his eyebrows, laughter in his eyes. 'I'm right where I want to be, Grace. Same as last night. Same as always.'

'Fair point,' I say with a breathy laugh. The release feels like a sneeze or, better, a mini orgasm, the tension I've been holding recoiling from my body and leaving behind a storm of fierce lust pulsing in time with my heartbeat.

We fall into silence.

He's wearing nothing but board shorts and his tan, his arms relaxed by his sides. I'm reminded how those big hands of his held my face, my waist, my back while his sensual mouth delivered kiss after kiss, his bold tongue duelling with mine, pushing me to higher, more reckless heights until I witnessed the moment of his glorious climax like a woman starved. My breath catches in the back of my throat—nerves replaced by drugging arousal.

His stare slides down my body. My core clenches. Last night I fuelled his fantasies. Drove him to touch himself. I want *that* passion.

'Sorry,' he says, 'no free show today.'

It's only when he speaks that I'm aware I'm ogling him back, my focus paused on his lean hips and the bulge in his shorts.

I laugh again, my audible sigh laced with a hint of disappointment. As if watching naked strangers jerk off in outdoor showers is one of my regular pastimes.

'Shame.' I glance again at his crotch. 'I kind of cock-blocked myself last night.' I look up from his brightly coloured board shorts, a lump of need lodged in my throat. Who am I around him, here in this place? Certainly not the woman I recognise—too contained to rock the boat, too fearful of disappointing people, too scared to demand more than a relationship grown stale, forced and passionless.

Last night, strung taut with unfulfilled desire and the hollow certainty that running back to my room was the action of the old Grace, I made a promise to embrace this thing with Ryan. Properly this time. No more holding back from what *I* want.

His eyebrows dip in that sexy way he looked at me last night while he rocked into his own fist. 'Well, today is another day in paradise. Anything is possible.'

He takes half a step towards me, and I look up, his eyes that intense blue of my fractured erotic dreams. At one stage I'd actually orgasmed in my sleep, waking up disorientated and far from fulfilled.

'I almost chased after you,' he says, 'but two

brush-offs in a row turns out to be my limit.' His tone is light, teasing.

'*You* have limits?' I want to touch him so bad, to reach up and kiss him again, but I need to respect the teacher-student boundary.

He shrugs one broad, golden shoulder, humour dancing on his lips. 'A few. Especially for women who interrupt a good wank, insist on watching and then scarper.'

Heat boils in my face. 'Yeah, well, no one is sorrier about leaving than me...' I say, emboldened to be honest by the way he's still mentally undressing me as if his orgasm barely took the edge off. 'I kind of...panicked. I was trying to...embrace the holiday-fling vibe, but I messed up, I guess. We should have gone for that drink, first.'

He watches with growing fascination, his eyes moving between mine and my mouth, staring as if entranced by my gobbledegook.

'Thanks for not standing me up this morning,' I whisper.

His shrug lifts those broad shoulders, reminding me of how it felt to be crushed against his chest.

'It's a small island, Grace.' His sinful smile is contagious. 'We were always going to bump into each other, but I'm glad you didn't allow a little thing like lust ruin a good paddleboard.'

I take a shuddering breath and compose myself while my mouth burns to reunite with his kisses until neither of us gives a toss about paddleboarding. I glance back at the deserted equipment hut up the beach wondering if I could persuade him to re-kindle where we left off last night.

Just then, two honeymooners emerge from the palm-tree-lined path that winds behind the hut. Each carries snorkelling gear and flippers in their free hands the other arms wrapped around each other. They stop so often to kiss they can barely walk.

My lungs grow tight with remorse. Greg and I would never have acted that way if we'd come here together. I look away, the comparison stealing my Ryan-induced high. Perhaps my brain is somehow convinced I'm betraying my ex by being intimate with another man, and that's why I fled last night.

Ridiculous. But my eyes burn as I avoid look-ing at the couple in love. I want more than regret of my past actions and holding back the unknown. If I want Ryan, I'm the only thing standing in my way.

'So…' Ryan grabs the paddles. 'You still keen for a lesson?'

I grasp the lifeline, desperate to be away from the resort and what it represents—my failure—for a short while. 'Yes. My sister raved about how she always wanted to try, so I'm definitely keen.'

He eyes me with curiosity so I march to the wait-ing paddleboards. 'Shall we get started?' I ask. The fierce attraction still hums through my veins but, no matter how tempted, I can't jump a man I met yes-terday before nine in the morning, not when I had my chance last night and blew it.

But I can change. Build on what I did last night. I can be honest and daring. Starting with standing on this damn paddleboard.

Face the fear and do it anyway.

That was Bryony's motto. Every time she pushed herself to do things most people take for granted. Every time she faced surgery, or a prolonged stint in hospital.

Ryan holds up a life jacket, his eyebrow cocked in question. 'How are your swimming skills? The lagoon is shallow enough for the first couple of hundred metres, but I recommend the jacket unless you're a confident swimmer.'

'I'm good—I used to do some lifesaving.'

He nods and drops the life jacket onto the sand.

'Anyway I'm sure this is harder than it looks, so the chances of me actually standing up on this thing long enough to get out of waist-deep water are pretty slim.' I scoop the board under one arm the way he picks up his and reach for my paddle.

But he doesn't relinquish it, forcing me to meet his eyes. 'What's the worst that can happen? You lose balance and get wet? Big deal.'

I shrug, my stomach twisted just from being this close to him dressed only in a bikini. My nerves frayed because I want him so badly.

He steps closer, holding my eye contact so I'm aware of every touch of warm air between us, aware of his hand above mine around the shaft of the paddle.

'You forget...' his voice dips low '...I've seen you all wet,' he says. 'It's sexy as hell.'

The ache in my clit returns, liquid heat pooling in my bikini bottoms.

His stare sweeps down my body to my feet. 'Nice ankle bracelet, by the way.' His lips twitch, the gesture making me want to kiss him again. Then I'm caught in the piercing beam of his bright blue eyes full of the knowledge that he noticed the delicate chain.

'Thanks. I had a pedicure at the spa.' A bonus of my sleepless night, which allowed me to snag the first appointment of the day. I don't add that I thought of him when I purchased the silver chain now adorning my perfectly pampered feet, imagining his face buried between my thighs, my legs draped over his shoulders, the silver glinting in the sun while I claim everything I want from this man in one big sexual exploration.

Between studying, supporting Bryony and my parents through her multiple hospital visits and meeting studious, like-minded Greg, there wasn't time for a misspent youth... But I can rectify that with Ryan.

He chooses that moment to release his hold on my paddle. I force myself to focus on his safety talk and technique tips. He applies the same confidence to teaching the nuances of paddleboarding as he did to his one-man al-fresco show last night, switching from flirt to teacher with easy relaxed competence so I almost forget about the wild kissing and the sexy way he stared at me as he came. I try my best to follow his instructions.

We wade out into the warm water and sit on our boards, side by side, Ryan watching me the way an instructor would.

'Grace—you seem distracted. Are you sure you want to do this?'

Of course I'm distracted—that broad chest with a sprinkling of dark hair I can still feel under my palms, his sexy abs contracting as he kneels on his board the way they contracted as he pumped into his fist, the mussed flop of his damp hair looking exactly the way it did when I left him after twisting that hair in my hands so I could kiss him deeper.

The want inside me bubbles up in a rush so strong, every muscle below the waist clenches.

'I'm good.' I groan in my head. I'll never get through this lesson without falling into a sexual-frustration-induced coma. 'Just nervous that I won't be able to do this and I'll make a fool of myself.'

Now why did I say that?

'Do you have to be good at it the first time? I'm the only person watching. I don't care if you can't stand up perfectly straight away. I fell plenty of times on my first attempt.'

I sigh. 'That came out wrong—I *don't* have to be perfect...' Liar. 'I just meant...it looks easier than it probably is.' My justification burns my cheeks. Of course I have to be perfect. Perfect daughter, perfect sister. More old habits.

Ryan nods, accepting me at face value, and continues the lesson.

My first attempt at kneeling on the board causes a wobble and a squeal. Ryan abandons his own board to steady mine while I attempt the move once more. Even with him holding it, it shifts beneath my knees. 'Ah...' I laugh, reaching for his muscular shoulder to steady myself but then I find my balance and look up to find him smiling.

'You're going to conquer this—I can tell by that determined look in your eye. Trust your instincts.' He releases his hold on the board and miraculously I stay in place, no embarrassing face plant into the ocean.

I mimic his paddling actions and try not to notice his beach-perfect body and how he could probably advertise water sports, or anything else, for a living.

When my heart rate settles and we're gently paddling side by side, I risk conversation. 'How long have you been doing this?' I ask.

'Oh, a few years. I find it very relaxing.' His lips press together and he doesn't elaborate on how long he's worked on the island. 'The conditions today are perfect, hardly any wind.'

'So is it time to stand up?' I say, because I can never go easy on myself. Push, push, push.

'So impatient. We'll master kneeling first. There's a small cove just past the lagoon. Let's head in that direction.'

Ryan must adjust his pace to paddle next to me,

because I'm certain he can go faster than the snail's pace I'm keeping, but every stroke feels more certain, my paddle planted a little more surely, adrenaline seeping away to make way for euphoria. I'm out of my comfort zone but doing it anyway.

Twice in twenty-four hours.

'So do you live here, on the island permanently?' I ask. He's a conundrum of a man—competent and confident, but laid-back and patient. Plus he's a gentleman. He could so easily have made this morning awkward, but he's professionally providing the lesson, with only a few inappropriate heated looks.

'No, I'm new here, like you. I'm filling in until the regular instructor returns from visiting his family on the mainland. To be honest, I travel around so much, I'm not sure where I call home.'

So he's a professional beach bum... 'Do you have family back in Ireland?'

He shakes his head, his easy smile dimming. 'My grandma is my only family, and she lives in London. What about you, Dr Grace?' he says, expertly shifting the focus my way. 'It's a fair distance to come to teach first aid and learn how to paddleboard.'

My titter of laughter sounds evasive. I can't confess I should have been on my honeymoon to a man I'm contemplating having casual sex with—he'll know I'm an amateur. I don't want to scare him and his strings-free offer away, and if he's in his thirties and still single, he's clearly anti-commitment.

Or perhaps he's had his heart broken...

Familiar regret at the enormity of what I did—the bills, the disappointment, the broken promises—shuts down my bout of curiosity. Admitting why I'm here means admitting that I settled for so long in a relationship I knew lacked vital elements. I should have simply enjoyed the view, of both Ryan and the ocean, and canned the conversation.

Now I have to brazen it out. 'It is a long way, but Fiji is a place on my bucket list and Taito made me an offer I couldn't refuse.' Not a lie. 'The hospital is a fair way away and he wants all the staff to be able to manage emergencies, including CPR, basic first aid and use of the very expensive new resuscitation equipment. You included, I'm afraid, so don't try and get out of my first class tomorrow.'

'I've told you before, I do what I want.' He grins, winks and I wobble again, so dazzling is his hotness.

'Your life must be one long holiday,' I say, glancing at a neighbouring island lined with palms in the distance. 'I can't imagine a more idyllic location.'

'I'm not complaining.' But his eyes don't carry the same degree of contentment as his words. 'Plus the company is great.'

I smile but the sense he's being as cagey as me tenses my shoulders. But this is how casual must work—superficial facts only. No talk of everyday life or real feelings…

'Look at the fish.' He points down at the crystal-clear water.

I look where he points, give my eyes time to adjust, wait for the surface ripples to settle and then gasp. The clumps of rocky reef below us teem with brightly coloured tropical fish darting this way and that as silver ribbons of sunlight highlight the surface currents. 'Wow. That's amazing.'

'I know, right. We have snorkel equipment back at the resort. This is the best spot if you want to give it a try.'

I watch the fish dart and dive for a few minutes, my face aching from my smile. 'Is this where you cut your ankle? Is it okay, by the way?'

He stares and I grow uncomfortable at my fussing over a graze. 'I, um…only ask because it's easy for cuts like that to become infected.'

'It's fine, thanks for asking. You don't have to worry about me, you know,' he says.

I laugh. 'Sorry…habit. And you may as well benefit from my being here.'

'Don't apologise. I'm just not used to the attention. So, ready to stand?'

'Sure.' But his cryptic response fires my curiosity—what happened to the rest of his family? Why is he single? And am I one of a long list of women to watch him masturbate in the shower?

He pushes up from his kneeling position to standing, making it look effortless. I copy his moves, follow his instructions, desperate now to master this for Bryony and to prove to myself that I'm more than a woman willing to settle, a woman who sticks out like a sore thumb on an island full of couples, a woman who runs from the offer of easy, commitment-free and probably amazing sex.

The wobble of the board under my feet intensifies, shunting my pulse sky-high, but before I know it, I'm standing.

'Okay, keep your eyes on the cove, not down at the water,' he says.

Flooded with adrenaline, I focus on the horizon, as he suggests, making small pushes with the paddle as I head for the beach.

The cove is little more than a patch of white sand nestled among the palms. I almost comment on how romantic it is, but then I remember who I'm with— casual and romance don't go hand in hand. I would know this if I'd actually had full-blown strings-free sex rather than the one-sided, frustrating encounter I orchestrated last night.

Ryan rests his paddle on his board without so much as a wobble. 'Do you want to explore the cove, look for coconuts? Or if you prefer, I can leave you to your own devices now that you've mastered paddle-boarding.'

Disappointment pinches under my ribs. I want him to stay. I want to kiss him again, to touch all the parts of him I didn't get to explore because I held back, and not stop until we're both sated and spent. If I allow him to go back to the resort alone, I'll send a message I don't want to send.

I stare at the deserted beach for a couple of beats,

my mind racing with his unspoken subtext and what *I* want.

I'd love your company if you don't have some-where else to be.

I want to kiss you again...pick up where we left off.

The words should be easy after what we shared, but instead I hear myself saying, 'I should let you get off to your next lesson.'

Bugger. Why is this such a hard habit to break?

'Should you?' he says, deceptively soft.

I'm focussed on staying upright so I can't see his expression but I feel his eyes on my skin as I paddle into the shallows, his words from last night in my ears.

Just do what you want, not what you think you should.

In my peripheral vision I see him step from his board and pick it up. I do the same as he wades in my direction, fine tremors skating down my legs to my toes as I meet him at the water's edge.

I look up.

His eyes burn bright blue with intensity. 'I'd like to stick around if you want the company, but it's your call.'

'I'd like you to stay,' I say, sticking with the hon-esty that served me so well in the shower. 'I'm en-joying your company.'

'Great. That's decided, then.'

I barely notice the breathtaking cove, fringed with palm trees, as Ryan carries his board up the beach and lays it on the sand. I place mine next to his, releasing the ankle strap while I grow hot and hyper aware that he's close. Before I can turn to face him, he grips my fingers, the shock intimacy of the gesture enough to jerk my head up into his line of vision.

I don't know what I'm expecting, but his face is relaxed, as if holding my hand is no big deal. And it shouldn't be, because we've kissed. Touched. But the wobble in my legs and the catch of my breath makes it a big deal. It feels as if we've been propelled from strangers to something full of possibility. Something tantalising, promising the kind of passion I hoped to find.

When he moves to walk further up the beach I tug him to a standstill. I step closer, my nipples aching against the fabric of my bikini top. I crave the heat and desire of last night as he pleasured himself and stared at me with challenge, or this morning when his eyes raked my body from my head down to my ankle bracelet. I want it all.

'Thank you.' My husky voice sounds sexy and sensual.

'What for?' he says.

'For being such an awesome instructor. For not making this morning awkward… If I knew you were such a gentleman, I would have gone inside in search of that condom. I've regretted it ever since.' I reach for his shoulder, stand up on tiptoes and press my mouth to his before he can speak. If I can stand on that paddleboard, I can do anything.

The kiss tastes salty from the ocean spray and still foreign, but it instantly transports me back to that moment in his shower, where I was too turned on to think straight, too boneless to act on anything other than instinct. And brave. So wonderfully brave.

Ryan grips my upper arms and pushes me away so our lips part before I've had a chance to devour him the way I want, but he holds me firm, still close enough to feel the heat radiating from his body, which douses the sting of what feels like rejection.

'Ever since I saw you on the beach on your first day wearing this bikini, ever since that mind-blowing hand-job, my thoughts have been anything but gentlemanly. Don't make me out to be something I'm not.'

'Okay, I won't.' My body incinerates so I'm certain the droplets of seawater clinging to my skin must be evaporating. 'Why don't you tell me about those thoughts, just so I'm clear?'

His eyes narrow. A tiny twitch of his decadent mouth. He looks as if he's about to drag me in for more kissing, but he holds back. 'Are you sure you want to do this? Because I can tell you that I wish I'd tasted your hard nipples last night. I wish I'd peeled off your bikini and seen you naked, touched every inch of you, tasted every inch, even after I came so hard it felt like the back of my head blew off.' His expression is pained, as if he can't quite believe he's talking instead of ravishing me on the sand. Or allowing me to ravish him, as I planned.

'I'm sure. I want you to do those things.' I slide

my arms around his waist, the heat of arousal burning through any self-recrimination I feel at applying the brakes. 'I was stupid last night. Overthinking.' But he makes me feel invincible, challenges me to be honest and demand what I want. Or perhaps it's this place. The pact. Bryony, my guardian angel. Who knows? All I know is that, with him, I'm reminded that my heart beats, that I'm breathing fresh air and that the sun warms my skin.

I slide my hands up his back, crushing my breasts and sensitised nipples against his firm, warm chest. 'Have you changed your mind?' I can barely utter the words for fear of his answer.

He offers me that lopsided grin of his. 'Feck, don't be daft.' He lowers his mouth to mine in a rush. He groans. I slide my fingers into his hair. His arms tighten around my waist, hauling me up so I'm crushed to his hard chest.

I surge into his heat, into the kiss with the same abandon of last night, pressing as much of my body to his as I can, the skin-to-skin contact adding rush after rush of arousal to my frenzied bloodstream so I can barely stand.

Kissing him here, on a deserted beach with only the sound of the lap of the waves onto the shore, releases a pressure valve. My heart climbs into my throat, its wild thudding robbing me of the ability to think, leaving me with only sensation. A place I want to wallow and linger until everything about my life feels this right.

I'm aware of movement and then my back hits the warm, dry sand. A sigh of almost painful relief leaves me. Ryan's thick thigh slides between my legs and I spread them wider, rocking my pelvis to rub myself and relieve the worst of the fiery tension burning my clit.

He breaks free, looking down at me, a halo of bright sun behind him. 'You're so sexy. This bikini, watching you move all morning…torture.' His mouth covers mine once more and then slides down my neck, the scrape of his stubble on my skin making my toes curl.

'I couldn't get you out of my head all night.' His lips glide over my skin as he talks.

'Me neither. I dreamt about you.' I grip his shoulders as if I don't want him to get away, riding his thigh with abandon while I pant to get oxygen, because need has enslaved me until I see a glimpse of the woman I was last night, a woman I fully intend to embrace. But then my mind blanks as Ryan peels the triangle of fabric from my breast, plumps the flesh in his palm with slow thoroughness and covers my peaked nipple with the heat of his mouth.

I cry out, not caring that, distance-wise, we're not that far from the resort. That other holidaymakers could at any time happen upon this tiny cove from the land or the sea. That I'm half naked on a beach with a man I barely know… But I'm done overthinking. I know enough—his integrity in seeking my consent and his concern about protection.

I'm about to ask him if he has a condom in the pocket of his board shorts when he releases the tie of my bikini top and shifts his mouth to the other breast, which is achy and impossibly more sensitive than the first.

Spontaneous combustion threatens. I'm drugged on the hormones raging through me. Paralysed. Cries trapped in my throat.

All the while he's laving and sucking, his hand rubbing the other breast, fingers toying and tweaking, his eyes are open and either glued to the attention he's lavishing on my breasts or watching my reactions to his touch. When I moan aloud, my hips jerking against his thigh so I rub both myself and his hard length, he repeats the soft stroking touch of his fingers on one side while he adds extra pressure to the other nipple by pressing it between his tongue and the back of his teeth. I've never been so turned on, every part of me tingling. An out-of-body experience.

'Ryan...' I don't know what I'm asking for, I only know I don't want him to stop worshiping my nipples, but I simultaneously want more, want everything he has to give. I've forgotten my pledge to touch and explore every inch of him, selfishly wallowing in his glorious attentions. But he's started a chain reaction in me and I can't stop.

He's rock hard against my hip but makes no move to hurry this along, as if he has all day to play with my breasts. Not that I'm complaining, because I'm too breathless, the tension building inside too over-whelming, the sight of him sucking and toying with rapt focus and sporadic grunts too erotic when com-bined with the incredible sensations.

'Ryan,' I gasp again. I want this. I want more. I want everything. But he ignores my incoherent pleas and continues, his face intense, as if he's enjoying what he's doing too much to stop. If I'd known this last night, I wouldn't have run.

I think of my dream, my sleeping orgasm, think of my fantasy of him licking between my legs with the sun on his back. I cradle his head, holding him tight, my fingers tangling in his decadent hair as my hips buck against his erection to their own, innate rhythm. The orgasm sneaks up on me, building with as much slow care and gentle stimulation as Ryan delivers to my nipples, and with a final grind of my clit against his thigh I detonate, slow rolling waves of biting pleasure consuming me until I'm spent and weak and almost part of the sand at my back.

I can't speak, but I want to sing hallelujahs. I've never had a nipple-only orgasm before. Is it just the excitement of a new partner? Someone different? The sexual frustration of last night? Or is Ryan some sort of sexual god rising up from the ocean for my pleasure?

When I open my eyes, he's gently blowing a stream of warm breath over one nipple, which is damp from his mouth, his face still intensely fo-cussed. Then he looks up. 'That was so fucking hot. I've never met a woman who can do that. You are so sexy...'

I'm still panting but I laugh too. 'I didn't know *I* could do that. You're clearly a breast man.' After the depth and intensity of that orgasm, I'm surprised he didn't feel the island shifting.

'I'm a Grace man.' He trails his hand over my stomach to my hip, his touch sure and firm and all-consuming so I want him to lavish my entire body with that degree of focus. I direct his mouth back to mine and then slide my hand to the front of his shorts where he's straining and hard against the fabric.

'Do you have a condom in your shorts?' I ask, grinding the damp, molten heat between my legs on his thigh. Still needy, still wanting.

He kisses me for a beat, two, three and when he pulls back, his face tight with arousal, I deflate, disappointment a bitter taste on my tongue because I see the regret in his startling blue eyes.

'I don't. I didn't want to assume. I thought I'd been...I dunno...friend-zoned or something. Thought I'd got you all wrong and you didn't actually like watching some bloke jerk off over you. Now I hate myself for being so...'

'Chivalrous?'

He snorts. 'No, not that. I wouldn't use that adjective to describe myself. I was going to say stupid.' A small frown settles between his brows. He reaches for my bikini top, covering my still-tingling breasts with the triangles of fabric. I take the ties from him and finish the job of refastening the bikini, my high draining away with the knowledge he's now the one applying the brakes.

He peels his body from mine and I instantly miss his heat, his strength, his size. He sits up and faces the sea, his arms propped on his bent knees, giving me some privacy to pull myself back together.

'I want you, Grace, don't doubt that for a second. It's just…' He looks back over his shoulder, and I try to force my body into some sort of relaxed, easy-going posture so he can't sense the disappointment boiling in my veins. 'It's just I don't want to give you the wrong idea about me. I'm not looking for a relationship. I don't really do relationships.'

Ah…so this explains why he's single.

'Neither am I, believe me. I thought we were just going to have sex, you know—no strings, a good time, holiday-fling kind of sex…' My mouth feels all sorts of alien speaking these oh-so-casual words, but it's a good feeling. Liberating. Because we want nothing from each other but pleasure, and now I've stepped out of my own way, I'm all in. 'That's what I want, anyway,' I add so there's no confusion.

He watches me closely, perhaps looking for re-assurance. But I didn't come here looking for love. A sarcastic huff blasts in my head. I came to the wrong resort for that. But now we've started this, my mind clears for the first time in what feels like years. I want what he's offering. Fun in the sun. A fling with an expiry date. No big deal, just the kind of sex I already know is going to be amazing, from the couple of bases we've already covered.

I can't help the smile that dances on my lips. 'But if you want to go getting all serious about it… *I love you, Grace…let's get married, Grace…*' I bump his shoulder with mine and grin wider.

His eyes search mine for a few seconds longer, and then he chuckles, slings his arm around my shoulders. 'All right, then.' His 'T' is hard in that Irish way so it sounds as if he said 'ten'. He must be accentuating the accent, playing up the brogue as if he knows how incredibly sexy it sounds.

'We're agreed—casual sex it is.' He tugs me close and presses a firm heated kiss to my mouth, a kiss filled to the brim with the sexual frustration I know he must be feeling because I'm there too.

I pull back, my voice playful. 'Although if you want to get beyond second base, you might want to start carrying a condom in your shorts.' I wriggle free of his arm and stand. 'Come on—we need to cool off.' I walk to the shore, leaving him seated.

At the water's edge I turn back, catching the moment his stare rises from my butt. 'And so neither of us has an excuse next time—' I tap one of the triangles of fabric of my bikini top '—I'll tuck one into my bikini.'

With a frustrated groan, he collapses back onto the sand.

CHAPTER FIVE

Ryan

WHEN I ENTER the bar that evening, after another call to the nursing home, my burning eyes seek out Grace in the crowd. Wearing a simple denim dress that cups her delicious figure, she's sipping a colourful cocktail and talking to the French couple that arrived at Lailai today. Laughing and carefree, her face alight with animation, she shifts something in my chest. A cold hard block of concrete there throughout my call to my grandmother's nurses. Just the sight of her makes me feel lighter somehow, dragging a small indulgent smile to my mouth.

I take a deep breath, trying to dissolve the gnawing and ever-present worry, despite the staff's reassuring prognosis. But I can't seem to shake the deep-seated kernel of dread that wants to sprout and expand.

What if I lose her? My grandma.

Despite the distraction of delightful and lovely

Grace, that haunting vulnerable place exposed near the surface like an open wound coils my muscles tight and presses on my temples with sickening pressure.

I break out in a fine sheen of sweat.

I'm seventeen again. Terrified for my grandma, who has just suffered her first stroke. Alone in the frigid dark. A homeless boy in a man's body.

The panic makes me latch onto Grace, a foreign, almost overwhelming urge to get her alone taking hold. Her company will crush the worst of the trepidation and impotence eating me alive. It happened on the beach last night and again this morning, her sometimes hard-won smile, her grit and sense of humour an anaesthetic.

And I crave that numbness with every daily reminder of my grandmother's frailty, even though I know not to trust another soul for my happiness.

Been there done that with my absent parents.

I prowl to the bar, wound tight, every nerve ending vibrating. I could play my owner's card. Clear the bar of everyone but Grace and me. Touch her freely, watch her eyes glaze with passion, splay her out on the table under the stars and pound us both to oblivion until my troubles exhaust themselves. Instead, I signal Charlie, the barman, for my usual, which he produces with a speed that pleases the businessman in me, and that's where I hang my pinballing thoughts.

Business.

The resort is perfectly placed to be the next Dempsey success. Some minor refurbishments to the communal areas, installation of Jacuzzis and plunge pools near the spa, a designated nightclub and some specialised rooms for the voyeurs and other kink-lovers and it will be good to go. A second call, to my assistant, confirmed that work can commence as soon as the current guests vacate. I take a drag of my beer, waiting in vain for the rush of satisfaction.

Thinking about catering to people's kinks draws my stare back to Grace. She's still laughing with the French couple, but she can't stop looking my way any more than I can clear her from my head.

But focussing on her is better than dissecting my thoughts. She makes a delectable conundrum. She looks classy, almost regal. When she lets go of her reserve, she's gutsy and determined, but beneath the surface there's a passionate goddess, candid and dauntless.

Who knew the hesitant woman who baulked at a drink with a stranger would enjoy watching me jerk off in the shower? How spectacularly uninhibited she was on the beach earlier... And how stupidly unprepared I was.

I spin my beer bottle on the bar, my fingertips against the cool glass—which is slick with condensation—the only part of me not on fire. Would she enjoy being watched, or having others watch her orgasm, the way she'd watched me? As if it fascinated her… As if her honest desires shocked the hell out of both of us.

Need roars through my blood. Here, away from the reality I managed to dodge in our conversation this morning, we can indulge in pleasure. Just what Dempsey resorts sell. But the idea of her at one of my establishments, her openness and fearless abandon, turns my stomach inside out, that possessive urge peaking once more.

What the hell…? I blame sexual frustration.

I'm still staring, trying to keep the alien feelings from my expression. The French couple smile in greeting before moving to the small dance floor, which is open to the gardens and lit by thousands of sparkling lights wound among the rough sawn timber rafters of the roof.

Grace cocks her head, her pretty eyes searching my face as if equipped with X-ray vision. 'Why don't you join me?' She taps the stool next to hers in invitation.

She sees it, the turmoil I battle.

'What are you drinking?' I ask, sliding onto the seat. 'It's making my teeth ache.' The purple cocktail is garnished with slices of star fruit and a perfect frangipani bloom. I lean my upper body close enough to detect her light floral scent and take an indulgent deep breath, which goes some way to calming the storm in me. 'You smell fantastic, by the way.'

She laughs, offers that little smile—half hesitant, half sexy temptress—that makes my blood pound

and renders me hard. There's a very satisfactory way
to banish my demons and have Grace all to myself.
Then I remember I need to confess my true identity.
Dammit—for the first time in years I wish my life
were as simple as the beach bum I've been acting
like since I arrived on the island.

Acting...? Try hiding.

'Thanks,' she says. 'While you were teaching
paddleboarding, I spent the afternoon back at the
spa. I had the most relaxing aromatherapy massage.'

Irrational jealousy grips me, my mind whirring
to remember if we have any male staff working at
the spa. Then Grace clinks her glass against the neck
of my bottle. 'Cheers. This is the house cocktail. A
Beachcomber.'

'Sláinte,' I say, taking a long refreshing swallow
of my beer, resting my arm next to hers on the bar
so our skin brushes and her pupils dilate. I could be
making her relax in other ways, ways that would help
me forget my woes for a while.

Her perceptive stare raises the hairs at the back of
my neck. There's an inquiry coming. I see it in the
set of her mouth against the tip of the paper straw
in her drink.

'You seem troubled tonight—is everything okay?'
Her voice is low, soothing, her compassion creat-
ing what feels like a safe space for any confession
I might have.

A dangerous feeling.

My first instinct is to reject her caring side. I

stopped myself relying on others years ago, learning those bitter lessons every time my grandma's
door slammed closed on my retreating mother. That's
why her concern over my grazed ankle made me uncomfortable.

I could lie, assure her everything is fine, but
there's something about her that I like. A lot I like,
actually. She's real and honest…smart and charming.
And now we've crossed that line into a physical connection we're trapped on the island until our flights
home. I can risk giving her a few breadcrumbs.

'I'm fine. Just distracted,' I say. 'My grandmother,
the one I told you lives in London, is unwell. I've just
finished talking to her on the phone.'

'Oh, Ryan, I'm sorry to hear that,' she murmurs
with understanding. 'Is it serious?' Her hushed voice
wraps warmth around me, when I hadn't realised I
was cold.

I swallow, look away, not ready to confirm something so definitive, even to myself.

'She had a stroke a year ago, which left her weak
down one side. It's not her first stroke. She has diabetes. But she's been fine, until recently.' A small,
unbidden grin tugs at my mouth when I think about
the powerhouse of a woman who raised me solo after
my grandfather died not long after I came to live
with them. 'Her mind is still sharp, and fortunately
her memory was unaffected.' I chuckle, shaking my
head. 'I'm in my thirties, but she still has enough
gumption to lecture me on wearing sunscreen and

remind me that she'd like a visit when I'm next home in London.'

I wince, guilt lashing me. The promise came easily—she's all the family I have. The only person to truly care about me, unconditionally. The only person to never let me down.

Why am I still here? I could leave tonight…first thing in the morning…any time I want, my private jet on standby at the airfield on the main island.

'Well, that's a positive,' says Grace, 'She sounds like a formidable lady—you'd best do as she says.'

We share a smile, my throat thick with memories and ghosts and what-ifs.

'So what changed recently?' she asks.

'She's developed a chest infection.' I sigh, spilling more details than I thought I'd share at Grace's gentle probing. 'She's on antibiotics. Oxygen.' I curl my fingers into a fist, the exposed feeling back. 'It's… I hate feeling helpless.'

Grace nods, her warm hand settling on my arm, her touch a comfort I didn't know I needed. 'It must be hard being so far away. But I'm sure she's in good hands.'

I take a swill of beer to stop myself blurting my darkest fears. She's so easy to talk to, opening me up when I'm normally a closed book.

A big part of me, the part my grandmother picked up and nurtured after my mother left, wants to jump on the first flight home and see with my own eyes that she's as well as she claims on the phone, to ensure she's receiving the best of care, even though I know she is, because I ensure it. And the other part—the part I bury deep inside—wants to pretend, to deny the ever-present knowledge that if anything happens to my grandmother I'll be truly alone.

My chest aches again, the pain reminiscent of so many times in my past.

I glance around for a distraction. Then I wish I hadn't. The place is wall-to-wall doting couples. Yeah, they all look loved up for now, but what happens when times get hard, when inevitably people lie and cheat and hurt each other? How many of these newly-weds will clutter up the divorce courts in years to come and how many children will be casualties of their parents' disappointed expectations and changes of heart?

I must make some sort of snort of disgust.

Grace follows my line of sight. 'What? You don't approve of PDA?' She watches the French couple smooch on the dance floor, a dreamy look on her face.

'I have nothing against PDA, I just—'

'I know you don't "do" relationships,' she says, quoting me. 'But you must see how romance is good for business in a place like this. You know, they're getting married here in a couple of days.' She inclines her head towards the dancing French couple. 'How perfect is that?'

When I don't comment, because I've clamped my jaw shut, she swivels on her stool, returning her undivided attention my way.

'I'm sorry.' She smiles. 'I don't mean to rant—I have happily married parents as role models, and, according to my sister, romance novels are an antidote to all the crap in the world…' She trails off, perhaps at the look on my face.

I grit my teeth. What can I say? That I don't believe in the bullshit people call love? That I hate what people do in the name of something that's supposed to be hearts and roses and for ever? People like my parents.

'Did you get hurt…' she asks '…by a woman?' At her hesitant question, all the sparkle dims from her eyes, replaced by a pained expression as if *she* were said fictional woman witnessing the fallout of her heartbreaking actions.

I hold in my skeptical snort. I don't want to insult her; she clearly believes in all this happily ever after bullshit. But the truth is, I've never risked my heart in a romantic way, so I have no idea what she's talking about.

'Don't look so sad,' I say, swigging my beer and looking away from the compassion in her eyes, as if she truly cares that my heart might lie in tatters. 'Nothing like that—I just don't do feels or rings or romance. Never have.' Spoken aloud to this woman, with her deep well of empathy and her optimistic outlook, the words seem small, beneath me, irrelevant. Perhaps simply because she's under my skin in a way I've never experienced.

I decide on a dollop of truth.

'I didn't have happily married parents as role models—my father cheated on his wife with my mother and then returned to his family when he discovered she was pregnant with me. I'm afraid I'm a cynical bastard.'

The empathy in her eyes scrapes at my skin, exposing the root of my trust issues.

Abandonment.

No doubt the doc here knows all about ways to screw up the human psyche the way my mother deserting me to chase after my father screwed me up. Good thing she's an anaesthetist, not a shrink, or I'd have to watch what I let slip.

'I'm not sad… I thought you might be grieving and I guess I can't help helping people—occupational overspill, I'm afraid. And something you said…you know, earlier…' She flushes, her skin that pretty pink that tells me she's remembering this morning. 'I realised this must be quite a difficult place to work if your heart was broken.' She tilts her head in the direction of the dance floor where several couples have joined the French in slow-dancing to some sappy love song.

I swallow, breathe a little easier. 'Well, thanks for your concern, but I guess I just don't believe in love. Half of these couples won't last. Hopefully it will be before they procreate and bring another life into their mess.' I watch her eyes round, astonishment flickering in their depths telling me she very much does believe. I grit my teeth and ponder saying more. I've been as clear as possible about my expectations, but I know from experience that some women see my stance on commitment as some sort of personal challenge…

I contemplate wrapping things up early, going back to London to spend time with Grandma. Most of my business with the experienced and competent team here can be conducted over video call. But…

My body plunges back into that dark and cold place of uncertainty, chills chasing away the warmth of a tropical evening. It's not just unfinished business with Grace holding me back. Going home may confirm things I can't bear to be true.

Incredulity hovers in Grace's small smile. 'You've never been in love?'

I shake my head, the pain lurking under my ribs since I hung up the phone returning with a vengeance. I take another drag from my beer. 'Nope, but don't feel sorry for me—I do all right with the ladies.' I wink, trying to steer us back to casual sexy banter. Back to numbness.

Of course she sees through me, her eyebrows raised in question.

I sigh. It seems Grace and I are going for absolute honesty. 'I can't imagine giving anyone that kind of power. It seems unnecessary in this day and age. Have *you* been in love?' I say to divert the spotlight.

Now why did I ask that? I don't want to know. It's irrelevant. And I can guess the answer. Her dreamy expression alone tells me she's a romantic.

My question dissolves her small frown, and she takes cover herself behind an elaborate swirl of her cocktail. 'Just once.' She pauses. 'I've not long been through a break up. And…well…' she swallows hard '…I was the one who ended it.' The pallor returns to her cheeks, her eyes taking on a haunted look that speaks of her guilt and concern for her ex.

Compassionate Grace, with her *should* and *shouldn't*, likes to do the right thing. She cares, about people, their needs and wants. It's who she is. Breaking someone's heart must have taken some serious soul-searching. I grow restless in my seat. I want to drag her out of here and kiss her so hard, we forget everything but what happens when we're together.

'I'd hate to think that my ex would abandon relationships altogether because of my change of heart. I guess I was extrapolating.' She looks up from her drink, her eyes shining.

My heart thuds with foreboding. What kind of man would Grace throw away? What did her ex feel, loving this woman? Was the risk worth the heartbreak she's worried she inflicted?

The block in my chest twists and turns, the burn making me wince.

This is why I prefer simple.

'See, my way is easier,' I say. 'If you avoid all the feels and rings and romance, you avoid all that messy stuff.' I'm trying to lighten the mood, predominantly for myself, because otherwise I'll have to probe those tender places she's exposed simply by looking hard enough, but then I catch her expression and sober. She's devastated to be the cause of someone's pain—she worried about my grazed ankle, for fuck's sake.

'Of course, you still care about him.' It's a statement, one that sees me sucking another swallow from my beer bottle to counter the acidic taste in my throat. What the hell? I haven't even had sex with her and I'm…jealous. I'm never jealous. This all-consuming Grace obsession needs dealing with, before it grows out of control. Hopefully I'll be less enslaved once we exhaust this chemistry we have brewing.

She fiddles with the straw in her cocktail. 'Yes, of course I care. He's not a bad person—we just wanted different things in the end.'

'I can't imagine you with a bad person. You're too smart for bullshitters.' Which begs the question, what is she doing messing around with me, the ultimate playboy, as the press would have her believe?

My stomach turns and I slide my unfinished beer onto the bar. She doesn't know who I am. She doesn't know my reputation or how I make my livelihood, because I've been evasive.

She offers a small sad smile I want to kiss away. My fingers curl into my palm. I can't believe I'm probing her past regrets instead of convincing her single really is the best medicine. 'So why did you break things off with this good man? Wasn't what you had with him real?' I ask, a metallic taste in my mouth. I can't imagine Grace leaving when the going got tough, not with her wide vein of determination…

Not like some. Selfish people who only think about themselves. People who commit to having a child only to abandon them when it no longer suits.

I try to relax. Now isn't the time to dwell on my parents. And her answer, her reason, doesn't matter. I shouldn't care, but I've never met anyone like her before and I've no idea what to do with the relentless way she fills my head, my blood, makes me as unsettled as I am infatuated.

She looks up, her expression earnest, reminding me of the way she looked at me last night in the shower. 'I wanted more than he did.' Truth blazes in her pretty eyes, stilling me, even my heartbeat.

'More?'

'Yes. We'd been together a long time, but we'd both lost our way somehow, as if both of us were no longer feeling it but still going through the motions. We prioritised work over our relationship, rarely making time to connect. It began to feel like a friendship. An obligation. And I realised I was more committed than him.' She swallows hard and I want to hold her, but instead I force myself to listen.

'Then one day I had an epiphany, and I knew that staying with Greg was the easy option, but I'd always wonder if I'd settled. I wanted to be braver than that, open to the possibility of finding more, not that I'm in any hurry.' She takes a huge gulp of her drink while I stare.

It's the most fearless, honest thing I've ever heard,

and I'm struck dumb for a few seconds. Then curiosity wins out.

'More of what?' If I wore a collar I'd be running my finger under it. On the beach earlier she said she only wanted sex—that I can do. And I quashed her idea that I'm a gent or chivalrous.

Grace shrugs, drains the remnants of her drink. 'I don't know... Sparks. Passion. Something extraordinary. Something that makes me feel alive. Something my future partner and I prioritise as first in our life. Isn't that the way love should be?'

I shrug, dumbfounded. 'I wouldn't know.'

'That's right—well, that's how *I* think it should be. Just like my sister's romance novels.' She laughs. 'Don't look so worried—you're not in any danger.'

The pounding in my head feels dangerous. I've never met anyone so fearless, not afraid to admit what she wants and to risk everything to find it. Is she scared of nothing?

She leans closer, her stare dancing with mischief and sensuality. 'You see, I want all the feels, and the ring, and the romance,' she whispers, quoting me again, her hair brushing my neck. 'So *you* are perfectly safe.' She glances at the dance floor, swaying to the music.

Panic courses through my veins—I knew the first time I saw her that she wasn't my usual type, yet I wanted her anyway. But, reality check. Despite her recently leaving a relationship, we're on the same page. And wanting what she wants isn't a character flaw, no matter how much our core beliefs differ. We're on holiday for all intents; by nature this is a fling. And then we'll go back to our real lives...

I ignore the way my skin seems to prickle, hollowness in my gut. 'That's good to know.'

'And when I'm ready,' she says, 'I'm sure I'll find it. But for now,' she stage-whispers, 'I have a condom hidden in my dress and I want to dance.'

Her sexy smile sends my blood thrumming enough to distract me from the irrational and entirely selfish spikes of jealousy for some future guy lucky enough to be the answer to Grace's dreams.

But dreams are pointless; I know first hand. Hope, wanting something, relying on someone for your happiness, rips out whatever heart you had, over and over again until all you can do is patch the ragged hole left behind.

Perhaps I should counsel her on her folly. Give her the benefit of my jaded wisdom...

She stands, takes my hand and heads towards the tiny dance floor. Her hand feels small, but sure and steady. Reliable and competent. I can't wait to see the doctor in action tomorrow.

We attract a few looks as I pull her close—the staff know my identity and the mushy newly-weds probably think it's cute that we, the island's only singles, found each other.

Another victory for true love.

My ribs pinch again, despite her assurances. I swallow, strangely livid. Irrational, because all she's done is accept my usual commitment-free spiel in her understanding, forthright way. I should be relieved. But, why do I feel I'm running but can't get ahead of myself?

After a few minutes of swaying together to the beat of the music, she looks up, hesitant. 'I feel I should tell you something. You've been honest with me about what you want... So I want to be honest with you.'

I wince; I'm a cagey, untrusting bastard who hasn't yet confided my true identity...but now's my chance. She'll tell me her secret and I'll confess mine. We'll laugh and then fuck and I'll shake off whatever spell Grace cast and be back to myself.

'And if you want to, you know, stop carrying *things* around in your shorts, then I'll totally understand.'

'What are you talking about? I'm totally happy with the contents of my shorts.' The foil packet may as well be radioactive; it's burning a hole in my pocket. I'm so aroused, so blown away by this surprising woman and all her contradictions, I can't think straight, let alone concentrate on the riddles coming from her kissable mouth.

She lifts her chin. 'Well, I'm sure you're...used to casual sex.' She whispers the last words in an adorable display of respect for our privacy. I want to tear her out of here right this minute and hide her in my bungalow until the end of the week.

'I know how holiday resorts work,' she says.

'Fresh bodies delivered every two weeks... The hunky paddleboard instructor must see quite a lot of action.'

I bristle. I *have* seen a lot of action; I'm thirty-six, for fuck's sake. Yet for some reason I can't get my head around, I want to shock her, to make her as unsettled and knocked sideways as I feel every time I'm with her. 'It's not Ibiza, Grace. It's a honey-moon destination.'

For now.

'Oh, yes.' She laughs. 'Well, I've only had one sexual partner and that was my ex. So I just wanted to be upfront about it, like you've been with the "no relationship" thing, so that our expectations are aligned.'

My face goes slack with shock. The fact she's a serious relationship person and that for some reason she's chosen me to test out a fling with should send me running. Instead, my mouth wants to twitch into a smile, while heat builds in my gut. She seems to think she's somehow lacking because of her...lack of partners, rather than the sexiest woman I've met. No wonder I'm completely enchanted.

I stoop lower, press the side of my face to hers, until the smell of frangipani fills my nose. My lips hover near her ear, but I don't make contact the way I want. 'You can orgasm from nipple stimulation alone,' I murmur. 'I'm not remotely worried about how good sex is going to be between us, so no need for the heads-up.'

The air around us feels like a furnace. I'm inebriated on Grace, my head actually light with need to slake every impulse I've had since we met, free and unfettered. I'm lost in her eyes, the scent of her hair, the memory of her pleasure-racked body splayed out on the golden sand…

'Neither am I,' she whispers, her eyes heavy-lidded with desire and sexy determination, a baser version of the way she mastered the paddleboarding this morning…before she shattered in my arms and called my name. Her voice is husky, arousal a palpable force around her when she asks, 'Wanna get out of here?'

CHAPTER SIX

Ryan

'Yes.' I step back, my body protesting. My pulse throbs in my temples to race to the finish. But I want to make it memorable for her, so that she can put away her 'should' and never regret this choice.

I look down, fierce need coiling in my stomach even as my shoulders tighten with the certainty that I'm not good enough for her. She's dauntless, demanding more from life, and I'm the lucky bastard who gets to tag along for the ride. For a while.

I want to reach for her hand, lace her fingers with mine, but a stronger urge to protect her from resort gossip keeps my voice low and my hands in my pockets. 'You head back to the bungalows and I'll follow in a few minutes—we don't want to give people something to talk about.'

She nods, tucks her hair behind her ear and makes her way out into the night, a saucy little glance over her shoulder the only sign that she's even remotely as desperate for this as I am.

Please let her be as desperate.

We've skirted this since we first spoke on the beach, the craving hot and heavy and impossible to ignore. Thank goodness, because it's keeping the other stuff in my head at bay.

I head back to the bar, finish my beer and chat with Charlie for a few minutes. Every second feels like a loud clang in my brain, as if I'm hurtling towards the edge of a cliff. It's my secret bearing down on me, that's all. Guilt. I'll tell her my true identity before this goes any further. I owe her that at least after her honesty and the open way she's embracing our chemistry. It's just a misunderstanding I've allowed to go on for too long. Hopefully we can laugh it off, or, even better, kiss it away.

After several torturous minutes, I cite needing to work and leave the bar. I'm nearing the lit path that winds around the resort's pool when she steps from the shadows and whispers my name over the sound of frogs and the gentle lap of the waves.

She's literally hiding in the bushes.

I duck from the path towards her, but before I can ask her what she's doing, she reaches for my arm and tugs me into the foliage.

'What took you so long?' Her mouth finds mine in the darkness, soft and demanding, bold and sensual, her kisses driving me close to breaking point.

I laugh, gripping her around her waist, and shuffle us deeper into her hiding place in an oasis of garden.

'I was trying to be subtle. How much have you had to drink? I don't want to take advantage.'

'Only one cocktail. I'm fine. I want you. No more false starts.' She tugs my T-shirt up, her grabby hands exploring my stomach and back while she kisses me until I want to peel her out of the denim dress right here.

'Grace, are you sure?' I can taste the hint of Charlie's famous house cocktail on her lips.

'Why not let *me* take advantage of *you*, if you're worried? Hurry. I need you,' she hisses, reaching into her dress and flourishing a condom as if she's discovered the cure for cancer.

I look around. 'Here?' I can't believe I'm hesitating, putting on the brakes after two incredibly frustrating encounters in the past twenty-four hours. What the hell is wrong with me? But I'm more determined than ever she have a good time after the secret she shared.

'I kind of had a whole seduction thing planned,' I say, lifting a curl of her hair and rubbing my thumb over the silky strands. 'A bottle of wine, some music, the view from my bure...' It's hard to talk past her kisses, which grow increasingly frantic with every passing second.

'I appreciate the gesture, but yes, here. Now. I'm not risking another false start.' She tugs my mouth down to hers, but not before I notice the small dart of her eyes at our relatively secluded surroundings. Al-fresco sex excites her, but the no doubt deeply ingrained conscientiousness that allowed her to qualify and practise as a doctor also makes her cautious of public indecency charges.

'Okay, but follow me.' I know every inch of this place, so I guide her deeper into the garden, to the rear of a small pool house, tucked out of sight of the path and surrounded by banana trees and hibiscus.

I want to reassure her that this island is privately owned. By me. That in a few weeks' time, when the singles arrive ready to party, there'll be plenty of sexual exploration going on here. That if she wants to experiment with voyeuristic sex, I can take her to one of my other, well-established resorts, where the exorbitant membership fee and NDAs everyone signs ensure the utmost discretion.

But her seductive smile and my need for her obliterate my good intentions.

Grace walks backwards dragging me with her until her back hits the wall of the pool house. 'I want to touch you.' She shoves my shirt up and I help her, tugging it overhead and casting it aside. Her touch roams my chest, shoulders and back, her hands on me a blissful form of torture. My mind grows foggy, my confession slipping away like a curl of smoke as Grace slides her hand inside my underwear and does eye-rolling things to my dick.

Fuck, I'm not the man I think I am, and I want to touch her too. I want to forget.

I slip the thin straps of her dress from her shoulders and trace the line of her collarbone with my lips until her breath catches.

'Ryan…' She abandons my dick to tug the loops of my waistband, shunting my hips closer to hers, impatient and uninhibited as she was on the beach this morning.

She wants to go fast and furious, and I'm greedy for more Grace. But I'm also determined that she'll never forget her first casual fling.

'Let's see these sensitive nipples.' I peel the dress down to her waist, exposing her to the cool night air. I look up from her perfect breasts, which rise and fall with her excited breathing, to find her eyes on me, and for a second we're locked in some sort of alternate universe, where only she and I and the sounds of paradise exist. My heart thuds against hers. My cock surges against the softness of her stomach.

'You sure you want to do this here?'

Her nod is all I need.

My patience snaps. With a groan of pent-up longing, I kiss her, pressing my body to hers until her naked breasts are flattened to my bare chest. I suck in her gasp of pleasure and kiss and nibble my way over her chest to those exquisite nipples, tonguing and laving more sexy cries from her. But Grace wants to set the pace. She shoves my shorts over my hips and grips my aching cock, tugging and pumping and hitting all the right spots until I'm cursing and fighting for control. I'm so high on her, wound so tight, I have to brace one hand against the stone wall behind her back, my fingertips digging into the rough surface to wrestle back some discipline. Why do I feel like a teenager with this woman? Why do I want to go faster and slower in the same breath?

She pushes my head away from her breast so she can cover me with the condom, and then she grips my shoulders as I hoist her around the waist and lift her from the ground. We're so in sync, it's as if we've rehearsed this a thousand times. She helps me get closer, tugging up the skirt of her dress and gripping my hips with her thighs, providing a haven of space I intend to occupy until, this time, we're both spent and sated and can barely walk.

I grip her waist with one arm and slide my other hand between her legs. She's wet and hot, her underwear damp. I push the crotch aside and notch the tip of my cock at her slick entrance.

'Are you okay?' I have no idea why I'm hesitating. Perhaps because she told me about her single sexual partner. Perhaps because all we seem to share is outdoor encounters. Perhaps I need to be what she wants. To make it memorable.

'Better than okay.' She releases her grip on my shoulders and traces one finger along the side of my face, her eyes locked with mine, the perfect blend of tenderness and sexy, just like Grace.

But I want to push her boundaries, to reward that daring erotic side.

'You want this, don't you? To be fucked against a wall where someone could hear or see?' My voice cracks with the pressure of holding back from thrusting inside her in a single, satisfying stroke.

Her lids droop and her head lolls back against the wall, a breathy 'yes' slipping past her swollen lips. She releases the hold of her thighs on my waist so that she slips down the wall an inch or two. Her tight heat swallows the head of my cock, forcing a groan from deep in my chest, razing my patience to the ground. I push home, gliding into her in a single thrust that leaves us both panting and staring, our hearts banging together like cymbals.

'Hold tight,' I say, loving the way her eyes are glazed with passion. She feels so good gripping me, the rush so profound, I almost can't speak.

She braces her arms on my shoulders. 'Don't stop.'

Stop…? Hell, I'd be hard pushed. 'No intention,' I growl as I thrust into her, shunting her hips against the wall while I grind my teeth to stave off the volcano of pleasure.

Every time I bottom out inside, she gasps, her warm breath mingling with mine, our lips only millimetres apart and our stares locked together as surely as our bodies. I use all my strength to hold her up against the wall with one arm and my hips, so I can tweak that sensitive exposed nipple with my free hand.

'Ryan,' she cries out, her eyes growing wide the way they did earlier when her orgasm seemed to shock the hell out of both of us. Man, she's incredible. The most honest woman I've ever met.

'Yes,' I hiss, because I'm close too, and I want this to be the best fuck against a wall she's ever had.

Time for some more dirty talk…

'You like taking risks, don't you?' I whisper over her lips, so I can watch the flare of shocked desire glow in her eyes. 'You liked watching me yesterday, and perhaps you even like the idea that someone might see us now.' I can't help the filthy visions filling my head featuring my demanding Grace, and I want her to know how her stark honesty makes me feel. If I'm going to debase the good doctor, bring her down to my level, I want it to be something she'll never forget.

Then again, perhaps she's debasing me…

'Oh, my…' She pants hard, nodding, and I flatten my tongue over one peaked, exposed nipple. 'Yes… yes, I do.' Her fingers curl, twisting my hair.

Her confession roars in my head, my hips powering harder, faster to reward her for it. So there's a part of her that enjoys the fear of discovery. I'm hoping that might actually aid and heighten her climax. That I can take her somewhere she's never been makes me feel invincible.

Then I hear giggling. Softly spoken French tells me company is close by. I hold my breath, my hips slowing a fraction but not stopping, because I don't think I could stop even if the entire island's population rocked up and started giving me points out of ten for technique.

Grace must hear them too, because alarm flashes in her eyes, but hot on its heels embers of excitement.

'Yes,' I say. 'That's my girl.'

I kiss away her reservations, the surge of my tongue against hers letting her know we're unlikely to be discovered in this secret tropical corner, and even if we were, would that be so bad? Doesn't our passion for each other, for this, justify the risk?

I keep moving, watch the way she bites her lip as she tries to fight the cries she released with abandon only seconds ago.

'Do you want me to stop?' My voice is hushed, but not a whisper. Grace needs to know that I don't give a damn about being discovered if she doesn't, the fact that we're on the same page evidence this woman could be made specifically for me.

She shakes her head, her mouth falling open, head thrown back. I tilt my pelvis upwards and add a grind to her clit with each thrust that has her breath hitching once more. I roll her nipple, applying extra pressure to make up for the interruption to her orgasm. I know that feeling. I've been walking around with blue balls for the past twenty-four hours.

'I'm not going to stop, Grace.' I pick up the pace again, my mouth hovering over hers so I can talk and kiss and capture her pants all at once. 'I'm going to keep fucking you right here until you come. Even if they hear us. Even if they watch.'

Her returned passion, her wild kisses and the clench of her internal muscles gripping my cock tell me she's fully on board with my plan. The knowledge that she's happy to continue with strangers in earshot goads me back to the rhythm that had her close moments earlier. I bite down, my jaw clenched and my thighs and abs on fire as I give her everything I've got. It's impossibly hotter now. More elicit. Risky and erotic. So perfect, I almost want to thank the French couple.

I rear back so I can watch the glaze of arousal in her eyes and the excitement on her face. We're silent apart from the soft gasps of air my thrusts force from Grace, the slaps of my hips against her thighs and the roar of my blood in my ears.

Grace drops her head to the crook of my neck, hiding her face, even as she grips me tighter and urges me to thrust faster with her hands clenching my buttocks.

A splash sounds, more giggling. The French couple are probably skinny dipping only metres away on the other side of the bushes. Gotta love tropical gardens. And these incredibly sensitive and talented nipples, which seem to have a direct link to the tightly gripping walls of her pussy.

'Don't stop,' gasps Grace.

'Nope,' I grit out, the eroticism of the moment clawing at me so my own climax builds at the base of my spine. I rub my lips over hers as I whisper between kisses. 'Part of me hopes they hear us, hopes they know exactly what we're doing. That we're doing this, that you couldn't wait to get back to the room…'

'Oh… Ryan.'

'That's it,' I whisper into her hair, which has fallen over her face and surrounds me in a fog of her scent. 'You're going to come all over me with people only a few steps away. You'll just have to come quietly. Or not, it's up to you.'

She must have been hovering close to the edge, because my words take her back to where she'd been prior to the French interruption. With a final cry, our eyes locked, she comes, milking my cock with hard, violent spasms until I too bury my grunt against the side of her neck and fill the condom with white-hot jets that leave me reeling and barely able to stand.

A long, drawn-out groan sounds in my head as I pump the last shudders into her still-pulsing heat.

Who is this woman? A woman of contradictions and extremes. A woman who takes relationships seriously but is embracing our holiday fling as if she's done this a hundred times.

When I raise my head from her shoulder, she's staring at me with something close to wonder.

'I can't believe we did that,' she whisper-giggles.

The French couple are still in the pool, no doubt having their own late night fun. For a heartbeat I'm lost for words, lost in Grace, my mind blissfully blank, my cock still hard and jerking inside her tight warmth.

'I can. You like the idea of being caught doing something you shouldn't.'

She turns serious. 'Perhaps I do…'

'Well, that was the hottest sex against a wall I've ever experienced.' It should thrill me, excite me that she's embracing what I'm guessing is a new daring side. Instead I drop my forehead to her shoulder and breathe through the almost violent urge to keep her—her pleasure and her honesty and her abandonment—all to myself, the possessive fire in my veins proof I don't want the French couple, or anyone else, intruding.

What the hell…? I've enjoyed being watched before with like-minded partners. Never have I felt such a bewildering ownership. My head pounds at the force of the alien feeling. Now would be the perfect time to tell her that when I make this a Dempsey singles' resort, she'll be able to explore and satisfy any kink she likes, that teaming sexually adventurous singletons in paradise is my speciality. But am I ready to lift the scales from her eyes, confess the fact I've pretended to be something I'm not to this woman, who seems to see inside me with a simple look? If only she knew what an oddity we make: the seller of sex and the saver of lives…

No—it's just a post-orgasmic thing. Good sex, the kind of chemistry we share are enough to leave anyone, even a cynic like me, seeing stars.

I step back, gripping the base of the condom as I withdraw and lower her to the ground. I clean up, wrapping the condom in a tissue, while Grace pulls her dress into position. But already I want her again, my greedy cock pulsing and thickening as I stuff it back inside my shorts. I want her to myself. In private.

How is that possible?

It feels dangerous, almost. She's dangerous...

'Can I walk you home?' I wince. I sound like some sort of old-fashioned suitor. Nothing could be further from the truth. The concrete block in my chest returns, only now it's sprouting wicked barbs, reminding me that there's nothing beyond the no-strings sex I peddle for a living. At least not for me. I don't do more than that.

She giggles again as she takes my outstretched hand. 'For someone who's just fucked my brains out, you're rather gallant, you know.'

I set off in the direction of the beach, focussed on the needs of my dick to combat whatever is going on inside my chest. 'Nah...it's just a vicious rumour. Besides, if I walk you home, you might invite me in for round two.'

Grace smiles. Breathes out a soft exhale. 'I might just do that.'

CHAPTER SEVEN

Grace

I OPEN MY EYES, seeking Ryan next to me in bed, to find only a single perfect frangipani flower on his pillow. Warmth spreads through me, the delicate bloom confirmation the last night really happened. I roll onto my back, my sappy smile directed at the ceiling. What an incredible night.

Then I sober, the high plummeting.

Ryan and I have nothing to do with romance, despite his parting gesture. This is just a fling.

I sit up, the silence and the sinking feeling confirming I'm alone in the bungalow. But what did I expect? That the king of commitment-free shagging had come over all sentimental, staying to spoon?

I swing my legs to the edge of the bed, doubts crawling over my skin like ants. Just because I'm on my dream holiday having amazing, life-changing sex is no cause for mushy romantic notions. Ryan made himself clear—he doesn't do feels, or rings or romance.

Just shattering orgasms and addictive sex giggles and flowers on the pillow. I sigh, my head a scrambled mess, but my body firmly stuck with the belly-fluttering memories. What happens now we've gone all the way? Will we revert to strangers sharing polite, awkward smiles when we meet on the beach or keep up the sex until it's time for me to leave? The keen heat between my legs answers for me.

But even if I can keep my head grounded in reality, what does Ryan want? I look back at the flower, wishing I could just ask him. Perhaps him leaving before dawn *is* his answer. Perhaps his no-strings rule means it's over after one night.

I worry at my lip as shivers pass over my exposed arms, then I plant my feet on the tiles with determination. I don't want it to be over. Messing around with him makes me feel alive and carefree. I want more. More of the incandescent passion that I feel when he smiles at me with that hint of challenge, so I know whatever comes next, be it paddleboarding or some impossible sex position, will be amazing and worth the risk of stepping out of my comfort zone.

I'll simply find him, tell him what I want, and if we're no longer on the same wavelength, it's no big deal.

Filled with fresh resolve, I head for the shower and step under the hot spray, embracing the new, improved me. The me that threw caution to the wind to explore something dangerous and uninhibited with a man who seems intent on being my dirty-talking guide. The me that woke up this morning and, for the first time since I called quits on my engagement, felt the rightness of that decision to my marrow.

I'm not naive—there's nothing on this island I didn't bring here. All these new and thrilling parts of me were there before. I just never gave them airtime.

But now I can.

With Ryan as my own private passion coach.

If he still wants the job…

The warm water touches the sensitive spots on my body—my nipples, the stubble burn on my neck, between my legs. Have I ever had so much sex in a twenty-four-hour period?

Even in the beginning, Greg and I found it easy to keep our hands off each other. I convinced myself the constant stress of exams, the pressure and competition of med school and then exhaustion of being junior doctors while pursuing our careers through a long-distance relationship were to blame. But I'm struggling to recall even the briefest of honeymoon periods. How could I have deluded myself for so long that the relationship, even from the start, gave me everything I needed? Just because growing up I'd put myself second in order to be a good sister and daughter, I should never have carried that attitude over into adulthood.

I stare at nothing, my movements automatic as I wash my hair. Greg and I became engaged around the same time that Bryony took a turn for the worse after a valiant two-year struggle with heart failure.

Her death was expected but no less devastating, so my distraction made sense. Did I love him, or just use him as a crutch, someone there for me at one of the worst times of my life, someone I latched onto for comfort without truly considering if our relationship had what it took to make it for the long haul? Just because we'd been together for years shouldn't have been the only reason to get engaged.

And after the grief, I wondered if I hadn't somehow forced him to ask. Our three-year engagement and the fact that we'd already postponed the wedding twice for 'work reasons' were red flags, if I'd needed them, that all was not hearts and flowers.

Shame heats every part of me from within.

You knew all along that it wasn't the bells and whistles roller coaster it should have been...

But I limped along out of obligation and inertia. The crushing fear of letting people—my parents, Greg's parents—down, the wasted years I'd already invested in our relationship, the feeling, one I was scared to acknowledge, that I was better off sticking with what we had than risk never finding love again.

Flashes of the day I lost my patient, Mr Burgess, on the operating table detonate in my head. Without the wake-up call of that horrible day, I might still be living in a deluded bubble, lying to both Greg and myself.

The high of my night with Ryan swirls down the drain with the soap-scented water. The anguish on Mrs Burgess's face when my surgical colleague and I broke the news that her husband of forty years hadn't survived the routine hernia operation materialises from the steam. He'd had a heart attack and never regained consciousness, despite our best attempts at resuscitation.

The enormity of her loss presses in on me from all sides once more until I'm conscious of my every breath fogging the glass.

Greg showed understanding that night, of course. Losing patients is a tragic but unavoidable part of our work, but my melancholy lingered in the weeks after, my memories returning time and time again to the night Bryony died, the years spent watching her live a kind of half life out of necessity, and the associated guilt.

Until one day, I woke up and saw my life with greater clarity—the beginning of the end for Greg and me. The beginning of the end of playing it safe and pretending.

Because had she been fit and able, Bryony would have grabbed life by the balls. She never once asked me to curtail my activities to stay with her through hospital visits or days when she didn't have the energy to get off the couch. I did that all on my own. Because she was my sister.

I owe it to her fearlessness to live the way she dreamed of living. And this holiday, my fling with Ryan, is a start.

I finish my shower quickly, eager to get to my first teaching class. Today emerges the new Grace in all her glory, one who came here from the other side of the world alone. One into risky outdoor sex with a sinfully hot paddleboarder within earshot of another couple. One who wants more than one night. One who'd go home a changed woman, with a fresh perspective on life and what she'd demand from it.

I pull on shorts and a tank top over my bikini, tie back my hair and grab my sunglasses before heading for the resort's reception on rejuvenated feet.

When I arrive, the small meeting room is packed with assembled staff members. My heart gallops for a glimpse of Ryan, sinking when he's nowhere to be seen. I slap on a smile for the staff and outline how I plan to structure the day's lessons.

I'm halfway through my introductory spiel on the basics of cardio-pulmonary resuscitation when the door opens and in saunters Ryan, casually dressed with his hair still damp from the shower as if it's just another morning, not the morning after he left me hoarse from crying his name. I look away, certain the evidence of my sex marathon decorates my face, as surely as Ryan's ripped physique under that T-shirt carries marks from my fingernails.

A pang of frustration gripes like a bout of colic. Him leaving denied me waking up to find his big, sexy body asleep next to me. Robbed me of waking him by taking him into my mouth the way he'd done to me in the night. Stolen another orgasm from me. Because if he'd been there when I opened my eyes this morning, I too would have been late for this class.

I clear my throat and keep my greedy gaze away from Ryan's handsome face, which gives nothing away—as if he didn't go down on me at least twice in the night, that wicked mouth of his quirked in a half-smile as he delivered such devastating pleasure I screamed into the pillow so as not to wake the neighbours. I had so many orgasms I lost count, just before I slipped into a climax-induced coma.

'So, once you remember ABC—airway, breathing, circulation—and you've established that the patient has no pulse and isn't breathing, you need to start chest compressions.' I undo the mannequin's Hawaiian shirt with a grin—someone has a sense of humour—and expose his rubber chest.

'The correct hand placement for chest compressions is two fingers above the edge of the breastbone.' I demonstrate the location, my head down to better ignore the heat of Ryan's stare, which tickles like feathered fingertips on my sensitive skin.

'Okay, let's have a volunteer. Who'd like to give it a try first?' I ask, my face flushing when for long silent seconds no one raises their hand. At last, Ryan stands from the back of the group. 'Great, a brave volunteer, but, the rest of you, don't get comfortable—everyone will be having a turn.'

Ryan drops to his knees beside me and I shuffle over a few inches, the hairs on my arms lifting and my pulse throbbing between my legs with him at such close quarters, as if my body remembers the source of my long night of nocturnal pleasure.

But unlike yesterday, the roles are reversed. I'm the teacher, his seriously impressed expression seeking my guidance. Why do I feel like the only woman in the room…the island…heck, the world?

I swallow down the renewed surge of lust. Whether the sex is over or not, the chemistry burns as fierce as ever.

'Place your fingers here to find the bottom of the sternum.' My voice feels rusty. I demonstrate the position again, sliding my hand away in time so our fingers don't touch. Because if I touch him, I'll want to kiss him. To press my mouth to his neck and feel his scruff against my skin. My breathy voice and nervous gestures alone are probably enough of a sign that Ryan and I are more than work colleagues.

'Good. One hand over another, fingers intertwined,' I say.

He follows my instructions, focussed and professional, where I struggle to forget the demanding touch of those hands now delivering chest compressions to a rubber mannequin.

Ryan performs the CPR in his trademark confident manner, topped off with a roguish smile for the other members of staff who all clap when he's done as if he's brought the inanimate casualty back to life.

This is his skill. People.

He makes them feel at ease, even while he nudges them out of their comfort zone, showing them that anything is possible, be it paddleboarding or screaming orgasms against a wall in a public place with people nearby…

From then I may as well be stretched out on a medieval rack, so gruelling is the simple teaching session. Where Ryan is relaxed and competent, I'm flustered and garble my words any time he's close or asks an intelligent, insightful question. He's a natural leader, encouraging even the shyest of the local women to step up and practise the techniques involved in CPR.

My mind is fudge; all I can think about is dragging him back to my room for a private anatomy lesson, or exploring all of the hidden nooks and crannies on the island—me, him and a jumbo box of condoms.

'Lets break for lunch,' I say, once the last staff member finishes their turn with the mannequin. I pack away the equipment as the small crowd departs, leaving the stragglers, Charlie the bar manager and Ryan, who stop for a chat.

Relief and anticipation play tug of war with my insides. He's waiting for me. As soon as Charlie leaves, I can persuade him to give our just-sex arrangement a few more days…

Be brave. Tell him what I want. Easy.

I tune into the tail end of their conversation.

'No worries, boss,' says Charlie. 'Catch you later.'

Boss?

I glance up, catch the flash of guilt, hastily concealed, on Ryan's face.

Every tiny hair on my body prickles to attention.

Why would Charlie call the water-sports instructor boss? Is it some sort of joke? But why Ryan's guilty look, unless he *is* the boss?

Have I been naive? Lulled into a false sense of security with sunshine and holiday vibes that I could trust him with my newfound sexual exploration?

Humiliation rushes through me. I don't really know him at all. I thought I was okay with that, but maybe I'm not... Perhaps this lesson proves I'm not a fling-with-a-stranger kind of person, after all.

I box up the resuscitation mannequin, my movements brisk and jerky, as I avoid looking at Ryan. It takes three attempts to fasten the clasps on the case as my head battles to make sense of what is clearly obvious.

Ryan deceived me about his identity. Why?

I hold my breath as the door whooshes closed behind Charlie, the air around me pulsing, my body attuned to Ryan's silent presence.

Sounds of the resort's comings and goings grow muffled. I feel Ryan's closeness like a bonfire burning my back. I force my shoulders back and plaster an overly bright smile on my face as I turn, every muscle screaming at me to scarper from my confusion.

'Hey, how's your grandmother today?' I ask, trying to keep my tone of voice neutral and devoid of my self-directed disappointment. I struggled to trust my instincts with Greg, a man I'd known for years. Why did I think I could trust my instincts for a man I've known for five minutes? I could have predicted that this situation, strings-free sex, wasn't really for me. Not even the brave new me. I'm a relationship person. I just need to find the right partner.

He presses his lips together, regret haunting his eyes. 'She's in good spirits, thanks. Grace, about—'

'That's good news. I'm glad.' I interrupt his excuses, already cringing. If only I could turn into a rubber mannequin and avoid this conversation, which feels like another failure.

But he wants to have it out. 'Can we talk?' he says, with a frown.

'Sure.' So breezy, when all I want to do is retreat and regroup my thoughts on casual sex. Yes, I hoped to enjoy it for a few more days, but he owes me nothing. It really doesn't matter who he is. But a part of me, the part that trusted him enough to share our incredible night, to step out of my comfort zone and embrace the chemistry we share, feels tiny stabs of defeat rain down like grains of sand flung by the wind.

'I was going to tell you.' He winces, trying to take the heavy mannequin case from my hand.

I shift it out of his reach, even though it twists my shoulder into an awkward position and the weight digs the handle into my fingers.

'Do you mean the boss thing?' I deposit the case onto the table near the door and swallow as much of the embarrassment from my voice as I can. I face him, lift my chin. 'Don't worry—we were just fooling around. You don't owe me any explanations.'

Ryan stares for one beat, two, his expression devoid of emotion, but fire brews in his eyes. The same fire in which, last night, I'd have happily burned alive.

He steps closer, his voice low. 'I want to explain. I meant to last night but we... *I* got carried away.'

'Hey, it's no big deal. I'd have fucked you even if you are the boss.' The words feel foreign; casual words for casual sex. 'So what are you? The resort manager? I thought that was Taito's role?' I ask, annoyed that I haven't pushed for answers before now. Not that it really matters beyond making me feel stupid for thinking I'd cracked the whole hook-up thing.

Bugger—I'll have to leave this part out of the story I tell Neve and Brooke.

He slings his hands in his shorts pockets and sighs. 'Look, why don't we get some lunch and talk? I wanted to invite you out for a boat cruise this evening...'

'I'm not hungry,' I say, snappy because I feel my resolve slipping, feel his magnetism drawing me back in. I can go willingly, continue to sleep with him because that's what I want, but no more seeing romance where it isn't. Yes, I want this passionate connection in my future, but I also want trust.

'A walk on the beach, then? Please, Grace. Give me a chance to explain. After last night... I thought we had a really good time—'

'We did have a good time, which is why I don't get that you couldn't tell me your true identity.'

He nods, contrite. 'You're right—I should have told you, but I got sidetracked. You're fun and smart and sexy enough to fry a man's brain.' He holds up his hands. 'That's not an excuse.'

Then I remember why *I'm* here and drop my stare to the floor. I'm hiding how I should have been accompanied by my new husband. But he's right. We can discuss this like mature adults—strangers, who just happen to have had lots of sex.

I take a shuddering breath. 'Okay. Let's walk and talk.' With a silent lecture on distinguishing orgasmic hormones from feelings playing in my head, I lead the way the short distance down to the water's edge, Ryan at my side.

Typically, the beach is busy with a group kayaking lesson for eight or ten of the resort's couples. By the time we've walked out of earshot, I've talked myself around in circles so many times, torn between booking the next flight home to avoid feeling foolish that I celebrated the success of my first fling too soon and demanding more sex until I'm an expert at casual.

I stop and face him. 'Listen, let's forget it. I feel a bit silly, if I'm honest. I got carried away by your hotness, too.'

He moves as if to touch me, his intense eyes searching, and then stops himself. 'You're not silly. It wasn't calculated. My intentions were more about self-preservation or… I dunno…laziness.' He scrubs a hand over his face. 'I should have told you. I own the resort. The island, in fact. Well, co-own it with a local businessman.'

'Seriously?' I gape. 'Wow. You really are cagey

and cynical. Were you worried I'd seduce you in your shower or lure you into a public sex act?'

He frowns at my sarcasm. 'Very funny.'

But I couldn't feel less like laughing. 'So you knew who I was, knew everything about me when we met on the beach.' I cross my arms over my waist, a shield. 'You're probably the person who hired me in the first place.'

Does he know about Greg? About my aborted honeymoon?

'No. Taito hired you. I instructed him to purchase the defibrillator and other equipment we might need for the resort and he suggested we employ someone to teach us how to use it.' He moves to face me and stops walking. 'I *was* genuinely covering the water-sports lessons when we met. Pita, the regular instructor, had a family emergency on the main island and there was no one else. So when you asked for a lesson but turned down my offer of a drink...' he shrugs '...well, further explanation seemed unnecessary. And then afterwards...once we'd crossed a line... I was going to tell you. I planned to tell you last night, before things went any further. But then... I guess I got caught up in the sex.'

'Okay,' I say, kicking at the sand, because I should make my own confession.

'Grace...' He steps close, his voice taking on that deep, seductive quality I now know well. 'I respect what you told me last night, about your past relationship. I don't want you to regret what happened between us. Last night was…incredible.'

'It was. I felt invincible when I woke up this morning. Stupid, because we don't know anything about each other and I thought I was okay with that, but…' I bite my lip, reluctant to admit my folly to a man so anti-commitment. But it won't be the bravest thing I've done since arriving here. 'But, perhaps casual sex and I aren't meant to be.' I awoke full of optimism, as if I'd cracked my own elusive code, my predictable and safe relationship with Greg nothing like this intense longing, as if I'm about to jump out of an aeroplane, every instinct telling me to back up, but knowing the fall will thrill and exhilarate.

He frowns, steps closer. 'I felt invincible too. If I could go back and tell you the truth in the bar, I would in a heartbeat.'

I feel the sincerity in his earnest stare with every thud of my heart. 'I don't regret it. I put myself out there, without my usual caution, but I'm not sorry.'

We fall into awkward silence as a couple of the keenest kayakers sail past.

'I should get back—I have to teach the rest of the class, but then you know about that. You're my boss, too.' I try to cut the hint of acid from my tone but fail.

'Grace…' He tries to reach for my hand the way he did last night when he walked me back to my room before a hundred other, more intimate, touches, but I step back.

'You don't have to feel guilty—I acted on impulse.

Blinded by sex hormones and novelty.' We met. We hooked up. There is no more than that. 'I just want you to know, it wouldn't have made a difference if you'd told me.'

He seems to bite back what he really wants to say, his jaw muscles bunching. Then he sighs. 'I guess I liked being just the paddleboard bum for a while, if I'm honest. I liked the way you looked at me, as if you had no expectations beyond me teaching you to paddle. I'm a loner, a distrustful prick, if you must know, and I didn't want to tell you that, because I like you and I didn't want to scare you off.'

This time I'm the one wincing, because I can relate. I know what it's like to have to live up to expectations and obligations, even your own, and I didn't want him to know that I'm on my honeymoon, alone…

We head back, silent for a short distance, as if neither of us knows how to proceed. Me because I presumed casual sex is free of angst, and exactly what it seems on the surface, and him presumably because he can usually walk away from his flings when they become awkward. But we're trapped here.

'Just for the record,' I say, 'I don't see you as a loner. You have a way with people. A gift for putting them at ease.' I smile because it's hard to make a big deal about this here, where everything is laid-back and simple. Where I'm different, but in some ways unchanged. The lesson a timely reminder—don't get carried away by romantic gestures.

Another couple walk past and Ryan steps closer on the path, his hand gently gripping my wrist. I turn to face him, allowing him to slide his fingers down to entwine with mine.

'So, if I say I'm sorry...' his voice is low, intimate, as it was last night when he demanded another orgasm from me 'introduce myself properly—Ryan Dempsey,' he holds out his hand, '...will you come sailing this evening, after your class?'

I draw a deep breath, my yes clogged in my throat, because I do want passion and adventure, but a hint of my usual caution will help me walk away at the end of the week without a backward glance of regret. 'There are lots of things I haven't told you about me, so I'd say we're even.'

Ryan frowns. 'Well, perhaps I want to know those things. I also want more than one night. Don't you?'

I nod, my pulse picking up at his honesty. 'Yes, I do.' As long as I hold something back, remember that this is just for the next few days, what harm can it do? And it's clarified one thing—the new Grace definitely wants a relationship for life.

With a relieved smile, Ryan steps closer, slides his fingers across my cheek and into my hair. 'I promise I'll make it up to you.'

It's such a fine line between letting go and holding something back, I feel as if I'm being tossed by the waves. But isolated here on an island with a man who literally rocks my world, what choice do I have but to try and walk that precarious line?

CHAPTER EIGHT

Ryan

'I'M GLAD YOU'RE HERE,' I say above the sound of the outboard, sucking in the addictive scent of Grace's hair carried on the warm breeze. I've given her the helm of the *Blarney*. It's torture to watch her small frown of concentration as she steers us around the many scattered islands in the archipelago that forms Fiji, her delight at being in charge of a fifty-foot motor yacht obvious, although its spec is so high, it could probably sail itself.

She narrows her eyes at me, a smile twitching her sensual mouth. 'I didn't want to miss this. Plus I'll think up other ways to make you pay.'

I laugh, but my stomach drops. How could I have been so stupid? This morning after an incredible night, all I wanted to do was kiss her awake and drag another orgasm from her beautiful, pliant body. I forced myself to leave, my spiel about casual boundaries fresh in my head, when in reality, I was the one craving more, craving everything she's willing to give in the time we have left. A realisation that caused my chest to constrict with panic that propelled me out of the door.

Is she the best form of distraction from my worries, or something more hazardous?

'That's a price I can't wait to pay.' I wink and fight the urge to kiss her.

What the hell is happening to me?

Despite her warning about her one sexual relationship, she blew me away. I can't remember ever finding sex funny, but it was with her, and hot and so addictive I want to drop anchor and remind her of how well we fit together. Instead I console myself with the wide-eyed excitement lighting up her sun-kissed face.

I feel her sigh as I bring my arms around her waist and allow my nose to linger in her hair. 'It's beautiful, here,' she says. 'Will you stay for ever?'

I stiffen. It's a thought that has never occurred to me. I could afford to retire here tomorrow, but ever since the day I had no choice but to sleep on a freezing concrete floor I've strived, hauling myself and my grandmother from relative hardship, singlehanded. And settling in one place? When it's easier to keep travelling, keep moving and forget the futility of craving a home, a constant.

A vision of Grace and I exploring the islands together on the *Blarney* flashes through my mind, both the image and my reaction jaw-dropping. There's so much we could do together, so much more I want to know about her if I indulged in relationships. And if she embraced everything with the abandonment, joy and determination I'm beginning to learn is her default setting, what a ride we'd have in store...

But I don't do that. I travel alone. I keep my casual relationships brief and superficial. I don't ask too many questions. Because then I can walk away.

I grow aware of that bloody concrete block crushing me. I know my grandmother would love to see me settled. But, am I ready to change? To re-evaluate my stance on love when I have first-hand evidence that love—if it is real—can end catastrophically and with collateral damage? Opening myself to the possibility of more with this woman also exposes me to the risk of loss.

And I'm already maxed out where that fear is concerned.

I try to exhale the tension gripping me. 'I travel a lot, and when I'm not travelling I stay in London to be close to my grandmother. I try not to be away for longer than a few weeks, but you're right. If ever there was a place to stop and smell the ocean, this is it.'

In many ways Grace reminds me of Grandma. Both strong, practical women with enormous capacity for compassion.

'So do you own other resorts?' She takes her eye off the horizon to cast me a sidelong look. 'Is this your only job? I'm determined to know more about you now. I won't be distracted by all this.' She waves her hand in my general direction, and I capture it, lift her hand to my mouth and press a kiss to her fingertips.

'I guess my official title would be entrepreneur, but in recent years the resort side has taken centre stage. This is my tenth.'

Her mouth hangs open. 'You own *ten* resorts?'

I nod. 'Yes, all over the world—hence the travelling.'

She pushes up her sunglasses, light dawning. 'This is your yacht, isn't it? You didn't just charter it…'

I shrug as if my lifestyle, the luxury of the *Blarney*, is no big deal, but I still have days when I wake up drenched in sweat, terrified because I'm seventeen again; alone, powerless and homeless.

She laughs, the sound humourless, not her usual delighted, contagious chuckle. 'Great. I thought you were the water-sports instructor when really you're some sort of undercover boss billionaire.'

'Well, hardly undercover…' I say, aware I'm still on thin ice. 'I'm just a normal bloke who worked hard and had some lucky breaks. Believe me—a smart, pretty girl like you wouldn't have given seventeen-year-old me a second look if we were the same age.'

I grow hot under her intelligent and inquisitive stare, aware I've revealed too much. 'Why don't we stop a while?' I say, as we approach one of the smaller inhabited islands. 'Drop anchor and grab a drink? Perhaps have a swim?'

'Sure. And you can explain to me what you mean by that.' She steps back, giving me the helm. I kill the engine and anchor us in place only metres from the shore, where a couple of local fishermen are dragging nets aboard their small fishing vessel.

Grace saunters off towards the deck loungers. I prepare us both a cold drink and sit beside her while I work out how much of my tawdry past to reveal.

'So tell me why I wouldn't have given you a second look at seventeen,' she says, taking a sip of her drink. 'Because at that age, I had my own issues, believe me.'

Every cell in my body wants to sidestep this topic with a distraction, to touch her, drag her into my lap and feel her warm, luscious body sprawled over mine. I'm usually past the infatuation stage by now and preparing to walk away but all I want to do is reconnect and resume the playful passion we discovered last night. Perhaps it's because I *can't* walk away. We're literally marooned here. Temporarily. Or is it that she challenges me, her fearlessness nudging me to probe my own contentment? There's something about this woman that makes me breathe a little easier, a calming presence that soothes the never far away urgency gripping my throat.

And now I want to know about her, too. 'I'll tell you mine if you'll tell me yours?' I hedge.

'Done.' She places her glass on the side table and offers me her full attention.

'Well, for a start, by seventeen, I'd left school. While you at the same age would have been studying hard to get into med school, I was working on a building site in the day and attending adult education classes in the evenings.'

If she's surprised she hides it well, her sharp, probing stare flicking over my face. 'What did a builder's mate study to end up with all this?' She spreads her hands to encompass the *Blarney* anchored in this idyllic place.

'Anything and everything going free—bookkeeping, IT, business management. You name it, I've done it. I couldn't afford to go to university until my mid-twenties, but I wanted more. So I worked hard, like you.'

The impressed look on her face puffs out my chest. 'You're very driven, some would say an overachiever…'

I incline my head in acknowledgement. 'Aren't you? Isn't that what it takes to make it? It's less about luck than most people believe. More about stubborn determination.'

She nods. 'Yes. But from night school to owning your own island is a lot of determination.'

It's not a question but it hangs there in the warm air demanding elaboration. And for once I trust this woman enough to know I won't regret telling her about my past. What's the worst that can happen?

She has too much integrity to run to the press with my sad little sob story.

'My drivers were more…basic than yours, I suspect. I was driven to be safe, warm and not hungry.' My voice is harsher than I intended, rough with the emotion that's never far from the surface when I think about my haphazard childhood and ad hoc parenting.

She sobers, her fingers flexing as if she's stopped herself from reaching out to touch me. 'We don't have to talk about this, although you should know I can relate—not to the hunger, but most of us have demons.'

I sigh, fighting the memories of having nothing but my own self-belief and a drive to provide for the one person who cared enough about me to stick around. Grandma. Until diabetes and her first stroke meant she could no longer cope with a teen-aged grandson.

I haul in a deep breath. 'I'm close to my grandmother because I lived with her. She raised me until she had her first stroke and moved into a nursing home. That's when I began caring for her.'

'At seventeen?' There's no pity in her expression, just the concerned look of understanding.

The rest of the story sticks in my throat. Do I spit it out or swallow it back, the way I have so many times in the past, whenever anyone strays too close?

But Grace is different. Or, with her, I'm different.

'Yeah. That's why I dropped out of school. Her

house was sold to fund her nursing-home care.' I swallow the bitterness that comes with the memories—a solicitor's letter from my mother informing me that, as Grandma's next of kin, she'd made the arrangements without thought of what would happen to her inconvenient son. 'I spent a week or so homeless, dossing at the building site until my pay cheque came through and I could afford hostel accommodation.'

Too proud to hunt down the parents who'd made it clear my whole life where I came in their list of priorities.

'Those freezing-cold nights sleeping on a concrete floor under a tarpaulin galvanised me. So yes, I'm driven.' And more, it confirmed what I'd always known, what I'd grown up fighting but finally came to terms with on that first soul-destroying night, when I'd spent my last pound calling my mother to tell her about Grandma's progress, for all the difference it made—that I was alone. That my mother, a woman who dipped back into my life whenever it suited her, usually after her latest break-up, really did care more about herself than her son and even her mother. And that I'd never give anyone that power over me again.

'Where were your parents?' Grace whispers.

I gaze out at the ocean so I can't see her expression. Pity is hardly conducive to attraction, and right now I need to know I can lose myself in the passion we share and the way she makes me forget that I'm alone.

By circumstance and by design.

I shake my head, shake away the memories of a scared, confused twelve-year-old being abandoned in London while his mother went back to Ireland indefinitely. 'I never knew my father. My mother was around for a while, but she'd always disappear to chase after him, to try and get him back, I guess. She'd leave me with my grandmother for longer and longer periods.'

'I'm sorry, Ryan. That must have been so hard on you.'

My body is too rigid to even shrug. 'I never knew if she'd show up again so I existed in a state of limbo. Hoping. Waiting. Powerless.' My voice drops, so tight is my throat. 'One day she disappeared for good, and I stopped waiting.'

I swallow, trying to regain my composure. I want to have sex with her, not freak her out.

'So you never had a chance to properly grieve, constantly reliving the feelings of loss?' she says with astounding insight. 'When did you last see her?'

Too restless to relax, I move to sit on the edge of the lounger, my arms braced on my thighs. 'Years ago. She crawled out of hiding when I graduated from business school with my first company. I made it clear I wasn't interested in a tender reunion. She didn't stick around.' And part of me never learns my lesson, a sliver of my psyche clinging to the hope that this time she'll be different. She won't let me down. She'll care.

'And now you're worried about your grandmother's

health?' Grace's hushed voice has taken on a soothing tone she must use on her patients. It grates at my eardrums, even as I suck comfort from her concern.

I nod, the worry tightening my chest eclipsing the pathetic wasted regret for my relationship with my mother, feelings I should have outgrown years ago.

'No wonder you're very close,' she says, the gentle back and forth swipe of her thumb on my arm registering.

I shrug, my chest burning because, in reality, I try not to be close to anyone. Closeness brings pain. Loss. Loneliness.

Better to be self-reliant. To avoid feeling. Except somewhere between Grandma and Grace that can of worms seems to have been cracked open.

'When I travel, I speak to her every day. Sometimes twice a day.' I close my eyes, numbing my mind to what happens the next time she has a stroke, or if she can't shake this chest infection. I can't contemplate my life without her keeping me grounded with her sharp wit and her shrewd wisdom and quiet, unconditional acceptance.

Grace falls silent for a long time, so when she starts talking again in that soothing, calm way, I'm thrown, as I have been since the minute we met.

'I had a sister,' she says, everything about her stilling, even her breaths. 'The one who loved romance novels and wanted to learn to paddleboard. She was younger than me. She was born with a heart condition.'

My own breathing stops; I'm desperate for the secret part of herself she's offering, and she's using past tense to describe her sister.

'She had lots of surgeries, lots of illness while we were growing up, always in and out of hospital. She missed out on things because she'd pick up germs easier than you or I, and they'd knock her sideways. She died three years ago waiting for a transplant.'

I stare at her profile, mute, my heart thudding. She's re-donned her sunglasses, perhaps as a shield. I find her hand, squeeze her fingers, suck the comfort from her touch. This caring, fearless woman is comforting me. Sharing her own pain to try and lessen mine.

'I'm so sorry.' I lift her hand, kiss the backs of her knuckles. 'You're amazing. Brave. So strong.'

She shakes her head, laughs a humourless laugh she conceals with a bright smile. 'This isn't the real me. This is the holiday me. People always present their best selves on holiday.'

She's right, but she can't hide the vulnerability in her tense mouth and rigid posture. 'I'm sure everything about you is incredible and real. And I've seen your bravery. Don't demean yourself.'

She shakes her head, growing serious once more. 'You know, it's funny. We never really had a normal relationship, Bryony and I. I don't remember a Christmas where she wouldn't get sick with pneumonia and wind up in hospital for a week. We couldn't go on foreign holidays because my parents wanted to be close to hospitals that knew her history. They didn't like to leave her home alone, so we spent a lot more time together than regular sisters. But when she'd gone, all I could think was of all the living she had left to do—amazing things she dreamed of wasted—and how I could have been a better sibling.'

'That's not true—'

'It is.' She cuts me off. 'As a kid I realised pretty early on that my parents had enough to deal with, so I tried to be perfect. Not rock the boat. But that didn't stop me feeling resentment. Towards my own sister. My very sick sister.' She looks down at our clasped hands, her fingers gripping tighter. 'I resented that she always came first, that our parents became consumed with her care, that I always had to be good and quiet and sensible.'

I wrap my arm around her shoulders, tug her close and murmur into her hair, 'You were a child too. That's normal. Understandable. I'm an only child, but I'm pretty certain most kids resent their siblings for something. You were just trying to deal with a stressful situation the best way you knew how.' Violent protective urges rush through me. We have more in common than I realised. We were both vulnerable, both struggling with things we were too young to handle.

I tighten my grip on her narrow shoulders, the thud of her heart against my chest grounding me.

She shifts, grunts as if she doesn't believe me.

'So you kept your head down?' I say, seeing a

young Grace in my head. 'Worked hard, tried your best to please? Hid your true feelings, your wants and needs to spare your family?'

She sits up, stares, looking close to tears, swallowing in between sniffs. When she takes off her sunglasses revealing her impassioned eyes, I spy a sheen of tell-tale moisture. 'Yes, I guess. And because all of my troubles seemed trivial next to what my sister went through. What about you?'

Tension coils in my muscles—I want to drag her close, engulf her in a hug so fierce, it will reset us both away from the vulnerable places we've exposed. Instead I answer her stark honesty with my own.

'At first I thought being good would keep my mother home.' My swallow scrapes my throat raw. 'It never worked. When I saw that nothing I did made a difference, that she was more intent on following my father, a man who would never love her, never leave his wife and family for her, I rebelled the other way. Gave my grandma a few extra grey hairs.'

We grip each other's hands, neither of us breaking the fragile spell.

'You called me fearless before...' She shakes her head and settles her gaze on the horizon while she takes some deep breaths. 'I'm not. I'm scared. I came here as a sort of challenge to myself. You see, I lost a patient in the operating theatre.'

'Ah, Grace...' I want to hold her so badly I ache. Skin-to-skin, every inch of her body pressed to mine the way it was in the early hours before the dawn while she slept and, for a terrifying moment, I imagined what it would feel like to have her in my life.

She shrugs, her chin lifting bravely. 'It happens sometimes. But it hit me hard, as if I'd bottled up all this guilt over Bryony and all my feelings that, somehow, I'd missed out on living too, right alongside her, because I'd held myself back. And suddenly the cork flew off.'

'You're being hard on yourself.' Of course she would develop a huge well of empathy for others. It's not only part of her personality, but how she developed too—nature and nurture.

'Maybe, but it's true.'

'You do a difficult job. I take my hat off to you. Fuck, I respect the hell out of you. Where would we be without diligent, caring people like you?'

She offers me a sad little half-smile. 'Thanks, but it made me realise how flat my life had become. All that conforming and caution and those self-inflicted limitations I'd grown up with continued to shape me long into adulthood. And I got scared that if I didn't change, I'd be wasting a life Bryony never had a chance to live. That's why I came here—fear, not bravery. But I'm hoping I'll go home with the beginning of a course adjustment. At least, that's the plan.'

'It's a good plan.' I pull her forwards, my hands trembling, impatient. I press my mouth to hers and hold us there, mouth-to-mouth, breath mingling until the worst of my chest ache eases. When we part, the passion is back in Grace's stare, the catch of my breath telling me how much of an idiot I've been to risk one second of this astonishing woman's company and how, if I were as brave as she is, I could pursue something more than a casual fling.

'You're awe-inspiring. Thanks for coming out on the *Blarney*.' I'm putting an end to our confessional, but I'm doing so as much for her as for my own comfort. After everything she's been through, she deserves her fresh start, and if I can be part of giving her some unforgettable memories to take home, perhaps I'll find it easier to watch her get on the plane.

Grace nods, a new understanding settling over us. For the first time in my life I welcome the intimacy, the connection, perhaps because I know my vulnerable place is safe in the hands of Dr Grace. Perhaps because she compels me to be a better version of myself. Perhaps because, around her, I feel temporarily less alone.

'Want to go for a swim?' she says, tugging me to my feet.

I nod, grateful for the distraction. The urge to touch her and lose myself is growing increasingly hard to control. She's cracked open a door I keep padlocked. Now I need to decide how far I can let her in and keep myself protected.

CHAPTER NINE

Grace

WE DIVE FROM the back of the boat and swim for shore side by side, our competitive natures turning the leisurely swim into a race. In the shallows, Ryan tugs me close, wrapping one arm around my waist and hauling my mouth up to his for a salty seawater kiss.

'If that fishing boat wasn't there, I'd be tempted to coax you into another session on the sand,' he says, his eyes bright and playful minus the haunting vulnerability that followed his confession earlier.

'You wouldn't have to coax. You're lucky I let you make it onto the beach—even watching you swim is sexy.' I suggested the swim to give him space to recover. I can tell he rarely talks about his feelings, and I needed a distraction after sharing my deepest regrets over Bryony.

We have so much in common. The glimpse of his inner fears inflames my desire for him higher, although I wouldn't have believed I could want him any more after last night. But the craving drags at my limbs, turning me molten so that I could barely keep pace with his relaxed but powerful front crawl.

Throughout our talk I wanted to climb into his lap and hold him, but I felt the tension radiating from his big, strong body, the set of his jaw, the pain in his eyes. Pain I wanted to kiss away so badly, I almost choked with longing. But he's a proud, confident man who'd hate any display that could be misconstrued as pity.

Now I understand his trust issues. Why he avoids commitment. He's been deserted by the one person who's supposed to love him unconditionally. Not simply abandoned, but repeatedly so, his hopes built up every time his mother reappeared only to fall to greater depths when she inevitably disappeared without warning. No wonder he can't allow anyone close enough to form a relationship. He's protecting himself. If he doesn't care, it can't hurt.

And now he faces the ultimate loss: his grandmother. The only family he has.

My heart clenches, climbing into my throat. I hold him close as I lose myself in the balm of the heat behind his eyes and the answering inferno between my legs.

I want him. More than ever. To a degree that steals my breath and reminds me that, without his stance on relationships, I could easily fall for him. But more than that, I want to comfort him, to burrow under his skin until I understand him a little more, to truly know Ryan Dempsey.

I swallow hard to dislodge the trickle of panic. This isn't supposed to happen. It's just a fling. Casual. Temporary. But in another life…if we wanted the same things…?

A commotion sounds from the moored fishing boat.

'That sounds like trouble.' I turn from Ryan's arms, adrenaline from my years of attending cardiac arrests and other medical emergencies kicking in. 'Let's see if they need help.' I set off at a run, aware of Ryan's footsteps splashing the wet sand behind me.

The fishermen's net is tangled around a green turtle. One of the locals attempts to slash at the nylon ensnared around the turtle's back leg with a knife, but as it's a metre long and, Ryan informs me, close to one hundred kilos in weight, the remaining man is struggling to hold on to the flapping creature. Ryan and I rush to help, each holding down the giant shell and freeing the fisherman to grab a towel from the deck to cover the turtle's head and front flippers.

The buzz of adrenaline fires my brain. I cast my eye over the magnificent creature for signs of injury, while checking the fisherman's hands for collateral damage—the knife is razor sharp.

With our extra two pairs of hands, it doesn't take long to cut the tangle of net away, but there's a bloody gash left behind where the turtle has twisted and dragged at its heavy burden. I look to Ryan to gauge what the men are saying.

He shrugs. 'I only speak a few words of Fijian— I don't think *hello* and *can I have a beer?* will help right now.' He's calm and controlled as ever, but there's deference in his expression as he looks to me. 'Do you think he needs to see a vet? There's a wildlife conservation centre on the mainland.'

The locals must understand some English because they both shake their heads. I scoop some seawater over the wound to wash away the blood. Then all three sets of eyes settle on me with expectation.

'We'll trust your opinion,' says Ryan and heat fizzes through me.

I peer closer at the wound, which appears superficial. 'I'm not a vet, but I think it will be okay. It's just a graze. Like a friction burn. It's not deep. But I wish I had some antiseptic, just to be certain.'

Ryan's worried frown disappears. 'I have a first-aid kit on the *Blarney*—I think there's some iodine inside. Will that do?'

'Perfect—it certainly won't do any harm,' I say, as he jerks to his feet, all action.

He strides into the sea, and then dives, striking out for the *Blarney* at a pace twice as fast as we swam to shore.

'He let me win...' I mutter under my breath, my lips twitching and my stare drawn to his muscular back as he glides through the water. He returns within minutes, rising from the ocean like a god, rivulets of water running down his ripped and golden torso as he brandishes a bottle of iodine solution in a waterproof bag.

It's all I can do to avoid drooling while I pour some of the iodine onto the turtle's wound. The minute I give the all-clear, the locals remove the towel from the creature's head and we all stand back. Awe steals my air as the turtle ambles back to the water, seemingly none the worse for wear and considerably lighter now he's free of his unwanted cargo.

My smile is so wide, there's a lump in my throat as it disappears from view under the waves. We thank our fellow rescuers and say our farewells. Ryan loops his arm around my shoulders, and presses a kiss to my temple. 'You were awesome. Lucky turtle.'

I laugh, wiping away the sting of moisture from my eyes. 'Me...? You're the one who undertook a supplies mission back to the boat like a competitive swimmer.' I can't stop my eyes from travelling his still-wet body, the memories of that first night in his shower bombarding my erogenous zones with hormones. Is there nothing this man can't do?

'You are so smart—it's a massive turn-on,' he whispers. 'I had a hard-on watching you teach CPR today. How inappropriate is that?' His stare turns intense, inflamed, full of promise. My body responds, pulse leaping, breath catching, temperature rising.

'Wanna go back to the boat and be inappropriate some more...?' I say. Because despite my warning to stay grounded, I can't get enough of this man.

'Hell yes!' He grabs my hand and we wade back into the sea.

On the boat, I head for the deck shower to wash off the seawater, every nerve alive with that feeling of invincibility I've had since the day I met him. How can he make me feel as if anything is possible if I'm brave enough to take a risk, or try, or confess my desires?

Ryan manoeuvres the *Blarney* to a tiny cluster of islands nearby that are little more than palm-strewn patches of sand. I laze on the lounger and watch him take his own shower, the droplets of water evaporating from my skin having nothing to do with the sun and everything to do with the heat my body generates.

Heat for him.

Heat that refuses to budge despite the fact that we want different things.

We couldn't work back in the real world away from the fantasy of paradise. Part of me would love to shrug off some of the responsibility that comes with my job and travel more. Do more. See more. Just like Ryan.

Or even *with* Ryan.

Wow—that's a full-on projection. Ridiculous.

Even if he wanted a relationship, we're too different. He'd probably find my life suffocating. I have obligations beyond my job and my friends. I've already let down my parents enough, and, after everything they've been through, I'm now their only daughter. I know they want grandchildren. I can imagine their faces if I introduced commitment-phobe, globetrotting Ryan.

'Are you hungry? The galley is fully stocked,' he asks as he towel-dries his hair and settles on the edge of the lounger, which is the size of a double bed, next to me.

'No.' Ravenous, but only for him. So what if we couldn't work back in London? We work here, just physical. I don't need to overthink. Just feel.

I touch his thigh, shivers of anticipation wracking my body. 'I want you. I've wanted you all day, since I opened my eyes to find you gone.'

He grips my hand, lifts it to his mouth and presses a kiss over my knuckles. 'I wish I'd stayed.'

I tug him down beside me on the lounger, our fingers still entwined as our mouths find each other with soft, exploratory and arousing kisses. The evening sun is so bright I close my eyes, every brush of his lips against mine heightened in sensation until my nerves buzz and I burn inside.

For him.

For the way he makes me feel. For bringing out the new Grace.

We kiss for ever, soft, languid kisses that make me melt into the cushions at my back, heated, searching kisses, so I grip Ryan's face and he holds mine, and passionate, fiery kisses, which leave me writhing against his hard muscles and digging my fingernails into his shoulders.

We break for air, both panting.

Yearning overwhelms me, until the only thing in my head is him. Until the only desire aside from sharing the physical ecstasy I know awaits me is to give him something not even close to all he's given me.

I hold his stare. 'I would have fancied seventeen-year-old Ryan.'

He smiles then sobers when he sees that I'm serious. 'I would have pursued you,' I say. 'Asked you out. I was braver at that age.'

He frowns, his expression pained while his eyes laser into mine.

I hold his face, because I want him to know the real me, the emerging me he's helped to bring out. 'I had a major crush on a boy like you must have been—laid-back, confident, good at everything.'

'I'm not good at—'

I press my fingers to his lips. 'You're good at the things that matter—people. I would have asked out a seventeen-year-old you, just like I asked him.'

He seems to hold his breath, his body braced over me on straight arms. 'What happened?' he whispers. 'Was he your boyfriend?'

I wonder if he's remembering his own teenage girlfriend, but then he had bigger things on his mind than girls, like his sick grandmother, his job and where he was going to live. Things I relied on my parents for, as he should have been able to do.

I shake my head, the memories painful. 'I arranged to meet him after school, but my sister ended up in hospital that day. She was really sick, so my parents and I stayed with her all night. When I went back to school the next day, I didn't have the courage to explain why I'd stood him up.' My voice drops to a shameful whisper. 'So I ignored him. Pretended I didn't care any more.'

'Oh, Grace, darlin'.' He drags me against his chest, and I breathe in the heat and scent of his skin to distract myself from the past.

'It's okay.' His voice rumbles under my cheek. 'You're still that fearless girl.' He presses his mouth to mine, punctuating his assertion. 'I'm in awe of you. Everything you do, you do with caring and passion and honesty.' Another firm kiss. 'So determined. And inspiring.'

His praise fills me to the point my head hurts, because he sees me the way I want to be. A woman to make Bryony proud.

I kiss him quiet, losing myself once more in our incredible chemistry. I want to make peace with my regrets and move on, and his touch, the safe harbour he provides when we're alone, brings that reality tantalisingly close.

'Ryan...' I reach behind my neck and loosen the straps of my bikini, my head falling back on the pillows when he pushes the fabric away and takes my nipple in his mouth. 'Yes,' I hiss, because here I'm free with him, safe to explore our physical connection, safe to reveal my vulnerable side, safe to demand this passion that burns, accepting nothing less.

'That's so good.' I cradle his head, meet his ferocious stare, which is harsh with a need matched in me. 'You make me feel so good.'

Arcs of fire lance my core as he sucks, and I grind my clit against his rock-hard thigh to appease the flutters and spasms inside, where I want to be filled. Ryan rises over me, his fingers seeking out mine, entwining and pressing my hands to the mattress while he keeps up the suction torturing my breast.

He says he doesn't do romance, and I now see that he would avoid the emotional pain of caring about someone too much, but I feel his desire, his passion, his attentiveness, to the tips of my curling toes. Not just for my body, but for all of me, even when he would deny its presence.

Words trap in my throat, words I know he'll reject, a new layer of regret blanketing and muting the waves of pleasure. If our younger selves had met in that parallel universe, would things be different? In another life, could Ryan risk giving a relationship a chance? Could I be content, as he claims to be, with just this live-in-the-moment passion?

I know the answer. I'm honest enough to admit that I want this, and more. I still want it all.

I cling tighter to his shoulders, as if simply holding on to him is a substitute for our differences. He abandons my nipple and I cry out, the sound smothered in a groan as he spreads my knees with his and rocks his hips forward so the hard length of his erection grinds against my clit through the layers of our swimsuits. His handsome face, haloed by the setting sun at his back, fills my vision, his fierce, burning eye contact paralysing me as he rocks above me.

'Do you want to move inside to the cabin?' he asks, bending forward to kiss me through the tremors he's creating.

'No. Do you?'

He shakes his head, his face serious. This is different from last night, where we laughed and teased. Different. Better. Because he's shown me a hidden part of himself, and he's seen the ugly, shameful part of me and wants me still.

'Let's stay here,' I say, my fingers flexing against the backs of his hands and my thighs spreading open a fraction more in an attempt to get closer.

His hand leaves mine to push the hair back from my cheek. 'You're beautiful. Irresistible. Addictive. I can't get enough of you.'

Heat builds behind my eyes. 'I feel the same.' But I swallow the spikes of emotion down; I won't ruin this perfect moment with what-ifs and maybes and shoulds. My thoughts turn practical. 'The condoms are inside, but I'm safe if you are?'

His eyes darken, fresh arousal slashing his already savage expression. 'They are, and I am. But are you sure? Because once I'm back inside you, we won't be moving for a while. I intend to spend every day you have left doing this, if you'll let me.'

The reminder that my days are numbered douses my high, like the sun ducking behind a storm cloud.

'I'm certain. In fact, from now on, take anything I say at face value, because I want that stark honesty we shared last night. I want to be that brave woman who isn't afraid to say what she wants. To chase what she wants. I know you can take it.'

'Fuck, yes, I can.' He groans, his eyes dropping half closed with arousal. 'Try me now. Ask me. Tell me. Let that woman free.'

My breath catches, the rush electrifying every nerve right to my fingers and toes. His gift, his safety net exhilarating. 'Go down on me.'

I bite my lip, a part of my brain blanking at the bold request.

His jaw clenches and his eyes rake down my body to the place where he's grinding his cock against the heat between my legs. 'My pleasure.' He sits back on his heels and slides my bikini bottoms off then he takes my hand, as if he's inviting me to waltz.

'Sit up.'

I obey, so turned on by this freedom, I'd do anything he asks in that moment, just as I know he'd do the same for me. He lies down beside me and guides me to straddle him, his hands on my buttocks until I'm astride his face. He even reaches for a pillow and shoves it under his head, getting comfy.

My body combusts; why is that so sexy?

I grip the back of the lounger, my thighs quaking, so acute is the excitement building. I look down, but Ryan is focussed on my sex, his thumbs parting me, and then his mouth covers my clit and he groans, his eyes darting to mine, watching me fall apart above him.

It's the hottest thing I've ever experienced, the sun on my back, his face between my thighs, his nods and grunts encouraging every cry, every gasp, every involuntary thrust of my hips over his mouth. The bites of pleasure are enough to drive me over the edge, so when he pushes first one and then two and finally a third finger inside me, I arch my back and my hands grip the lounger with cracking force.

'Ryan…' His name has become my favourite chant. I wanted to come full of his delicious cock, but I'm not going to make it. This is too good. And I'm fully invested in his plan—to spend the rest of our time together chasing this high.

He's groaning, his eye contact searing, stripping me bare, so for a perfect moment I'm freer than ever before, just me, naked, exposed, taking what I want without hesitation, apology or concession.

My climax sends my body rigid, the air forced from my lungs on a protracted wail I can't hold inside, each spasm stronger than the last. When it's over, and I collapse next to Ryan, his arms holding me and his kisses bringing me back into my body, my brain stutters back to life.

My first thought?

Shit, I'm in deep trouble.

CHAPTER TEN

Ryan

I HOLD HER TIGHT, willing the gallop of my heart to subside. My chest burns as I try to suck in calming breaths. But she's everywhere. Her scent, the warmth of her sun-kissed skin, the tickle of her hair, which is splayed over the pillow next to me, strands even clinging to the scruff on my chin.

What the hell is happening to me? Perhaps I'm having some sort of cardiac event. I grip her tighter, my pulse easing at the knowledge that if I do die, there's no one better to have on hand.

Ever since she told me about her sister, opened up about her teenaged self, ever since she probed my dark places with the care and gentleness she must give to her patients, that pressure, the concrete block shifting inside me, has built. Is this what I've avoided all these years? The sprouting, alien feeling of a deeper connection? A bond with the real Grace, one who has hang-ups, but also has the balls to put herself out there emotionally, time after time, where I'm a snarling emotional hermit, protecting himself at all costs?

We've both dealt with crap in our lives, but our reactions couldn't be more different—hers to care and help people, to improve herself and demand everything from life, and mine…? To acquire all the trappings of wealth, but to hide from real, honest, human connection. Am I truly that spineless? That terrified of being alone?

I ignore the lust still pounding through my blood as I hold a languid Grace, and probe my memories for the last time I felt this way.

It's dark in there, the vulnerable place in my head, certainly not as brilliantly white lit as being here in this moment with this dauntless woman. But where I would normally dodge those vicious talons designed to make me feel twelve years old again, I want to challenge, to test their power.

Do I, for the first time ever, want more? To try to be close to what Grace deserves, whatever the hell that looks like?

No, I can never be that. Even Grace couldn't make her long-term relationship work. What hope would someone like me have? This is all I know. And the timing sucks—I couldn't possibly face two major life adjustments at once… Back in London, Grandma has to be my main focus.

I release a long sigh, resolved to ignore the clamour in my head every time I think about the countdown of days left and just enjoy this and all the moments. That's where my instincts lead. But are they instincts, or merely habits?

She shifts against me, her fingers tracing patterns on my chest. 'Are you okay?'

'I'm fantastic.' Physically. But my head…? It's fucked seven ways to Sunday. I kiss her, because I know that will ease the worst of this burn in my chest and the warning siren deafening me. I know she can shift the concrete a fraction so I can breathe. 'There's nothing better than watching you own your feelings. You make me crazy—'

Words fail me, so I kiss her again and again, succumbing to my physical needs, which are easier to embrace than the doubts and questions meeting her has thrown up.

I pull back at last. 'Do you want to spend the night on the *Blarney*? It has everything we need,' I ask, the idea materialising from that dark place. 'I want to be selfish, to keep you all to myself for as long as I can.'

She laughs then, pushing at my shoulders so she can level those bright intelligent eyes on me. 'I could be on board with that, excuse the pun.'

'Good,' I say, my head already time-travelling to the end of the week, when we'll go our separate ways. Will that be enough time to gorge on Grace? Will I have exorcised this foreign craving? Be all cured of the hold she seems to have over me?

'What about whales? They might capsize the boat

while we're asleep?' She sits up, gorgeously dishevelled, eyes wide.

'It's too shallow here for whales.' I palm her waist, her warm, soft skin like silk. 'And I have a perfect solution—we won't sleep.'

'I hadn't thought of that—I like the way your mind works.' She licks her lips, a devious smile tugging at her perfect mouth as she shoves the waistband of my swim shorts down over my hips. I help her to remove them and then roll on top of her, my hands stroking the hair from her still-flushed face. My body aches, the need to plunge inside the tight warmth that awaits me driving me to distraction, but still I hesitate.

'You're the bravest person I know.' My heart thuds against her ribs and I pray she can't tell how fast it's beating. 'I can't stop thinking about a teenaged you—I want to go back in time, be that boy you wanted and tell you it will be okay.' God knows where this is coming from, but I've never spoken truer words.

Grace's brow pinches in a tiny frown. 'Ryan...' Unlike moments earlier when she screamed it, my name is a whisper on her lips, almost a question laced with longing. She presses her mouth to mine, her thighs spreading so I sink closer, my cock scalded by the wet heat between her legs.

I focus on this, us, mentally rearing back from that place that makes me restless.

I have no answers for her unspoken questions, no

solution to her longings except the physical. Grace was bold enough to embrace her first one-night stand, but I've never had a serious relationship. And it's stood me in good stead up to now.

I tilt my hips back, the head of my cock sliding to her slick entrance to distract us from the intimate abyss. The doubts filling my head have no place, because I wasn't good enough for a girl like seventeen-year-old Grace then, and I'm seriously lacking for the woman she is now. What do I know about feelings and relationships and commitment?

I push inside her, the streak of pleasure making me groan. This is different from the night I spent in her bed. I know things about this Grace, the knowledge leaving me tense and uncertain, when I've always relied on absolutes.

Grace shifts her hips, bites her lip, sighs. 'Can we sleep here, on deck? I want to watch the sunset and rise.'

'We can do anything you want,' I say through gritted teeth. Because I want to give her everything I can, as shallow as I know it will be.

She grips my face so she can kiss me—my lips, my cheeks, even the tip of my nose—and then looks deep into my eyes. 'Stop holding back, Ryan.' Her voice is low, a sexy demand, but her stare carries that insightful caring I want to shield myself against.

I press inside her to the hilt and then bury my face against the side of her neck while I try to get a handle on the rage of feelings bombarding me.

The boulder in my chest expands. I yank my head away and roll us so she's on top, sprawled over my chest, her squeal of surprised laughter morphing into a groan as I thrust up into her from underneath.

I want her too shattered to look at me that way. Too debauched to notice I'm reeling on the edge of previously uncharted territory. Too spent to say more than 'yes' when I take her again and again until I've exhausted my demons.

'Yes.' She pushes back, sitting up over my hips and rocking in time with my thrusts.

I grip her hips, moving her to the rhythm I want, shutting out everything but her naked, honest desire. 'Ride me harder. You feel too good.' I cup her breasts, rolling my thumbs over her nipples so she clenches me tighter as she throws her head back. I need her so much, need to come so badly, for a second I'm worried I won't get there. Worried that the weight crushing my chest has spoiled even this for me. But then she calls my name once more, and I join her in the free-fall, one certainty in my head.

I'll never forget this moment, this holiday, this woman.

CHAPTER ELEVEN

Grace

THE SUN SITS low on the horizon by the time we sail back into the lagoon the next evening. Ryan heads for the Lailai's jetty and moors the *Blarney* while I watch the preparations taking place on the beach. The staff are busy laying the final touches to a make-shift altar decorated with tropical flowers near the water's edge. A carpeted walkway lined with lit torches and a handful of chairs faces the ocean. It's hard to imagine a more exquisite location to share vows.

I sense Ryan behind me at the top of the gang-plank. 'The French couple—Evie and Remy. They're getting married tonight.' My heart flutters at the ro-mance of their nuptials, even though my joy is damp-ened by the last traces of my own personal regret. Regret I can finally let go. There's no doubt that I did the right thing by halting my own wedding and coming here alone. What seemed monumental in that West End bar over margaritas with Brooke and Neve—the pact, the challenge I set myself—now seems so simple. Because I found the kind of passion I crave.

But the chills cooling me on this tropical evening remind me that, just like bleached coral washed up on the shore, I can't keep what I found. Not with Ryan, who isn't long-term-partner material. Longing swells in my throat. Trying to make us work, back in London, would shunt me back where I began, fooling myself I had something real and enduring.

I can't force Ryan to be something he's not and I can't settle like that again.

'Let's go wish the groom good luck,' I say, the impulse bittersweet.

Ryan grunts, grabbing his backpack, his face that of a man about to sit in the dentist's chair.

'Oh, come on. Surely you can appreciate how romantic this is. And, at the very least, it's good for business,' I say, recalling the photos of similar weddings I saw on the resort website when selecting this as our honeymoon destination.

After our magical night on the *Blarney*, I felt as if we'd moved closer together, but it seems he's in no mood to be teased. If only I could dissect his thoughts and feelings and find the slightest chink in his armour, a place to anchor my hope.

He takes my hand with only a cursory shrug of acknowledgement as we head for the beach. I lean into his side, keen to prolong the bubble of existence we've shared in the past twenty-four hours. It's there still, our deeper connection. I feel it in his stares and the grip of his hand.

Confessing the enormity of his childhood abandonment was a big step for him, and I'm humbled that he shared his secret with me. And now he might lose his beloved grandma, too.

He'll be alone. But he doesn't have to be.

I squeeze his fingers, walk a little slower, prolonging the moment when I have to drop his hand. Because deeper connection or not, it's temporary.

He's not mine to hold or fix or console. He's an island. Rocky and invincible on the surface, but afraid of the attrition and erosion of the waves that pound his defences.

Could he ever overcome those fears and be open to more than a few nights of stolen passion? Could I wait on the slim chance he might, one day, change his mind? Or is delaying the inevitable just another form of settling for something I know in my soul isn't right for me?

At sea, on the *Blarney*, it was easier to live in the moment and not think about the clock ticking. Easier to deny the depth of feelings building inside me, changing me, making me want impossible things. Easier to believe that Ryan and I could part in a few days, with a 'thanks for the memories,' the new and improved Grace swapping her bikini for scrubs without a backward glance. But I'd be lying to myself, and I've given up that pastime.

I'm not ready to face the end with him, but I know I want more than he's capable of, some day. A partner for life. Marriage. My happy ever after.

With a heavy heart, I head for the wedding party, trailing a reluctant Ryan.

I must be gripping his hand too tightly, or perhaps he's still protecting us from resort gossip, because he drops my hand and leans in, his voice low for my ears only, his message dimming my smile for Remy, the groom.

'This will be the final wedding to take place on the island. Next week, the builders move in, refurbishments begin and a whole new website launches.'

His words aren't spoken with malice, but they feel like a slap or an unwanted secret—a drunken uncle no one invited who sneaked into the ceremony to shout, 'I object.'

I look up, my forehead scrunching as I try to gauge his meaning from his tense expression and shifting stare, but then I'm engulfed by Remy's hug, laughing while he adorns my neck with a salusalu, a Fijian lei of delicately scented tropical flowers, followed by a very European kiss for each cheek.

'Please, you must come. Both of you. Evie will be delighted.' Remy turns, offering Ryan a garland from the scented stack draped over his arm. Dressed in cream linen shorts and a white shirt open at the neck, he's as low-key as a groom can be, but also perfect.

'I'd love to,' I say, my eyes darting to a distracted Ryan, whose cryptic statement quashed all the lovely feel-good hormones Evie and Remy's sunset wedding induced. But why shouldn't I be gooey? It's a wedding. Even the hardest cynic would find it impossible not to share a fraction of the joy and excitement on Remy's face as he waits for his bride.

My heart plummets at the irony.

A hardened cynic like Ryan. A man who, with good reason, doesn't believe in love and marriage and keeps the risk of pain at bay by avoiding relationships.

'Excuse me.' Ryan leaves, summoned by Taito, who loiters under the palms, while I offer sincere congratulations to Remy.

I watch Ryan's retreat, trying to recall the look on his face as he kissed me awake this morning with the sun rising on the horizon, just as I'd wanted.

I feel like you're in my blood,' he whispered, his lips feathering mine, and I gasped past the stricture in my throat as he pushed inside me and we started another day in paradise as lovers.

Where has that Ryan gone? I haven't asked anything more of him, knowing what a huge step admitting feelings is for someone so anti-commitment. And even though his sentiment, spoken at a moment of physical intimacy, can't be trusted, his eyes shone with the vulnerability of opening up on an emotional level.

But now? He's gone. Reverted to the man I first met. Secretive. Closed off. Scornful.

Doubts swirl, making me feel sick. I clutch my elbows, crossing my arms over my waist.

Two other couples arrive, greet Remy and take their seats. I look down at my cut-off shorts and strappy top, wishing I had time to change into a sundress. But my casual outfit seems somehow appropriate here among the natural beauty and simplicity of the location.

I take a seat as Remy and the celebrant take their positions at the altar, a gnawing discomfort in my chest. Not for my own happy ending, which was an illusion I created by mentally cutting and pasting Ryan's head into my couple's photo, but for the absolute certainty that I want this, what Evie and Remy have, in my future. And Ryan, the man to bring me back to life, and long-term relationships are mutually exclusive.

As Ryan slides into the seat beside me, I turn a bright smile on him to hide the reality-check downer I've been plunged into. I ache to touch him, to reconnect the way we did on the *Blarney*, but the look on his face—tense, maybe even angry—keeps my hands in my lap and my heart in my throat.

'What's wrong?' I hiss, looking around at a retreating Taito, concern for Remy jolting my pulse. Has Evie changed her mind? Does she plan to stand him up?

'Nothing's wrong.' He looks straight ahead, mouth a flat line, jaw muscles bunched. 'I guess I just feel how you did yesterday when you discovered my true identity.'

When he does turn to face me, there's hurt in the down-pulling of his mouth and glittering fury in his narrowed eyes.

For long seconds I'm mute as I try to make sense of what he means while I cling to memories of the Ryan of last night, this morning aboard the *Blarney*. Then the fog clears.

He knows.

About my booking here, which should have been with Greg, my new husband.

Shame lashes me, sealing my breath.

'Ryan—'

At that moment the bride arrives, wearing a simple white sundress and radiating happiness. Flowers adorn her hair, her small smile for Remy only.

My ribs pinch as flood after flood of emotions leave me speechless.

I should have spoken up yesterday. But I knew he'd freak out.

'I wanted to tell you,' I whisper to Ryan once Evie has passed on her way to her groom. I touch his leg, his muscles steel under my palm.

I try again. 'I didn't want you to think…you know, that I was looking for a substitute or something…'

'It's no big deal,' he says, his eyes trained on the French couple, his emotional withdrawal as complete as if he'd risen from the chair next to mine and departed. I touch his arm, uncertain of my reception if I were to hold his hand.

He turns towards me, a fake smile on his devastating mouth. A mouth I've kissed and watched laugh and murmur and confide…

Then he presses his index finger to his lips. 'Shh,' and he turns his focus back to the ceremony.

I bite my tongue and sink into my seat. I've had ample opportunity to tell him how I happened to come here alone. But I didn't. Out of shame at being the kind of woman to go so far down the wrong path?

The remainder of the beautiful, intimate wedding passes in a blur. Hot anger simmers in my blood, followed by chills as I try to figure out if I'm the one in the wrong, and why Ryan would care that I was engaged. From day one he's been clear this is temporary. And that suited me fine. In the beginning…

I sit up straighter, shake off the feeling I'm a naughty toddler. I refuse to slip back into old, people-pleasing patterns. So I was engaged. He'll have to get over the idea. I've learned how to be honest and demand what I want without apology, and he helped teach me I could voice those desires, but now I want more than he's willing to give.

I want a future. Commitment. A lifetime.

I just can't have those things with him.

The weight dragging me down, the confusion stealing my attention from the ceremony, the anger at Ryan blowing hot and cold all provide clarity. I bite the inside of my cheek to stave off panic. Of course I want more of Ryan. How could I not when he makes me feel alive? When, with him, I feel like myself for the first time in my adult life?

But it's all an illusion, a mirage in the sun, the very nature of a holiday fling, the fantasy of something too good to be true. There's no point in falling for Ryan, no matter how much I want to believe in a possible happy ever after. Because despite our closeness on the *Blarney*, despite sharing our pasts, until he learns to trust and risk his heart, this fleeting, hedonistic whirlwind is his limit.

When the ceremony ends with a small round of applause, I wipe the sheen of happy tears from my eyes and stand. I won't let Greg or Ryan spoil this for me, diminish what I want from life. I don't *need* a fairy-tale ending—I'm perfectly fine alone—but I *want* to find that one person who fires enough passion in me and vice versa that we share the same goals, the ups and the downs and a million moments in between. Committed to putting each other first. Putting us first. So desperate to start that romantic adventure together, that we're of the same mind, there's no putting off the commitment or prioritising work.

Ryan takes my arm. 'We need to talk.'

I nod, my heart heavy with all I want to say. 'Yes. We do. But right now I'm going to change for the party.'

'Later then.' He presses a chaste kiss to my cheek, his face behind a rigid mask. 'I'll see you there.'

I swallow the lump in my throat and walk away to prepare.

We're back to strangers, but is there any point in fighting for more?

CHAPTER TWELVE

Ryan

HER VIBRANT DRESS, shades of reds and orange, mimics the flames burning me up inside. Burning for her, because discovering she was engaged, that she planned to come to my resort with her new husband, doesn't diminish my need for her one little bit. If anything the jealousy is back, a leaping beast snarling at the fire.

She glances my way and I can almost see the flecks of amber in her eyes that, no matter how hard she smiles, still harbour a flicker of disappointment.

Of course I let her down.

I warned her to expect nothing from me but orgasms.

She turns back to the bride, gifting me a view of her bare back and shoulders. I can't see them from this distance, but I know her skin is dotted with freckles. I even tried to count them this morning while she slept in the first rays of dawn, before I could no longer deny myself and I woke her, my mouth tracing all her sensitive places until she kissed me as if I'm the last man on earth.

Or the only man she needs.

But it's not me she needs, or wants. Her ex-fiancé seals our fate, because she's exactly what I guessed the first time I saw her on the beach—a woman who wants it all.

Love, marriage, for ever.

Things I've never craved, because relationships aren't for me.

My fist grips my ice-cold beer bottle as that weight in my chest scrapes me raw. It doesn't matter that she was engaged. It shouldn't matter that she'd planned to be another man's wife. I wasn't jealous when she told me she'd broken someone's heart. But I can't get it out of my mind, can't get *her* out of my mind.

When I'm with her, I want to crawl inside her head and see what she's thinking, feel what she feels. When she's out of sight, I want to find her, to see her smile and laugh and tease. And when she looks at me with her kind, compassionate eyes… I want to fall to my knees in worship. She seems to understand me, without me speaking a word. It's intuitive for her, part of who she is—respectful, caring, empathetic.

I slam the beer bottle onto the bar. I'm buggered. Stuck between the razor-sharp coral reef of my self-imposed limits and the unknown fears of the deep fathomless ocean.

I catch her eye again. She's deep in conversation, but she's thinking about me, looking over at me, probably worried about me after my fucked-up display of jealousy and denial earlier.

After the ceremony, I spent an hour in the shower picking apart the mess in my head to come up with that conclusion. I'm jealous. Of a man I don't know, for a situation—marriage, commitment, a lifetime— I don't want.

But it's her. Grace. She's filled my head with what-ifs, not from anything she's done or said, but because of who she is. How she makes me feel. As if, with just a fraction of her guts and determination, I could be a better man. A more whole version of myself. Worthy of belonging with a woman like Grace.

I didn't even know there was anything missing before I met her.

But I've allowed myself to peer through the curtain and see a glimpse of a different life. A life I thought I'd passed up long ago. A life I rejected as bullshit. But she makes me crave. Makes me restless. Makes me want more.

It hits me then, the sting of a million grains of sand. I'm lonely.

But that's not a good enough reason to crave a relationship.

I drag a hand down my face and slug another swallow of beer, but there's no shifting that concrete block in my chest.

When Grace finishes her conversation with Evie, I stand. I need to apologise for being an arsehole earlier. For spoiling her delight at the French couple's nuptials. But before I can make my way over to her, she makes a beeline for me, her shoulders back, her chin up and her signature fearlessness glowing in her eyes.

'You look beautiful,' I say. It's not a stalling tactic or a diversion—I can't keep my eyes off the way the fiery dress hugs her body or her softly flowing hair reflects light from the lanterns. Words and crippling feelings force their way to the back of my throat, bursting to be free. I grit my teeth.

'Thank you—can we talk?' she says.

'Of course.' I indicate a free table for two near the ocean and we head there side by side, my hand aching to caress her bare back. But I've sacrificed that privilege with my behaviour and the shit going on in my head.

I pull out her chair and slide next to her, when I should perhaps sit opposite, remove her far from temptation. But the other side of the world wouldn't be far enough. I'm infected, incurable. My only hope for survival to attempt to keep a lid on the craving once she leaves.

I pull in a breath. 'Let me start by apologising for earlier—I sounded accusatory, and I had no right.'

She nods, sips her champagne, her entire demeanour relaxed when there's a volcano grumbling inside me, a need to right the wrong, but a bigger need to take a giant leap into the unknown…

Admit feelings.

She looks out to the ocean. 'I told you I had a long-term relationship, and I was the one to call it off. I left out the fact that happened a month before our wedding.'

I make a fist. I want to reach for her hand so bad, I have to grip the leg of the chair. Oh, how she must have agonised over that decision. I know her—she does nothing lightly. She would have analysed the fallout, taken everything, everyone, into consideration. She probably still feels guilty for letting those people down. Perhaps why she didn't mention the fiancé and the aborted wedding.

'You could have told me that too.' My throat is scratchy as I swallow. 'It doesn't make any difference.'

'Could I?' Her stare pierces into my soul. She sees into my darkness; she showed me that yesterday on the *Blarney* when she clutched my face in her palms and shattered under me.

And she's right. If she'd told me she was reeling from a failed engagement, I'd have fought my attraction to her, tooth and nail.

'At first,' she says, 'I was a little embarrassed that I'd come here alone, to a place for couples. That I'd look pathetic and needy. I wanted you to see me as more than a woman clueless to what she wanted. But more than that, I felt guilty for abandoning a man who'd been there for me when Bryony died. For letting down my parents, who loved my ex and looked forward to grandchildren one day. They splashed out for a wedding I cancelled.'

Her voice breaks and I reach for her hand.

She shakes her head, a warning that she needs to say this. 'And most of all, I was ashamed, because I spent a long time pretending that my ex and I wanted the same thing, when I knew we didn't anymore.'

'Later…once you told me your stand on relationships, I didn't want to spook you, because we were on the same page, neither of us looking for more than sex. It seemed too…heavy a confession for my first fling.'

I nod because she's right: a week ago I would have baulked. To hear her pinpoint my fears pierces my eardrums. 'You didn't want me to think you were getting any ideas after I'd spun you my casual spiel.'

Tension builds in my head. I don't want her caution, her withdrawal. I want her passion, her honesty, her bravery.

She nods, her usually open face shrouded in restraint. 'Right. And I didn't think it mattered. Because we only have days, and then we'll never see each other again.' I hate her shrug, a sick part of me not ready to see her preparing to move on.

'You're right, it doesn't matter.'

This is why I'm better off alone.

I force out the hardest words. 'I felt jealous, so I tried to make it matter.' I look away from her small frown, my revelation rattling the handle of that door I keep locked. But knowing that she was engaged, almost married…it forces me to take a second look at Grace. To admit things I want to be a lie. That there's a barrier to seeing her again back in London, the growing idea I land at whenever I think about saying goodbye.

I'm the barrier. My fear of reliving that pain of losing someone I care about. A pain I lived and re-lived so many times as a kid, and now I face it once more, with Grandma.

She wants romance, rings and a relationship.

All the things I can't give. Things I've shied away from so often, I wouldn't know where to begin. Can I, in good faith, suggest we meet back in London, knowing how vastly our expectations differ?

My throat burns, but I force myself to ask. 'So you were supposed to come here with your new hus-band?' I can barely say the word.

'Yes. I called it off after I lost my patient. That's when I forced myself to be honest. To admit what I had wasn't enough any more.' She places her unfin-ished champagne flute on the table. 'I realised that marriage had to begin with extraordinary passion. How else could it hope to last? Starting it with such low expectations as apathy, almost as if it was an inconvenience, nothing more than an official stamp on a certificate…

'And now you're not scared to go after that pas-sion?' My muscles tense, because I feel as if I could flee at any time. Flee from how she makes me feel.

Flee from pitting myself against her fearless soul-searching. Flee from myself.

'No.'

I shrink at the courage of her conviction.

'For years I struggled with guilt over Bryony, so I put limitations on myself. But she'd want me to be happy. Alive. Not just coasting.'

She sucks in a breath, her shoulders rolling back. 'I want to live the life she couldn't. I want it all, for real next time, not just for convenience or out of habit or for the time already served. I want passion and adventure and fearlessness. No holding back. If that makes me selfish, so be it. We only have one shot at this life.'

'You have balls of steel, you know that?' Respect for her builds like pressure, threatening to split me apart.

She laughs, but quickly turns serious. 'Not really. Bryony was the bravest person I know. She knew what she wanted—she dreamed of travel, adventure, meeting Mr Right, straight from the pages of her books—and if her body had allowed, she'd have gone out and done that. That's my inspiration. I just wish I'd started sooner.'

I can't speak.

Just then Remy and Evie approach. 'We're sorry to interrupt,' says Evie, 'but we just wanted to thank you for upgrading our bure, Mr Dempsey.'

'No problem.' I feel the heat of Grace's scrutiny

on the side of my face. 'I hope you enjoy the rest
of your time at Lailai. And congratulations again.'

They saunter hand in hand back to the dance floor
as an itch of unease intensifies under my shirt collar. Do *I* have it wrong, the rest of the world, right?
Is monogamy, lifelong commitment, love worth the
risk? The pain? The potential loss?

Would I have these doubts if Grace and I never
happened? If she'd come here with her husband, just
another couple to scoff at?

'Upgrade?' Her lips twitch, as if she's holding
back a grin.

I hide behind a swig of my beer. 'I gave them my
bure—it's the best. I gave the staff some extra work,
but it turns out that nothing is too much trouble at the
Lailai. They prepared the bungalow for them while
we were at the wedding ceremony.' I don't want to
talk about why, or hear her theories on how I'm a
romantic at heart. 'During the shuffle, Taito mentioned something about your original booking of the
second superior honeymoon bungalow and I probed.
That's how I discovered you were booked here for
your own honeymoon.'

'I see. I thought you didn't believe in romance?'
She blinks in that slow, sensual, all-knowing way
that has enslaved me from day one.

'I don't. It was a business decision.' I try to bluff.
'They'll blast their social media with photos.' I shrug.
'Free advertising for the resort.'

The dewy look in her eyes, her small feline smile,

tell me she doesn't believe a word of it. 'We've both always been honest about our wants, Ryan. That's why I'm a little confused by you blowing hot and cold today. It seems to me you're the one uncertain all of a sudden.'

I swallow, because I'm helpless in the face of her frankness. Helpless and reeling with confusion.

'My wants haven't changed,' I say. It's partly true, as sure as I am of myself. I refuse to make false promises I'm not sure I'll be able to keep.

Should I end this? Here? Tonight?

'Mine neither.' She lifts her chin. 'I'd like to enjoy my last few days, before I have to get back to reality.'

She's so strong.

And addictive. We're better than good together. Surely I can keep my shit together so we can stay on track for a couple more days…

'I want that too.' The roar of truth deafens me, because how could I not want her? 'I'm sorry that I blurred the boundaries earlier with something as pointless as jealousy. I'll do better.'

She nods, her intelligent eyes full of heat and understanding. 'And when it's done, no regrets.'

I'm paralysed in my seat, so deep is my longing to undo this calm, composed woman who has all but turned my life upside down. To make her as desperate and agitated as I feel. To bend under the force of the passion I know her capable of. But she's right.

Keep it simple. Walk away. Same as always.

'Will you come back to my new bungalow? If the

clock is ticking, I want to get my fill, starting tonight by peeling you out of that stunning dress.'

She smiles her first genuine smile since the *Blarney*, full of arousal and mischief and promise. 'I will, but let's be real with each other from now on. Give me that.'

I nod, too choked by my own regret and stupidity to speak. I lost sight of real the minute I met her. But just because I can't be as brave as she is, doesn't mean I can't give her everything until it's time for her to leave.

That's what a selfish, superficial bastard would do, and if the cap fits...

CHAPTER THIRTEEN

Grace

I'M STILL IN Ryan's bed, in the bure he shifted to last night, the French doors open to a slightly different, but equally beautiful view of the sea and another perfect day in paradise. Before I can wonder where he is, he strolls back into the bungalow carrying a tray full of breakfast delights. His smile pins me to the pillows, his sleep-rumpled hair and board shorts low on his hips adding to the delicious sight that makes me want to weep.

After yesterday's bump in the road, I promised myself I'd focus on the truth and not become caught up in my feelings for this man, because they're ridiculous. Ingenuous and unrealistic, especially in light of what I've just read about Ryan Dempsey on the internet. More evidence if I needed it of the dead end we're hurtling towards with every tick of the clock.

'I hope you're hungry,' he says, his voice still sleepy, 'because I raided the kitchen. Perks of being the boss.' He winks, sets the tray on the table on the balcony and crawls onto the bed to kiss me, long and hard.

I pull back, my heart sore and happy and all kinds of confused.

'I did something.' I grip my phone and hold my breath.

His brows pinch together and he collapses beside me, throwing one arm under his head in a lazy sprawl of his big, manly body that wakes up the rest of my anatomy.

'Something I should have done the first day I met you,' I say, because we agreed to keep it real. 'I looked you up.'

'Oh...?' He stills, his dipped stare telling me every word I've read is true.

My pulse gallops. Throat tight. 'Are you seriously planning on changing all of this?' I wave my hand at the breathtaking view through the open French windows.

'I see. Well, I'm not going to rip up palm trees and build a shopping mall on the reef, but yes. That's why I'm here. To turn this into a Dempsey resort. I presume that's what you've read.'

He swings off the bed and strides to the balcony, snagging a croissant on his way to the kitchen. 'The only major change will be the clientele—singles instead of couples.' He shrugs as if it's no big deal, and to him I guess it isn't.

An ache settles behind my sternum. How can I be

so wrong about someone? When I heard he'd given his superior bungalow to the French newly-weds, I saw that, despite what he believes about himself, out of pain and fear of getting hurt, he is romantic and generous and caring. Saw that he has so much more to give than the bare minimum he allows in order to keep his distance.

But now…

Is it about the bottom line? Or is he so cynical that he would change something that works, just because he'll never need to personally use the facilities?

'You shouldn't believe what you read on the internet.' He flicks on the kettle and grabs a couple of mugs to make tea.

I pluck my phone from the sheets, finding the article I've just read with a pounding pulse. '"Irish entrepreneur and founder of Dempsey Holdings today announced his purchase of the latest Dempsey resort. Famed for the 'anything goes' luxury singles' resorts all over the globe, Dempsey, at thirty-six and one of Europe's most eligible billionaires, remains, himself, determinedly single. 'I don't believe in marriage,' boldly says Dempsey. 'It's an outdated lie, an excuse for people to behave selfishly hidden behind a veneer of respectability.'"'

I look up. His face is blank, but a muscle twitches in his jaw. 'So…?' he says. 'That's what I believe. I told you that. Everyone is entitled to their opinions.'

'So that's what you meant when you said Remy and Evie's wedding would be the last on the island?'

'Yes.'

'And there's no part of you that sees this as a waste of a good thing? That you have a perfect investment here as it is?' I say, my voice rising.

Is this the ultimate gesture of contempt to his past? To the love he doesn't believe exists?

'No.' His eyes harden. 'It's business, Grace. A money-making decision—the way I make all my business decisions.'

'But why change what isn't broken? It's perfect here.' I sigh.

His jaw hardens, eyes blank. 'Because I'm not in the happy-ever-after business.'

I cringe. Inwardly collapse as if his words are blows. For the first time I see the other side of Ryan Dempsey, so far from the laid-back, patient paddle-board teacher. The ruthless businessman. Driven. Single-minded. Formidable.

My throat burns for the pain and fear I know lies behind his cynicism. For that lonely and scared boy waiting for the door to open. Waiting to be accepted and loved and deemed important by the one person he should have been able to count on.

His mother.

'I know you're entitled to your opinions, and I don't care that we want different things from life.' *Liar.* 'I just wonder if it's good business sense motivating you, or something else.'

My head pounds, danger signs flashing. It's none of my business. The world is full of idyllic honeymoon locations. One less won't matter. But I can no longer deny how much I care. I want him to be happy, and my greatest fear is that I'll leave him behind on this island knowing he isn't. Knowing that perhaps he never will be until he faces what's holding him back.

'You're reading too much into it. My resorts are wildly successful. Lots of people, wealthy people, want somewhere discreet and luxurious to play and mingle.'

'Of course. I have friends who'd probably love one of your resorts. I'm not making a judgment.'

His face hardens, his next words deceptively quiet. 'Perhaps you'd love it too. You're honest about your desires, and really that's all it's about.'

He can stand there and calmly visualise me as a paying guest at one of his hook-up resorts?

My temperature spikes, red-hot and fiery. The need to lash out. To open his eyes. 'Yes. Maybe I would. And maybe I'll try one out.'

The twitch next to his eye gives me no satisfaction, because his lips are mashed together, when the fool in me wants words he'll likely never say. 'Only, eventually, I want to meet someone. I'm sure most people who go to a Dempsey resort do so hoping they'll find a connection. It's human nature.'

A connection like the one I've found with him.

All the fight leaves me in a rush. What's the point of arguing? He's him and I'm me. We can't work off this island. Can't work beyond really good sex.

I clamber out of bed, avoiding his stare. 'Breakfast looks divine. I'm just going to jump in the shower first.' I head to the en suite bathroom, finally releasing my trapped breath as I press my back against the closed door.

What am I doing?

I switch on the shower and then brace my arms on the edge of the basin, staring at my pale face in the mirror. All I need to do is keep it together for one more day and then I'll be gone.

No, I don't want to lie to myself any more. I should tell him I want more of him. Stop pretending it's still just about the sex for me. Admit out loud how much I care that he's happy.

When I step under the hot spray, the water numbs my outside to match my inside. I close my eyes, my head full of self-talk as I try to grasp at reality. Perhaps when I'm away from here, away from him, perspective will return. My feelings will dissolve. But either way, I don't regret coming here and meeting him. Without that leap of faith—long-haul journey of faith more like—I'd still be stuck with my guilt and regret and inertia. Still living a half-life. Still pretending I had everything I needed.

Don't I owe it to myself, to the new me, to tell him how I feel, even when I know I'll be rejected?

The door opens after a single knock, and a naked Ryan strides into the room. He opens the shower door and steps inside, his face fierce with need and the passion I've come to expect.

'Let's not fight. Not when we have so little time left.' His hands grasp my face and he tugs my mouth up to his kiss under the spray.

I pull back, panting. 'We're not fighting.' I grip his wrists, squeeze, and look deep into his eyes, unable to contain my feelings. 'I just want you to know…that you're not the loner you think you are. You're a caring people person. Your staff adore you. You muck in where needed. I'm pretty sure Evie and Remy will never forget you.' My voice breaks, the rest emerging as a whisper. 'And neither will I.'

His stare burns bright with emotion, even as a deep frown slashes his brow. He doesn't want to hear what I'm saying, but I'm running out of time. If I don't say it now, I'll miss my chance.

I place my hand on his chest, over his heart, which thumps against my palm. 'You care from the heart, Ryan, not just from the head. You have so much to give. Always remember that.'

He grips my face harder, his eyes burning into mine, seeming to say all the things I want to hear. But he would never vocalise them. He can't. I knew that from day one.

'And you don't have to do things to please anyone but yourself,' he says. 'You're brave and true and breathtaking. Keep being that, Grace. Keep being you.'

His mouth covers mine and I whimper, leaning into his heat and strength. My arms hold him as tightly as he's holding me. If I could squeeze the broken pieces of him back together with my bare hands, I would. But he'll never want the same things I do. All I can do is hold him now, and respect him and his choices anyway.

We head back to the bedroom, still dripping, too impatient to towel dry. I push him backwards onto the bed and crawl over him, my mouth tracing every droplet of water, every ridge of muscle and valley of soft, Ryan-scented skin.

By the time I take his erect length into my mouth, his eyes burn with that familiar passion we share, his fingers tangling in my hair and his hips lifting from the bed, his demands honest in a way I suspect he can't be with his heart. But I live for the moment. This moment. Us.

One of a dwindling number of moments we have left.

'Grace...' His voice warns me he's close as I suck and stroke and take him as deep as I can. If I could mark him somehow, I would, so that he'd always remember how good we are together when everything else, the world, our pasts, others' expectations, are stripped away.

'I want to come inside you.' He caresses my cheek, his stare locked to where my lips are stretched around his beautiful thick penis.

I release him and straddle his hips, sinking onto him with an ecstatic groan. He joins me in vocal pleasure, his head thrown back, and then he quickly recovers, his hands cupping my breasts as I ride him with only the warm, scented breeze from the open doors on my skin.

Jackknifing into a sitting position, Ryan wraps his arms around me and presses me to his chest so hard, I struggle to breathe. 'I'll remember you too,' he says against my throat before dipping his mouth to capture one nipple.

His declaration fills a place inside me; if this is all he can give me, I'll take it. Carry it home with me, a holiday souvenir I can pull out and inspect any time I find my newfound search for this kind of passion wavering.

We rock together until sweat coats us, neither of us in a hurry to the cross the finish line. When we eventually come, him seconds after me, it's all I can do to bite back my words and stop myself from confessing just how hard I've fallen.

CHAPTER FOURTEEN

Ryan

I GRAB GRACE'S hand and drag her out of the shallows, tossing our snorkel gear into the kayak so I can pull her close for a kiss.

'That was amazing. Thank you,' she says when I release her for air, even though every bone in my body protests. She's leaving tomorrow after her final first-aid class, and while the reasons and arguments that it's for the best sound through my head, that confused, churned up part of me wants to lock her in my bungalow so she misses her flight.

So fucked up. Because it would only delay the inevitable. We can't stay here for ever. *I* can't stay here for ever. Even if I could, I'm still the same person I was a week ago and Grace deserves better. She deserves her passionate life and a partner who shares her dreams.

Not a cynic like me. A loner, in spite of what she might think. A coward.

Our kiss turns heated. I wrap my arms around

her waist and drag her closer, wishing we could stay here, like this, trapped in this moment for ever, like cursed lovers.

'Ryan,' she whispers, rubbing her lips against mine while my eyes stay stubbornly closed. 'I need to tell you…' The sound of a stormy sea rages in my head, but I open my eyes, powerless to deny my beautiful, fearless Grace.

'I know you don't want to hear it,' she whispers, tracing my lips with her fingertip, 'but I could so easily fall for you.'

I watch the words I'm dreading emerge, then hide a wince, because it's disgust with myself I feel. Disgust for touching her in the first place when I knew I shouldn't. For selfishly gorging on every minute I could with her, even when I saw the way she looked at me, knew what she felt, because I feel it too. Disgust for not being brave enough to deserve her.

'Don't…' I crush her close, breathe in the scent of her hair and formulate words worthy of this amazing woman I wish I'd met in another life. As another me.

But she's too honest to stay silent. 'I wanted you to know. But I don't expect anything of you,' she says against my skin, tearing out another chunk of concrete from that block.

I ease her away, a burning Grace-shaped imprint left behind on my chest. 'I don't deserve someone like you, Grace, even though if I were in the happy-ever-after business, I could fall for you too. But I'm

in the singles business. I don't know how to do anything else.'

She's frozen with my hands on her shoulders. Or
I'm frozen…terrified to break the moment, to acknowledge the full circle we've reached only to find
ourselves back at the place we started.

I hear my name being called, turning away from
Grace to see Taito heading our way across the beach.

'Boss, there was a phone call for you. From Manor
Court,' he says, mentioning the name of my grandmother's nursing home.

Acid fills my throat, my heart leaping, fear nudging aside all other feelings. 'Did they leave a message?'

He shakes his head, and my blood actually runs
cold. I reach for Grace's hand, automatically, and
stride towards my bure, aware that her stride matches
mine in urgency. 'Thanks, Taito. I'll call them back.'

I find my phone and stab out the international
number I know by heart, my stomach lurching into
my mouth.

Please don't let it be too late.

I'm wound too tightly to sit, but neither can I
move, frozen in place facing the view I'm blind to
with a silent, stoic Grace by my side.

The conversation is brief—terse yes and no answers from me and an avalanche of alarming medical terms from them.

*'Atypical bacteria…worsening pneumonia…acute
renal failure…lapses of consciousness…'*

I disconnect the call and try to suck in enough oxygen past the panic choking me. This is it. This can't be it. I'm not ready. I knew this day would come... eventually... But... I pace to the kitchen and back, the movement making me seasick.

'You should go. I'll help you pack.' Grace's scent buffets me through the fog, her hand warm and soft and comforting on my arm. It's bittersweet, pleasure and pain, comfort and confrontation, her touch burning my skin while her words sink in.

'I need to think...' My temples throb. I should have gone sooner.

'Ryan—you need to go to her.' Calm. Hushed. Her doctor's voice. 'You'll never forgive yourself if you don't.'

I scrunch my eyes closed, wishing I could switch off my hearing and the drum inside my head that beats out the certainty I've dreaded all these years. Perhaps if I ignore it, it won't be true. Just as I learned not to feel after my mother abandoned me for the umpteenth time, just as I've shoved down my feelings for Grace.

Deny. Ignore. Hide.

'Listen.' She stands in front of me, her hands gripping both my arms, fingers digging into my biceps. 'You can't hide from this. Not this. You might save yourself the pain of not going today, but in the long run, the consequences will be greater. I know. I hated saying goodbye to Bryony. I cried and bargained and begged the universe to make it untrue. But I'm glad every day that I had that chance. Because I miss her and every day I wish I could speak to her, but at least I got to say goodbye.'

I shake my head. Step back from her wall of concern and sense and courage. 'I understand, but she's only seventy-eight. We've been here before—she's recovered before. I will go, but—' I move away from her scalding touch and compassionate eyes, my scalp prickling with apprehension. I curl my fist into my hair and relish the sting.

I'm wound so tight, there's no room in me for feelings. I welcome numbness, the automatic pilot that makes me fire a series of emails and instructions to my assistant to set the wheels of my imminent departure from the island—and from Grace—in motion.

When I turn back to Grace, she's looking at the view, her arms crossed over her waist, her back rigid. I step up beside her, my own hands curled into impotent fists inside my shorts' pockets.

Her concerned expression cuts me like a knife. 'I hope you're right, about your grandmother. I hope more than anything she recovers, that she tells you off for your sunburnt nose.'

Her words sting like acid. Even now she's trying to lesson my worry. The urge to take her in my arms one last time almost weakens my knees. But I hold my body still, every muscle focussed on keeping me together when I feel like I'm crumbling into a million fragments.

'And more than anything,' she whispers, 'I hope you find contentment in your life.'

I recoil, too shattered to hear this now. 'I can't do this,' I say. 'The end was always coming for us. We both knew that. It's just one day early.' And there's only room in my head for one sickening storm.

She faces me with a brave smile. 'I know. It was just a holiday fling,' she says, letting me off the hook.

I feel her distance even though she doesn't move. She's giving me space. Letting me escape gently, so great is her empathy and understanding.

'I'll be okay, you know,' she says. 'And if you need to talk, I'll be there. Any time.'

Irrational rage bubbles up, an inferno of need and denial and powerlessness. Part of me bows under the weight of gratitude, and the darker part, the part snarling in a corner for fear of being dragged into the light, wants to test her passion, to know that it isn't just me reeling and rudderless.

'You know you can't fix this, Grace. You can't fix me.' I ignore the flash of hurt in her eyes, the foul words spewing unbidden. 'It's okay—just walk away and see what happens.' My eyes burn, so intent is my stare, but I don't back down; my sanity demands this vile display. 'I'll survive. I've survived before. We'll still be the same two people who want different things. The world won't end.'

It will just feel that way.

But I can't give her any more than I have, and

the evidence that it's not enough may as well gouge out my eyes.

She swallows, her huge heart boldly on show as she tries to conceal the pain I've caused. 'I know I can't fix it—I would if I could. But at least try to be honest with yourself going forward. Yes, you'll survive, but is that living? Is fear a good enough reason to never allow yourself to be loved?'

Her sad smile, the stoic tremble of her lip, kills me, chews me up and spits me out. She presses a kiss to my cheek and steps away, heading for the door. I watch her go, my feet glued in place by the very fear she thinks is easily overcome. I'm only strong enough to face one loss.

Grace slips outside, but before she closes the door, she levels her courageous stare on me, stealing what's left of my air. 'I lied before, on the beach.'

I frown.

'About how easily I could fall for you.'

My pulse pounds in my temples, a sick mix of relief and longing.

'I know I shouldn't have,' she says with bleak eyes, 'but I've already fallen.'

And then she leaves.

CHAPTER FIFTEEN

Grace

THE FIRST WEEK back at work after a holiday is the toughest. I tell myself that's why my feet feel as if they're dragging, and I'd rather sleep in one of the sterile on-call rooms at the hospital than go back to my empty, cold apartment. But even in the temperature-controlled hospital I feel frozen to my core. It's as if I'll never be warm again, as if I left all the available sun in the world back in Fiji.

The same place I left a piece of my heart.

It's ridiculous to pine for someone I met two weeks ago, someone who wants the opposite of what I want. But *pine* is too mild a word for the soul-deep ache rendering me morose and chilled to the bone.

No, it's not depression; it's heartache. I'm the ultimate cliché. I fell for a man I met on holiday. A man so emotionally unavailable, he should have come with a health warning. And now I need to get over it.

Please let me get over it.

I toss my disposable hat into the bin, scan my access card and leave the operating theatres, still wearing scrubs. I walk on autopilot past the wards and head for the exit that will take me to the staff car park.

That's when I see him.

Ryan.

If he weren't permanently stuck in my mind since we parted in Fiji, I might not have recognised him. Wearing a sharp, charcoal business suit and tie, he leans up against the wall near the exit, one hand slung in the pocket of his trousers and the other holding his phone, which is where his focus lies.

I stand stock-still, hold my breath, drinking in the sight of him with greedy, burning eyes. He's had a haircut, his decadent dark waves shorn around the sides and back; even the top, a place my fingers know all too well, is tamed. It's only been a week since I last saw him, but he appears to have dropped some weight, dark circles under his eyes.

My heart clenches, the violent spasm stealing my breath. How can I still want him so badly? How can every cell crave him, need to comfort him? It's a lost cause. Even now, I'm bargaining, making deals in order to kid myself for a little longer, so I can have what I want.

Just one last night... I'm strong enough to be his fuck-buddy... Perhaps I don't want commitment after all...

Lies, all lies. And I've stopped moulding myself for others. No matter how crippling this pain, I have to stay strong.

I must move, because my theatre shoes squeak on the hospital linoleum and Ryan looks up from his phone. His gaunt, tired face lights up for a second, and hope soars inside me, and then the shutter falls on his expression and we're back to strangers who shared a week of incredible sex. Strangers who aren't even friends. He never contacted me after he left Fiji. No call. No text.

Not surprising.

'Hey, how are you? How's your grandmother?' Immediately I see the answer in his eyes, the pain he's battling as he pushes away from the wall and walks towards me. We meet in the centre of the corridor.

'She didn't make it. I buried her yesterday.' He speaks without inflection, as if he's challenged himself to say the words minus the emotions I know are stacked behind them.

I sway in his direction, my grief for his loss acute and violent. But he's not mine to console.

'I am so sorry.' I swallow my own feelings and reach out, touch his arm. I can't stop myself. I need him in this moment, even if he doesn't need me—but it's poor substitute for touching his bare skin, even though the wool of his suit is so fine, I can feel his tightly coiled muscles beneath the fabric.

I want to whisk him back to the island, to strip

away all our pretences along with our winter clothes and just exist with the sun on our skin. But no, he gave as much as he could give, and I'm a stupid woman for wishing it could be different.

He doesn't want me.

He doesn't even need me.

Even just to hold his hand at his lowest ebb.

If he'd called, told me about his grandmother, I'd have dropped everything, been there for him in a heartbeat.

'How did you know where to find me?' I ask, forcing my hand to drop to my side, because Ryan has made no move to return my touch. No polite cheek-to-cheek greeting.

'I didn't, really, I just hoped if I hung out near the staff car park I'd see you eventually. Hospital security is really tight—turns out you can't just phone up and ask for the location of a member of staff because if you don't see them, don't speak to them right that minute, your head is going to explode.'

I smile, although the threat of tears burns my throat. 'Who knew…?'

The light-hearted moment seems to take its toll on him. He swallows, visibly struggling. 'Can we go somewhere? For a drink?'

My pulse leaps, my heart clamouring to be heard. *Yes… Oh, please, yes.*

Then I shuffle my feet as his request tears a big strip off me, leaving a fresh wound, raw and gaping. Because he doesn't want me. He made that clear on the island. He's grieving. He wants the pain to stop. And together we can patch the hole for a while. But it won't hold for ever.

And at what toll to me…?

'I can't… I'm… I'm meeting a friend.' A friend who would understand if I cancelled, but am I strong enough when all I want is to be the person he turns to? Not just in the acute phase, but always and for ever.

He presses his lips together, glances away and then steps closer, filling the thick air between his body and mine with his delicious scented heat, a potion designed to enslave me.

'Right, the thing is,' he says, his stare dark, 'I miss you.'

My stupid heart talks to my pituitary gland so a cascade of endorphins joins the protests in my weak body. 'I miss you too. We had quite an intense holiday, didn't we?'

He frowns and I bite my cheek. Don't interrupt a man when he hunts you down to get something off his chest…

'But I'm not done. I'm not ready to move on like it never happened. I want you back, Grace. I want to keep seeing you, take you on dates, get to know you in the real world…'

I sway towards those words. The urge to kiss him—to snuggle inside his suit jacket and steal his warmth, suck in the scent of him and agree—is so strong, I have to curl my nails into my palm to stop myself from moving. My body clamours in triumph while my brain rocks up with the police and noise control, breaking up the party.

'Ryan,' I whisper, 'I'm heartbroken for your loss. I know how important she was to you. You're grieving and that's horrible, worst of all because it's a process and there are no shortcuts—you just have to go through it until, one day, it won't hurt so bad.'

He looks annoyed, furious even. 'I am grieving, of course I am, but I still want you.'

I swallow down scalding heat, my eyes burning. 'I want you too. And, sure, we could see each other for a while, but... I still want to find a for-ever person. I want a relationship and romance, and a ring one day. And you don't.'

He shakes his head but I plough on, my courage for rejecting what my heart truly craves dwindling as I cling to the last threads. 'I made myself a promise that I'd stop hiding the real me, stop being apologetic for what I want. You helped me do that, helped me see that the passion I want is out there, I just have to find it with someone who wants the same. There's no point forcing it if it's not there. I made the mistake of fooling myself before.'

He steps closer, still not touching me. 'You can't deny we're good together.'

'Of course not, but the cracks had already begun to show before we left Fiji. We tried to patch them up with sex and that worked fine on the island, because it was a magical, fantasy place, but it won't work here in the real world. You know that. You even tried to remind me of that before we left. And you were right. I can't settle again. I can't put others' feelings before my own.' I swallow hard, scrape out the next sentence, which cuts me to shreds. 'Not even yours.'

I want my words to be lies more than I want my next breath. I want him to be in a place where I see a glimmer of hope for us. I wish I could settle, be okay with what he's offering.

I feel myself waver, so strong are my feelings for this man. 'Perhaps—'

'No.' His voice is a whip crack. 'Don't do that. Don't relent. Demand what you want—always. You deserve it.' He scrubs a hand down his tired face, and my pulse trips, missing a beat, compassion for the man I think I'm in love with oozing from every pore.

'I was just going to say that perhaps you could give me a few days to think it through. Perhaps we can go for a drink Friday, after my shift. I really am meeting my friend Brooke tonight.' I step close, press a kiss to his cheek and force myself to back away when the feel of his skin under my lips is so right, I'm leaving a part of me behind with that final kiss. 'I really am sorry for your loss. Call me if you need to talk before Friday.'

I turn away before the tears fall, rushing to my car on wooden feet while every cell in me wails and wheedles. I tear out of the car park as fast as I can, silencing the voices in my head with the blaring radio.

Otherwise I'd cave.

* * *

'I made the wrong decision, didn't I?' I down half of my pint of lager and wipe my mouth with the back of my hand, my body twitching to run out of the pub and find Ryan. I'm still wearing my scrubs, but it's not that weird a sight as Brooke and I chose to meet in a pub close to the hospital. More strange is that I'm seconds away from throwing myself on the floor and wailing like a toddler.

'I don't know,' says Brooke, her usual unflappable stare wary. 'Where does it hurt the most? Your heart or your pussy?'

I give her a death stare and then lean into her side for a comforting hug. 'Tell me I haven't just made the worst mistake of my life.'

'You haven't just made the worst mistake of your life,' she replies, deadpan.

'I'm serious.' I swallow another glug of beer. 'What should I do? Don't force me to call Neve for advice while she's on holiday.'

'Okay, okay.' Brooke sips her gin and tonic and props her elbows on the table, her expression that of a mother about to deliver a bollocking. 'The thing is that men aren't good with expressing their feelings—universal knowledge. So the fact that he sought you out at work to tell you he made a mistake and still wants you is *huge*.'

She spreads her hands, indicating just how monumentally I've messed up.

I drop my head into my hands, the pulsing throb

at my temples palpable. 'No, no, no…' I look up, searching for validation in my friend's expression. 'I thought I was being strong, standing up for what I want. Refusing to settle…'

'You were, sweetie. You did all that. But did you ask him how he feels about you? Give him a chance to be eloquent? Did you tell him you love him?'

I shake my head, my throat closing and my head light. I didn't say those exact words to him in Fiji. 'No, because he's grieving. He'd say or do anything right now to make himself feel better. I know.' My stomach clenches for Ryan. How could I have left him when he needed someone, a friend, the most?

'Of course you know.' Brooke reaches across the table to squeeze my hand.

'I'm in love with someone who doesn't believe in the concept. And the minute I touch him again, hold him, everything I feel will rise to the surface.' I laugh to stave off tears, but they build regardless. 'I want to be there for him, but I just need time to strengthen my guard, because casual isn't going to be enough for me anymore.'

'And of course you wouldn't marry him tomorrow if he proposed, but guys don't say stuff they don't mean. Just because he's grieving doesn't mean he doesn't want you, for real.'

I glance at the door, debating a mad dash back to the hospital. 'I suck at relationships. I suck at long term and I suck at flings.'

'No, you don't—this stuff is complicated. And

you don't have to be perfect at it.' She pushes my hair from my face, her eyes soft with understanding. 'The important thing is to do what you want, what feels right in your heart. You can't go far wrong that way, and whatever the outcome, at least you've been true to yourself.'

'You're right. If I want my happy ending, I have to be honest.'

I should have told him that I love him, put everything on the line, no matter how crazy it sounds after only two weeks, or how crappy the timing. I tug my phone from my pocket and compose the first lines of a text, my thumbs flying over the screen.

'That's my girl,' says Brooke. 'Go get him.'

CHAPTER SIXTEEN

Ryan

I STARE AT the texts, the words blurring. I don't need to read them. I know them by heart.

Grace: I've had time to think about what you said. Do you still want to meet Friday for a drink?

Me: Something has come up. Out of the country on business for the next three weeks. I'd love to talk on my return. Bailey's Bar, seven p.m. on the twentieth?

Grace: I'll be there.

I blow into my hands, my gaze following the inky black ribbon of the Thames. My breath mists in front of me. The bar heaves with Friday night revellers, this table outside the only way to ensure privacy. No one in their right mind would choose to sit outside on a night so cold.

But I'm not in my right mind. I haven't been since meeting the woman who turned my life on its head, ripping through me with her guts and compassion and courage.

Perhaps she won't come. Perhaps she's changed her mind… I've veered back and forth for the past three weeks, certain of what I want, but offering Grace enough space so she'll believe I speak from the heart and not simply out of grief or loneliness or desperation.

A man learns a lot about himself in the dead of a sleepless night. And everything I learned led back to Grace, time and time again.

'Ryan…?'

I spin and she's there. She looks small, fragile, wrapped up against the cold, a bobble hat covering her head, but she's the bravest person I know, her inner strength contagious.

I press my mouth to her cheek, which is ruddy from the cold, when all I really want is to bundle her into a bear hug and never let her go. To look into her eyes and have her read my mind, because, even now, I've no idea if what I want to say, need to say, will make it past my frigid lips.

'Do you mind sitting out here near the heater? It's chaotic inside.'

Don't talk about nothing. Tell her how you feel about her.

I pull out a bar stool at the high table facing the river. 'I ordered mulled wine—it's still hot.'

'Thanks.' Her eyes light up as she sees what I arranged with the bar staff. 'They have frangipani flowers here?'

I shrug. 'I organised that. It's been so cold...' In my heart, my soul, my life, without her. 'I wanted a reminder that somewhere in the world, the sun is shining. And frangipani remind me of you.' I stare, lost in her eyes, struck dumb. How will I ever convince her to take a chance on me? How will I ever convey all she means to me?

'How are you?' she asks, taking her drink in both gloved hands and blowing across the steaming surface.

'I'm doing okay. I still miss Grandma every day, miss picking up the phone and checking in with her, even just for one of her tongue lashings.'

She nods, that trademark compassion in her eyes. 'It will get easier with time, I promise.'

My throat tightens. I shift in my seat, inching closer because I'm as drawn to her now as I was on the beach, that first day. She's a beacon on a dark night.

'Grace—'

'Ryan—'

We smile and I indicate she speak first.

'I need to apologise for the way I behaved at the hospital that night,' she says. 'You needed a friend and I wasn't there for you. I was scared I'd lose myself, because I need to be brave one last time. To tell you something I know you won't want to hear, but—'

I press my fingers to her cold lips. 'Shh… Please let me say this first.'

She nods, her eyes wide.

I take a deep breath. 'I should never have let you go that day in Fiji. The timing sucked, but I should have told you my feelings when I had the chance. I should have been as brave as you are. As honest. Because the feelings were there. I just hid them, denied them. Lied to myself and to you.'

She leans away from my touch, a half-smile emerging from behind my fingers. 'That's an awful lot of shoulds.' The amber in her eyes sparkles. 'Why don't you just do what you want?'

Warmth sings through my blood. 'I love you, Grace. A part of me loved you that first day, when you worried about my grazed ankle.' I take her gloved hands. 'It's not grief talking, or loneliness, or fear. I love you because you're dauntless. Your heart is the size of Big Ben and you see things others don't see. You cared and you cared and you cared until you infected my blood, made me care too. You're perfect as you are, but you're still trying to improve, to be the best version of yourself, and you give me hope. That one day, if I embrace just a fraction of your bravery, I can be worthy of you.'

Moisture shines in her eyes. I cup her frozen cheeks, bring her face closer, my lips on fire to taste her once more. 'I can't promise to be everything you deserve, but you need to know that you make me want things. The same things you want. Us. Commitment. Marriage. I'm scared to promise for ever, but I'll try. Every day I'll try. Because you were right. I can't live without love. Without *your* love.'

She laughs, tears spilling over onto my thumbs and then she's out of her seat, her mouth on mine while her arms hold me so tightly, the air whooshes from my chest.

She pulls back. 'I love you too. I wanted to tell you that in Fiji and again at the hospital. I've been carrying the words around every day, stopping myself from texting them. I love you, Ryan.'

I drag her into the space between my spread thighs, kiss her until my heart, thundering behind my ribs, settles.

She grips my wrists, her eyes searching mine. 'Don't say you're not worthy. You're as worthy of love as the next person. And I'm going to prove that to you. Every day.'

When we surface from kissing, I wrap my open coat around her and clutch her to my chest, the reassuring beat of her heart against mine sweeping away every doubt I've had these past three weeks.

'There's one other thing to address,' I say, keeping my tone serious.

She looks up.

'You said we fix things with sex. I want to convince you that's not true, so I propose we don't have any for the first year of our relationship. I want you to feel secure that I'm serious about wanting more. Wanting it all.'

She yanks free of my arms. 'What? No sex for a year? Are you insane?'

I hide my smile. My forthright Grace was never going to take this lying down. 'I think we're up for the challenge.'

'I think you're deluded. I won't last a day. An hour.' She presses her mouth to mine with a delicious little moan.

My grin twitches my lips. 'Ah, my Grace, so honest about her desires.'

'Too right,' she says, snuggling back inside my coat. 'Now take me home or we run the risk of public indecency charges. I don't care how cold it is.'

I press my lips to her forehead, that place in my chest that she unearthed filled with this incredible woman. 'Whatever you say, my love. Whatever you want.'

EPILOGUE

Grace

MY BARE TOES curl into the warm sand, every step forcing my pulse higher with delirious anticipation. But also taking me one step closer to the man I love.

He's so handsome. So brave waiting for me alone under an archway of scented tropical flowers, back lit by the setting sun. Just a few more steps and I'll be able to hold his hand. To whisper, 'I love you,' and see my feelings reflected back at me in his eyes.

I pass our tiny gathering of guests—my parents, Brooke and Neve and their plus ones, and a handful of friends we've acquired as a couple over the past year. A year filled with highs and lows, compromise and laughter, as all real relationships are.

'You look so beautiful,' Ryan says as I arrive before him at the altar. 'You're the best risk I ever took.'

'I feel the same way.' I kiss him, ignoring wedding etiquette, and smooth one hand over the white linen shirt that covers his deeply bronzed torso. Ryan in board shorts turns out to be my favourite thing about Fiji. All I have to do is suggest a paddleboard and I get to watch all his tanned, toned body in action.

We're supposed to face our local celebrant for the vows, but neither of us drops the other's hand as we stand and stare, wearing matching sappy smiles. It's our day, we can do what we want.

It's only much later, after the vows and the cake and speeches, when I'm in his arms as we slow dance under the stars near the water's edge, that it hits me I have a husband. I press my mouth to his, a distraction from counting the minutes until we can abandon our guests, and I can get him alone in Lailai's best honeymoon bungalow.

'I would have been happy to keep on living together,' I say. Turns out happily ever after comes in all forms, once you meet the right person.

His smile is knowing, indulgent. 'I wouldn't, Mrs Dempsey.' He lifts my left hand to his mouth, pressing a kiss over the wedding ring he placed there only hours ago. 'I'm never letting you go. Best to make it official.'

I laugh because, in the end, he was the one adamant we tie the knot. The one to set the date. The one to make all the plans. 'You mean Dr Dempsey.'

He picks me up, swirls me around and then kisses me.

'Are you glad you didn't change the place to singles only? We could hardly have come here for our wedding otherwise.' I slide my hands under the hem of his shirt, caress the warm skin of his back.

'Of course I'm glad. As a very smart and beautiful woman once told me, romance is good for business.'

I laugh and then press my mouth to his. As we move towards our guests, snag ourselves two glasses of champagne, I catch a glimpse of Brooke and Neve dancing with their dates under the palm trees.

'Yes, it is. Cheers to that.'

'And to us,' says my husband.

We clink glasses.

* * * * *

UNDER HIS OBSESSION

CATHRYN FOX

MILLS & BOON

For my dear friend Claudine Laforce.

You are kind, generous and supportive and I'm lucky to have you in my life!

CHAPTER ONE

Khloe

"THERE'S THE DOOR. Feel free to use it."

Stomach in knots, I stare wide-eyed at my boss, hardly able to believe what I'm hearing. Then again, is it really so inconceivable that he's canning my ass? Disobedience comes with a price, and like all other men in power, Benjamin R. Murray, owner of *Starlight Magazine*, can do what he wants and say what he likes. Privileged men like him think the world is theirs for the taking and will walk on, or over, anyone who gets in their way.

"You're really firing me?" I ask, as Manhattan's midday sun shines in through the floor-to-ceiling windows, warming the blood zinging through my veins and stirring the nausea in my stomach. My skin begins to moisten, but no way will I let this man see me sweat. I don't want him to think he holds all the cards. Even though he does. But I'm not a girl to go down without a fight.

"That depends." Benjamin drops the chicken leg he's been gnawing on and wipes greasy, sausage-thick fingers on the stack of paper napkins before him. His chair groans under his impressive weight as he pushes away from his desk and stands to square off against me. The situation is clearly dire if he's abandoning his beloved bucket of chicken. "Are you going to do the exposé on Will Carson or not?" he asks. His deep voice is hard and unwavering, letting me know my future at the magazine depends on what I say next.

Though I can't afford to lose this job, I refuse to dig up dirt on Will Carson, a brilliant software developer—aka, the Millionaire Rocket Scientist of Wall Street. Partly because the exposé done on him a few years back by one of *Starlight*'s reporters ruined his life and partly because my father used to work for Will's grandfather, James Carson.

James isn't like other powerful men—he treats those who work for him fairly, respectfully. He was always generous and kind to my late father, going above and beyond to make sure a single father and his daughter were looked after. I have no doubt those care boxes containing food and clothes came from him—he knew my love for M&M's and somehow my size—even though he vehemently denied his involvement.

The man owns half of Manhattan, and after I graduated with a journalism degree, he offered me a job at the *Grub*, a magazine that reviews restaurants.

I politely declined, since I live off frozen food and know nothing about fine dining. Although it might have been a better jumping-off point than *Starlight*.

I want to write meaningful articles, to earn my place in the cutthroat news business and to get there on my own merit. From watching my father, I learned to work hard and to never take handouts—he didn't like it when those care boxes materialized on our doorstep. And I won't abandon my principles by twisting information for a headline like I'm some damn bottom-feeder.

Then why are you working at Starlight*?*

Because I can't get hired at a reputable magazine without experience, and I can't get experience without getting hired. So, *Starlight* it is. Or was…

"Well, are you?" he asks again, pulling my focus back to the matter at hand.

I cross my arms and plant my feet. "No," I say through gritted teeth. It's not a smart answer, considering rent is due next week, and my groceries consist of a single sleeve of stale crackers and a half-eaten box of pizza pockets.

"It's my way or the highway, Khloe," he says, his beady blue eyes arctic cold.

"Why me, Benjamin?" He doesn't tolerate anyone saying no to him, but what do I care? He can't fire me twice. "Why take me off sensationalized crime stories and put me on celebrity gossip, especially when you know I have a connection to the Carson family?"

His grin is sardonic. "That's your answer right there. You have an in, and any good journalist would use that connection to get information."

"You already ruined Will's life. Why twist the knife?" I ask, even though I already know the answer. Money. That's the answer to everything in a rich man's world.

"The public is interested in the famous Carson family. It's time we told them what Will has been up to since his fiancée left him."

Starlight's front-page spread on Will had never sat well with me. I've never met him, but from the stories James told, Will didn't seem like someone who'd get drunk and jump into bed with another woman at his bachelor party.

The pictures splashed across the front cover, however, painted a different story. Money and power. They mess with people. In the end, Will proved to be no different from any man with millions and authority—and because of the spread, he lost his supermodel fiancée. But I still refused to do the exposé. My father would turn over in his grave if I suddenly sank to slimeball level.

"I guess this is goodbye, then." I turn and see a flurry of activity in the hall. Great, my colleagues were eavesdropping. At least they'll have something to talk about at the watercooler. "I'll clear my desk."

"If you change your mind…"

"I won't," I say. Heads duck and eyes are averted as I walk down the hall. Despite the storm going on in my stomach, I straighten my back and calmly walk to my four-by-four pod.

I reach my desk and stare at the papers strewn across it. Nothing truly belongs to me, but I spitefully shove the stapler into my purse. I'm about to walk away but can't. Dammit, I'm not a thief. I put the stapler back and go still when a pair of heels tap rapidly on the floor, growing louder as they approach.

Breathless, Steph skids to a stop. "I just heard." My only real friend at the magazine—all the others would slice and dice anyone who got in their way— Steph takes my hand. Thick painted lashes blink rapidly over caramel eyes. "What happened?"

I lower my voice and explain, even though I'm sure everyone knows—around here, rumors spread faster than a Sean Mendes You Tube video.

"He's such a worm," she says.

"Hey, don't insult worms. They have their purpose."

"Wait, I got it." Hope fills her eyes. "Just say you couldn't find anything on Will. I mean, he might be a grade A asshole—"

"Will's an asshole?"

"Yeah, that's what every reporter who tried to get a story on him says."

"They do?"

"Oh, yeah." She holds her hand out and starts tapping one finger after another as she says, "Opinionated, arrogant, bossy, patronizing."

"What you're saying is he's no different from any other Wall Street millionaire."

She nods. "I also heard he doesn't keep any of his assistants around for long. They're fired for the smallest of mistakes."

"I guess I haven't been paying close enough attention to the Carson family drama."

"Well, anyway, he's become a bit of a recluse, taking privacy to the extreme. You could just say you didn't find anything."

I give her a look that suggests she's insane. "Steph, come on. If I don't bring the story Benjamin wants or twist it to his liking, I'll be fired anyway."

"But I don't want you to go." She pouts. "You can't leave me here with all the two-faced piranhas."

"You have that interview with the *Cut* next week, right?" While it's Steph's dream to write about trends and designs, I'm more interested in politics and current events. My ultimate dream is to write for the *New Yorker* magazine, and in my spare time, pen a novel.

"Yes, but—"

"No buts. You got this. And something will come my way," I say. I hike my purse up higher and lift my chin, showcasing confidence I don't currently feel.

Steph steps to the side to let me pass. "If he offers it to me, I'll tell him to shove it up his—"

"Thanks, Steph, but I don't want you to lose your job, too."

"The *Cut*, remember." She jabs her thumb into her chest. "It's mine."

"Good girl," I say, and give her a hug. "I'll text you later."

"Wait, Khloe." Her gaze moves over my face. "Are you sure you're okay? You look a little pale."

"I'm fine."

Her eyes narrow. "You need some sun."

I run my tongue over one of my molars. "A piece of filling chipped off this morning." There had been something strangely hard in the sausage on the left-over pizza I had for breakfast. "Maybe if I put it under my pillow, the tooth fairy will leave enough money for us both to go on a vacation."

Steph laughs. "Your sense of humor is still intact. I guess that means you're all right."

"I'll be okay," I assure her with false bravado.

I make my way to the elevator and realize that while I refused to do the exposé, the next person likely won't. Dammit. I hurry downstairs, step out-side and hail a cab. But instead of going to my small apartment in Brooklyn, I give the driver directions to James's mansion on Sixty-Fourth. I have no idea if he's home, but he's well into his nineties, so I doubt he'll be out for long.

When we arrive, I pay the fare and step out, lift-ing my eyes to take in the looming building before me. I haven't been here since I was a teen. The first time I ever saw James's mansion was when I was five. I'd had the chicken pox, and the after-school day care teacher had sent me home. Dad had put me in the back seat, and I'd sat quietly as he'd driven James to wherever he needed to go. We'd picked up one of his grandsons from swimming lessons— apparently, he'd already had the pox, so it was safe to sit him in back with me. For all I know, it could have been Will beside me that day. I was quiet and shy, and other than answer a few questions James directed my way, I stayed silent.

Until I vomited all over the back seat.

I take a deep breath and step up to the front door of the mansion. Unease presses down on my shoulders as I jab the bell. I haven't seen James in years, and part of me worries he might think I was behind the last exposé. I wasn't, of course. I'd had no idea Avery Roberts was working on an article that would ruin a man's life.

Behind me, people rush by, always in a hurry. One of these days I'd like to go somewhere with a slower pace. Maybe write that book. But with the meager funds in my pocket, the farthest I could trek is to Starbucks, two streets over. When I got there, I'd have to order a water, no straw. I snort at that thought and pray that the tooth fairy comes through. But I'm quick to pull myself together when the door creaks open.

I expect to be greeted by a servant. Instead, James Carson himself is standing in the foyer, his hazy blue eyes moving over my face. I wait for recognition to hit, and I can tell the second awareness creeps in by the way his eyes widen.

"Mr. Carson," I begin, and place my hand over my uneasy stomach. "I don't mean to bother you—"

"Bother me. Of course you're not bothering me, child. Come in, Khloe. Come in, and please call me James."

"It's been a while. I wasn't sure if you'd remember me."

"You haven't changed a bit."

I can't say the same for him. Over the last decade, his winter-white hair has thinned, and the lines bracketing his milky eyes and pale lips have deepened. He's a little shorter, his body much frailer than it was when I last saw him.

"Come along," he says. Gnarled fingers tighten around a cane, and his gait is slow as he guides me down the hall.

"Maybe I changed a little," I say for lack of anything better. "It's been quite a few years."

"Ten, to be exact," he answers. While his body is deteriorating, it doesn't appear that his mind is following suit. I shadow him into his den and admire his extensive library as the vanilla smell of old books fills my senses. James turns and offers me a warm, grandfatherly smile, and my heart squeezes. He was like the grandfather I never had and always wanted. It was only Dad and me growing up. We lost Mom to cancer when I was just a child. I only have a few fleeting memories of her.

He winks at me. "Have you decided to take the job at the *Grub*?"

"The only thing I know about food is how to eat it, and even then, I make a mess of it. Believe me, I'm not cut out to cover restaurants and do reviews. I'd be a detriment, not an asset, to your company. But thank you for the offer."

"I always loved your honesty." He taps his cane on the wooden floor. "Max did a great job raising you."

Warmth fills me at the mention of my father. "You were always so good to us. My dad talked fondly about you."

"He used to tell me your dream was to write for the *New Yorker*."

"Still is," I say.

A beat of silence takes up space between us as we both get lost in our thoughts. A moment later, James breaks the quiet. "Then to what do I owe the pleasure of your company?" he asks, his voice gravelly as he smooths his hands over an imaginary tie and nods at the ebony leather chair.

I lower myself and sink into the soft cushion. It's heavenly, and if I weren't so anxious, my stomach roiling, I'd love to curl up and have a nap. Although I'm not sure why I'm so tired. I get enough sleep most nights, and it's not like I could be pregnant—unless it was immaculate conception.

"There is something I think you should know."

He walks up to his bar and picks up a brandy decanter. "Drink?"

After the morning I've had, I sure could use one, or two, but I politely decline. I'm not sure I'd be able to keep it down. He pours a generous amount into a crystal snifter, swallows it in one smooth motion, and refills his glass.

I wait as he slowly makes his way to the sofa across from my chair. I take stock of the room, my gaze going from the colossal desk in front of the window to the Polaroid camera on the side table. I note the stack of what looks like wedding photos beside it. I cringe, knowing they're not happy photos of Will's wedding, considering he never had one. While a part of me is mortified about the terrible invasion of privacy, I can't help but think his fiancée had a right to know what was going on. I sure as hell would have wanted to know. But I'd have to have a fiancé before he could cheat on me. Aren't I a real catch now? Jobless, penniless and soon to be homeless. I can't understand why men aren't lining up.

"You still work for *Starlight*?" James asks, like he's reading my mind.

I fold my hands in my lap. "As of today, no."

He straightens. "You quit?"

"Fired, actually. That's why I'm here."

The lines around his eyes deepen as he squints at me. "What is it you want me to know, Khloe?"

"First, I'd like you to know I had nothing to do with the exposé on Will. I had only just started at the magazine and had no idea they were doing a story on him."

"Never thought you were involved, child," he says quickly, and my shoulders relax slightly.

I lean forward and put my hands on my knees. "I was asked to do a follow-up today because I had connections."

He nods slowly and takes another swig. "And you were fired because you refused?"

"That's right." Yeah, the man is still sharp. "But I wanted to warn you and Will. I might have said no, but the next reporter won't."

"I appreciate you coming to tell me this." He sets his glass down, and his curled fingers adjust the gray cardigan around his shoulders. His eyes shut, and at first I think he's deep in thought, but he goes quiet for so long, I fear he's fallen asleep.

I'm about to rise and tiptoe to the door so I don't disturb him when his lids open and his blue eyes pin me in place.

"Do you have work lined up?" he asks.

"No, it just happened, but I'm about to start pounding the pavement."

"I have a job for you."

I shake my head fast. "While I appreciate your kindness, I—"

"As stubborn as your father." His chuckle is deep and raspy. "But you see, Khloe, you'd be doing me a favor."

"What kind of favor?" I ask, settling back in my seat.

"Will needs an assistant for his upcoming trip to Saint Thomas."

Oh God, a trip to Saint Thomas sounds heavenly right now. A Caribbean beach, sand, water... But I suppose if I'm in some boardroom taking notes for Will Carson, I'll see none of the island. Still, getting out of New York for a while does sound nice.

"It's a temporary job, until you find something in your field, of course."

I consider my meager savings. I'm adamant about making my own way in life, but a paying job until I can find something else, well, that would cover next week's rent and put food in my belly—once it stops churning. Plus, James did say I'd be helping him out.

"What would I have to do?" I ask.

"You can write, can't you?"

"Of course."

"I must warn you. He's not always an easy man to work for."

"I've dealt with worse, I'm sure."

James chuckles. "I'm sure you have. Will, however, is very regimented and has high expectations of those who work for him."

"I have high expectations of myself," I assure him. After Steph telling me Will was pretty much an ogre, I'm not sure why I'm working so hard to sell myself. Oh, right... I like having a roof over my head.

"He also has a strict dress code."

"A dress code? Really?" From what I know about software developers, they go to work in jeans and wear T-shirts with sayings like Cereal Killer or I Paused My Game to Be Here. Then again, people think all reporters are heartless sharks. I'm not heartless, and for all I know Will is a suit-and-tie kind of guy, like James used to be. But a dress code means I'd need to go shopping. I consider my budget and there is very little room for new clothes. Maybe I won't be able to take this job after all.

James finishes the brandy in his glass and sets it on the table. "An assistant is an extension of Will and is expected to act and dress a certain way. Is that a problem for you?"

"I...uh...what does he expect his assistant to wear?"

"No worries, your clothing will be supplied."

"Oh, okay." A measure of relief washes through me.

"You'll find a new wardrobe in your closet when you reach your destination." He glances the length of me, like he's trying to determine my size. I debate whether I should outright tell him, but in the end, I don't want to say the number out loud. Honest to God, from the little amount I eat, I should be thinner than I am. But no, my body likes to store every damn calorie I take in. While I've come to terms with it, that's one of the many things my ex-fiancé, Liam, wanted to change about me. Apparently, I didn't fit in with what was expected of his affluent family. Douchebags. Every last one of them.

"Anything else I should know?"

"You'll have to sign a nondisclosure agreement. Anything you see or hear cannot be repeated."

Jeez, the more he talks about Will, the more intrigued I am about the secretive, regimented asshole who provides clothing to his assistants. The same man caught in bed with another woman during his bachelor party. The more I think about it, a man like him getting caught seems rather contradictory to his character. If I hadn't seen the pictures with my own eyes, I might not have believed it. Will flat on his back, some random girl riding him like he was her own personal pony. It's rather disgusting that Avery sneaked in and took the pictures.

James sits back in his chair and lifts his head. He riffles through the Polaroids beside him, finds what he's looking for and hands it to me.

"That's Will," he says, but he doesn't need to tell me. Nor does he need to tell me I'm looking at the hottest guy on the planet. One who can't keep it in his pants, even when he has a beautiful fiancée.

"Whose wedding?"

"Will's brother Alec and his beautiful bride, Megan. Married in Saint Moritz near my resort." Under his breath he says, "Now there's only one left."

"I'm sorry, what?"

There's a new spark in his eyes when he says, "You're perfect for Will."

Perfect for Will?

Something feels a little off in the way he phrased that. Then again, he is in his nineties, and perhaps he's not as sharp as I thought. "You mean I'm the perfect *assistant* for Will, right?"

"That's right. Isn't that what I said?" That spark is back in his eyes, and before I can answer he continues with, "You'll do it then?"

"I'd never say no to a favor for you, but can I ask how it *is* a favor for you?"

"Will is a very private man. He hires a new assistant for every trip. He's not so trustful, you see. Doesn't let anyone get too close or hang around too long. There is no room for complacency in his world."

"I can understand that."

"Every assistant is vetted through my agency, and I'm their last stamp of approval. Unfortunately, no one quite fits what he needs."

"You think I do?"

"I think you're perfect. But there is one more thing, Khloe." He leans toward me. "It's very important."

I eye him carefully, not at all sure I like the sound of this. "Okay…"

"I realize you don't put articles out in your own name at *Starlight*, but please don't mention you're a journalist, or anything about the magazine."

I'm about to question him on that, but quickly realize why it's important to keep that information private. Will, undoubtedly, has a deep hatred and distrust for reporters after the exposé done on him. "I don't like to lie."

"It's not a lie. It's just not something he needs to know."

"Why hire me if he hates reporters? I'm sure there must be at least one temp at the agency who could give him what he needs."

"Not the way you can. Now you'd better get a move on—his plane leaves in a couple hours."

When I catch what looks like mischief in his cloudy eyes, unease trickles through me. While I'm certain James would never steer me wrong, I can't shake the feeling that I'm about to go down the rabbit hole and not come out the same.

CHAPTER TWO

Will

AT THE SOUND of hurried footsteps on the metal stairs of Granddad's Learjet, I lift my eyes and say, "You're late."

"Excuse me?"

I take in the breathless woman glaring at me. Damn, if looks could kill…

I sit up a little straighter, fold the newspaper I'd been reading and carefully set it on my lap.

"I said, you're late."

One hand planted on her hip and one foot tapping restlessly, she says, "I do apologize," her dark brown eyes flaring hot. "I'm usually punctual, but not only did I have little time to prepare for this trip, traffic was horrible, and my driver was a maniac. I'm lucky I made it here alive."

"You didn't use Granddad's driver?"

"No. I left from home and didn't see the need for him to backtrack to pick me up."

I raise my brows. "That's what his service is for."

"I just didn't want to put anyone out," she says, and it surprises me, considering most temps love to ride in Granddad's limo.

She rakes agitated fingers through a mess of wavy chestnut hair, her chest rising and falling as if she's been running. Her tight yoga pants hug her curvy hips like a second skin, and the relaxed V-neck T-shirt she's wearing showcases an abundance of creamy cleavage. Something inside me twitches at the sexy sight and reminds me I haven't been with a woman in far too long.

Nevertheless, despite the fact that the mere sight of this woman rouses something primal in me—reminds me I'm a man with needs—I'm not about to get involved with her. My traitorous dick might be showing interest, but I never mix business and pleasure. It's one of my many hard rules. After the exposé done on me, I don't let anyone get too close. Which means, while I can acknowledge my desire for her, I'm not about to act on it.

"I thought I'd be taking this trip solo until Grandfather called and said he found someone suitable last-minute."

"Yes," she says, her breasts jutting out a little more as she squares her shoulders. "I'm Khloe."

"Khloe," I say, trying the name out on my tongue. "Have you signed the nondisclosure agreement, Khloe?"

Her eyes drop to my mouth when I repeat her

name. Is she, too, wondering how it would sound on my lips if she were in my bed, beneath me?

Cool it, Will. She's an employee, and that makes her hands-off.

"Yes, at James's house," she says quickly. "He has a copy. We both do." She taps the big bag slung over her slender shoulders.

I eye her for a moment, and with a lift of her chin, she stares back unflinchingly. There's no denying that she's different from the women who normally travel as my assistant. Most don't look me in the eye, and are all fidgety and nervous around me. It's rather irritating. This woman, however, has a confidence about her and doesn't look like she'd put up with any kind of bullshit, especially from me. Which begs the question—why did Granddad hire her? It's not that I'm a complete asshole, although I've been called that and worse a time or two. It's just that I'm careful and private, a guy who likes things done in a certain way, and most importantly, a guy who trusts no one.

"I don't tolerate tardiness, and I certainly expect my employees to dress in a certain way. There are rules."

Her teeth clench with an audible click, and I can almost hear her brain spinning as a violent streak of pink colors her cheeks. If I had to guess, she's about to tell me where to shove my rules. Either that or she's contemplating which foot to use to kick me in the nuts. It's rather odd how I find her reactions amusing. But I can't give that any more consideration. No, not when she's smoothing her hand over her mess of hair and arousing my dick all over again.

"I'm well aware you have rules, and while your grandfather mentioned that you expect those in your employment to dress a certain way, I assumed for travel..." She pauses and runs her hands down the length of her body, and my eyes follow in appreciation. "I assumed that this would be more comfortable for the long flight." She takes a breath, lets it out slowly, and I grin as she works fervently to tamp down a flash of temper. I'm pretty good at reading people, and my gut tells me those weren't the words she wanted to throw my way. This woman is becoming more intriguing by the moment. "When we reach our destination, I'll be sure to dress appropriately."

"Very well. You should settle yourself in for take-off, and once we're in the air, I'd like a brandy."

Her head rears back at my request, and instead of sitting, she stares at me, mouth dropped open, like I've grown a second head.

"Wait, what?" she asks, then glances around the private jet.

I'm not sure who or what she's looking for, but her attention returns to me when I say, "A brandy. Is that a problem?"

"No... I just..."

I take in her narrowing eyes and tightening mouth and can't shake the feeling that something about her is...off. Granddad is pretty particular when it comes to my assistants. Then again, he's not getting any younger, and I do worry about him. Can I still trust his judgment?

"My grandfather explained your duties, did he not?"

"I…" She briefly looks down, her dark eyes stormy. A second later, her head lifts and she shakes her wavy hair back, her composure returning. "Yes, of course."

"Then you know you'll be running errands, cooking, cleaning, taking care of my needs while in the air and at my beach house."

"Yes. Right. Exactly. Your needs. I'll get you a brandy as soon as we're in the air."

"Please, have a seat so we can take off." I gesture to the leather recliner across from me, and she quickly lowers herself and buckles in.

The copilot secures the cabin door, and I give him the all-clear nod before he disappears into the cockpit. My attention travels back to Khloe. Her gaze flits to the window, then to the magazines and newspapers flared out on the round table between us. Brows angrily squashed together, her hand goes to her stomach, and her fingers splay.

"Are you a nervous flyer?"

"No, I've just never flown in a private jet before." She smiles, but it's forced. "It's nice."

"Help yourself to something to read," I say. She shakes her head and pulls what looks like a hard-covered journal from her bag. I go back to reading my paper, but every few seconds I glance over the top, curious about the woman my grandfather hired. She's young and fresh-faced, but there's a light of intelligence and experience in her eyes—unlike the recently graduated college girls who normally sign up at the agency.

I never delve into the personal, and I'm about to ask her what she does, or rather did, for a living, and why she is no longer employed, but my buzzing cell phone draws my attention. I tug it from my suit jacket and slide my finger across the screen.

"Hey, Jules," I say, and don't miss the way Khloe's eyes lift and travel to mine. They latch on briefly, hold for a second too long, then she goes back to the pages of her journal as if uninterested. My niece begins to talk a mile a minute. While I love and miss her, I have no idea how my cousin Tate and his wife, Summer, stay sane. "No, I can't come over tonight. I'm going to Saint Thomas. Remember I told you that the other night." She jabbers on some more, and I can't help but smile when I hear Summer in the background, telling her to slow down. "Of course I'll be back for your birthday party, and no, I'm not telling you what I got for you. You're really going to like it, though."

Summer takes the phone. "You tease."

I laugh at that, but it's true. I am a tease. I've been known to push buttons as well.

"Hey, be nice." I steal another glance at Khloe, who's looking out the window and feigning disinterest in my conversation. How would she react if I pushed her buttons? She didn't like it when I reprimanded her for her tardiness or her clothes, and I can't deny that I enjoyed that quick flash of anger in her eyes. What would she do or say if I fueled that fury?

"You promise you'll be back for her party?" Summer asks.

"I wouldn't miss it for the world." I love hanging out with Jules and spoiling her. I used to want kids of my own, thought I'd have them with Naomi, until I fucked everything up between us. Jesus, I have no idea how I got so drunk at my party and found myself in bed with another woman. What kind of guy pulls a shitty stunt like that, anyway? Not one worth marrying, that's for sure. I thought I was different from the generation of men who'd come before me. All of them had been unfaithful. I prided myself on my ability to engage in monogamous relationships, but I guess after a few drinks, my true colors had come through. I'd never meant to hurt Naomi—I'd loved her, for Christ's sake. But at the end of the day, she's better off without a bastard like me in her life.

I talk to Summer for a few more minutes, and hint at Granddad's old age. I am worried about the man's judgement. As a doctor and Granddad's former aide, Summer assures me he's well and fine. We're well into the air by the time I end the call. I catch Khloe's eye, take in the pallor of her skin. Perhaps she's lying about being a nervous flyer. If that's the case, she never should have agreed to this job. Then again, it pays well, and she might have circumstances I don't know about. But I'm not about to ask. Her business is hers, mine is mine.

"Seat belt sign is off," I say. When she nods, I arch my brow at her, and she looks puzzled for a second.

"Right, your drink." She's quick. Damned if I don't like that about her.

She unbuckles and turns to set her journal down on her seat. When she gives me an up close, unobstructed view of her curvy ass, it captivates my cock. Goddammit. It's all I can do to swallow the groan rising in my throat.

Jesus.

She turns to me, and I scrub my hand over my chin. "How would you like your drink? With ice, cola, water?" she asks.

"Brandy on the rocks," I say.

She gives a curt nod and makes her way to the small kitchen area at the rear of the plane. My gaze is latched onto her backside as she walks away, and I shake my head to pull myself together. I've been working so goddamn hard lately, long into the nights, developing a new algorithm platform for Carson Management Investments, the hedge fund company I run for Granddad. I've forgotten what it was like to crawl into bed with a soft, curvy woman who smells like sweet vanilla.

I turn back to the newspaper, and while my focus is usually laser sharp, the clanging at the back of the plane pulls my attention. What the hell is she doing back there, busting the place up? Something falls and smashes, followed by a round of muted curses. I unbuckle to see what the hell is going on. Khloe has her back to me as I walk toward her, and I'm about to look over her shoulder when I reach her. But she turns at that exact moment, and the large glass of brandy in her hand hits my chest, soaking us both.

"Dammit," she says, and tries to jump away, but with the counter digging into her back she has nowhere to go. I, on the other hand, have plenty of room behind me. So why aren't I distancing myself, putting a measure of space between our vibrating bodies?

My dick twitches.

Ah yes, and therein lies the answer.

"I'm so sorry, Mr. Carson," Khloe says.

"It's Will," I grumble.

Back arched, she fishes a cloth off the counter and dabs it to my chest. Tension arcs between us, sizzling down the length of our too-close bodies. I haven't felt this kind of arousal in a long time. It's definitely not something that comes along every day.

I slip off my suit jacket and work the buttons on my shirt.

"What are you doing?"

"Getting changed. I'd rather not spend the next four hours in a wet shirt."

"Oh, right. Of course."

"Do you have a change of clothes?" I ask.

"Someone on the ground put my luggage in the outside baggage compartment."

With only a breath of distance between us, I peel

my shirt off and take the cloth from her. I mop the brandy from my chest, and a strange little squeaking sound rises in Khloe's throat.

"You okay?"

She blinks twice, rips her focus from my chest and straight-up asks, "I suppose you're firing me for this?"

My attention drifts from her eyes to her mouth as she drives her teeth into her bottom lip. "You think I'd fire you for something as trivial as this?"

"I heard things about you."

I let loose a laugh and shake my head. "What's the latest I'm being called, Khloe? Asshole?"

A grin flirts with her lips as her eyes cut to me. "Well, maybe."

"Don't believe everything you hear," I say.

I hand the cloth back to her and step away to grab a clean shirt from my bag. I pull my case from the overhead bin and take out a dress shirt and T-shirt. Khloe still hasn't moved from her spot.

"Which would you prefer?" I ask.

"Both will probably float on me." She shrugs. "But I guess I can tie the dress shirt at the waist."

"Dress shirt it is," I say, and tug on the T-shirt as I move to the back of the plane to hand the button-down over. Her fingers curl around it, and she glares at me as I stand there.

"Do you mind?" she finally blurts out.

"Mind what?"

"I'm not about to get half-naked in front of you. I don't even know you."

"Are you saying if you knew me, you'd get half-naked?" I ask, and keep the smile from my face as her cheeks flame red. Look at that. I guess now I do know how she'll react when I push her buttons. Truthfully though, I shouldn't be teasing her.

"Either turn around or point to the bathroom so I can change."

I jerk my head to the left. "Bathroom's right there."

She slides past me, her warm body brushing mine, and her sweet vanilla scent reaches my nostrils.

"What do you like to drink?" I ask, switching focus.

She turns back to me. "I'm easy."

That makes me smile, because I don't get the sense that anything about her is easy.

"But leave it. It's my job. I'll fix us both a drink after I change."

"And I can fix us both one while you change."

She eyes me like she doesn't know what to make of that. "Fine, I'll just have what you're having then."

"Brandy on the shirt?" Her eyes widen at the joke. "See, not always an asshole," I say, and turn my attention to making the drinks. I reach for two tumblers and add a splash of brandy to both. I take a sip of mine as I head back to my seat. Newspaper back in hand, I begin to read again. My mind drifts to the real reason I'm headed to Saint Thomas. While I have a home there and plan to work on my algorithms, I need to check on Granddad's luxury hotel. It was destroyed by hurricanes, and a lot of people were out of work because of it. It's back up and running now, and I want to make sure everything is proceeding smoothly. I also need to work on staffing for Leonard Elementary, the school we're building to replace the old moldy one. As I consider that, I realize Khloe hasn't returned to her seat. What the hell is she doing in that bathroom? I check my watch. Christ, she's been in there for a good twenty minutes.

Pushing from my seat, I go to the door and knock. "Khloe, is everything okay?"

"Uh, just not sure about this shirt."

"You'd prefer the T-shirt?" I ask, and reach over my shoulder, about to peel it off.

"No, that won't help either."

"Come out here. Tell me what's going on," I demand. A second passes, and the sign on the door finally changes from Occupied to Vacant. Her damp T-shirt is balled up in her hands, and she's pressing it hard against her chest as she steps from the lavatory.

"I had to remove my bra," she says, "and this shirt is white."

"All my shirts are white. So are my T-shirts."

"That's why I said nothing you have will help."

"Help with what?" I ask, and when her chest heaves, understanding dawns. She's worried her nipples are going to be visible. But now that I'm thinking about her nipples… Shit, that's a distraction I don't need. "Hang on." I open the overhead compartment again and pull out a blue blanket. "This should help."

For the first time since she boarded the plane, a

smile makes an appearance, and something inside me twists. "Thanks, Will." She adjusts the blanket over her shoulders, and my gaze drops to take in a hint of pink brushing against the fabric before it's hidden from my view.

Jesus.

Her body is ripe and lush, and my hands itch to slide down her back and grab a fistful of her sweet ass. Not only is she different from the young, fresh-out-of-college girls who do temp work for me, she's the opposite of the rail-thin women in my social circle. I loved Naomi, but she needed to eat more than a salad. No matter how much I encouraged it, she always refused.

I clear my throat. "When we land, I'll get your bag, and you can change before you deplane."

I wave my hand for her to sit, and she tightens the blanket around her shoulders as she hurries to her seat. I follow, all the while admiring her curves. As she settles herself, I wonder what her story is. Married? Single? Boyfriend? Then again, it's none of my business. Still, I might ask Granddad how he found her and why he thought she was a good choice. I hand her drink over, and she takes a sip, her skin paling even more. Something buzzes in the back of my brain, something just out of reach as my gaze rakes over her white face.

"Do I know you?"

CHAPTER THREE

Khloe

"Ah, I'm not sure," I say, the cold pizza I'd eaten for breakfast threatening to rise up and make a second appearance. I thought I was nauseous from my ordeal at *Starlight* this morning. Now I think I might be coming down with something. Either that, or I shouldn't have eaten that leftover slice sitting on the kitchen counter all night.

Will's eyes narrow in on me. "Khloe," he says, and the way he says my name, like he's savoring it, does the weirdest things to my insides. Then again... leftover sausage pizza.

He sits forward, and I catch a hint of his aftershave. Sandalwood, beach and... Will. I inhale slowly. That scent could magically melt the panties right off a woman. I'm pretty sure mine are currently on fire. Honestly, if someone bottled it and called it Panties Be Gone they'd make a fortune.

Strength and power radiate from Will's hard body

as he inches closer, his long legs stretched out before him. I do my best not to envision them wrapped around my body.

Sometimes my best just isn't good enough.

"I think I might know you," he says.

"You...think?" I ask, trying to focus on what he's saying to me.

"Is your last name Davis?"

Oh, God, he knows. He knows I'm Khloe Davis, sensationalized crime reporter from *Starlight*. He's liable to open the deck door and toss me out mid-flight. But I don't think that's possible at our flying altitude. At least I hope not. I gulp, and the world spins around me.

"Yes, it is," I manage to get out as bile punches into my throat. I'm not sure if it's from his revelation or my upset stomach. Either way, this isn't good. Not good at all. James wanted to keep my identity a secret, and this man hates reporters.

"Your father used to work for my granddad, right?"

"He did," I say quickly and realize there is no way he could put it together since I use a pen name. A wave of relief hits me, but it's short-lived. I take a few deep breaths as an invisible fist grips my tightening throat.

"You were in the car that day Granddad picked me up from swimming lessons."

"That was you?"

"Yeah, and you were as pale then as you are now."

"I...I had the chicken pox."

Don't get sick, Khloe. Don't get sick.

"Right, I remember." Alarm widens his eyes. "Wait, you don't have them again, do you?"

"No, I think I have..." We hit an air bump, and before I know what's happening, Will has me by the elbow and is rushing me to the bathroom. No. No. No. I am *not* going to throw up in front of the hottest guy on the planet.

Wrong.

Two seconds later I'm on my knees bent over the toilet heaving my guts out, and Will is standing directly behind me. He pulls my hair back, and in that instant, with my head buried in the porcelain bowl, I pray to God I get sucked out into the abyss. But no, I don't have that kind of good luck.

"I'm...okay," I say. "Can you please leave and shut the door?"

My hair tumbles gently over my back as he lets it go, and I'm grateful when he leaves me to die alone. I groan, but then he's back. He's saying something, but I can't quite hear with my head in the toilet.

He drops to his knees behind me, his pelvis pressed up against my rear end as he leans over me and puts a cloth to my forehead. I moan against the damp coldness. "That feels soooo good," I say. Will's body goes rigid, and a soft hiss leaves his mouth.

Oh, wait, crap!

"I mean the cloth," I hurry on, my voice muffled

as I stick my head deeper into the bowl. "The cold cloth feels good."

"You probably shouldn't talk."

No kidding, since I'm not thinking with any sort of clarity, and my words could be construed as sexual. It's not like I was saying it felt good to have his pelvis pressed up against me.

Even though it does.

Good God, how desperate am I that I'm enjoying the feel of Will's body—well, one part in particular—while I'm losing my breakfast in his toilet? Even if I had a chance with this guy, not that I want one, my current predicament would no doubt quash any interest on his part.

"I think you have the flu," he says.

While I'd like to come back with some smart-ass comment that involves Einstein, the sarcastic retort dies on my tongue. We might have gotten off on the wrong foot, but he's trying to take care of me as I die a slow and agonizing death. I vomit again, and Will reaches past me to flush the toilet. I heave a grateful sigh and wait to get sucked into space, but no. Like I said, I don't have that kind of luck.

"Here," he says, and puts a plastic cup to my mouth. I take a drink of water, rinse my mouth and spit. Not a dainty girlie spit either, if there is such a thing. No, it sounds more like a baseball player hacking up a sunflower seed.

And this, my friends, has become my life.

I moan and lift my head from the bowl.

"Feeling better?"

"A little." I take another big drink and spill half the water over my shirt as the plane lurches. "Goddammit." A sound crawls out of Will's throat, and I glance at him over my shoulder. "Are you laughing?"

"Not even a little bit."

"This isn't funny."

"Never thought it was. But I have to say, you're handling it better than most." Concern dances in his eyes.

Okay, maybe he wasn't laughing, but I've been on the defense with him since I boarded the plane.

"Mouthwash?"

"Yes, please." He pulls a travel-size bottle from the vanity, opens it and hands it to me. I rinse repeatedly and go back on my heels, only to end up sitting in Will's lap. I'm about to apologize and slide off when his hand goes around my waist to hold me in place.

"It's okay. I got you," he says, and my heart does a ridiculous thump at his thoughtfulness. Truthfully, I'm not used to anyone taking care of me, and this is actually kind of...nice.

Nice? What the hell am I saying? I just vomited in front of Will Carson. There's nothing nice about that—for either of us.

"You don't have a parachute on this thing, do you?" I ask.

He chuckles slightly. "No, why?"

"I'd like to get off."

I'd like to get off.

"I mean…"

"I'm actually getting a complex," he says, a hint of teasing in his voice.

"What are you talking about?"

"I've met you twice now, and you vomited both times. How's a guy not to take that personally?"

I groan and reach for a paper towel. My cheeks burn from sheer mortification. "I am so embarrassed."

He puts his hand to my forehead. "You're cold and clammy and slightly warm."

"Pizza for breakfast," I say. "Wasn't my best decision."

"If it was food poisoning, it would have hit you earlier. How about some ginger ale?"

"Not a bad idea."

"Maybe some toast? It might help settle your stomach."

"I don't think I can eat anything."

"Do you think you're going to be sick again, or do you want to go lie down? The sofa opens to a bed."

"I think I'd like to lie down. I guess now I know why I was so tired when I met with James today." Worry grips my stomach, and I clutch Will's arm. "I hope I didn't give it to him."

Will holds me by my hips and repositions himself so he can stand. "I'm sure he's fine, but I'll call him just to make sure." He hauls me up with him and turns me around. With infinite tenderness, he slides a strand of damp hair from my face, and I let out a shaky breath. His arm drops, but his gaze stays locked on mine. His gorgeous blue eyes bore into my face, his gaze probing, searching.

"I'm okay," I say. "My stomach is settling."

"Yeah?"

I nod, and he slides his arm around my waist, but the damn plane hits another air pocket, and Will stumbles backward. I fall with him, until he's splayed across a table and I'm on top of him.

I yelp and unsuccessfully try to push off of him. "I can't get up."

His arms lock me in place. "Hold on," he says, his voice a degree deeper. What the hell? Why is he still holding me? Does he like me on top of him like this?

"Rough air," he explains.

Guess not.

The plane bumps again, and for a split second I'm floating over him. But then I drop, press down on his hardness, and arousal slams into me as our bodies collide.

"We need to ride it out for a second longer," he says.

Ride it out.

A strange, inappropriate giggle rises in my throat and a crinkle appears between his brows at my bizarre reaction. I swallow—hard—and pull myself together. Good Lord, this flu has me acting completely out of character.

Yeah, blame it on the flu, Khloe.

"How long do you think it will last?" I ask, and when a grin tugs at the corner of his mouth, my cheeks once again flare hot.

What is wrong with me? No matter what I say, it comes out sounding sexual. Why is that? Oh, probably because I'm flat out on top of the sexiest man alive, and even though I just finished losing my breakfast, everything about this guy reminds me I'm still a woman—one who hasn't been touched in a long time.

"Shouldn't be too much longer," he says. "The pilots will adjust flying height to get us out of the wind shears."

"I'm probably squishing you," I say, and wiggle as I try to shift to the side of the table.

"Please stop moving." His hands tighten around my body, and that innocent touch seeps beneath my skin and burns through my blood. "At least we managed to get you horizontal."

"For your sake, you'd better hope I don't get sick again."

He laughs. An honest-to-God belly laugh. "You'll give me a heads-up, right?"

"It's possible. But the words might come out too *late*." I emphasize the last word to let him know I'm still pissed off at his greeting. And seriously, James totally misled me with this assignment. I thought I'd be attending board meetings and taking notes, but no. I'll be getting this man his brandy and whatever else his assistant does for him. Why would I need writing skills for that?

"Khloe," he says, his voice a bit more serious.

I blink slowly, and when my lashes lift, I'm staring at blue eyes brimming with questions. "Yeah?"

"It's not my business, but you're different from the other girls who apply for temp work."

"I was fired recently," I say.

"Oh, shit. Sorry." He goes quiet, his mouth tight.

"It wasn't my fault." I roll my eyes and can't keep the disgust from my voice when I add, "Men in power, they're all alike."

"What's that supposed to mean?"

"My boss wanted me to do something, and when I refused, he canned me."

His expression turns angry. "Jesus, sorry."

I know what he's thinking. That my boss wanted sex, or something equally disturbing. The sudden visual of a naked Benjamin batters my uneasy stomach. I think of a naked Will instead, but that just batters another part of my body.

"Yeah, he was a real jerk, but I don't want to talk about it. I just want to move forward, okay?"

"Just so you know, I would never put you in any position you didn't want to be in."

Even though he doesn't strike me as a missionary sex kind of guy, I glance down at our vanilla position—the only one I'm familiar with, sadly—and take in the two hundred pounds of rock-solid muscles beneath me. Lord, he's everything fantasies are made of, and a thousand new ones begin to run through my brain.

"Um," I say.

He laughs. "Current position excluded. This was for your own safety. But you know what I mean, right?"

"Yeah."

"I have rules." His eyes narrow, and the muscles along his jaw ripple. "A lot of them."

"James warned me."

"Getting involved with an assistant is a hard no." Too bad my nipples didn't get the memo.

I let out a shaky breath. "Getting involved with my boss is a hard no for me, too."

"Then we're on the same page."

And the same table.

I nod. "I think we can get up now," I say, throwing up a silent prayer that he can't feel my pebbled nipples pressing into his hard chest. "The plane has stabilized."

"Slowly," he says. "Any fast movement could turn your stomach again."

I inch up from his hardness. And my God, every movement is agonizing, like slowly tearing a bandage off—if said bandage were covering every erogenous zone in my body. Will follows me up and stays close as he guides me to my seat.

"Sit here," he commands in a soft voice, and while I'm not one to take orders, a shiver goes through me at his. "I'll open the bed."

I do as he says, noting the way his T-shirt strains against his biceps as he opens the sofa and makes me a bed. I wipe my mouth with the back of my hand and smooth my hair from my face. I glance down, and groan when I see the water stains on my shirt. In all the commotion, I left my blanket behind and now my nipples are staring straight at the man turning my way. Is the universe trying to play some cruel joke on me? I'm a good person. Kind to the elderly and animals. Yet…this.

Before I can cover up, his glance drops, and his eyes linger on my puckered nipples for a brief second.

"Khloe."

"Yeah?"

"Your blanket," he says gruffly, but I'm already reaching for it.

Get it together, girl. I might be attracted to him, but clearly I'm not his type. Not only does he date model-thin girls, he made it clear that I was hired to cook, clean and cater to his needs. Those needs don't involve sex. Which is a good thing. I'm not about to mess around with my boss. Even if he asks me to.

Okay, maybe if he asks me to…

CHAPTER FOUR

Will

I CRACK OPEN a new bottle of water, pour it into a clean glass and make my way to Khloe's room. She fell fast asleep on the plane the second her head hit the pillow and has been coming in and out of consciousness ever since. I've been giving her ibuprofen every four hours, and her temperature has come down, but this flu has definitely kicked her ass to the curb.

At first light I called Granddad, but Summer, who's been checking in on him, answered, saying he wasn't showing signs of the flu but was resting. She assured me she'd give him the message and have him call back, but I've yet to hear from him.

As I approach Khloe's door, a low, agonized groan reaches my ears. I slow my steps and walk softly. After the night she had, I'm sure her head must be killing her. I inch the door open and find her sitting up in the bed, dark circles under bloodshot eyes as she catalogs the unfamiliar room.

"Will?" she asks when her gaze lands on me.

"Welcome to the living," I say.

She smooths her hand over her wayward curls, and I can't help but grin. With bedhead hair, cheeks puffy and red from fever, and big glassy eyes, she's a hot mess, but goddammit, she's still as sexy as hell. She's off-limits, I get it, but no red-blooded male could possibly be immune to those full round curves and thighs I could really sink my teeth into. I had a handful of her lush body when I carried her from the plane to the car and then again to this bed. Not a single bone jabbed me, and I have to say I damn well liked it. Perhaps that's why all her sexy curves infiltrated my dreams a time or two last night.

How is a girl like her still single?

Not your business, Will.

She smacks her lips together, peels her tongue from the roof of her mouth and cringes as she swallows.

"Here, drink this."

I hand her the glass, and she gives me a grateful smile.

"Thank you." She swallows half the contents and sets the glass on the nightstand. "You didn't happen to get the license plate of the truck that ran me over, did you?"

"Afraid not." I lean into her and place my hand on her forehead. "How are you feeling?"

"Like the walking dead." Her eyes narrow. "How long have I been asleep?"

I give a low, slow whistle. "You've had one hell of a night, Khloe. Tossing and turning and moaning for hours on end."

"Hours?" Her gaze goes to the closed curtains, a hint of morning sun peeking in through the cracks.

"It's eight in the morning," I say.

She presses the heels of her hands into her eyes and rubs. "My God, the last thing I remember was lying down on the plane. I have no idea how I got here."

I sit down next to her on the edge of the bed, and she sways toward me as the mattress dips. "I brought you here, put you to bed and have been waking you every four hours to give you ibuprofen."

"You have?" she asks, her eyes big.

I rake my hands through my hair. "Is that so hard to believe?"

"What I can't believe is that I threw up in front of you."

"Again, you mean?" I say, hoping to coax a laugh out of her. I don't.

"Yeah, again," she groans. "I haven't been sick like that since I was—"

"In the back seat of Granddad's car?"

"Ugh."

"Projectile vomiting. I've never seen anything like it."

"Yeah, it's quite the gift." She covers her face, hides behind her hands. Suddenly she pulls them away and her gaze flies to her chest. Her shoulders drop from her ears when she finds herself still in my button-down. At least it was dry when I put her to bed, and I didn't have to suffer the visual of her gorgeous full tits, nipples poking through the dampness.

Oh, the hardship.

Seriously though, her body is, to sum it up with one word…banging.

As my blood starts to leave my brain, she tugs the sheet up to her chin.

"Ugh, I need to change into some clean clothes."

"I didn't want to put you to bed in a dirty shirt, but I wasn't about to undress you." I put my hand over my crotch. "You know…with me being fond of my nuts and all."

That brings a smile to her face, for about two seconds. "Did you get any sleep at all?"

I give a casual shrug, but her concern for me is appreciated. "I dozed."

"I…feel horrible," she says her voice so soft and sincere it tugs at something inside me. "I hope you don't get it."

"I've had my shots."

"Me too, and yet…" Her eyes widen. "Wait—"

"I called Granddad, and he's resting. No signs of flu."

She relaxes. "Thank God. At his age…" Her nose crinkles, and as I take in the sprinkle of freckles, I note the tinge of sadness in her eyes. "I really appreciate you taking care of me. You didn't have to… I mean I never expected you to…"

What, has no one ever taken care of her before?

"See, not a total asshole."

"I'll give you that."

"Mighty generous of you. How about I get you to the shower and then make us something to eat." Her stomach takes that moment to growl. "I'm starving."

I stand and hold my arm out to help her up.

"What?" she asks, looking at my hand like it might grow a snake head and bite her.

"I'll help you to the shower."

"Oh." She pushes the sheets down. "I can get up myself."

I drop my arm and shove my hands into my jeans pockets. Her gaze follows as my pants slide lower on my hips.

"Granddad used to say your dad was stubborn. I see the apple hasn't fallen far from the tree."

"I've put you out enough." She swings her feet over the edge of the bed.

"I don't mind putting out."

Jesus, Will. What the fuck are you doing?

Her feet stop seconds before hitting the wood floor, and her gaze flies to mine. Dark eyes narrow, like she's trying to figure out if I'm flirting or not.

I am, but I shouldn't be. She's an assistant, and the last girl I should be screwing around with. Yeah, sure, she signed a confidentiality clause, and Granddad vetted her. But sex with the help is wrong, and something the media would leap at and twist if they got wind of it. The last thing I want is my face splashed all over the papers again. I've brought enough shame to the Carson family as it is, and I'm sure Khloe doesn't want her history out there for all to examine and pick apart.

"Believe it or not, when someone needs help, I help," I say, getting my head back on right and redirecting the conversation. "That, and you're a friend of Granddad's. He'd kill me if I didn't treat you properly." She nods, and I continue with, "Why don't you shower, and I'll make us something to eat."

She scurries off the bed and wobbles a bit as she stands. "Whoa," she says, and puts her hand to her head.

"Let me help you." I wrap my arm around her waist and tug her against me. She's stiff at first but then relaxes into me. "You're still pretty weak."

She takes in the big room as we head to the en suite bathroom.

"This place is gorgeous." Cold air blows down from the overhead vent, and she shivers.

"I'll adjust the air-conditioning, and when you're up to it, I'll show you around the place." I slowly guide her across the room, taking short steps to match hers. "Your room has a spectacular view of the ocean."

"Really?"

"Yeah, mine is next to yours, with an equally great view." I point to the curtains. "Behind those, you'll find a patio door and a private deck, just for you. We have amazing sunsets here in Saint Thomas. Unlike anything I've ever seen."

A happy sigh catches in her throat. "Will, I think this is just what the doctor ordered."

"Good," I say, although I'm not sure why seeing her this happy has suddenly turned me into the grinning village idiot. Maybe it's because she got fired and was violently ill all on the same day and could really use a break.

"Just yesterday morning, I was thinking how much I'd love to get away," she says, and her smile is a little off-center when she adds, "Talk about fate."

"If you believe in such things."

She arches a brow. "A skeptic?"

"I believe our destiny is in our own hands, not someone else's."

"If I hadn't decided to go see James, I wouldn't be here. I believe everything happens for a reason."

"Why did you decide to go see Granddad, anyway?"

Her body tightens ever so slightly. If I wasn't holding her, I might never have noticed.

"Someone mentioned his name, actually." She gives a casual shrug. "Thought I'd pay him a visit."

I nod but get the sense that she might not be telling me everything. I think about pushing, but she's not feeling well. When Granddad calls, I'll get answers from him.

I flick the light on in the bathroom, and her eyes

widen. "This is bigger than my entire apartment." She steps away from me and makes her way to the tiled shower. She runs her fingers over the taps. "I have no idea how to use these."

"Simple." I move around her to turn on the water. "This is for the rain shower nozzle," I say as it sprays down. "This one is for the body, and this one is for the feet."

"All angles covered. Literally."

I adjust the temperature and step back. "I'll make us something to eat."

"I'm supposed to—"

"Yeah, well, not today." I tilt my head when she gives me a confused look. "It's for my own good."

"Isn't cooking part of my duties?"

"Yes, but if you were me, would you let the Ebola monkey touch your food?"

She puts one hand on her hip, and her brown eyes flare. "Did you just call me a monkey?"

I chuckle. "Get a shower, Khloe. There are towels in the cabinet, and you'll find everything you need in the vanity, even a new toothbrush."

She glares at me a moment longer, but today the fight just isn't in her. She softens and says, "You thought of everything."

"Part of the assistant's job is to stock this place for the next assistant."

She opens and closes the vanity and pulls out a few drawers to check the contents. "I heard you went through assistants fast."

That gives me pause. I don't like anyone knowing too much about me. "Who told you that?"

Her hair tumbles as she gives me a quick glance over her shoulder. "Ah, I don't remember. I think maybe your Granddad."

"There's a reason for that," is all I say.

"Okay." She shrugs. "Not my business."

I'm about to leave but turn back and say, "You should probably know you talk in your sleep."

A streak of red flares across her cheeks. "I do not."

I grin at her, and despite myself I say, "Yeah, I'm afraid you do."

She pulls in a deep breath. "What did I say?" she asks, and when her fingers grip the sink hard, I cut her some slack.

"Mostly mumbling, but I did hear you say my name a time or two."

Her eyes narrow. "You're making that up."

"I believe you said something about my cologne." I tap my finger to my chin. "What was it you called it again…?"

"I was delirious, Will. High fever, remember?"

"Then you mumbled something about bad or being bad. Wait, maybe you were saying I wasn't so bad."

"I vomited the two times I met you, or have you forgotten?" she counters, and I keep my grin hidden.

"We may have gotten off to a bad start, Khloe. With you showing up late and all." It's true, we did. But honest to God, she's like a breath of fresh air.

"I told you, I pride myself on my punctuality, but James offered me the job at the last minute, and traffic, and...and...ugh, forget it. I'm wasting my time."

Under the guise of strengthening my next point, I let my glance race the length of her. In reality, I'm simply enjoying the view of her in my button-down. "And of course, you were dressed improperly, but for what it's worth, I don't think you're so bad, either."

She pulls a big round brush from the drawer, and I step outside and close the door before she can throw it at me. It hits the door with a thud, and I laugh out loud. I shouldn't enjoy pushing her buttons so much. But goddammit I love the way she gets all fired up.

I head to the kitchen and busy myself with making the coffee, anything to keep my mind off her curvy naked body in the shower. The woman is a distraction I don't need. I'm here to work on my algorithms and check on the hotel and school. What I should not be contemplating is all the ways Khloe and I could get down and dirty.

Once the coffee is brewing, I boot up my laptop and answer a few emails. The shower turns off, and I power down my computer and grab eggs and bacon from the fridge. I'm not sure how she likes her eggs, so I decide scrambled is safest. I drop bread into the toaster and fish the jam from the fridge. Soon enough everything is ready, but Khloe is nowhere to be found.

I retrace my steps to her room. Her door is slightly ajar, the way I left it, and I catch a flash of black inside.

I knock softly. "Everything okay in there?"

"As good as it can be," she says, her words tight.

"You're not feeling sick again, are you?"

The door swings open, and I nearly swallow my tongue at the unbelievable sight before me.

Sweet mother of all that is holy.

"Is there a problem?" she asks, one hand on her hip, her expression far from amused.

"Um...no," I lie. Because yeah, there is a problem, and it's between my legs, growing thicker by the second.

She pushes past me. "I hope you made coffee. I'm going to need a gallon."

"I made coffee," I mumble as my eyes latch onto her backside, which sways sexily, spilling out of the too-tight French maid uniform. Her heels tap the floor as I steal a glance at the lacy stockings hugging her thighs. This...this is what she thought Granddad meant when he told her I had a dress code? I think the tables have turned, and now she's the one who's going to be pushing my buttons, every last one of them.

She disappears from my sight, mumbling angrily about men in power and how they're all the same, and I gulp. Cupboards open and slam closed, pulling me from my trance, and I force one foot in front of the other, rounding the corner to find her filling a mug with coffee. She plasters on a smile, but there is anger in her eyes as they bore into me.

"Coffee?" she asks, her smile saccharine sweet.

"Uh, yeah. I can get it."

"I believe that's my job." She grabs a mug, slams it onto the counter and fills it to the brim.

"Thanks," I say. She tugs on the hem of her small skirt, but it doesn't budge. She grumbles something and turns to me when a sound I can't control rumbles in my throat.

"Is there a problem, Will?"

If I were a gentleman, I'd tell her she didn't have to dress like a French maid straight out of my fantasies. Yeah, if I were a gentleman, I'd tell her that a costume is not required in my home, and that if she insists on wearing it, I might break my hard rule and tear it from her lush body. For a brief second, I lose myself in that erotic fantasy. My hands on her soft flesh, slowly sliding those stockings down, then licking a path back up her legs. Of course, in my fantasy, she's quivering and moaning my name—not cursing it under her breath and glaring at me like she'd like to fillet me with the biggest damn knife in the drawer. Yeah, if I were a goddamn gentleman, I'd yell abort, but unfortunately, it's not my brain calling the shots.

"Well, is there?" she asks.

Come on. Tell her, Will. Tell her this isn't what you meant by a dress code.

"Uh, no…no problem at all," I say.

I am so fucking dead.

D.E.A.D.

CHAPTER FIVE

Khloe

I TAKE A much-needed sip of my coffee, when what I actually want to do is throw it at Will, mug and all. What the hell? After taking care of me, holding my hair back and wiping my face when I was ill, not to mention checking on me through the night, I thought he was a decent guy, was more like his grandfather—until I looked in my closet and found a dozen French maid outfits.

I mean seriously!

This…this ridiculous costume—two sizes too small for me—is what he insists his help wear? Maybe I should have told James my size. But who in their right mind could have foreseen this insanity? Yeah, that must be it. Will Carson is insane. What other explanation can there be? I can see the headline now. *Woman dies of suffocation in a too-tight French maid outfit her rich, clearly insane employer forced her to wear.*

Okay, I might have to trim that a bit. But that's certainly the gist of it.

Anger courses through my blood, and I swear to God if I didn't need the money that came with this job, I'd toss my coffee at him—although it's possible I'd wait until the second cup, since I really need this one—and storm out the door.

"Breakfast is ready," he says. I take a breath and let it out slowly.

"I lost my appetite," I grumble through clenched teeth.

"You should eat something."

My stupid stomach takes that moment to growl. "Fine." If I catch him grinning, that's it. I'm out of here. I spin, and his expression is thoughtful and maybe even a bit confused. I'm about to ask what his problem is, but the smell of breakfast hits me. My mouth waters at the sight of two plates with toast, bacon and eggs.

He waves his hand toward a patio door. "We can eat here or on the deck."

"Deck," I say, and scoop up my plate. "Lead the way."

Will gathers his plate, and I follow him. I'm pissed off, and the last thing I should be doing is admiring the man's ass in his low-slung jeans as he heads to the patio door. He opens it, and a warm breeze washes over me. I step out into the sunshine and breathe in the briny scent as waves lap against the sandy shore below. I glance down at the infinity pool overlooking the turquoise waters. My anger instantly dissipates, and I forget all about the stupid outfit. Well, not entirely. But if the ridiculous getup is the price I have to pay for this unbelievable Caribbean view, then so be it. Cripes, I'm such an easy sellout. But the view...

"My God, this is beautiful." I glance around, the wind blowing my hair from my face, but there are no other villas close to us. Will's home is at the end of a strip of land, the ocean on all sides. "And so private."

"That's why I bought the cottage. I value my privacy."

Cottage? I think he means mansion.

"That's Magdalen Bay," he says, and I take in the strip of secluded white sand below.

"I could go skinny-dipping and no one would see me."

"I'd see you," he mumbles, his voice an octave deeper.

I turn, watch his throat work as he swallows— like he's afraid I might really get naked.

"I'm not going to go skinny-dipping," I blurt out. "I don't even know why I said that. It's just that I've never seen anything like this, and I love how private it is. I value my privacy, too, Will."

"Well, I'm glad you like it."

"Wait, how long are we here?" I ask. I was in such a rush to get ready, I never had the time to ask James.

"Granddad didn't tell you?"

"There's a lot James didn't tell me," I mutter.

"Three weeks," he says as he pulls a chair out

from a small round table and gestures for me to sit. "That's not a problem for you, is it?"

Moisture dots my forehead as the warm wind whips around my body. "You could have said six months and that wouldn't be a problem for me."

"Not in a hurry to get back?"

"No." I lower myself into the chair and set my plate down. A bird sings in the tree near the deck, and it smooths all my ruffled feathers. "Why would I ever want to leave this place?" I take in the opulence a second time and shake my head. "Why do you?"

Will drops down into the seat across from me. "My work is in New York."

"Can't you write code from here?"

"Yes, and that's what I plan to do these next few weeks, but I want to be close to my family. Grand-dad is…" His gaze lowers, a deep sadness in his eyes.

Without even thinking about it, I place my hand over his. "I understand that. He's the patriarch that keeps you all together." It was something my father once told me. He'd also told me all of James's sons had a penchant for younger women and had left a trail of broken homes behind them. It saddened me, although Will isn't the kind of guy who'd want any-one's pity. I can relate. I don't want pity, either. He nods, eyes locked on my hand as I give his a gentle squeeze.

"It was just you and your dad growing up, right?" he asks.

My stomach tightens, and my heart misses a beat

at the mention of my dad. He died right after I graduated from journalism school, and I miss him terribly. At least his dream of seeing me walk the stage to receive my diploma was realized before he passed away. That gives me a measure of comfort.

I slowly pull my hands back. "I was three when we lost Mom."

Sympathy lurks in his eyes when he says, "That's tough, Khloe."

"I had my dad, though. We were very close."

Will makes a strangled noise, and his lips twist painfully.

"What?"

"Dad left us when we were young."

"I'm sorry."

"I mean, he didn't die, he's still in our lives, but…"

I dig into my eggs and slide the fork into my mouth. "Delicious," I murmur, and note the way Will's attention turns to my mouth. "Sorry, go on."

He shrugs like his father's leaving was nothing, but I get that it's something. "He bailed. None of the men in our family have staying power."

My Dad pretty much said the same, but I don't believe it's a trait passed on from generation to generation. "You truly believe that?"

"Yeah, sure. So does my mother. She warned my brother Alec not to get married." He laughs, but it holds no humor. "You read the papers, don't you?"

For a secretive guy, I'm a little shocked at how open and honest he's being with me. I guess he wants to ensure that I know exactly what kind of guy he is and where the two of us stand so I don't go and get any ridiculous notions about us. With his power, money and looks, I'm sure he has women throwing themselves at him. I find none of those things appealing. Okay, maybe that's a small lie. He's drop-dead gorgeous, and fine, my traitorous body finds that appealing.

"I read the paper," I say, the eggs catching in my throat. Not only do I read them, I've written some of the articles. At least I didn't twist things to ruin a man's life.

"Right," is all he says.

I pick up the toast and nibble on the corner.

"Going down okay?" he asks, his brow quirked, and that concern does strange things to me. Blunt and demanding one minute, caring the next. He's quite the contradiction.

"Yes, thanks." I wash the toast down with my coffee. "Your brother ignored your mom and did get married, right? Those were the pictures James showed me, weren't they?"

He laughs at that. "Granddad and his damn Polaroids." Big fingers curl around his cup, and he looks at me over the rim. "Alec is married, yes."

"So how is that working out?"

His left shoulder rolls. "Time will tell, I guess."

"Wow, you are so jaded."

He looks at me long and hard, and I get the sense

he's not sure if he should ask the question dancing in his eyes.

"What?" I finally ask.

"What about you, Khloe? Why aren't you married?"

I exhale. "Damn, I should have seen that coming."

He chuckles, and the rich, deep sound sends a current of heat zinging through me, teasing every erogenous spot as it settles deep between my legs. I squeeze my thighs together, but all that does is arouse me even more. Damn, this man's charm is like a high-voltage jolt. If he harnessed it for good, he could be our next superhero. The lace on my ridiculous outfit takes that moment to itch, reminding me he's no Prince Charming. No, he's an insane millionaire who abuses his power and authority. Why can't guys like him use their assets for good instead of evil?

"I was close," is all I say. "So what are my working hours? I'm hoping to get in some sightseeing on the weekends."

"Way to change the topic, Khloe."

"You liked that, did you?" I blow on my fisted knuckles and wipe them on my shoulder. "I am a woman of many talents."

"Your weekends are yours. Monday to Friday, you're mine."

You're mine.

My pulse leaps when I catch what looks like lust in his eyes, but it disappears so quickly I'm sure

I must be hallucinating. Yeah, this warm weather is simply messing with my brain…and my libido. I need to get a leash on that right away. Because I am so *not* Will's type. Not that I want to be. I don't.

Tell that to your aching nipples.

He clears his throat, and the corners of his mouth tighten. "Your duties are written out for you in my rule book," he says.

Come again?

"You have a rule book?"

"You don't?"

"Well no, that's kind of…" I want to say insane, but he doesn't look like a man who would appreciate bluntness from a subordinate, and I can't forget what Steph said. He goes through assistants in the blink of an eye. "Different," I say.

"I'm a man who lives by certain rules." His tongue slips from his mouth and brushes over the groove in his top lip, sending a shiver through me. "It's best for all of us this way."

As I study the streak of moisture on his lip, a blast of heat warms my blood, and I'm pretty damn sure it has nothing to do with our tropical location. I tamp it down and try for normal when I say, "Whatever you say, sir."

Will goes still for a second. What? Does he not like being called sir? Damned if it doesn't make me want to do it more.

He smooths his hand down his chest. "I think you should take the rest of today to rest, and make sure you're germ-free before you touch any food. My workload is light today, so I can pick up the slack."

"Sure thing. Maybe I'll go for a swim in that gorgeous pool or lounge on the beach."

"Whatever you like. You packed a suit?" he asks, like he's worried he's going to see me naked after all.

Yeah, I get it. No one wants to find a beached beluga on their private piece of paradise. My God, my ex was a jerk. If a man can't appreciate a woman with curves, then he can go to hell. Although I'm beginning to believe no man in Manhattan does. At least my battery-operated friend doesn't judge when I get naked.

"Khloe?"

"Yeah?"

"You disappeared there for a second."

"Right, I do have a bathing suit. Is wearing one in your rule book?"

That brings a half grin to his face. "Of course."

I resist the urge to roll my eyes. He goes back to his food, and I do the same, eating slowly when I really just want to scarf it down and put some much-needed distance between myself and my new boss.

He finishes and stretches his arms over his head. I try not to stare, or admire the way his muscles flex and bulge, but I do it anyway.

"Are you up for a tour of the place?" he asks when I set my fork down.

"I'd love a tour, sir." I note the tension on his face as I push away my plate and stand. We make our way into the kitchen. "How long have you owned this house?"

"A few years now. I bought it after… Let's just say, it's a secluded location that no one knows about, and the locals respect my privacy."

"So the locals know who you are, then?"

"Yes," he says. I wonder how they feel about a famous millionaire living among them, especially when there are some very poor areas, not to mention the damage done from the hurricane a few years back.

"You get along with them?"

"We get along just fine." He waves his hand. "This is the kitchen, obviously. You decide what meals you want to cook. I like breakfast at seven sharp, lunch at noon, and dinner at seven. You don't have to use local culture recipes if you don't want to, although one of my assistants left a cookbook if you're so inclined. My likes and dislikes are in the rule book."

"I bet they are," I murmur.

"What's that?"

"Nothing. Want to show me the rest of the place?"

We leave the kitchen and move through the mansion. He shows me the airy living room, a dining room that could comfortably seat eighteen, his large den with a massive desk and not much else, all the bathrooms, and all the bedrooms—most decorated in beach decor. I think there were six. I take in the opulence of the place, but it saddens me. There are no pictures, no homey touches, no stamp of a guy who entertains friends and family, a guy who welcomes love and laughter into his home. He's become quite the recluse after the exposé, and damned if I don't feel a niggling of remorse myself. I might not have written the article, but I worked for the magazine that did.

He goes on to explain more of my duties: shopping, cleaning, laundry, running errands. Our last stop on the tour is his bedroom, and he doesn't invite me in. Instead, we stand in the hall and his eyes cut to mine.

"Just remember, anything you see or overhear doesn't leave the confines of this house."

I glance into his room, take in his perfectly made bed. It doesn't even look like he slept in it. That brings a pang of guilt to my stomach. He stayed up to take care of me and probably never even got a wink of sleep. Maybe he's not such a bad guy after all.

My gaze roams to the comfy-looking soft blue bedding, and I engage my mouth before my brain. "What kind of noises are you worried I'm going to overhear?" His throat makes a sound, and I turn to him. "Oh, right. I get it. You…visitors…women."

Things would have been so much easier if I'd just been flushed out into space.

"No one is to come into this house unless they are vetted by me." He dips his head, and as he pins me with a glare, his mouth is right there. If I wanted to kiss him, all I'd have to do is go up on my toes. But I don't want to. The man is the most gorgeous specimen on the face of the earth, but clearly insane. Not to mention he can't keep it in his pants, and straight up admitted it. "Do you understand?"

"What I think you're trying to say is you're allowed 'visitors.' But I'm not."

"I never said that—" He runs his hands down his chest, a gesture that is becoming familiar, and that crinkle is back in his forehead. "Do you want visitors, Khloe?" he asks.

He's been honest so far, so I don't see the need not to return the favor. "For the record, my days of Netflix and chill are over," I admit.

His eyes narrow in on me. "Why is that?"

"They just are, okay?" I am not about to admit that men don't find me attractive, and that my ex wanted to change me, and that I've given up finding anyone because I no longer believe there is a match for me. No, it's best I keep my deepest flaws to myself.

He studies me too closely, too intently. He opens his mouth like he's going to push, but the door chimes.

"Expecting a *visitor*, sir?" I ask with a raised brow, even though it could end up in him canning my ass. But for some reason I just can't help myself.

"No," he grumbles, but I catch a hint of caution in his tone, a rigid restraint in his body as he heads to the front door. My teasing turns to concern as I follow him. He opens the door, and a gorgeous olive-skinned woman who looks to be in her early thirties stands on his steps. She gives him a sexy, come-hither smile when their eyes meet.

"Will," she says in a singsong voice, heavy with a creole accent.

His smile is back in place. "Bevey," he says, his body relaxing slightly.

"I heard you were back," the gorgeous Bevey says. "I came as soon as I could. I brought your favorite dish."

Yeah, I just bet she did. And I also bet it's called Bevey, with a cherry on top.

CHAPTER SIX

Will

"Come in," I say to Bevey, and stand back to allow her entrance. Her dark brown eyes widen, and her smile turns a bit forced when she sees Khloe in her ridiculous uniform. "Bevey, this is Khloe, my new assistant."

Bevey shifts the plate of johnnycakes from her right hand to her left and extends her arm to greet the shorter, curvier woman beside me. "Nice to meet you, Khloe."

"Nice to meet you, too," Khloe says, and points at the dish in Bevey's hand. "Would you like me to take those for you?"

"Yes, thank you. I made them this morning. They're Will's favorite." She gives me a big toothy smile that lights up her pretty face. "He says my johnnycakes are the best."

"I bet he does," Khloe says under her breath. "I'll put these in the kitchen, sir. And if you need me, I'll be in the pool."

Sir.

Okay, she's seriously fucking with me. Maybe I should fuck back.

Maybe I should fuck *her*.

Khloe disappears, and I will my dick to behave as I turn to my dear friend. Bevey and I go way back. I came to the island with Granddad years ago, when he was first looking to buy a resort, and Bevey was the one who greeted us at the airport. She drove the shuttle bus, but after one taste of her johnnycakes I knew her talents were being wasted. Granddad bought the resort, and I promoted her to chef.

"It's so good to see you." I open my arms, and the bright yellow scarf covering her hair tickles my face. After a firm hug, we break apart. I gesture with a wave, and we walk farther into the house. "How are things? How are Samuel and Chardane?"

"We're doing so much better now, thanks to your generosity. The new housing complex is more than we ever expected, and—" she sighs and claps her hand together "—running water."

That brings a smile to my face, but it falls quickly. "The school should be completed this month. I'm back to check on progress." It kills me to think the middle school kids at Leonard Elementary, including her daughter, Chardane, are being educated in an old building that had once been waterlogged. I can't even imagine the mold and mildew they're subjected to on a daily basis.

Her big brown eyes widen, and her full lips curl. "The kids are all very excited about the new school."

I guide her through the kitchen, and the delicious scent from the johnnycakes reaches my nostrils. I'm tempted to have one, but I'm full from breakfast. Besides, Khloe might enjoy one with me later, along with a cup of coffee. I had a hard time swallowing mine this morning with her sitting across from me, her body barely clad. Wait, what am I doing? Khloe is here to work for me. I shouldn't be thinking about taking coffee breaks with her or how much she would like Bevey's johnnycakes.

Shouldn't be thinking about how hot she is in or out of that ridiculous uniform.

"Any more news on filling the positions?" I ask.

"Applications are still open for English teachers. After Jess and Mari went back to the States, we haven't been able to fill their spots."

I open the patio door and we step outside. "I'll run that by Granddad. He can check at the staffing agency." I widen my arms. "Who wouldn't want to spend their time here?"

"It is a beautiful island, yes," she says in her creole accent.

I pull the chair from the table and gesture for her to sit. "Is everyone well?"

"We are well," she says, tucking her long white dress around her knees and lowering herself into the chair that Khloe had recently occupied.

"Can I get you a coffee, tea?"

She waves her hand. "I'm fine." Her eyes narrow in thought, and her full lips pinch tighter.

"What?" I ask, worry invading my gut. She clearly has something on her mind. "Are you sure things are good at home and work?"

"It's not me I'm concerned about."

"You're worried about me?"

She leans in. "I'm worried about your new assistant. What is that silly costume she's wearing?"

That brings a laugh to my throat. "Granddad told her I had a dress code, and I guess that is what she thought she had to wear."

She grins and points a finger at me. "And I take it you aren't planning to tell her the difference anytime soon."

"Where's the fun in that?"

"Oh, Will. You are trouble, but I am glad to see you having fun." She leans in and lowers her voice even more. "She's a beautiful woman, no?"

I smirk. "That she is."

"It's time you settled down, Will. Found yourself a nice wife."

"Bevey," I warn. "You know I'm not interested in marriage." Not anymore, anyway.

"Foolishness. It's not natural to be alone. You just have to find the right woman."

I don't bother telling her I had the right woman and ruined it.

"Don't you be too hard on this one. She has potential."

Hard on her?

Yeah, I think it's the other way around, judging by my dick's response whenever she's near.

"I'll be my usual charming self."

Bevey laughs and glances around. "Has James come with you? I do miss that man."

"No, he's home. I'm actually waiting to hear from him. I'll let him know you stopped by with the johnnycakes. He'll be disappointed that he missed out."

"Before you fly back, I'll bring a fresh batch for James."

I put my hand on hers. "You're too kind."

"You're the kind one, sir."

Sir.

Jesus, when Khloe called me that earlier, a streak of anger behind the word, my dick stood up and took notice. I have no idea why I want to hear that on her lips in the bedroom.

"Things are good at Great Bay Resort?" Her husband, Samuel, had been injured in the hurricane, and after millions of dollars' worth of repairs to Granddad's resort, he's back working. But now he's out of maintenance—the lifting had aggravated his back—and working in the kitchen with Bevey and the rest of the culinary crew.

She steeples her fingers and looks at the sky. "Give me strength."

I laugh. "I take it he's underfoot."

"He needs to leave me to the cooking. The man can't boil water without burning it."

"How about I pay him a visit and see what other job he might enjoy."

"You are a savior," she says, and a big splash below catches our attention. I glance through the glass-panel decking and catch a glimpse of Khloe swimming from one end of the infinity pool to the other. A bead of sweat travels down my back when she surfaces on the other end and I glimpse her breasts barely tucked in to a too small bikini top.

"I won't take up any more of your time," Bevey says, and when I turn to her I catch a knowing grin on her face.

"Don't be silly. I enjoy spending time with you."

"Something tells me there is someone else you'd rather be spending time with."

I cock my head, a playful challenge. "Then you'd be wrong."

She laughs and stands. "You're selling, but I'm not buying," she says. I just laugh and follow her back inside the house. The cool air-conditioning dries the moisture on my flesh. "You'll be attending the Carnival in the village, yes?" I open my mouth, and she cuts me off. "You need to work less and play harder."

"Have you been talking to Granddad?"

She laughs. "He's a wise old man, Will. You should listen to him."

I glance at my watch. "I would listen to him if he'd ever call me back."

We head to the front door, and I give her a hug to see her off. Back inside, I'm about to go to my den but instead find myself wandering to the deck. I lean on the rail and look out, but Khloe is no longer in the pool. Now she's making her way down the wooden steps that lead to the ocean. A warm breeze washes over me as I enjoy the view—and I'm not talking about Magdalen Bay.

Khloe steps into the water, slowly going deeper. For a moment, she disappears in the rough waves, then she jumps to the surface a little farther out. Her squeal of delight carries in the breeze and reaches my ears. It brings a smile to my face. I tug at my T-shirt and consider joining her, but that could only lead to trouble. It's best I lock myself away in my office and get some work done. That and I should call and check on Granddad again.

I pull my phone from my back pocket, but my heart jumps into my throat when Khloe's squeals of delight turn into a cry of pain.

What the hell?

She disappears under the water, and I take off running. I bolt through the house, push open the door leading to the lower back deck and take the steps to the ocean two at a time. I tug off my shirt and toss it as I go, then kick off my shoes. I reached the edge of the water and search for Khloe, but Jesus, I can't find her. As full-blown panic burns through my blood, I splash into the surf and dive under. I swim, search, the salt water stinging my eyes. I break through the surface for air and catch a glimpse of Khloe trying to swim ashore.

"Khloe!" I call out.

"Will," she whimpers, and I hurry to her. Her lips are twisted, and tears prick her eyes, but I can't see any physical injuries. "What happened?"

"My leg. I don't know what happened."

I scoop her up and fight the tugging waves as I carry her back to the shore as quickly as possible. The second the sand goes from wet to dry, I set her down and take her leg in my hand.

"Damn," I say, and study the spreading red rash.

"Shark bite?"

"No," I assure her, but her eyes are so big and wide, so worried she was attacked by a shark in five feet of water, it's all I can do not to smirk.

"Are you laughing?"

"I'm not laughing. This isn't funny."

"You seem like you're laughing." She reaches for the red spot and winces. "It hurts." I catch her hand before she can touch the sting.

"A jellyfish sting is nothing to laugh about." I search her face. "Are your tetanus shots up to date?" She nods. "Okay good, the sting isn't too bad. You likely only brushed up against the jellyfish, but we need to treat it right away."

"No way, Will." She tries to push me away. "Get away from me. I mean it."

"What the hell, Khloe. We have to remove the tentacles. There looks to be about two. That's not many, but we have to remove what's there."

"You are *not* peeing on me. Ohmigod. Could this week get any worse? First I vomit in front of you and now you're going to pee on me." She covers her face with her hands. "And this bathing suit. I have no dignity left. None."

This time I do laugh.

She pushes me again. "See, I knew you were laughing."

"I'm not laughing. Well, I am." Only because she's so wildly sexy when she gets angry, and she was worried I was going to pee on her.

She gives me the death glare. "Stop it."

I shake my head, seriously thrown off my game by this woman. I brush her hair back and meet her wild eyes. "You're really having a bad week, aren't you?" My heart misses a beat, an imaginary band squeezing it as she curls into herself.

She softens against me, and I catch a hint of vulnerability in her. This woman is strength and independence, and I'm sure helplessness is not a trait she'd like for me to see in her. Although I must say, it does bring out the protector in me.

"I've had better," she murmurs.

"I know you have," I say in a soft voice. "And I'm going to take care of this sting, okay?"

"Will…please…"

"Don't worry, my pants aren't coming down anytime soon." I scoop her up and head back toward the house. "Peeing on a jellyfish sting will cause more pain than relief. Urine can actually aggravate the jellyfish's stinger to release more venom."

"But I thought—"

"You thought wrong." Guilt worms its way into my gut. "Goddammit, this is my fault."

"How is it your fault? Did you tell the jellyfish to sting me? Or maybe you stock the ocean to keep people away?"

Is that what she thinks of me? I know I take privacy to the extreme, but I'm not a monster who would purposely hurt anyone.

I frown at her. "I should have warned you. In the rule book, it says to wear water shoes."

"How would that have helped? The sting is in my calf."

"Yeah, true, but it could have been worse. Could have been a stingray. I was...distracted when you told me you were going swimming."

She gives a very unladylike snort. "Oh, is that what you were?"

I get the sense she thinks I'm talking about Bevey distracting me—she is a beautiful woman—and maybe it's best I let her believe that. Khloe doesn't need to know my brain has been working at half capacity since she first boarded Granddad's plane. I don't want her to get the wrong idea...or the right idea. Or any idea.

"Did you pack water shoes?" I ask.

"No."

"I'll go to town and get you a pair." I look at her feet. "Size eight?"

"So the size of my feet you know?"

I have no idea what she's talking about but come back with, "Apparently you're not the only one with special gifts."

"Shut up," she says, clearly catching my reference to her projectile vomiting skills. Her lush mouth twists into a grimace. "Maybe I'll stick to the pool and just admire the ocean from the deck."

"Jellyfish tend to come to shore on windy days. I think you'll be okay to get in again. It'd be a shame for you not to enjoy the Caribbean waters. Let's just make sure it's when the winds are down, and I'll go with you."

"I'm not going to put you out like that, and I'm supposed to be the one taking care of your needs, not the other way around."

I hold her tight and think about that as her arms wrap around my neck. "Still believe in fate, Khloe."

She snarls at me, and I must say I love her spirited nature. "I don't think getting stung by a stupid jellyfish had anything to do with fate."

Warm sand squeezes between my toes as I hurry my steps, well aware of the way my body is reacting to having her lushness pressed up against me. I shift her an inch higher in my arms before she feels all eight inches of me against her sweet ass. "Didn't you say everything happens for a reason?"

"Well, yeah, but..."

"What do you think the reason for this is?"

She opens her mouth, but it doesn't matter what she says, not when my swelling dick has come to its own conclusions.

That my pants do indeed need to come down... soon.

CHAPTER SEVEN

Khloe

MY LEG MIGHT be hurting, but that's not the only part of my body that's throbbing. Okay, so I might not really like rich guys who say and do what they like—ones who make their help wear revealing costumes—but I can appreciate his hard body and lean muscles as he runs to the house like I'm a light weight in his arms. Trust me, I'm not. And Will has been kind to me, even depriving himself of sleep to watch over me.

I press against him and breathe in the scent of his skin as he opens the door and carries me down the long hall to *his* bedroom. He sets me on his big comfy bed and steps back, studying my face. A thoughtful, concerned look backlights those gorgeous blue eyes.

"How are you feeling?"

I give an exaggerated exhale to hide my arousal. "Like I really pissed someone off in a past life."

He laughs and sinks to his knees. "No dizziness or nausea? Do you feel like you're going to be sick?"

I slap one hand to my forehead. "Please tell me that's not going to happen again."

His big fingers circle my wrist, firmly removing my hand from my face to place at my side. "No, you'll feel sick to your stomach only if you're having a severe reaction." He cocks his head. "No abdominal pain, numbness or tingling, muscle spasms, or breathing troubles?"

Well, I am having a bit of trouble breathing, but I think it's from the strong and steady way he moved my hand to my side. Would he move me around like that in bed? I'm a take-charge kind of girl, so I have no idea why the idea of surrendering my needs to Will arouses me so much.

"No, I'm good," I push past my lips.

He takes my leg in his hand to examine it, and I suck in a fast breath. His gaze shoots to mine.

"Am I hurting you?"

"I'm good," I lie, as he gently holds my thigh. Honest to God, his touch is one thing, but his current position on the floor—between my spread legs—is something else altogether.

"Don't you think I should go to a doctor?" I croak out, trying to get my focus on something other than how good his touch feels.

"If you're not experiencing any of those symptoms, I say no. For the next twenty-four hours I'm

going to have to watch you for signs of a serious reaction, though."

"I'm not going to keep you up all night again,
Will."

"I don't mind you keeping me up all night."

His head is dipped, and I can't see his face, can't
tell if he's teasing or not. But when he says things
like that, and things like he doesn't mind putting
out, my thoughts go off in an inappropriate direction, and damn the flush crawling up my neck and
warming me all over.

"We'll worry about that later, okay?" he says,
"Right now, we have to clean this and spray it with
vinegar."

I crinkle my nose. "Vinegar? Are you kidding
me?"

"Do I look like the kind of guy who would kid in
a situation like this?

I lift my chin an inch. "I don't really know you
that well."

"Then you're just going to have to trust me on
that."

"I don't trust anyone." Working at a cutthroat
magazine like *Starlight* is enough to make anyone
jaded. And I can't forget my ex promised to love me
forever. Look how that turned out.

"Makes two of us," he says quickly. "But I do
know what I'm doing?"

"You've been stung?"

He nods.

"The vinegar worked?"

"Yeah. The pain you're feeling, I can relate." His eyes hold a measure of sympathy as they meet mine. I study him for a second, debating my next move. His jaw clenches, and he finally breaks the silence. "Am I doing this, Khloe?" he asks, and even when frazzled with my obstinance, he's still so goddamn sweet and charming I think I might get a toothache.

"Has anyone ever said no to you?" I ask.

He responds with, "The vinegar works. I promise."

"Vinegar it is, then," I say.

"Stay put, okay?"

I nod and he disappears into what I assume is the master bathroom. Drawers open and close, and a minute later he comes back with a spray bottle and tweezers.

"I'll be as gentle as I can," he says, his mouth tight, like he knows this is going to hurt. "But this might sting a bit."

"It's already stinging. Besides, I can handle a little pain." As soon as the words leave my mouth and I catch a grin curving his kissable lips, I wish I could get them back, swallow them down into the depths of my stomach, never to be heard from again.

What the hell is wrong with me?

Maybe I should sleep with him, get this insane arousal out of my system so I can talk and act like a woman who isn't obsessed with sex. But he's my boss, and we both have rules about that.

"Good to know," he says, his voice an octave deeper. "Take a big breath, Khloe."

I do as he says, and his gaze drops from my mouth and moves to my expanding chest. That's when I become acutely aware that I'm in a revealing bathing suit, and my nipples are pressing hard against the thin material, making my current arousal painfully obvious. Why am I constantly in revealing clothes around this guy?

"Okay," he says gruffly. "Okay, okay," he repeats, like he's talking to himself and trying to pull it together. He mutters what sounds like a curse and turns his attention to my sting.

"Tell me what you used to do for a living," he says, and I get that he's trying to distract me as he uses the tweezers to pull the first tentacle off.

"My dream is to someday write a book," I say, hedging the question.

"Oh yeah? What kind of book?"

"Maybe a thriller. I love psychological thrillers and horror."

He casts me a quick glance. "Really? I never would have guessed."

"No?"

"I would have thought something along the line of satire."

"And why is that?" I give him a sassy look that suggests he knows nothing.

"That's why," he says with a laugh. "You've got a sharp tongue."

"You don't know anything about my tongue," I shoot back. His hand stills over my leg, trembles a tiny bit, and my mind once again goes off in an erotic direction, envisioning him getting to know my tongue better by pressing his lips to mine.

"Just one left," he mutters and steadies his hand enough to pull off the last tentacle.

"Not so bad," I say, until he sprays the open wound with whatever is in that bottle. I let out an ungodly scream, and I'm pretty sure I pierced Will's eardrums judging by the way his face is contorting.

I grab the spray bottle from him. "What is this fresh hell?" I read the label. "Sting No More. It's clearly mislabeled. It stings twice as bad."

"Give it a second," he says, a grin playing with the corner of his mouth. "The vinegar will neutralize the venom."

"My day is just getting better and better." I toss the bottle to the bed, but lo and behold the pain starts to settle.

"Good?" he asks.

"Better."

"Now we have to put your leg into very, very hot water."

"Sure, why not. It's been fun so far."

He presses his hands to my thighs, leaving a burning imprint as he pushes off me to stand up. "You really are a good sport about all this, Khloe."

"Yeah, that's me, good sport Khloe."

"I actually admire that."

I meet his eyes, and it's rather silly how that simple compliment managed to jump-start my pulse, speeding it up enough to make me breathless.

He holds his hand out to me, and I let him lift me to my feet. I'm about to put pressure on my leg, but once again find myself in his arms. Good thing, considering the muscles in my legs have dissolved. He carries me to his master bathroom, which is twice as big as the bath in his spare room, and sets me on the marble countertop. I take in the room as he fills a claw-foot tub. Steam rises, dampens the sliding glass shower doors and the mirror behind me. I don't dare turn to look at my tear-streaked face and beach hair. I had enough of a fright with the jellyfish.

"All set?" he asks.

I nod, and he lifts me from the counter and sets me on the side of the tub. I wince as I plunge my leg into the water, bracing the other on the edge of the tub. My flesh instantly turns red from the heat. "When you said hot water, what you really meant to say is water so hot you can boil an egg."

He sits on the tub beside me, his feet on the floor. "You okay?"

"I will be." I let out a sigh. "Thanks to you."

He nudges me with his shoulder. "Was there a compliment in there somewhere?"

"Probably not."

He laughs, and it comes out rough. His body rumbles, and I become acutely aware of his close proximity and what it's doing to me.

"Can you get me a towel, please?"

He grabs a towel from the cabinet and hands it to me. I drape it over my shoulders.

"Are you cold?"

"No." I'm pretty sure I'm going to spontaneously combust. "I just… I'm in my bathing suit."

"I've noticed."

My gaze cuts to his. My ex spouted some pretty harsh comments the last time I wore a suit around him. The thing is, I have no problem with my curves. I rather like them, and I'll be damned if I'm going to starve myself to fit society's expectations. But I get that men prefer waif-thin models, and Will here is no exception.

"I wasn't expecting anyone to see me in it." I shrug into myself, but my breasts only spill out more. "It's last year's, and I didn't have a chance to go shopping."

"You don't like it?"

"I never said that."

"But you did say something about it earlier. I wasn't sure what you meant."

His hand moves, brushes against mine as I grip the edge of the tub. "I wouldn't have worn it if I thought you were going to see me in it. It's just that it's a bit small."

"Yeah." A sound catches in his throat as his gaze slowly skims downward. "I noticed that, too."

I'm about to die of mortification, until I catch the heat in his eyes. And his breathing is a little more labored. Am I reading this situation right, or has the venom gotten to my brain?

"In the rule book, two-piece bathing suits are prohibited."

"Are you kidding me?"

"No," he grumbles, and scrubs his face.

"That's really in the book?"

His jaw tightens, his muscles rippling. How is it possible that he's getting better- and better-looking by the second?

"It's going to be in about two minutes," he murmurs.

The air around us charges, and my heart speeds up. "Will…" I say, his name coming out a little soft, a little husky around the edges.

He shifts closer, his breath warm on my face. "You remember my rule about not getting involved with those in my employment."

"Yeah," I say, and he touches the cotton towel, rubs his fingers over it in a way that has my thoughts sliding off track. I take a moment to envision the rough pad of his thumb touching another part of my body in much that same manner.

"You're a beautiful woman with a killer body, Khloe, and if you wear this again…" He lets out a slow breath, and it blows a tendril of hair from my face. He moves closer, breathing me in as his mouth goes to my ear. "Let's just say, I've never been tempted to break that rule. Until now."

I take a few deep breaths. Is this guy for real?

Wait, I've already established the fact that he's insane.

"My ex," I begin before I can think better of it. "He wanted me to lose weight, fit in more with what a woman is expected to look like." I turn my head slowly, and there's a mixture of heat and anger in Will's eyes.

"Your ex is obviously an idiot."

"That's why I left him."

"You shouldn't change yourself. Not for anyone."

"I don't plan on it. I like myself just fine." He smiles at that, and heat arcs between us. I take a fast breath to get my head together. "Even if you were tempted to break the rules, I'd never sleep with another woman's man."

"Bevey is an old friend," he explains.

"That's not who I'm talking about."

He stares at me, his brow furrowed. I give him a moment to process—personally I'm not thinking straight, and I suspect a lot of blood has left his brain, too. Damned if I don't want to glance down to check. A second later, his eyes widen in understanding. "You're talking about Jules."

"That's right." I lift my chin a little. "I have rules, too, you know."

His grin is slow, sexy as hell. "So you *were* listening in to my conversation."

"No… I…" Shit. Busted.

"It's okay, you signed the nondisclosure agreement."

"It was hard not to listen. You weren't trying to

be quiet. I am curious, though. What is the present you got her? Diamonds would be my guess."

"What would a four-year-old want with diamonds?"

"Four?" Okay, now that I didn't expect.

"Jules is my four-year-old niece."

A thrill I wish I wasn't feeling races through me.

"Don't you keep up with the news, Khloe? My cousin Tate and his wife, Summer, have a little girl."

"Now that you mention it."

He leans into me, his mouth grazing my shoulder. "Is that the only thing stopping you…?"

My left leg drops from the edge of the tub and plunges into the hot water. It splashes up on us, dousing the lust bubbling between us.

He pulls back, fast, and his face hardens, his eyes a blazing mess of lust and regret. "Khloe… I. Damn. I don't know what I was thinking." He inches back, putting a small measure of distance between us. It does nothing to extinguish the heat in my body. "We…ah…probably shouldn't let this happen, right?"

My brain is so fuzzy, I can't tell whether he's making a statement or asking a question. "You're right," I say. Getting involved with my boss is wrong on so many levels.

And why is that, Khloe?

Oh, because…

I rack my lust-induced brain, but can't come up with an answer. He's single. I'm single. He's made it clear he's not the settling-down type, and I'm not looking to settle down with him. I don't even like rich, entitled guys. But there is no doubt we're physically attracted to each other, and we're both consenting adults. Why can't we have a little fun if we're clear on the rules from the get-go?

"Here," he says, the deep tenor of his voice dragging me back to the present as he hands me another towel. "I'm going to lift you out, and you can drape that around your leg." He bends into me, hooks his arms under my legs and gently lifts me from the tub.

I put my hands around his neck, and he hisses quietly as I spread my fingers to touch more of his skin. I slide my hand down his back, palm his muscles. His jaw is so tight I fear something might snap as he sets me back on the counter, takes the towel from me, and with the utmost care pats my leg dry. I widen my thighs a little more to make it easier for him, and maybe to tease him a bit. Now that I know what I do to him, that he too feels the heat between us, I plan to torment. I'm not going to make things easy on Will. In fact, I'm going to make things very *hard* on him.

As a delicious, devious plan forms in my mind, I say, "I think I need to see this rule book of yours, sir."

CHAPTER EIGHT

Will

WHAT THE EVER-LOVING hell is going on in my life? It's been three days since I touched down on Saint Thomas. Three long, torturous days with Khloe prancing around in her skimpy uniforms and bending over to dust every possible low spot. At night, when she's not driving me insane, she sits on her deck, her head buried in her journal, her soft humming sounds filtering in through my bedroom window and caressing my cock.

I glance up from my laptop as she hums a tune and bends to run a feather duster over the baseboards—again. I only have so much control, and with her aiming that sweet ass my way, it's about to shatter.

"Haven't you cleaned that already?"

"Yes," she says and goes back to her humming.

"Do you think you could stop humming?" I command in a deep voice.

She blinks innocent eyes at me, although I'm be-

ginning to believe there is nothing innocent about
her. She's been reading over the rule book for the last
two nights while I've been in my office working on
a new Do Not list.

My phone pings, and I reach for it. It had better
be Granddad. I've put a call in to him every day, and
he's yet to call me back. This time it's Tate.

"How's Saint Thomas?" he asks. "Is the view still
as spectacular as always?"

I lift my eyes slightly as Khloe sways her hips to
an imaginary song inside her head. "More spectacular than ever," I grumble.

Tate laughs. "Sure doesn't sound it."

"Just a lot on my mind. Like how is Granddad?
Why isn't he calling me back?"

"I'm not sure. I was with him earlier, and he never
said anything about you calling."

"Is he okay?"

"As good as can be expected. He's midnineties,
after all."

"Do you think… Do you think he might be losing his mind?" I blurt out.

"I've been thinking that for years, but why are
you suddenly asking?"

Khloe leaves my office, and I lower my voice.
"The woman he hired to accompany me to Saint
Thomas. I'm not sure what he was thinking."

"She's not working out?"

"She broke the vacuum, a few dishes, everything
she cooks she burns, and she…"

Papers rustle in the background. "She what?"

"I'm not sure you'd believe me if I told you."

"Now I really need to hear."

"She wears these French maid uniforms. Hang on, I'll send you a link of what the outfit looks like." I do a quick search, find the image on Amazon, grab the link and shoot it off to Tate.

I wait a second. As soon as a low, slow whistle followed by a hoot of laughter comes through the line, I know he's opened it.

"Lucky you," Tate says.

"No, not lucky me. You know my rules."

"Yeah, fuck the rules, Will. If she's hot, and I think Granddad said something about your new assistant being a looker, then I'd go for it. What do you have to lose?"

"Right now, I'm losing my mind."

Tate lets out another roar. "Hey, you never know. She could be the one."

"Tate, you know—" I stop when, from the kitchen, something hits the floor and smashes.

"What was that?" Tate asks.

"Lunch, I'm guessing."

"Sounds like things are in bad shape."

Khloe's not. Her shape is just perfect. My cock, however…

I lean back in my chair and look out into the hall. Pinching the bridge of my nose, I say, "Maybe I should cut this trip short."

"Nah, just don't work so hard. Put your feet up and have some fun for a change."

"Wait, you called me. Did you need something?"

"Nope, just checking in. Jules is excited about her party, and I'm just making sure her uncle Will is going to be there," he says, but I have a feeling that's not entirely true. I never get calls when I'm here in Saint Thomas. Everyone knows I come when I need solitude, and I'd assured Summer I'd be there for Jules's party. What is this really all about? Before I can ask, Tate says, "So you'll be there?"

"I'll be there. If I don't spontaneously combust first."

Tate laughs again. "Yeah, you need to get laid, man."

I'm beginning to believe he might be right.

"While that sounds about right, I haven't had a chance to check on the resort or the school's progress yet. I've been afraid to leave Khloe alone. She nearly lit the kitchen on fire the other day. I was thinking of getting Bevey to give her a few lessons."

"You're good in the kitchen. Maybe you could show her a few things."

Goddammit, the things I want to show her involve the use of a mattress, not a stove.

"I better go check on her. Can you get Granddad to call me?"

"Will do."

We say goodbye, and I push from my chair to check on the commotion in the kitchen. I don't smell smoke, which gives me a measure of relief. I step into the kitchen to find Khloe at the table, writing something in my rule book.

She closes it and flashes me a smile when she sees me.

"What are you doing?"

"I was just finishing my notes," she says.

I shove my hands into my pockets. "In *my* rule book?"

"I've given that some thought, and since I'm working for you, I believe it's *our* rule book, and I thought I should jot a few rules down, too."

Since I'm not sure I like the sound of that, I change direction. "I heard a crash."

She crinkles up her nose—her freckles are more prominent now that she's spent time in the sun. "Sorry, broke a plate. You can take it out of my pay, like the last couple I broke."

"I told you I'm not going to do that."

She puts the end of the pen in her mouth, nibbles a little and says, "I've given that some thought, too. I made notes in the book on how I could repay you, *sir.*"

Jesus, she's fucking with me. I'm sure of it.

"How's that?"

She just grins and says, "Your lunch is made. It's in the fridge. The wind has finally died down, so I thought I'd take my hour lunch break and go for a swim."

"Don't forget your water shoes," I say. I went into

town yesterday with Khloe to stock the fridge and pantry, and we picked her up a pair of shoes as well as a few new one-piece bathing suits and a couple of cover-up dresses.

"I do need to pay you back for the shoes and all the clothing. But it's all outlined in the book." She taps the leather cover, giving me a small grin that pushes all my buttons.

I make my way to the fridge, pull the door open and find a sandwich and salad. "Have you eaten?" I ask. "We could sit on the deck..."

She wipes the back of her hand across her forehead. "I'm not hungry yet. I'll grab something after my swim."

I curse the disappointment in my gut. Dammit, I shouldn't be trying to find ways to hang around her longer. I should be trying to find ways to avoid her.

"I'll just eat in my office," I grumble, and keep my head down.

"Whatever you prefer, sir."

"Khloe," I say around a thick tongue. "Call me Will."

I snatch up my lunch and make my way to my office. I toss the sandwich down and catch a glimpse of Khloe on her way to her bedroom to change. I'm pretty sure the new suits will look amazing on her killer body, and damned if I don't want to sneak a peek. Her soft humming sounds reach my ears as she makes her way to the door. It opens, closes with a soft click, and my dick urges me to head outside to enjoy the show.

I bite into my sandwich and shake my head. How the hell can anyone screw up a turkey sandwich? I peel it open to see that she used mustard instead of mayonnaise. I'm beginning to believe she didn't read the rule book at all.

I toss it aside, my appetite dissolving, as a new kind of hunger takes up residence in my body. I push my chair back, my heart thumping a little faster.

Don't do it, Will. Don't give in to temptation.

Then I remember what Tate said. I need to get laid. The man's not wrong. What *is* wrong is sleeping with the help.

Unless she wants that, too…

I jump up and make my way to the kitchen. The rule book sits on the table where Khloe left it, like she wanted me to flip through it. Who am I to disappoint? I scoop it up and run my thumb over the leather as I step out onto the deck. The warmth of the day falls over me, and I scan the beach for Khloe. Her head pops from the green water as she leisurely swims in the bay.

I pull out a chair, sit and flip the book open. I leaf through the pages with my writing and stop when the script changes. I settle myself to read, but the first line has me sitting up a little straighter, sweating a little harder.

This…this is what Khloe's been up to? I take a couple of deep breaths before I begin to read *her* rules. And from the title alone, I'm ready to blow my load.

> *Ten Rules for Sleeping with Your Assistant:*
> *1. The affair is secret.*
> *2. Sexual pleasure only.*
> *3. No dating.*
> *4. No overnights in the same room.*
> *5. No kissing.*
> *6. No gifts.*
> *7. No getting personal.*
> *8. Life goes back to normal when we return to the US.*
> *9. For every plate I break or any inappropriate behavior, there should be some sort of repri-mand. I should also be required to pay for the things you've purchased for me.*
> *10. I'll leave the details up to you.*

The world closes in on me, goes a little fuzzy around the edges. All this time, Khloe has been making rules of her own, rules that totally make sense. Rules I can live by. Humming sounds reach my ears. I push from my chair, look out over the ocean, and nearly bite off my tongue when I find Khloe standing on the sand, staring out at the ocean, dressed in nothing but her goddamn water shoes.

Sweet Jesus.

CHAPTER NINE

Khloe

I DON'T NEED to turn around to know his eyes are on me. I can feel them boring into my naked flesh as I admire the green waters of the bay. Every nerve in my body is alive and on fire, knowing Will is either going to send me packing or meet me on the sand and accept the rules of the game. The move is risky on my part, but from the way he looks at me to the tortured curses I hear in his throat when I bend to dust… Yeah, he wants this as much as I do.

A noise sounds on the stairs behind me, but I don't turn. This is Will's private paradise, and the only one who can be coming my way is the man I want in my bed. My heart crashes against my ribs, pounds behind my eyes. His vibrating energy, volatile heat, reaches out to me, slides over my skin as he closes the distance. Staying perfectly still, I breathe deep, catching his scent.

He steps up behind me, his harsh breath so damn

hot on my skin, I'm sure I'm going to ignite. I'm about to turn to face him when he stops me.

"Don't move."

I have no idea what it is about his strong commands that get to me. He runs his fingers from my shoulders to my elbows, and I shudder.

"I read your rules." Warm lips brush my shoulder, and erotic sensation shoots straight to my sex.

"And?" I ask, a thrill going through me. If he's kissing me, it must mean he's in agreement.

"There are a lot of them."

"Not compared to the two hundred rules you have. But enough to keep us on track. No mistakes. No misunderstandings."

"Yes, that's why rules are important."

"Very important," I agree.

His teeth graze my flesh as his hands drop to my waist, shape my curves. "New rules for sleeping with the assistant. I never would have thought of that."

"But you agree with them?" I ask, my voice coming out a breathless whisper.

Touch me already.

"Arms above your head."

My pulse leaps, and I swallow as I do as he commands. A warm breeze washes over my naked body as Will steps close enough for me to feel his hard cock pressing against the small of my back.

"I'm still trying to decide," he says, and I feel a moment of panic. Him being here, touching me, his blatant arousal...aren't they all signs that he's made up his mind?

"Decide what?" I ask, doing my best not to sound as needy as I feel.

"What the punishment for breaking my dishes should be."

I scrape my teeth over my dry bottom lip. "It's a big decision."

"Very big," he says, his fingers biting into my hips as he pulls me against his hardness. I wiggle, grind against him, and his deep groan of approval is my glorious reward. Damn, I love how I get to this man.

His big warm hands leave my hips, begin a heated journey up my stomach until he has two handfuls of my breasts.

"These," he begins, as he kneads my flesh, "have been driving me crazy for days now."

"Sorry, sir," I tease.

"Jesus, Khloe." He growls into my ear, and my body shudders. "You've been fucking with me, haven't you?"

"Who, me, sir?"

"Yeah, you." One hand leaves my breasts, and he shifts his stance to grab my ass. He squeezes, pulls his hand back and gives me a small slap. I let out a little yelp.

"What...what was that for?" I ask, a new kind of pleasure dancing on my flesh.

"For pushing my buttons." He takes my hands, puts them by my sides and steps back. He goes silent for so long, I'd think he'd retreated if not for the tortured sound of his breathing.

"Like what you see, sir?" I ask, just to get a rise out of him.

"Turn around."

Sand squishes beneath my shoes as I slowly spin, and my breath catches when the heat in his eyes burns my flesh. I have never seen that look on a man's face before. Intense, frustrated, excited… needy.

"Yes, I like what I see."

My gaze leaves his face, takes in his loose blue T-shirt, going lower to examine the bulge in his khaki shorts. My mouth waters, and my fingers itch to close around him, weigh him in my palm.

"I'm not seeing enough," I say. His body stiffens, and as he grumbles a curse, I bite back a grin. I have no idea what it is about this man that brings out the bold side in me, but I love his reactions.

"Widen your legs," he commands.

I spread my legs, and my sex moistens, my inner thighs becoming so wet, I'm sure he can see them glistening. His deep groan confirms it.

He rubs his hand over himself. "Every night in bed, I take my cock in my hands and think about burying my mouth between your legs."

Holy…

I figured this man was the opposite of vanilla, but I've never had anyone talk dirty to me before, and I have to say…I love it.

"I believe in rule number two," I say. "Sexual pleasure is on the table."

"The table, huh? How about the bed, Khloe?"

"Yes, sir," I say, and his nostrils flare as he steps up to me. He lightly runs the rough pads of his thumbs over my hard nipples, plucks at them, and once again slides his tongue over the dip in his upper lip.

"Have you been touching yourself, too?" he asks. "Thinking about me with my mouth between your legs, licking you until you explode?"

A whimper catches in my throat as my sex squeezes.

"Yes," I manage to say. "When I'm in bed at night, listening to the waves, I widen my legs and touch myself, imagining it's your fingers inside me."

His hands leave my breasts, slide down my body and slip between my spread legs. The black in his eyes bleeds into the blue as he runs a finger along the length of my pussy.

"God, you're so wet."

He slides a finger into me, and my muscles hold him tight. I take a few deep breaths and make a move to touch him. "No," he commands. "Just stand there."

"Will," I murmur as he slides another finger in and strokes me a few times.

"I can't wait to get my cock in here," he says.

"What are you waiting for?" I ask.

His grin is slow, so damn sexy when he scoops me up and hurries to the house. I hold on to him, reveling in the strength of his body, the rippling of his hard muscles. I'm pretty sure I won the man lottery with this guy.

"My room or yours?" he asks. "It wasn't in the rule book."

"Your choice," I say. "Just please…hurry."

He carries me to his room, and I slide down his body as he lets me go. We stand there for a moment, and he cups my face. His head dips, and for a second I think he's going to kiss me. I'm about to remind him of the rules when he steps back.

His gaze roams the length of me, a leisurely inspection. I'd feel self-conscious if it were my ex, but all I feel as Will looks at me is desirable. I put my hands on my stomach and slide them up until I'm cupping my breasts. His eyes never leave my hands as he reaches over his back, grabs a fistful of his T-shirt and peels it off.

"That's better," I murmur as I revel in his glistening skin. His big fingers fumble with the button on his khakis. I drop to my knees, release the button and tug down his zipper. His hand goes to my hair, and he fists it tight. The little tug sends sensations straight to my pulsing core.

"Mmm," I moan as I free him. I take my time to admire his length and girth.

"Like what you see?" he asks, his voice a tortured growl.

Instead of answering, I stick my tongue out and hold it there. He tugs my hair, and our eyes meet.

His breath hitches as he grips his cock and cants his hips forward, rubbing the crown over my tongue.

"That is the hottest damn thing I've ever seen," he says.

"More," I say.

He pushes against my tongue, and I widen my mouth to accommodate his thickness. My fingers slide around to cup his beautiful ass, gripping him tight as I take him deeper than I've ever taken a man.

He pumps into me, his cock swelling as I eagerly suck. I've never been into giving oral sex like this before. My nipples tingle, anxious to feel his mouth wrapped around them, and my sex is so needy, I'm sure the second he touches me I'm going to soar higher than ever. He pulls out of my mouth, and I whimper at the loss.

"I'm about to come down your throat, Khloe."

I lift my chin and meet his eyes. "I want that," I protest.

"You'll get it," he says, shoving his thick thumb between my lips. I suck on him, lick him, and he lets loose an agonized cry.

"On the bed. Right now," he growls. I bite back a smile, and he reaches down, lifts me from the floor and sets me on the bed.

"I was fighting a losing battle, wasn't I?" he asks, and just to be bad, I flip over so he's looking at my ass as I crawl to the center of the bed.

"You tease," he says.

"Who, me, sir?"

"I should tie you to that bed and make you pay for what you've been doing to me."

"I believe that's covered in rules nine and ten." I flatten myself on the bed and roll onto my back.

"My God, you'd like that."

"I'm merely pointing out a rule, Will."

"I want you so goddamn much, I can't think straight. You bending over in that little French maid outfit…"

I bite on my finger. "I had no idea what I was doing."

A sound of disbelief rumbles in his throat. "This might not be slow or easy."

"Did you read anywhere in the rules that I wanted slow or easy?"

"I want you so damn bad, I might just wreck you."

"Yes please," I say, and run my tongue over my lips. "Can I taste you again first?"

He tugs his shorts and boxers off, climbs onto the bed, and straddles me. He not-so-gently shoves his thumb back into my mouth. "You want me to come in here, Khloe."

Since my mouth is full, I nod, and he strokes himself. In a fast move, he pulls his thumb out and replaces it with his erection, filling my mouth. My entire body quakes, and I suck hard as he rocks into me. I reach for him, run my hands over his sides, but he takes my arms and puts them over my head, positioning my body so I'm entirely open to him. He slides deeper into my throat, and I moan around his cock.

"Fuck," he cries out. I make a move to reach for him when he pulls back, but the intensity in his eyes as he slowly shakes his head stops me and fills me with a new kind of excitement. I take a fast breath.

He repositions between my legs, his eyes going from my wet mouth, to my breasts, to the needy juncture aching for his fingers…for him.

"This sweet pussy. I'm going to own it."

"Yes, sir," I say.

Falling over me, he takes my breasts into his big palms. He tugs at my nipples and squeezes my breasts to form a channel.

"You have the nicest tits."

I reach down and take hold of him. "You're not so bad yourself."

He grunts as I stroke him, but I lose purchase as he backs up and sucks a nipple into his mouth. A moan erupts from the depths of my throat, and I squirm, arch into him, giving him everything. He backs off and lightly flicks his tongue over my nipple.

"Oh, yes," I cry out, and put my hands back over my head, gripping the headboard. The heavy weight of his body presses down on me, fueling the need between my legs as his cock presses into my outer thigh. Pleasure sweeps through my veins, burning me from the inside out.

He strokes my clit, and I rock my hips shamelessly. His chuckle vibrates around my nipple.

"Are you laughing at me?" I ask, as I take deep

breaths. As long as he keeps doing what he's doing, I don't much care.

"Nothing to laugh at here, Khloe. No, this sweet pussy is something to admire, appreciate and enjoy." He slides a finger into me, and I swear to God my eyes roll back in my head.

I lift my head, but he's not looking at me. He's staring at my pussy like it's the most fascinating thing he's ever seen. When was the last time this man had sex? Then again, when was the last time I did?

"Spread your legs wider," he commands, and I do. He grips my inner thighs and opens them a bit more, putting me on full display. "Jesus."

His head slowly lifts, and his gaze collides with mine. "I knew you'd have a nice pussy, Khloe. Christ, when you bent over and I could see your panties hugging you, your sweet lips, I knew. But this—" he rubs his finger down my lips, spreading them "—is so fucking pretty. The hottest pussy I've ever seen."

My throat tightens with the way he's admiring me like I'm a national treasure. I like it. A lot. Holy shit, if my ex could see me now, see the way Will is worshipping my body. Wait, no. I don't want to think about that jerk.

"You know, if you come into my office and bend over like that again, you'll probably be sorry."

Okay, so I'm definitely doing that. "You have a problem with me bending over?"

"I sure as hell do. How am I supposed to work

with my cock standing up to take notice every single time?"

I grin.

"You like that, huh?" he asks, and slides another finger in.

"Will…" I murmur.

"Khloe," he says, "we shouldn't make this sweet pussy wait a second longer." He slides down my body, and my hips rise with that first delicious swipe along the hot length of me. Hot sensations fill me as the soft blade swirls around my clit, coming close but never touching. "Is this what you wanted?" he asks.

"I'm going to add no talking to the list," I say, and he chuckles softly.

"But don't you want me to tell you how much I love your body, the taste of you?"

"Yeah, okay. Just don't stop."

"Khloe, I'm not going to stop until you come."

"Thank you," I murmur, my head going from side to side as delicious waves course through my body. He goes quiet, licking, probing, doing magical things between my legs until I'm shaking mindlessly. He moans and works his fingers inside me, his tongue taking me higher and higher.

"You've been in need of attention," he says, his voice raspy.

"Yes…" My breathing changes as he returns to his task, and it becomes almost impossible to fill my lungs as everything in me focuses on my building climax. "Will… Will…"

He sharpens his tongue, applies more pressure to my clit, and like a damn bursting, I let go. His moan of approval sends a tingle down my spine.

His head lifts, his breathing rough.

"Come here," I say.

He climbs up my body, his weight pressing down on me as his lips hover over mine. My lips part automatically. Shit, no kissing. "I'm not the only one in need of attention," I say, and shove until he's on the mattress beside me.

I roll over and crawl across the bed. The position isn't all that different from when I'm dusting.

"What are you doing?" he asks. The gruffness in his voice brings a smile to my face, and I glance at him over my shoulder.

"Getting a condom. I just assumed you had them in your nightstand."

I turn, give an extra wiggle of my ass and pull open his nightstand. I tug out a condom, and I'm about to hold it up, but Will is right there, his body pressed over mine, his hard cock between my thighs. His heat burns my skin, and my heart gallops like I've just run a marathon.

"You're such a tease," he whispers into my ear as he slides his hands around my body, covers both breasts and lifts me until I'm upright on my spread knees. I slide my hand down, capture his cock as he pivots forward, and I give it a stroke, wishing I could taste it. My God, this man brings something out in me—something wild and adventurous, something I was too afraid to allow myself to feel with my ex. Knowing Liam, he'd simply have shamed me, reprimanded me for my behavior. But I'm done with that. I've accepted my body the way it is, and now I'm going to accept my needs, too.

I bring my fingers to my mouth and taste Will on my tongue. He growls against my ear, the heat of his breath caressing my bare flesh.

"Jesus Christ that's hot," he growls.

"Good. I want to try everything with you."

He stills for a second. "Try?"

"Will," I begin, deciding if I'm going to have the best sex of my life, then I need to be open and honest. I go down on my breasts, press them into the sheets and keep my ass in the air.

"I've never been fucked like this."

He goes quiet, thoughtful for a moment, like he's struggling to make sense of my words. Hesitation tightens my gut. Maybe I shouldn't have taken this position, or opened up so readily. Maybe it's too soon to admit my inexperience. Will it scare him away? But all worry evaporates when he grips my ass, squeezes my cheeks.

"No?" he asks, his voice a bit shaky.

"No," I say. "I've never even been on top. Sex was never something my ex and I excelled at, and he was kind of my..."

"First?"

"First and last."

He slides a finger into me, and we both groan. "Not your last, Khloe. Not your last by a long shot."

"No, not my last," I say, even though I'm sure once my time here with Will is over, my sex life will go back to dormant. I'm still sure no man out there is right for me, and I refuse to change who I am to suit someone else. Besides, when I return I have a career to focus on. But I can't think about that when Will is ripping into the condom and sheathing himself.

"That's something I want to do, too," I say as I look over my shoulder, note the way he's rolling on the condom.

"You want to suit me up?"

"Yeah, is that weird?"

He grins. "Not weird at all. In fact, I think you should write out a list of all the things you want. Put it in the rule book. We'll work our way through it and check things off as we achieve them."

I smile at him. "I like that idea."

"And here you thought I was insane for having a rule book."

"I never used the word *insane*."

"Khloe," he says in a commanding voice that tugs at my clit.

"Yeah."

"You can keep talking if you want." He presses his crown to my wet pussy. "But I'm going to put my cock in you. Right now."

"Okay," I say, and let loose a breath.

"This position is going to allow me to go deep. It might hurt."

"I like a little pain, remember?"

He runs the rough pad of his thumb along my spine. "Baby, I don't think you know what you like," he says in a tone so soft and so full of genuine concern, it nearly knocks me off my knees. "But when you leave this island, you're going to know what you want and what you love. I promise you that."

"Yes," I say as he pushes inside me. I grip the sheets, curl them around my fingers as he slides in, going deeper and deeper, stealing the breath from my lungs with every delicious, glorious inch. My walls spread, clench, tighten around him. My God. "This is what I've been missing out on," I say.

"Feels good, right?" he moans, his hands gripping my hips harder, biting into the flesh for leverage. He slides in so deep I lose all train of thought, can't even answer his question. He pulls almost all the way out, and in one swift movement, he's filling me again. I gulp.

"Khloe," he says in a soft voice, his thrust slowing.

"Yeah," I manage to say when I get my voice working again.

"You with me?"

His thoughtful check-in does something weird to my insides. "I am," I say.

"I don't want to hurt you."

I move my body, back up against him, wiggle

and encourage him to take me the way he needs to. The way I need him to, even though I'm not sure I know what I need.

"Talk to me." His grip loosens and he draws circles with his thumbs. "Tell me how this feels."

"Good. So good."

"Too deep?"

"No, Will. I want all of you in me. I want everything."

"I'll give you everything." He lowers himself over my back, once again seated high inside me, pushing on my walls, brushing the sensitive bundle of nerves inside. He moves slightly, rotates his hips, and I groan. "Thattagirl. Tell me how you like it."

He pulls out and pistons into me. Hard. My nipples scrape against the mattress, and the tingles spread to my sex as the headboard bangs against the wall. Pain mingles with pleasure, and so help me God, I love it.

"Like that, Will. Yes, please," I whimper.

"You should see the way I'm sliding in and out of you. I've got an amazing view, Khloe."

My sex clenches. "I want to see."

"You will, but not tonight. Tonight I'm just going to keep fucking you like this until you come. That's what I want, I want you to quiver around me when I come inside you," he says. Beneath his even tone, there's a hint of tension, a shakiness that I'd easily miss if my attention wasn't on everything he was doing to me, everything he was saying. Will Carson is teetering on the edge, and I've done this to him. Me. Khloe Davis. He grips my ass cheeks and massages.

"You've got the nicest ass." He slides a pillow under my hips and pulls my knees out from under me. I fall until I'm flat on the pillow, my ass slightly raised.

"You're going to like this," he says, and when he slams into me, my clit rubs against the soft pillow-case.

"Oh, God, Will. More, please. Harder."

"Greedy girl. I like that about you." He traces my curves. "I like this about you, too."

As he touches me, worships me, I lift my ass a bit more, a shameless move I never would have tried in the past, and I'm rewarded with a deep groan and a smack to the ass.

He changes angles, thrusts, going deeper. Hard. Pounding. Every purposeful slide stimulates my breasts and clit until I'm drowning in heat and need. An erotic throb crashes over me until nothing exists but pleasure.

"Will!" I cry as my muscles clench around him, each determined drag in and out of my sex causing more friction, more sensations. I lose all control of my muscles as he coaxes orgasm after orgasm out of me. I whimper, fist the bedding, and I know he's reached his limit when he seats himself high, goes still and calls out my name. Nothing has ever been more satisfying than hearing my name on his tongue as he reaches his ultimate pleasure. The sweet, beautifully seductive sound wraps around my closed-off heart.

He falls over me, his hot body moist and hard. His rapid breath flutters my damp hair. "You good?" he asks, and I smile, taking a moment to enjoy the post-orgasm bliss. He rolls off me fast, his brow pinched as he moves my body around like I weigh nothing. Our eyes meet.

"Khloe?"

Oh, crap. He's worried he hurt me. I touch his face, enjoy the feel of his bristles against my hand. I'm guessing it's a rare day when he forgets to shave. "I'm good," I assure him. He examines my face a moment longer, then a slow smile curls his mouth. My lips tingle, but no, I'm not about to kiss him. I can follow the rules—my own rules, anyway. "There is one little thing, though."

His brow pinches again, and the muscles in his shoulders grow taut. "What?"

"If we check this position off the list, does it mean we can't do it again?"

He laughs, relaxing. "We can do whatever you need, however many times you need it."

"I mean, I have to be sure, right? Have to nail down what I like and don't like."

"Yeah, we're going to nail it down. Over and over again…"

CHAPTER TEN

Will

I TAP A finger against my desk as I wait for my call to Granddad to connect. Outside my door, Khloe is struggling to figure out how to get the new vacuum to work. I can't help but grin and shake my head. Yesterday, having her beneath me in my bed, should have helped get my thoughts off her. But now that I know what her soft body feels like, the way her tight walls squeeze an orgasm from me, I only want more.

I turn to the window, and in the near distance, I spot Vin, the groundskeeper, a man I entrust with my place when I'm back in New York. He comes once a week to do the shrubbery and does a walk-through of the house every day in my absence. Since he knows everyone on the island, he's also my go-to guy for everything from furnishing the villa to repairs on the house. He glances up as if he feels my gaze and waves to me. As I wave back, an idea takes shape, and I can't help but grin. If Khloe wants to experience everything, then I'm damn well going to make that happen.

"Hello…hello…"

"Oh, hey, Summer."

"Everything okay? I said hello like four times."

"Yeah, I was just distracted."

"What's her name?" she teases.

"Summer—"

"Oh, we have the same name."

"You are not funny."

"So this call is not to say you finally found someone and you're getting married."

"No, I was distracted because of work. Nothing more," I lie.

I stare at the open computer on my desk, the algorithms that need my attention. I just can't seem to focus lately.

Summer chuckles, and it pulls me back. "Something funny?"

"Nothing funny at all." Her voice takes on a serious tone. "What's up?" she asks, and I can hear Jules squealing in the background.

"How's Jules?"

"Good. Granddad is showing her a rope trick. Remember the one where he threads it through his fingers and you put your arm through a couple times?"

I laugh softly. "I remember," I say. He used to do that with me when I was sad, missing my dad. "Can I speak to him?"

"Hang on." From the muffled sounds on the other

end, I suspect she's put her hand over the phone. "Ah, he said he's busy with Jules right now and asked if he can call you back later."

"What is going on with him?" I frown and rub the center of my forehead. "I've been trying to reach him for days."

"What about?" Summer asks.

"I just… I guess I wanted to know more about Khloe."

"Khloe?"

"The woman he hired to assist me on this trip."

"Is it not working out?"

I lower my voice. "She can't even cook, plus she broke the vacuum and numerous dishes."

Summer laughs. "Meaning she's making your life chaotic. I like her already."

"Not funny." I eye the door to make sure she's not within earshot. "I'm not sure how Granddad thought she was good for the job."

"Are you disappointed in his choice?"

"No."

Shit, that one word jumped to my lips rather quickly. And I'm sure I hear Summer chuckling again.

"Well then, what's the problem?"

"You know I like things done a certain way."

"Oh, I know, Will. Believe me, I know."

"There's a reason for that, Summer." I sit back in my chair and watch a yellow bird perch on the shrubbery outside. The sky is a perfect blue, the sun shining brightly, and for some reason it takes me back to a time when I used to enjoy the outdoors. Enjoy life.

"I know that, too. Look, why don't you try to enjoy yourself while you're there. This Khloe sounds like a breath of fresh air. Take her out, show her around. She's probably breaking things because you're an ogre and she's intimidated. I know how you are."

"Believe me, she's not one bit intimidated by me," I say quickly.

"Oh? I thought all your assistants were afraid of you."

"Not this one."

"Are you saying she likes you?"

"I wouldn't go so far as to say that." We might be physically attracted to each other, and she might be seeking lessons, but twice now, in her most disgusted voice, I heard her say something about men in power all being alike. I'm not sure what she means by that and I hope she's not lumping me into the same category as her last asshole boss, who wanted more than she was willing to give. What's between us is consensual. That much I'm sure of. I wouldn't make her do anything she didn't want to, and the French maid outfit was her doing, not mine. I must say I'm growing quite accustomed to her attire.

"That doesn't change the fact that you should get out of the house, go do something fun."

Yesterday I did something fun...and I didn't even have to leave the house.

I chuckle softly.

"Something funny?" she asks.

"No." I quickly straighten. "I do have to go check on the middle school and get to Granddad's resort. There are some staffing situations I need to look into."

"When are you going to take that stick out of your ass?"

My head jerks back. "What the hell, Summer?"

"Motherhood. It changes you." She laughs. "What I'm trying to say is checking progress at the school and the resort is not fun."

"It needs to be done."

"Lots of things need to get done. I need to bake a zillion cupcakes for Jules's party. It'll happen but not today. Get it?"

"I don't like to procrastinate."

"And you like rules. I know, I know." I can almost hear her rolling her eyes at me. Oh yeah, motherhood has definitely changed her. "But sometimes rules are made to be broken. Sometimes really good things happen when they are," she says, a hint of mischief in her tone.

"Summer—"

Her exaggerated sigh cuts me off. "Do we want to talk about the stick again?"

"No."

"Okay, then. Go do something that doesn't *need* to be done. What about running the ninety-nine steps at Charlotte Amalie? Granddad said you used to love to do that. And take Khloe with you. She deserves fun for having to put up with you. That in itself is just cruel."

"Why don't you tell me what you really think," I say, and shake my head.

"Fine then. Get your pasty white ass out of the house, and go do something fun for a change."

"Pasty white ass? Jeez, I love you, too."

"Love you, Will. Now go, do what I say. Doctor's orders."

"Fine, fine." I end the call and drop my phone onto my desk.

Curses reach my ears along with a lot of banging and clanging.

"Khloe," I call out.

She appears at my door, blinking innocently. "Yes, sir?"

I take a deep breath and work to keep the blood in my brain. "I have to run some errands. It's a beautiful day. I thought I could show you around Saint Thomas. Unless, of course, you prefer to stay here and abuse the vacuum."

"Your vacuum hates me."

"Vacuums can't hate, and it's brand-new. You broke the last one, remember?"

"I remember." She plants a hand on one hip and sticks it out. "Then why won't it turn on?"

"I don't know. How about I look at it later?"

"Why not right now?"

"Because right now I'm thinking about all the

ways I need to reprimand you for breaking the first one."

Her mouth goes slack, and her chest rises and falls at her fast intake of breath. "Oh, I see. Don't let me interrupt you, then." She makes a move to go, but stops when I push from my chair.

"Want to get out of here? Go for a drive, get some fresh air?"

"And ice cream?"

That brings a smile to my face. "Sure, we can get ice cream."

"Let's go then."

"I…uh…think you might want to get changed first."

She glances down and laughs. "Good catch."

"Khloe." Christ, I sound like I've just swallowed sand.

"Yeah."

I scrub my face. "You don't have to wear that around here. You can wear whatever you want. Yoga pants. Whatever makes you comfortable."

What are you doing, dude?

Being the goddamn gentleman I should have been from day one.

She blinks up at me. "Really?"

"Yeah"

"But the rules…"

"We can write new rules."

"We could…" She sticks one leg out and her skirt lifts to reveal the garter belt holding up her stocking.

Whoa.

She makes a soft, throaty noise that instantly takes me back to yesterday afternoon, and all the little moans I pulled from her. "I've grown rather fond of these suits, actually."

"Yeah, me, too," I grumble.

"Then it's settled." She straightens, and her beautiful tits jut out. "I'll continue to wear them."

"And I'll continue to be rock hard all day long."

She grins and magically pulls a feather duster out from behind her back. "I think I missed a spot." She bends down, points her ass directly at me, and swipes at some imaginary spot of dust on the baseboard. I have zero control over the hungry growl that crawls out of my throat.

"Sir, is there something wrong?" she asks.

"I just asked if you wanted to get out. Bending over isn't conducive to that plan."

"Oh, I apologize, sir."

My dick thickens. "Actually, since you have that duster in your hand. I think I do have a spot on my desk that needs some attention."

"Of course." She walks across the room, my gaze latched on the sexy sway of her hips. "Oh, yes, I see it right here."

She leans over my desk and concentrates on a spot, all the while gifting me with an up-close view of her gorgeous tits.

I stand, circle the desk and grip her waist. She yelps as I spin her, lift her from the floor and set her ass on my desk. I cup her chin, press my thumb to her lush lips, and since kissing is off the table, I slide my thumb inside her mouth. She sucks on me, and the sweet sensations wrap around my dick. Her legs envelop me, and she pulls me against her until she's pressed against my cock. She's so goddamn hot between her legs, my mouth waters for a taste.

I reach around my back, lock my hands on her ankles and remove her legs. She whimpers, but I step back, take one foot and brace it against my stomach. Her breathing changes as I run my hand along her thigh and unsnap the garter holding up the lace.

"What are you doing, sir?" she asks, and I love the role she's playing.

"We're going out, and you can't go out dressed like this. You're so goddamn sexy it will draw attention, and I like to keep a low profile, as you know."

"I do know."

"I thought I'd help you out of these clothes. That is, if you want me to."

"Oh, I do. I do," she says quickly, and I love her enthusiasm.

I grip the band and slowly roll the lace down, tossing it away. I repeat the motion with the other leg, and step back to admire the woman before me. Her dark eyes are ablaze, her thighs wide.

I'll never look at that desk the same way. I step around her and clear my desk, my hands shaking with need. She's practically quivering when I circle back, widen her legs even further and position myself in between them. I cup her breasts, run my thumbs over her nipples until they're poking through the thin black material. She shivers.

Her hands lift, but I grab her wrists and place them at her sides. "Keep them here. Only I get to touch. That's your punishment."

"Yes...sir."

I unzip her outfit from the back, and it falls to her waist, showcasing those gorgeous full tits.

"Fucking beautiful," I grumble, and give her shoulder a light nudge until she's flat out on my desk, spread wide open, mine for the taking. I push the skirt up, exposing a flimsy pair of lace panties. With the pad of my thumb, I brush her clit through the material, and her whimper curls around me, tugs at my cock.

"Ever been fucked on a desk?" I ask, pretty sure of her answer.

"No."

"You want to be?"

"So much..."

I chuckle at that, and in one fast movement tear the lace from her hips.

"Oh God," she moans.

"So pretty," I say, and bend forward to lick her. Her hips writhe restlessly as her heat reaches out to me. She's so damn responsive, it fucks with me in the strangest ways.

I suck on her clit and slowly slide a finger into her tight channel. She clamps around me. "Look at you, so needy and wet and ready for me."

"Yes…" she murmurs and tosses her head from side to side.

I stroke her until she's whimpering, but I don't make her come. I want to be inside her, to feel her contractions around me. I push my shorts to my knees, and she goes up on her elbows, watching as I tear open a condom.

"I want to do it," she says.

"Yeah?"

"Please, sir."

I take her arm and sit her up. "Make it fast, okay?"

Her teeth dig into her bottom lip as her small hand takes hold of me. Her soft fingers glide over my shaft as she fits me with the rubber, and I curse under my breath.

"That wasn't so hard."

I laugh. "Yeah, not hard at all." I nudge her a little. "Go back on your elbows so you can watch."

Her breath catches, and the excitement in her eyes thrills and infuriates me. I'd like to hunt her ex down and punch him. It pisses me off that he never properly cared for her in the bedroom. Then again, I kind of like it that I'm the guy giving her lessons and letting her explore her body and fantasies. Yeah, I like that a lot, and I want to make this great for her.

I rub my crown over her clit, get it nice and wet. Her moans vibrate through me, and the heated look in her eyes is a thing of beauty. "You like the idea of that, Khloe."

"Yes," she moans. "I want to watch."

I press my head to her opening and give her an inch.

"More," she says.

I give her more and grip her legs. My fingers dig into her lush thighs as I widen them. I thrust forward, sliding deeper.

"Will," she says, "that is so hot."

"Yeah, you got that right," I murmur, a grunt catching in my throat as I clench my teeth. Watching her take every inch of me into her body, watching her watching me…oh yeah, for the rest of our time on this island, this woman is mine. I move, rock into her, my body curling toward hers.

"No visitors, Khloe," I say without thinking.

"What?" she asks, her lids falling closed, ecstasy written all over her face.

"No visitors, for either of us. Just you and me while we're here, okay?" Christ, why would I want to be with anyone else when this beautiful woman has dropped into my lap. The truth is, in the past I've brought a woman to my bed while here, for physical release, but I've lost interest in one-night affairs. This three-week affair, where I'm helping a beautiful woman blossom, that's where it's at.

"Okay," she agrees, and I don't want to think too hard on how happy that makes me.

Her hand slides down her body, and she tentatively strokes her clit. Holy shit. My gaze flashes to hers, and for split second I catch the vulnerability in her eyes, the uncertainty. Everything inside me softens.

"You never touched yourself with your ex, did you?" I ask.

"No," she says.

I slide in and out, and her finger stills. "You like it?"

She nods.

"Then keep doing it, because baby, that is so damn hot."

Her eyes widen a little. "Yeah?"

"Oh, yeah. Do it, Khloe. Rub yourself. Let me watch."

Her finger moves faster, her inhibitions ebbing, and I fuck her the way I think she needs to be fucked. Hard. Fast. Strokes that hit all her hot spots. One of these days I'll go slow, show her the pleasure in a softer touch. But for right now, we fuck.

Her gorgeous tits jiggle with each thrust and her ass slides on the desk. I grip her hips, pull her back to the edge of the desk, and let her rub herself a little more. But I need to touch her, too, so I join her, my fingers mingling with hers as I play with her clit, and her gaze flashes to mine. The admiration in her eyes, the appreciation at what I'm doing, the freedom I'm giving her to explore, messes with me a bit.

She removes her hand, giving me full access, and leans on both elbows. Her head falls back slightly, and I touch her body, learn her likes from her sexy little noises. I change the pressure on her clit, experiment with my touch until I get it just right.

"Like that, just like that," she says, and a second later she's tightening around me, squeezing and milking me as she gives herself over to the pleasure.

"Khloe," I groan, and every muscle in my body tightens as I let go. I feel so goddamn happy it's a little strange. When was the last time I was this happy? I open my eyes to find her staring at me, a smile on her pretty face.

"Wow," she says, and I can't help but laugh. "Sex on the desk wasn't even on my list. Maybe I should get you to make the list."

"I can help you add to it, if you like." I brush a strand of hair from her face and swipe my thumb over her wet bottom lip.

"I like," she says, and we both chuckle. We stay like that for a long time, both basking in the afterglow.

"Come here." I pull out of her, quickly discard the rubber and stand back between her still-open legs. "Let's get you out of this." I tug at the dress bunched around her hips. "It must be cutting off circulation." I peel the outfit over her head. "You made the…?" I begin, but my gaze drops to her beautiful breasts.

"Made the what?" she asks.

"I can't remember what I was going to say." I cup her breasts. "Do you have any idea how beautiful these are?"

"Breast man, are you?" she jokes.

"Khloe, with you I'm every kind of man. Ass, legs, breasts…" Her mouth parts slightly. What would she taste like?

Wait, no. Can't go there. It's in the rule book.

Rule book, right. That's where I was going earlier, until her beautiful breasts sidetracked me.

"Did you make your list already?"

"Yesterday, after we had sex."

I shake my head. "I like a girl who gets right at her tasks."

"I thought you might."

"Oh, you think you know me now, do you?" I say.

"I watch, learn, listen."

While I like to keep a measure of distance from, well, everyone, I'm not as upset as I should be, normally would be, to know she's been observing.

"So do I," I say.

"I like the way you watch, learn and listen," she says in a teasing voice.

"How about tonight I take a look at your list, see if you missed anything?"

She runs her hand over the top of my desk. "I'm guessing I did." Her grin is slow, seductive. "What other tricks do you have up your sleeve?"

"We have lots of time for me to show you," I say, and make a mental note to talk to Vin before we leave the house.

CHAPTER ELEVEN

Khloe

MY BODY IS blissfully sore, my mind still a bit woozy from that glorious climax, but I'm not complaining. I loved every minute of it. I stretch out my legs in the passenger seat as Will drives us to town. The windows are down, and I breathe in all the fragrant scents from the local foliage and blossoming flowers. I slowly turn my head his way, take in his freshly shaven face. It's late morning, and he's dressed in cargo shorts and a T-shirt. He suggested I dress in casual clothes and wear comfortable footwear, yet he never said where we were going. Not that I care. I'd go bungee jumping if it meant getting away from that mutinous vacuum cleaner.

I sigh contentedly and rest my head against the leather seat. It's odd how comfortable I am with Will after such a short time. Yeah, okay, so he's an asshole. At least, according to Steph. Although, outside of scolding me for my appearance and tardiness, he's been pretty decent. But of course, I can't forget he admitted he's a cheater. And when it comes right down to it, I don't *really* know him. It's possible he only took care of me when I was sick because his granddad would kill him otherwise.

Do you really believe that, Khloe?

I'm not sure. He did ask me to be exclusive for the next few weeks. I said yes in the heat of the moment, but do I expect him to keep it in his pants? Not really, and I don't care one way or the other. I have no ownership over him, and vice versa. We're just having fun. Things will go back to normal when we return home.

"We're a long way from New York," I say, pulling my phone from my bag to shoot a picture, then send it off to Steph. After I'd left James's mansion, I texted her to tell her about the job. She was both thrilled and worried for me, but I assured her I could handle any entitled millionaire. And handle him I did. I snicker quietly.

Will's hand slides across the seat and gives mine a squeeze, and I turn my attention to him as he drives.

"What are you doing?"

"Sending a picture to my best friend."

"Khloe, no one is supposed to know you're here in Saint Thomas."

As his brow furrows, panic invades my gut. Shit, I'd forgotten all about that in the nondisclosure agreement. I wasn't supposed to give away the location. There's nothing I can do to get the picture back.

"I'm sorry, Will. She's trustworthy. She won't tell anyone." Worry creeps into his eyes, and a chill goes up my spine.

"I understand that, but things have a way of getting out."

He's not wrong about that. "Am I fired?"

He winks at me. "Not this time, okay. But if you break the rules again…"

There's a teasing note in his voice, but beneath it I understand he's serious. His life had been put under a microscope, and it was a horrible invasion of privacy that resulted in a lot of loss. Yes, he did something wrong, but was it the world's place to dissect and judge? No. It was no one's business but his and Naomi's. It's certainly none of mine.

"It won't happen again, I promise. And I'll tell her not to share my location."

"You're sure she's trustworthy?"

"Yes, best person I know. You'd like her a lot. Not that you'll ever meet her. I'm just saying—"

The jerk of his chin cuts off my rambling. "Look."

Up ahead I see two gigantic cruise ships in dock. I sit up a little straighter.

"My God, those are magnificent. Look at the size of them. How do they even float?"

"They float because the gravitational force is less than the buoyancy of the upward force."

"Ah, okay. I'll have to take your word for it. I was an English major. If you want to know how to fix a dangling modifier, I'm your girl."

He chuckles. "I'll be sure to remember that. Have you ever been on a cruise?" he asks.

I shake my head, and a few loose tendrils fall from my ponytail and slide down my neck. His eyes follow, and the hairs on my nape tingle under their appreciation.

"Nope, never even been out on a sailboat," I say.

"Let me guess, motion sickness."

I crinkle my nose at him. "Funny, and no," I say, and in that instant, I realize how different we truly are. But I'm not about to bring up that I had only the basic necessities in life, and unlike the people in his social circle, I never went on elaborate trips, flew in private planes, sailed in fancy boats and cared only about getting richer—no matter who got hurt in the process. I'm not resentful that I never had material things. Hell, I'm a strong, independent woman because of it, and I like who I am. Instead I say, "The opportunity just never presented itself."

He arches a brow. "You know I have a sailboat, right?" He points downward. "Right here on Saint Thomas."

"How would I know that?" I ask, even though I'm not one bit surprised. The man has everything he wants. Well, except for a wife. Does he still want that? My guess would be no, considering the lifestyle he lives.

He follows the winding road. "I guess you wouldn't."

"No one knows anything about you, Will. You take privacy to the extreme."

"You know why that is, right?"

"Yeah," I say, a measure of guilt worming its way through me. I consider the front cover spread again. Yes, Benjamin insists we sensationalize. But the fact is, Will was caught with his hand in the cookie jar, so to speak. It seems out of character for him, though.

"I'm sorry about Naomi," I say.

"I'm sorry I hurt her, too, but she deserves better than me."

"Are you…" Ugh, how can I word this?

"Still in love with her?" he asks.

"Yeah."

"I'll always love her, Khloe." He casts a quick glance my way, his blue eyes showcasing pain and regret. "We had something great. I ruined it, and something like that doesn't come along every day."

I stiffen at that admission, jealousy zinging through me. What the hell? No way should I be feeling anything other than sadness for this whole situation.

"Maybe something better will come along." Not that he'd ever know. He's locked up tight and not about to open himself to love.

He grunts a response.

"Do you still keep in contact?"

He runs agitated fingers through his dark hair. "No, and I don't read the tabloids, either, but the last I heard she was in Milan and seeing some guy there. I have no idea if it's serious or not, but I want her to be happy."

I'm totally shocked by his maturity. He loves the woman yet wants her to find happiness with another man. Not quite the asshole everyone says he is…but the pictures. I press my hand over my stomach as it takes that moment to tighten, and I make a mental note to do a little research of my own.

"Where are we going?" I ask.

"I need to stop at Granddad's resort."

"James has a resort here? I knew about the one in Saint Moritz because he showed me pictures of Megan and Alec's wedding, like I mentioned. Actually he showed me a picture of you at the wedding."

"Why did he do that?"

"I guess he wanted to show me the ogre I would be working for."

"Ogre, Khloe. Really? Do you want to go talk about how I took care of you when you were pro—"

"Okay, not an ogre," I say, laughing. "Tell me about James's resort."

"It's called Great Bay Resort. I think he bought it because the first time we came here, I fell in love with the place. Granddad's like that. And he's always been there when we needed him." He chuckles, staring into the distance like he's remembering happier times.

"What's so funny?"

"I'm just thinking back to when he told Tate he wanted to gift half of his million-dollar estate to

Summer Love. And Tate thought she was a con art-ist out to steal millions from him, so he flew to Saint Moritz to take her down." He chuckles again. "She took him down instead."

"What do you mean?"

"He fell in love with her. Sometimes I think Granddad orchestrated the whole thing, but other times I realize he's in his nineties and probably couldn't pull off a scheme like that even if he had a team working for him."

You're perfect for Will.

For a moment, James's words ping around inside my brain. During our meeting he seemed so lucid at times; other times, I thought he was dozing off. Is it possible that he was trying to find a wife for his grandson? No. The man barely knows me. What would make him think I was perfect for his grand-son? He wouldn't, simple as that.

"That's a great story, Will. So romantic."

He makes a noise—a half laugh, half groan. "It's crazy how it all played out, if you ask me."

We pull up to the resort, and my eyes go wide to take in the opulence. "It's beautiful."

"It was practically destroyed in the hurricane."

"The damage and loss broke my heart when I heard about it on the news. So much devastation."

"You remember Bevey?"

"How could I forget her?"

He chuckles again. "She's head chef at Granddad's resort. Her husband, Samuel, was injured in the hurricane."

"I'm so sorry to hear that."

"Her daughter's school was destroyed, too. The kids are in an old school that's been waterlogged. It's dirty and mold-ridden. Not healthy for them at all."

"My God, I had no idea. I wish I could help out some way," I say. "I don't really have anything to offer, though."

He casts me a quick glance, and I can't quite figure out his expression. He drives under a roofed-in area, pulling up in front of the grand resort.

"It's even more amazing up close." I examine the sprawling resort painted in bright yellow, orange and blue. Each room has a balcony overlooking the emerald waters.

"How come you don't stay here when you visit?" He arches a brow and reaches for his door handle. "Right, privacy," I say, answering my own question. "This doesn't look like it was destroyed by the hurricane."

"We rebuilt quickly."

"I'd imagine that really cut into the bottom line," I say under my breath.

He opens his mouth to speak, but the valet steps up to the driver's side.

"Good morning, Mr. Will."

Will smiles at the valet and turns back to me. "I have some things to take care of. Do you want to wander around, check out the pool and gardens?"

"Sure, but I thought you said we were getting ice cream."

"We are, soon."

Will opens his door, and the valet gives him a big smile. "Mr. Will, it's so good to see you."

Will shakes the man's hand. "Anthony, my friend. It's been too long. How is Hannah?"

He sticks his stomach out. "Another little one on the way," he says, his big brown eyes beaming.

"Congratulations. Is Hannah well this time?"

He holds his hand out flat and wavers it a little bit. "Just slight morning sickness. Not like last time."

"No hyperemesis, then?"

"No, thankfully."

"Glad to hear it."

I stand there and listen to the exchange. Not only does Will know the valet, he appears to know his wife and the circumstances surrounding her last birth. I'm beginning to believe there is more to this man than meets the eyes.

Will looks my way. "Anthony, this is my assistant, Khloe. Khloe, if you need anything at all, Anthony is your man. You can trust him to help you." Anthony appears to grow two inches taller at Will's compliment. I exchange pleasantries with Anthony, and Will hands his keys over. He circles the front of the vehicle, puts his palm on the small of my back, and leans in. "I'll only need about thirty minutes, I think. I have some staffing issues that need my attention."

"Who are you firing?"

He shakes his head. "I love the high opinion you have of me." Before I can say anything, he holds out his hand. "Pass me your phone?"

I reach into my purse. "What do you want my phone for?"

"I'm going to put my number in, call myself, and then I'll have yours."

He takes my phone, puts his contact in and a second later his rings. "Don't venture off the resort, okay?"

"Why?" I shoot a glance over my shoulder. "Is it dangerous?"

"It's safe enough, but easy to get lost. Although I'm pretty sure you can handle yourself," he says with a smirk.

"You know I can." He gives me a nudge and the double glass doors open, inviting us into the posh lobby. I glance around, take in the buttery yellow sofas, the chandeliers, the curving staircase that leads to a restaurant on the next level.

"Through those back doors, you'll find the garden, the pool and the bar. Grab yourself a drink. Charge it to me."

"I can buy my own drink," I say, and frown as I recall the meager amount of money at the bottom of my purse.

"You're my guest, Khloe." His blue eyes narrow, go serious. "You'll charge it to me."

"You're kind of bossy."

"Which is why you call me sir," he says, but the

heat behind that one word fills me with luscious memories.

My gaze travels back and meets his. "Right, thanks for the reminder, sir," I tease, and I'm rewarded with a groan. With an extra little shake of my ass, I head toward the back door, not bothering to glance over my shoulder. My cell pings. I lift it and read the text from Will.

Will: You're going to pay for that.

Khloe: Looking forward to it.

His growl follows me outside, and the sound is muted as the double doors close behind me. In the courtyard, men, women and children lounge at the pool. There are a few people sitting at the bar, nursing things that look quite refreshing. The fragrant foliage fills my senses as I walk the brick path to the outside bar. I slide onto one of the stools, and the bartender comes right over. He looks to be in his midthirties, a light beard covering his jaw. He's handsome, but let's face it, he's not Will Carson handsome. Few, if any, are.

"I'd like something fruity and refreshing," I say, and tap my chin as I look past his shoulders at the chalk menu listing the drinks.

"Strawberry daiquiri?" he suggests.

"Perfect." The man two stools over picks up his icy beer and begins to spin my way. "Oh, and please put it on Will Carson's tab. I'm his assistant," I add, as per Will's request. The man does an about-face, sets his drink back down and stares into the glass like it holds all the answers to the universe.

Wow, it's almost like the simple mention of Will invokes fear in others. Maybe he actually is an ogre to the staff working here. In all seriousness, he's been nothing but a perfect gentleman to me. Well, okay, maybe that's pushing it. Other than ensuring I'm having a good time and climax first, he's no gentleman between the sheets. But I wouldn't want it any other way.

I pick up my drink and wander around, taking time to smell the flowers and smile at the child laughing in the pool. The longing pulsing through my body doesn't go unnoticed. Here I used to think Liam and I would marry and have a family of our own. Now I'm convinced there is no right man out there for me. And that's okay. I don't need a man to make me happy. Kids? Well, if I do decide to have them someday, there's always in vitro.

The warm sun beats down on me as I meander through the gardens, greeting guests and staff. My phone pings and I grab it.

Will: All done. Meet me out front? Let's go get you that ice cream.

Khloe: On my way.

I tuck my phone back into my purse, take my empty glass back to the bar and head toward the front of the resort. Will is leaning against his car talking to Anthony. I don't want to interrupt, so I open my door. Will turns at the sound, and a smile touches his mouth, like he's extremely happy to see me. Weird thing is, my heart is speeding up a little, too.

"Hey," he says turning to me. "Did you get a drink? Enjoy a walk?"

I nod. "Did you get your staffing situation straightened out?"

He nods, says something to Anthony and slides into the car. I drop into the passenger seat next to him.

The drive is a short one, and the next thing I know he's parking on a street.

"Where are we?"

"Historic downtown. Have you heard of the ninety-nine steps at Charlotte Amalie?"

"I've been busy wrestling a vacuum into submission, so I haven't had time to do much research."

That brings a smile to his face. "Well, you're about to get a firsthand look, and I'm going to race you to the top."

"So this is why you told me to wear comfortable footwear."

"Yup." He unbuckles and slips from the car.

I do the same, and the heat beats down on me. "I am not running up ninety-nine steps, Will. I'll die."

"It's fun, trust me."

"Trust you? I don't trust anyone, remember?"

He briefly looks past my shoulders, his smile faltering. "First one to the top wins."

"Wins what? A drive to the hospital in an ambulance, or worse, to a funeral home?"

He laughs out loud, circles the car and steps close to me, very close. His warm breath feathers over my face.

I plant one hand on my hip. "I thought we were getting ice cream."

"You can have ice cream and anything else you want. If you beat me."

I spin around and glance up and down the busy street. A man with a cart full of coconuts stops to hack the top off one with a huge knife and hands it over to a customer, who dips a straw inside. I make a mental note to try one. Then I see the brick stairs. My gaze goes from the bottom to the very top.

"That looks like a lot more than ninety-nine steps to me."

"Only by four. They added some cement steps."

I eye Will. "You've done this before, right?"

He rolls one shoulder. "Sure, numerous times."

"Okay, since you have an advantage, I get a head start."

He thinks about it for a second. "Fair enough."

"You have to count to ten before you can start up."

We walk toward the stairs, our knuckles brushing innocently, but damned if it doesn't send shock waves straight down my body. Maybe the rush of adrenaline will help me beat him. We reach the bottom step, and I glance up to see the green wooden rail on the right, and foliage popping with bright purple flowers on either side of the steps.

"It doesn't look so bad up close."

His mouth is close to my ear when he says, "It's not."

"What does the winner get?"

"Whatever they want."

I take a second to think about what I want. But the vision of myself living happily ever after in a cozy house with a family, writing articles I want to write, is a dream not even Will, a man with all the resources in the world, could fulfill.

"Go," he says.

"What?"

"One, two..."

"Oh, shit," I say, and dart up the stairs. Will is laughing from the bottom. "Count slow," I yell, but when I look back he's already closing the gap between us. I start laughing so hard I can barely climb, but I'm competitive, and clearly Will is, too. I pick up the pace and hurry onward.

I push harder, but his long, strong legs have no trouble reaching me. His breath is hot on my neck, and I do everything to block his way. I spread my arms, but he grabs me by the waist, picks me up and spins me until I'm behind him.

"That's cheating!" I yell at his back, but my gaze quickly drops to his ass as he easily negotiates the steps. I reach the top, panting like a Newfoundland dog…in Hawaii. Will doesn't appear winded at all. Jerk.

"I won," he says.

"You cheated."

He takes my hand, leads me through a crowd I hadn't noticed from the base of the stairs, and my breath catches when I see the spectacular view below.

I turn to see Will's reaction to the view, but it's me he's looking at. I swipe at my damp forehead. I must look a mess, but from the appreciation in his eyes, you wouldn't know it.

"Fine, you won. But I want a rematch after I get in shape."

"You're in great shape, Khloe," he says, and despite the crowd of tourists at the top, all standing by the rail taking pictures of the most breathtaking view of Saint Thomas, he comes close and puts his hands on my curves. For a private guy, this public display of affection surprises me. Then again, the place is full of tourists who don't know either of us.

"Want to know what I want?"

CHAPTER TWELVE

Will

"WHAT DO YOU WANT, Will?"

I open my mouth, about to tell her how I plan to take her tonight, when my pants start pulsating. She glances down, arches a brow.

"Ah, you're vibrating down there," she says, and grins at me. "Maybe instead of asking you what you want, I should be asking what kind of kinky things you're into." Her voice is playful, and if we weren't in public, I'd strip her bare and show her exactly how kinky I like it.

I grin. "Since I won, you'll soon find out."

A visible shiver moves through her as I pull my phone from my pocket. I hope it's Granddad. When I see it's Alec, I frown.

"Hey, bro, what's up?" I ask.

"Not much. Just wondering how things are going in Saint Thomas."

Why the hell is everyone calling and checking in on me?

"Since when do you call me when I'm here?"

"Never. Just missing my big bro is all." My gaze slides to Khloe, who is wiping her brow with the back of her hand. Her big eyes are full of awe and wonder as she steps away to give me privacy and takes in the view below.

"Have you been talking to Granddad?" I ask.

"Yeah, I was with him yesterday. Brianna is back from Italy. She was hoping to see you. Megan wants to have a big family barbecue."

Shit, it's been months since I've seen my cousin and her husband. "How long is she home for?"

"Just a couple weeks."

A thread of worry weasels its way down my spine. There was no talk of Brianna coming home. Is her marriage breaking up? "Is she...okay?"

"Why wouldn't she be okay?"

I step away from the chatter of the crowd and lean against a tall tree. "If she's back suddenly and Luca isn't with her..."

"That's where your mind goes?" Alec asks. "Straight to divorce?"

"You know we've seen a lot of it."

"We're a new generation, Will," he says, his voice full of conviction.

I snort. "Yeah, well, tell that to Naomi."

"She was never right for you anyway."

"Alec—" I begin.

"Listen, Luca is flying in next week. He had some work commitments. So you see, they're still happily married like the rest of us, and we're hoping for a big family reunion."

I don't miss the dig. "I probably won't be back in time."

"You could come home early." I let my eyes travel Khloe's length, admiring her curves in her V-neck T-shirt and the shorts that show off her curvy ass and hips. I suppose I could cut this trip short, but do I want to? "I'm ah, not sure that's possible."

Alec snickers. "Yeah, that's what I thought."

"What are you talking about?"

"Work comes first over everything for you," he says, humor gone from his voice.

"You're one to talk."

"Priorities change when you're married. You'll see."

"No, I won't see, and we're not having this conversation again." Why the hell can't they all just leave me alone? I'm married to my job now, and I'm content. Happy.

I'm also having the best sex of my life with Khloe.

"Come on…" Alec goads. "Humor me. You, of all of us, wanted to get married."

"Things have changed," I say. "When you see Granddad can you please ask him to call me? Also ask him to check the staffing agency. Leonard El-

ementary needs English teachers. Surely there must
be one unemployed teacher on the list."

"Will do, bro."

I end the call and step up to Khloe, my chest to
her back. She leans against me.

"Hey, are you okay?"

"Fine, why?"

She turns and presses her hand over my heart.
"It's beating a little fast."

I shake my phone before shoving it into my
pocket. "My brother."

"You two get in a fight?"

Not really wanting to get into it, I hedge with,
"Something like that."

"I always wanted siblings," she says quietly, a look
of longing in her dark eyes.

"You can have mine." I snort. "My brother and my
cousin and his wife are driving me crazy."

"I love that you're all so close."

"You'd love them, Khloe. I think you'd really hit
it off with Summer." I laugh.

"What's so funny?"

"After Summer had Jules, she lost all her filters.
She tells it like it is."

"Then I probably would like her."

"She told me I needed to get you out of the house
today, that you deserved to do something fun for
having to put up with me."

"You have been doing something fun for me."

I grin. "Yeah, it has been fun." I put my hand

around her waist and lead her back to the stairs. We descend slowly, and she runs her hand along the wooden rail. But my grin turns to a frown as I go over my conversation with my brother. Khloe studies me, concern etched in her eyes.

"Are you sure you're okay?"

"Yeah, it's just. Alec and Tate and even Summer are on me about getting married."

"Ah, I see."

"I don't need a wife to make me happy."

"Just like I don't need a husband," she says.

I eye her. "Do you still love him?"

"My ex, you mean?" I nod, and she exhales.

"No, I don't. I'm glad I woke up before I found myself in a controlling marriage."

"But someday you'd like to get married?"

She gives me a very unladylike snort, and it makes me smile. I like that she's herself around me, doesn't pretend to be something or someone else. I'm used to pretense from the women in my circle, especially the ones looking to marry up. It's hard to know who's real and who isn't. I appreciate Khloe's honesty.

"I've given up on the idea. Besides, right now, after my last job, I need to concentrate on me."

I give her a nudge. "Maybe while you're here, you can write that book you talked about."

"I would." She pauses and gives me a seductive smile. "But I think my boss is about to start keeping me up late at night. He's an ogre, you know."

I laugh, the tightness in my chest easing a bit, as we talk openly. I'm not usually like this with women. But she's not any woman, is she? She's open and real, and I kind of like that we have this easy banter. I chuckle inwardly. Christ, with the ease she can get things out of people, she'd make a good reporter.

"You know, I have a lot of connections in the publishing ind—"

She holds her hand up to stop me. "Will, I appreciate that but—"

"But you need to do everything on your own."

She nods. "I want to get there on my own merit, you know. I want the validation that I can do it."

"I understand." Her dark eyes are serious as they move over my face, like she's not sure if I really can understand. "I get it, Khloe. Sometimes, though, it's okay to get by with a little help from a friend."

She smiles. "Is that what we are?"

"Friends?" I nod. "Yeah, I like that. I like the idea of us being friends."

"With benefits," she says, and nudges me.

"I like that, too," I say, and laugh. "Come on, let's get that ice cream, and I have one more stop to make before I take you home and have my way with you."

We go down the rest of the stairs, the noonday sun beating on us. We find an ice cream stand and both get double scoops. A few minutes later, we're in the car, headed to the middle school. We finish our cones as I drive.

"Where are we?" Khloe asks, as she takes in the old school and the new one in construction behind it.

"This is where Bevey's daughter goes."

"Oh, you wanted to say hi to her?"

"Something like that." I look into a field where the kids are seated at picnic tables. "Do you want to wait here?"

"No, I'll come."

We slide from our seats and walk toward the kids, who are all dressed in the same uniforms and eating boxed lunches. When they see me, they jump up and run our way.

"Whoa," Khloe says, as they huddle around me. "I guess you're well known here."

"Kids, kids," Amelia says, and claps her hands. "Come finish your lunches." After a few grumbles the kids all file back to their seats.

Khloe casts me a curious look. "Aren't you popular?"

"I have a way with kids," is all I say.

"Uncle Will. Uncle Will," Chardane says, and waves me over.

"Come meet Bevey's daughter."

"She calls you Uncle Will?"

"I've known her since she was born." Khloe follows me across the sunburned grass, and I note all the girls at the table are coloring as they eat their sandwiches. I go down on one knee to talk to Chardane. She gives me a hug, and I introduce her to Khloe.

"Is she your girlfriend?" Chardane teases in her

childlike voice. All the girls around the table chime in and rib me about my "girlfriend."

"She's my friend," I assure them.

"Good, because Chardane wants to marry you," one of the girls says.

Chardane turns red and glares at her friend. "Annie!" she cries out. "That was a secret."

Beside me, Khloe is muffling a laugh, and I catch Amelia's eye as she looks on with concern. I scrub my hand over Chardane's head.

"I'm an old ogre," I say. "Just ask Khloe." I look past Chardane's shoulders. "Besides, I think that boy two tables over might like you." Chardane spins and then makes a face.

"Chad is a butthead."

"And he picks his nose," the girl to Chardane's right adds.

I laugh at that and stand. "I need to go talk to your teacher. Will you girls take care of Khloe for me?"

They snuggle together to give Khloe room on the bench. "Will you be okay for a minute?"

"Coloring is my favorite pastime."

I walk with Amelia until we're out of earshot.

"It's good to see you, Will." Amelia pushes her thick dark hair from her shoulders, her brown eyes full of concern.

"You, too. How are things?"

"Overcrowded classrooms and overworked teachers."

"I'm waiting to talk to Granddad, to see if he can

find someone at the staffing agency that can take the position."

"Even one more teacher will make a difference," she says.

"No sicknesses, with the mold?"

"We keep the window open and the school ventilated. The new school will be ready before the rainy months, and we have you to thank for that."

"You don't have to thank me. It's the least I could do."

She looks beyond me, and I follow her gaze to see Khloe laughing with the kids. It brings a smile to my face.

"Bevey told me you had a new friend. That her?" She fiddles with the bright pink scarf around her neck, lifting it over her head to block the sun.

I laugh. "Oh, is that how she put it? And yes, that's Khloe."

"Bevey is just happy to see you enjoying more than work."

"Why is my love life suddenly everyone's concern?"

"It's not right for a man to be alone."

"I'm fine alone, and Khloe is nothing more than my assistant."

Who I sleep with.

"Uh-huh," she says, and I shake my head, letting it go.

"I need to speak with the foreman." I nod toward the new schoolhouse.

"You go. I'll take good care of your assistant until you get back."

"Amelia," I warn, and she laughs and brushes me off. I head to the new school and stand back to take in the progress.

"Will." I turn at the sound of Lyron's voice. I extend my arm and his big palm closes around mine, squeezes with a firm handshake.

"Lyron, my friend. It's good to see you."

Lyron takes off his ball cap and uses his arm to wipe away the moisture on his forehead. "She's coming along good, no?" he says, his accent much like Bevey's. "Right on schedule."

"That's good to know. The sooner we get those kids out of that old school the better."

He shakes his head. "Not healthy at all."

"How's the family?" I ask.

"Raeni is no longer coughing, now that we've moved into the new housing complex. Clean running water and no mold. It's heaven."

I put my hand on his back. "Glad to hear it."

"How is your family?" he asks in return.

"Doing well. Granddad is still as stubborn as ever." I wink.

"And a wife for you?" he asks. I just shake my head.

"I can't get away from it," I say, and he laughs.

"It's not natural, Will," he says.

"You've clearly been talking to Bevey."

He whistles innocently. "Come, I'll show you through."

I follow him into the building, and I'm pleased to see how fast it's come together. After the inspection, I bid him a farewell and make my way back to the girls.

My girl.

Whoa, where did that come from?

Khloe glances up when I block the sun from her table. Her eyes are alive, full of happiness.

"You really do like coloring," I say, and she sets her crayon down.

"The girls were just telling me a funny story about the time you went scuba diving and panicked when you thought you saw a shark, but it turned out to be a sea lion." The girls all laugh again, and Khloe joins in.

"My goggles were foggy."

"Sure," Khloe teases.

I shake my head, defeated. "I'm going to have to have a talk with your mother, Chardane." I say, and she just grins up at me. "No more talking about me." I turn to Khloe. "And you...didn't you have your own incident where you thought you encountered a shark?"

Khloe stands. "All righty then," she says quickly, a grin playing on her mouth. "Thanks for letting me color with you, girls."

I put my arm on the small of Khloe's back, and we head back to the car. "Sweet kids," she says. "I'm glad they're getting a new school."

"Now we just need to find teachers to fill the classrooms."

"There's a shortage?"

I nod. "I've been trying to get a hold of Granddad, to check the staffing agency for qualified English teachers."

"Will," she says quickly, and touches my arm to stop me.

"What?"

I turn toward her. "I can help out. I have an English degree, remember?"

"Yeah, I remember." I stare at her for a moment, and see nothing but open honesty on her face.

An odd lump settles into my throat. "Are you serious, Khloe?"

Her eyes widen like she's excited by the opportunity. "Very serious." But then her demeanor changes, her enthusiasm waning, and she frowns. "Oh, but wait. I already have a job here."

"Well, so far you're pretty shitty at it," I tease.

"Hey," she says, feigning offense. A second later a grin pulls at her lush lips. "Okay, well, maybe you are right. But your granddad—" She stops talking, like she's about to say too much.

I frown and narrow my eyes. "What about him?"

"I don't want to let him down."

"Okay, so maybe you can't cook, and you break things, but he is going to lose his mind when he hears you're going to help out in the classroom."

"I think he's already lost his mind," she says.

"You're probably right."

Her teeth dig into her bottom lip, and it draws my attention. Once again, I can't help but wonder how her lush mouth would taste. "Would you mind? I could work around what you need."

"You could take a few hours in the afternoon to help while you're here. If that's what you really want."

"I do," she says, a new purpose about her. I start the car and can't help but feel this woman is too good to be true.

Could I be right?

CHAPTER THIRTEEN

Khloe

I STEAL A glance at Will as we drive back to his villa, feeling excited. I've never taught school before, but at least I'll now be doing something useful. I study the man who has given me this opportunity—he has a strange, unreadable look on his face.

"Hey," I say.

He smiles. "What?"

"You never told me what you wanted for winning the race." I lift my chin. "Although I do want a rematch."

His hand slides across the seat, and there is a new kind of tenderness, a mellowness in him I've not seen before.

"How about I show you instead."

"Ooh, I like the sound of that," I say, as the heat from his hand seeps under my skin and arouses my body.

"There's a festival coming up. Have you heard anything about it?" he asks.

"No, what's it about?"

"It's a cultural fair with a mix of food, drink, plants. Things like that. It's a fundraiser for the church and schools. They play traditional games, and nightly performances by schools and organizations display various aspects of Virgin Islands traditions and culture."

"That sounds like fun."

"We should go."

I eye him carefully. "As long as it's not a date. Rule number three."

He frowns at me. "I know the rules. And it's not a date. I just thought since we both want to go, and we're going in the same direction, we might as well go together."

"Good. Then okay, let's go." He looks ahead as he navigates a turn, and my gaze settles on his mouth. Why, again, did I say no kissing?

Because it's too personal.

Yeah, maybe, but damned if I don't want to feel his lips on mine. They've been pretty magnificent on other parts of my body.

I sink back into my seat and enjoy the scenery as we make our way home. I'm a little sleepy by the time we reach Will's villa. But I sit up straight when I see a big truck pulling out of his driveway and a man standing on the path waving the driver off.

"What's going on? Who is that?" I take in the stocky man dressed in long white pants and a long white shirt that contrast with his dark hair and skin.

"Right, you haven't met Vin yet."

"Vin?"

"He's the caretaker when I'm not here. He was overseeing a job for me today while we were gone."

The mischievous smirk on Will's face raises my curiosity. "What kind of job?"

"Oh, just a little something I thought you'd like."

I frown at him. "What have you done?"

"You'll see."

I give him a warning glare, but he just laughs and exits the car. I hop from the passenger side, and Vin comes to greet us.

"Vin, meet Khloe. She's my new assistant."

"Nice to meet you, Khloe."

"You, too," I say, and shake his outstretched hand, noting the warmth about him. Most people here on the island are so laid-back and welcoming.

"Everything is in order?" Will asks.

"Exactly as you asked," Vin answers.

"Excellent," Will says, and puts his arm on my back to lead me inside.

"What is going on?" I demand when we're alone.

"Come with me and find out."

He guides me down the long hall into his bedroom, and when I step inside a gasp climbs out of my throat.

"No. Way."

Incredulous, I spin to face Will, my cheeks flaring hot.

He arches a brow at my reaction. "You don't like it?"

"Vin," I begin. "He knows." I cover my face with my hands. "This is so embarrassing."

Will chuckles, puts his arms around me and backs me up until we're standing in front of the huge floor-to-ceiling mirror he had installed beside his bed. "Don't be embarrassed."

For some reason, with Will I have no problem being open. But maybe deep down I'm still scarred from my ex, still shy and embarrassed about my needs. "What must he think?"

"That we're adults, doing what adults do. I'm pretty sure he's not judging, Khloe. Even if he is, so what?"

As his words sink in, my hands drop from my face. *Fuck you, Liam.* "You're right, Will. I'm a grown woman, single, and what I do is no one's business but my own. No one has any right to judge me."

"Especially your asshole ex," he says, and that's when I get that he really understands me and where I'm coming from. I'm a little—okay a lot—touched by his insight and what he's trying to do here. My heart beats just a little faster.

Careful, Khloe. You don't want to start feeling things for this man.

"Especially him," I say.

He brushes his knuckles over my cheeks, and the touch is so tender and sweet my pounding heart races just a little faster. Dammit.

"I only hire trustworthy people. People who respect my privacy. What we do here stays here."

"Did he have to sign a nondisclosure agreement, too?" I tease.

He gives me a lopsided grin. "What, did you think you were special?"

He's joking. I get it, so I shouldn't feel like I've just been slapped in the face. I freaking hate that I do. But in all seriousness, his words are a good reminder that what's between us is sex, and I'd be wise to remember that. But everything from the way he cared for me to the fun we've been having—even running the stairs and getting ice cream together— makes it a little hard to keep my head on straight. Is it any wonder women throw themselves at him?

"Well, good. Because I don't want the world to know my business, especially in the bedroom."

He cringes. "That makes two of us."

I soften. "I'm so sorry that happened to you."

"You know what I'd rather talk about?" he says, and repositions me until I'm looking at myself in the mirror.

Light shines in through the open curtains and slants off the wall, lighting up our bodies as we admire each other in the mirror. "I think I might know."

He walks around me, his fingers lightly touching my stomach, hips and back as he circles. I let loose a feathery breath, my legs a little shaky. I have to say, I'm a bit surprised that he went to the trouble of installing a mirror so I could get the full experience, see exactly what we're doing to each other. There's a thoughtful side to Will. Have reporters been judging him too harshly?

He was caught on camera, Khloe.

But it had never sat right with me before, and after spending time with him, even less so.

I can't think about that right now, though. Not when he's gripping the hem of my T-shirt and running rough knuckles over my flesh.

"Hands up," he commands, and grins when I physically react to the direct order.

I lift, and he ever so slowly peels my shirt over my head, tossing it onto the bed. I wet my lips, and his gaze drops from my mouth to my breasts, which are cresting over the top of my bra, almost like they're eager for his touch, his tongue.

He cups them, weighs them in his hands. "I'm going to fuck these," he says with conviction, and a moan catches in my throat. He meets my eyes. "I'm going to fuck you everywhere. That's what I want for winning." He waits for me to react, and I nod. "You want that, don't you? You want to figure out what you like and what you don't."

"Will, I'm pretty sure I'm going to like everything you do to me."

That brings a smile to his face. He steps closer, slides his hands around my back and unhooks my bra. He tosses it away and stands beside me. We both look at my half-naked body in the mirror.

"So beautiful," he says, and I appreciate that he loves my curves.

"When you look at me like that, Will," I say, wanting to be completely honest with him, "it truly makes me feel beautiful."

"Good, because there are two things I want you to feel when you're with me. One is beautiful…" He steps behind me, and his hard cock presses against my back as he slides his big hands around my body and palms my breasts. His thumbs brush my nipples, and as they harden even more, his low groan reverberates through me.

"From the moment you stepped onto the plane, I haven't been able to stop thinking about these. Then… Jesus, Khloe…then when I saw you in that sexy French maid outfit, I knew I was a goner, knew I'd have to have you or risk a bad case of blue balls for the duration of our stay."

"I wasn't going to wear it. I mean, of all the things to make your—" My words fall off when one hand leaves my breasts and dips into my shorts. His finger finds my swollen clit and brushes lightly. "Will," I moan. "That feels so good."

"Yeah, and this is the second thing I want you to feel when you're with me."

"I like those rules," I say as he slides a thick finger into my body. My head falls back, rests against his shoulder, and he puts his mouth to my ear.

"Take your shorts down, Khloe, and look in the mirror. Watch me touch you."

I grip the button on my shorts, rip it open, and bend forward slightly to shove them down my legs. My ass connects with Will's cock, and his groan turns me into a tease. I stay bent, like I'm having trouble with my shorts. But what I'm really doing is wiggling my ass against him. His groans grow louder when he clues in.

"You're such a tease."

"Who, me?" I say, and blink my lashes at him in the mirror. He backs up an inch and gives my ass a whack. I jump, secretly delighted by the sting left behind.

"Now watch," he orders, and puts his finger inside me. I spread my legs, catching his eyes in the mirror before my gaze drops to his hand. I move my hips, grind against his palm and moan without care. I love what this man is doing to me, the way he's freeing me and taking me to new heights as I get to watch it all.

"Like that, baby?" he asks, his breath hot on the shell of my ear.

"You know I do," I say, and cup my breasts. I pinch my nipples.

"Yeah, like that," he says. His lips slide over my skin, and he buries his mouth in the crook of my neck, kissing softly as he slides a second finger into me.

"God, yes," I groan. My hips move faster, and his fingers go deeper, stroking the hot bundle of nerves inside me. I can barely catch my breath as I take in the action in the mirror. I swear to God this is the hottest thing I've ever seen.

"Like what you see?" he asks, his breathing a little rough, too.

"I'm so close, Will," I cry out, my body quivering, all sensations centered between my legs, where his deft fingers are about to make me come.

"Take what you need, baby," he says, and my body lets go. I gasp, and he puts one hand around my waist to hold me upright. "I got you," he murmurs into my ear. My body shudders around his fingers as he slowly brings me back, lightly stroking in a soothing motion.

He guides me to the end of the bed and sits me down. His blue eyes are drenched with lust as he pushes my hair from my shoulders. "Comfortable?" he asks.

I nod, touched by his check-in, and turn my focus to the big bulge before my eyes. Eager to touch him, taste him, I unbutton his shorts and shove them to his knees. His gorgeous cock springs free, and I open my mouth to take him in, wishing I could swallow every inch but knowing it's impossible. Still, I'm not a girl to go down without at least trying.

"Oh God yes," he sighs, and I take his balls into my palm to massage gently. I move to the very edge of the bed and tilt my head as he slides in and out of my mouth. "So damn hot," he growls.

Moisture drips from the tip of his cock, and instead of licking, I dip my finger into it and rub it between my breasts for lubrication.

"Oh, yeah," he says when he realizes what I'm doing.

"I want you here," I say, and squeeze my breasts together. "Right here."

"Baby, I want that, too."

He bends and thrusts upward, easily sliding between my breasts, and I open my mouth to give him a lick with each motion.

"I must have died and gone to heaven."

If my mouth wasn't full, I'd laugh at that. He reaches behind me and fists my hair, and I steal an upward glance and catch the way he's watching the action in the mirror. Wanting to give him the best show of his life, I rub my breasts around him and suck him into my mouth. He grows harder, blood filling his veins, and that's when I know I've got him right where I want him, and my efforts are about to be rewarded.

"Khloe, I'm going to come," he says and tries to back up. But I squeeze my breasts harder, locking him in place. "Oh fuck, yes."

Now that we're on the same page, I loosen my hold, and he thrusts once, twice, and slides into my mouth the second he lets go. I lift my eyes to find Will's face twisted like he's in sweet agony as I drink him in. I swallow every last drop and let my breasts go.

When I do, he holds the back of my head and

brings my cheek to his stomach. I bask in the warmth, the soapy scent of his skin. Contentment falls over me as he rakes his fingers through my hair. It falls over my back, tickling me. My eyes close, sleep pulling at me.

"You're incredible, Khloe."

The hitch in his voice, the waver in his words, combined with the intimacy in his touch pull me wide awake. I glance up to see his eyes closed, his head tilted back. If I didn't know better, I'd think what just happened has touched him on a whole different level, too.

Too?

Oh, Khloe, don't go there.

CHAPTER FOURTEEN

Will

I wave to Vin from the window over the kitchen sink, and he waves back. A week ago I gave him a big bonus—a thank-you for taking care of the mirror installation—and it had put a huge smile on my face. Similar to the ridiculous smile I'm currently sporting as my mind goes back to all the fun Khloe and I've been having inside the bedroom and out. Sex with her has been phenomenal, and the way she opens to me, the way she's game for everything, is mind-blowing. I had fun adding to her to-do list, and we've rapidly been making our way through it, but there is one thing, one act, I didn't add. One I knew better than to add. This is sex, with no emotions, and the last thing I plan to do is make love to her.

We only have a little over one week left here in paradise before we go back to the grind of New York. I have no idea how the time went so fast. Then again, what is that old saying? Time flies when you're having fun. It's strange, because normally I'm happy to return home after being away for an extended period, but this time is different. I'm not sure I'm ready for this trip to be over. Oh, and why is that?

Khloe.

Simply put, I've become totally obsessed with the woman who is wide-open and honest in the bedroom. The same woman who is currently giving her time to a classroom full of elementary school kids. She's been spending a few hours there every day for the last week, and I've never seen her happier.

I step away from the window, take the steaks from the fridge and flip them over in the marinade. A laugh bubbles up in my throat. Here I hired Khloe to take care of the household chores while I worked, yet I've been cooking for her every night and damn well loving it. I especially love all the gratuitous moans she makes when she slides the fork into her mouth as she savors a home-cooked meal. The women I know love to eat at fancy restaurants, but Khloe prefers home cooking. Probably because before this week she lived on takeout pizza and nuked food. Something she confessed to me earlier in the week when she burned my eggs. Which once again takes my thoughts back to Granddad and why he hired her in the first place. Not that I'm complaining. I chuckle quietly to myself as I think about thanking the old man.

While Khloe and I have stuck to the rules for "fucking your assistant," it's getting harder and harder to watch her leave my bedroom after my lips have been all over her body, save for her mouth, and my cock has been inside her. Christ, I might be cashing in my man card here, but I kind of like the idea of her snuggling in next to me, and more importantly waking up next to her in the morning. I shouldn't be having those thoughts, but there doesn't seem to be a damn thing I can do to stop them.

I put the steaks back in the fridge and wander outside. Warm air falls over me, and I step up to the deck to glance at the pool and ocean below. Papers rustle on the table near the pool. Shit, Khloe must have forgotten her journal.

I make my way down the stairs and pick up her hard-covered journal. I consider opening it, but that would be a huge invasion of her privacy, and what kind of man would that make me when I go overboard to protect my own? I carry it into the house and deposit it on the kitchen table. Perhaps she's started work on that novel she's talked about. The sound of my car pulling into the driveway reaches my ears, and I nearly bolt to the door like a lovestruck teenager.

Jesus, I can't fall for her. I'm not looking for more, and neither is she. Even if I was, I've already proven I can't stay committed, and I'm not about to hurt her the way I hurt Naomi. Khloe put important rules in place for a reason, and that reason was to ensure we keep this physical. So I'd be wise not to get any notions that she might want more.

I force myself to walk slowly and pull the door

open to find Khloe jumping from the passenger seat, a wide smile on her face. Goddammit, I like her. I like her a lot.

"How was your day?" I ask, my heart picking up tempo at the mere sight of her. I let my eyes skim the length of her, admire her T-shirt and skirt, which both hug her curves.

"Amazing," she says. I can't help watching her mouth as she excitedly goes on to tell me all about today's lessons and how well the kids are doing. She never did tell me what her last job was, and it's not important, but I have to say, I think she's found her calling here. Would she like to stay on permanently? I mean, she could live in my house, use my car, and I could fly here often, maybe even move—

Jesus, what the hell am I thinking?

I shut those thoughts down quickly, and as she talks, I lead her into the kitchen. She comes to an abrupt halt, her voice falling off when she spots her journal on the kitchen table. She points at it, worry backlighting her brown eyes.

"What's that doing down here?"

I jerk my thumb toward the deck. "You must have left it by the pool earlier."

Her eyes widen. "I did? That's not like me."

"Guess you must have had other things on your mind." I step up to her, put my hands on her hips and pull her against my body. "Don't forget, these past couple weeks you've been doing all kinds of things that you don't normally do." I hope to pull a smile from her, but her startled expression doesn't go away. I soften my voice and ask, "Hey, are you okay?"

Her eyes flicker to mine. "Did you...read it?"

"Of course not," I say, a little offended that she thought I would. "I would never betray your trust like that, Khloe."

"Yeah, I know," she says, and it calms me. She visibly relaxes, and my mind briefly goes back to the way I betrayed Naomi's trust. It seems like a lifetime ago now.

She glances at me like she wants to say something, then closes her mouth again.

"What?" I ask, and step back to examine the way she's still staring at her journal. "Do you have the secrets to the universe in there?"

"Something like that," she says, and picks the book up. She jumps at the sound of her phone ringing in her purse. She pulls it out, checks the caller and casts me an apologetic glance. Over the last week, I've gotten used to that look, considering her phone has been ringing like crazy, and she'll only ever answer it in private. It's possible she's lining up work for when we return, but I don't ask, and she doesn't supply. That's rule number seven for "fucking your assistant." No exchanging personal information.

"I'll be right back." She darts upstairs, and my curiosity deepens. I fully understand and respect that whatever she has between those pages, and whoever it is calling her, is none of my business. It shouldn't bother me that she's being secretive and almost cagey.

Why then does it feel like she just kicked me in the teeth?

I light the barbecue, and when it reaches temperature, I place the steaks on the racks. Khloe has a strange expression on her face when she comes back downstairs and steps outside.

"Everything okay?" I ask.

She hesitates for a second, and I can't help but get the feeling, again, that she wants to tell me something. "Yeah, sorry about that." She jerks her thumb toward the kitchen. "I had to take that call."

I eye her for a second. "You sure you're okay?"

She briefly looks down, like she's considering that, and when her head finally lifts her demeanor changes. "Positive," she says, and gives me a big smile that's obviously forced. "Should I make a salad?"

"Already made." She turns to go back inside, and I follow.

"You always think of everything," she says, her smile genuine this time. Her dark eyes light up, "Speaking of thinking of everything, this girl at school told the funniest story…"

I smile to encourage her to continue as I grab the bottle of white wine I've been chilling, pour us each a glass and head back outdoors. The whole time Khloe is following me around and talking animatedly with her hands.

We both laugh at the end of her story, and she takes a sip of wine. That gives me a chance to pipe in. "Khloe, have you ever thought about becoming a teacher?"

Her brows pull together, and she stares into her wineglass. "Actually, no. I never considered it before. Never thought I'd like it."

"You're so good with the kids."

She smiles. "I'm having fun. I can't deny that."

Before I can help myself, I say, "You could always stay on here." Shit, what am I doing? "I mean, if that's something you'd want. You said you loved it here, and the school is desperate for help."

She sets her drink down and stares past me, like that thought had never occurred to her—and why would it?

"I...don't know." She flips her hand over until it's palm up. "My life...friends... New York."

"Sorry. I don't know what I was thinking," I say. "You once asked me why I didn't live here, and I gave you the same answer."

"Yeah," she says so quietly I have to strain to hear. She fiddles with the stem of her glass and takes a deep breath as she looks out over the ocean. "The truth is, Will, I don't really have a reason to go back." Without looking at me, she continues. "I lost my dad and have no family to speak of, other than my best friend, Steph. I used to think I was going to be a part of Liam's big family." Her smile is shaky, and her eyes are a bit glossy as she looks up at me. "I've always wanted that, you know. I always wanted to be a part of something great like that. I think I liked the idea of belonging to his family more than anything."

I step away from the grill and sit facing her. Sliding my hand across the table, I take her palm in mine and lightly brush my thumb back and forth over her flesh. "You should have that. Just not with him, because you shouldn't change yourself for anyone. You're perfect just the way you are."

She chuckles. "Look at that. The one guy who likes me the way I am is an anti-marriage recluse."

"Khloe—"

She holds her hand up to stop me. "It's fine, Will. I'm not asking you for anything."

And now why does it feel like she kicked me again, except this time lower?

"Anyway, I'm far from perfect, but thank you for the compliment." She gives a humorless laugh and glances at our enclosed hands. "Steph is in my corner, but…" Her head lifts. "But we could always visit each other, I guess." She looks at the ocean. "The people here are much nicer, more accepting." She shrugs. "I said there was no right man for me in Manhattan, but here in Saint Thomas you never know, right?"

An ugly burst of jealousy tightens my throat. The thought of another man's hands on her curvaceous body…hell no.

I swallow. Hard. And I try to sound normal when I say, "You're a beautiful woman, Khloe. The right guy for you is still out there. You just haven't found him yet."

"What about you, Will? You've locked yourself away in this villa. Do you really believe the cheating gene runs in your family?"

"I did a bad thing, Khloe. Now I'm paying for it. I deserve to pay for it."

"You made a mistake. People make mistakes, and most times they get to deal with them in private. What happened to you, *Starlight* broadcasting your mistake all over the newsstands, it wasn't fair. You deserve happiness. You're a good guy, whether you think so or not."

"Do you know something I don't?"

Her entire body stiffens. "What do you mean?"

Jesus, what is going on with her? Her body language is a clear giveaway that she *does* know something I don't. But what? "You said I'm a good guy. Many think differently."

"Ah…" She takes a sip of wine and meets my eyes. "Amelia told me everything."

Unease worms its way through my veins. "What are you talking about?"

"She told me you personally funded the new school. And the lunches that are delivered to the kids every day come from your granddad's resort."

I frown and go back to the barbecue. With my back to her I ask, "Why would she tell you that? That's not information I want out there."

"At first I thought you wanted to get the repairs

done on James's resort fast because it affected your bottom line, but you care about these people, don't you? You wanted them back to work for their sake, not yours."

"I don't like people knowing my business," I grumble.

She stands up, and when I turn to her, she walks over to me. Her palms lie against the sides of my cheeks. "Why don't you want people knowing about all the good you do?"

"I just don't like it. My business is my business."

"After the spread in *Starlight* it might—"

"I don't need adoration, Khloe. I just need privacy."

"You have so many secrets, Will."

"Don't we all," I say, and her lashes fall quickly, hiding her expressive eyes.

"I suppose," she says, then goes quiet for a few seconds. "Wait, we're breaking rule number seven here, and I know how important rules are to you," she says. She sniffs the air. "How are those steaks coming?" she asks, changing the subject.

"Medium-well, right?"

"You got it."

"Then we're good to go." I take the steaks from the barbecue and set one on each plate as she disappears into the house and comes back with a salad. But when she sets it down, I see that look on her face again, and I'm convinced she wants to tell me something but isn't exactly sure how. And I have a feeling I'm not going to like it.

CHAPTER FIFTEEN

Khloe

WE STAND BEHIND a barrier and watch the adult parade make its way down Main Street. Honestly, I've never seen a carnival quite like the one they throw here in Saint Thomas. Women dressed in pink boots, colorful bikinis, headpieces and fluffy angel wings dance down the street to the music of "Soca Kingdom." Another troupe comes behind them, and I gasp when I see the women bending forward, twerking, and the men holding their hips, simulating sex.

"Whoa," I say to Will, who turns and grins at me.

He playfully wags his eyebrows. "A little racier than you thought?"

"Definitely not the kind of parade I'm used to."

He jerks his head to the left. "Want to go?"

"Nope."

Chuckling, Will puts his arm around me, and the guilt circling my stomach jumps into my throat. For the past week, I've been making secret phone calls, gathering information. And just the other night, I finally got hold of Avery Roberts, the journalist who'd caught Will with his pants down.

I sort of told her I was doing a follow-up story, a small lie, and asked how she managed to get him in such a compromising situation. I hinted that I wanted something just as racy for the headline. She was reluctant to talk at first, but when she mentioned that she had a hatred of rich, arrogant men and I fully agreed, she loosened up a bit and admitted she once hit on Will and he stone-cold rejected her. That's when it occurred to me she was out for blood, and I was determined to get to the bottom of it. Those pictures had always felt a bit off to me, and now I know why.

The more we talked, the more she let slip, and I eventually learned she was behind the pictures—she'd personally set Will up to fall. Apparently, she'd contacted the girl who was to dance at Will's bachelor party and paid her off to slip a roofie into his drink. Later that night, the stripper had led him to the bedroom and left a window open in the back of the house so Avery could get in to take the illicit pictures.

The sheer horror of what she'd done—that she could destroy a good man's life on purpose—left me speechless, and that never happens to me. Avery hadn't just been out for a headline, she'd been out for revenge. As I mull that over now, my heart aches for the man and all he lost simply because some reporter wanted to get even.

As my stomach cramps, I once again try to figure out how to tell him. I can't keep that information to myself, but I'm not sure how to say it. I nearly blurted it out the other night when he was barbecuing, but something horrible and selfish had stopped me. I'm stupidly falling for the man—how could I not—and once he knows the truth, he'll go back to Naomi, the woman he's never stopped loving. I hate myself right now, and I have to figure out how to tell him because he's a good man, and he deserves the truth. He deserves the happiness he was denied.

My phone buzzes, and I unzip my purse to grab it. My damn heart jumps into my throat when the word *Starlight* lights up my screen. Crap, it's my old boss. I angle the phone so Will can't see it and shove it into the back pocket of my shorts.

"Aren't you going to answer?" he asks.

"No, it's not important."

He looks at me for a moment, his eyes narrowed, and I'm grateful when he doesn't push. In a few short days, we'll be headed back to the real world, and I'll deal with Benjamin then. For now, I'm going to ignore his calls. But I can't deny that I am curious. Why is he suddenly reaching out to me? Has he had a change of heart? Even if he has, I'm not going back to *Starlight*. I'd rather starve. But that won't happen for at least a couple of months. Assistant to Will Carson pays well. One of his rules is he never hires the same woman twice. But I wonder if he'd make an exception. Bend the rules for me.

Good God, girl, get it together.

He doesn't want more, and once he finds out he was set up, he'll be begging Naomi to come back.

Why, oh why, did I go and fall for him?

We watch the parade until the end, and when the crowd begins to disperse, Will puts his hand on my back and leads me down the street.

"How about we try some local cuisine?" he says as music blares from a band playing on the corner nearby and people bustle about. Will pulls me closer before I get lost in the hustle.

"Sounds like a great idea," I say, trying to push a little enthusiasm past the lump in my throat.

His eyes narrow in on me. "Are you okay?"

"Yeah, fine." I give him a little nudge. "Just thinking about what we might cross off the list tonight."

He laughs at that, and we make our way to the food tables. Will points out all the traditional food— everything from fungi, which is made with salted cornmeal, water and okra, to callaloo, a soup made from leafy greens, okra and meat. He stops at the table serving deep-fried pastry stuffed with chicken, beef, fish or vegetables. He rubs his stomach.

"Pâté. Mmm. My favorite."

"They look yummy."

"Want to try?" Since I can tell he does, I nod. "I'll grab us a couple," he says, and pulls his wallet from his pocket. He hands over a stack of bills and in return receives six different pastries. "There's a free table over there." He gestures with a nod. "Grab it, and I'll get us a couple painkillers."

"Painkillers?"

He laughs. "It's a local drink made with rum, pineapple juice, coconut and orange juice."

"All things I love."

I take the plate from him, weave my way through the loud, excited crowd, and drop down into a chair. I push my hair from my face and wonder how I'll be able to eat when my stomach is a roiling mess. I almost laugh at that. I feel as ill today as I did when I first met Will—all those years ago in the back seat of the car. The truth is, we've been having sex, and it's been great, but as I sit here, I actually miss his presence. I miss his tenderness, the gentleness in his touch. I spent my entire adult life taking care of myself, doing for myself, and this is all so…nice.

"I thought that was you."

I glance up at the sound of a woman's voice. "Bevey, it's so nice to see you," I say, and gesture for her to sit across from me. She readily accepts the invitation and sinks into the café chair.

"I'm so glad I ran into you. Chardane talks about you nonstop."

I smile at that. "She's a wonderful girl."

"I wanted to thank you for all you're doing." She makes a tsking sound. "It's a shame you can't stay on permanently."

"My life…well, New York," I say, and she nods like she understands. Once again, I think of the offer

Will made. I'm sure that offer will be rescinded once I tell him the truth and he goes and finds his true love. "If the circumstances were different," I say.

"Where is that man of yours?" she asks, and runs her hand over her pretty yellow-and-blue head scarf as she searches the crowd.

"He's not my—"

"Oh, girl." Her gaze flies to mine, and she waves a dismissive hand. "Don't even go there with me." She gives a big laugh. "I see the way you two look at each other." She leans in. "Between us girls, I've never seen the man happier."

"Not even when he was with Naomi?" I blurt out without thinking, and then slam my mouth shut, wishing I hadn't brought her up. I probably sound like a jealous teenager. Which wouldn't be too far from the truth. Except I'm a twenty-seven-year-old woman, and I knew what I was getting myself into when I wrote the rules for having sex with your assistant. I just never knew at the time Will was so sweet, loving and caring. I'd once told him I trusted no one. He'd said the same. Things have changed for me, and after everything we've been doing, is he capable of letting down his guard and trusting me?

Bevey taps a long finger on the table. "Not even with Naomi," she says with a slow shake of her head. "No one makes him smile the way you do."

My stupid heart jumps in my chest, and a smile I have no control over shapes my lips. My God, I must look like a fool.

Bevey laughs again, confirming my suspicions that I do look like an idiot. "That's what I thought. Girl, the first time you answered that door in that outfit, I knew you were going to give him a run for his money."

I cover my face. "I can't believe he makes all his assistants wear such ridiculous outfits."

"Excuse me?"

I drop my hands at the surprise in her voice. "I said I can't believe—"

"I know what you said." Her brow furrows, and she briefly looks down. "Who told you he makes all his assistants wear those outfits?"

"His grandfather, James. He told me Will had a strict dress code and that my closet would be full when I arrived. Why?"

She grins like she's privy to something I'm not, then lets loose a hoot of laughter. "That old son of a bitch, and two sizes too small at that."

"What?"

"Nothing. Ignore me, I've had too much sun."

She turns from me when a shadow falls over our table. "There you are," Bevey says, and stands to give Will a hug. He sets the drinks down and pulls her into his arms.

After a quick embrace, she says, "I have to get back to my table. Raising good money with my johnnycakes." She squeezes Will's hand and gives him a wink. "You take good care of this one, Will."

He frowns thoughtfully as she leaves. "What was that all about?"

I shrug and my phone rings in my back pocket. I continue to ignore it and take a sip of my drink. "Wow, this is delicious," I say, and try not to think too hard on what Bevey told me. She can't be right. Will can't be happier with me than he was with Naomi, right? He pretty much said he still loves her.

Will takes a bite of the pastry and moans. "You have to try this." He holds it out to me, and his eyes focus on my mouth as I bite into the pastry. For a second, I can't breathe or even chew. All I can do is stare back as heat and energy arc between us. My pulse picks up tempo, and I finally manage to chew and swallow.

"You've got..." He leans toward me and brushes a crumb from my lip, and before I realize what's happening, he's leaning closer, then his mouth is on mine. Tender, exploratory at first, tasting, testing. But when I lean toward him, he deepens the kiss, and his tongue tangles with mine. His hand slides around my head and he grips a fistful of my hair. We exchange hot, hungry kisses born of need and frustration, but he halts abruptly when someone catcalls and tells us to get a room.

He pulls back, and we're both breathless. Silence falls heavy, our heated gazes locked. I bring my finger to my kiss-swollen lips and touch them lightly, the burning imprint of his mouth still there, ruining me for any other man. I am in so much trouble.

"The rules," he says, his voice rough and gruff. "We broke rule number five."

My brain races, spins, and I work to quiet it. "Remember how we replaced your rule for not sleeping with your assistant with ten new rules?"

"Are you suggesting we replace the no-kissing rule with something else?"

"Yes."

"Okay, what do we replace it with?"

"No expectations," I say. He doesn't flinch, doesn't even bat an eyelash. If he wanted more from me, wouldn't he have reacted? Bevey can't be right.

"Fine," he says. He continues to stare at my mouth, and I resist the urge to squirm. What is going through his head? His gaze lifts slowly, and as the black in his eyes bleed into the blue he asks, "Want to get out of here?"

Before I can answer, he's standing and taking my hand. People blur around me as he quickly guides me through the crowd, and I'm not sure I've ever seen him so intense before. We get in his car, and less than ten minutes later, we're entering his villa. As soon as I step through the door, he locks it and pushes me against it.

"This mouth," he says, and runs his thumb over my still kiss-swollen bottom lip. "It's been making me crazy. I've wanted to taste you for so damn long now."

"Why didn't you?"

"Rules."

"Right," I say, barely able to fill my lungs as his entire focus falls to my mouth. Adoration, affection, worship dance in his eyes, and my heart crashes harder against my chest. I swipe my tongue over my bottom lip, and the groan that follows trickles through my body and settles deep between my legs.

I place my hand on his hard chest and slide it down until I'm cupping his swelling erection. His eyes briefly close, and I reach for his zipper, but he stops me. I frown, and he steps into me, scoops me into his strong arms and carries me to his bed. He sets me down on the edge of the mattress and steps back, his gaze roaming over me, a slow, leisurely inspection. There's a change in him, but it's so slight I wouldn't have noticed if I wasn't familiar with all his nuances. Over the past couple of weeks, I've gotten to know this man…have fallen in love with him.

"We go home soon," he says.

"I know," I answer, and hold my breath, praying he wants more after we leave paradise but knowing it's impossible. I fight the tears in my eyes, and while I should blurt out the truth and stop this before it goes any further, I can't. I want—need—this one last night with him.

But instead of asking more from me, his eyes scan my face, and he sinks to his knees. He lightly traces my chin and dips his head until his lips are on mine, tasting softly, exploring thoroughly. And I shut down my thoughts, wanting to enjoy this moment for what it is.

"Baby, you are so beautiful," he murmurs into my mouth, one hand pushing my hair from my shoulder to expose my neck. He runs a soft finger down my neck until he reaches my T-shirt. He tugs it from my shoulder and slides my bra strap with it. His lips leave mine and brush lightly over my skin, and goose bumps follow in the wake of his wet mouth.

I put my hands on his broad shoulders and touch him, my fingers moving over his skin in much the same way he's touching me. His mood is mellow yet deeply intense. Normally our sex is frantic as we try out new, fun positions. I have no idea what he intends this time, but I like this slower, softer version of him.

He nudges my arms and I lift them, knowing full well what he wants. He strips my shirt away and unhooks my bra. His gaze drops, and a quiver goes through me as he takes my breasts into his hands, leans in and presses soft, openmouthed kisses to my nipples.

My heart misses a beat and then another, and I try to swallow down the things this man makes me feel with every touch, every kiss, but this time I can't. I can't smother the love blossoming inside me, filling me up and making me whole again.

"Will," I say quietly, and his eyes lift.

"Yeah."

I swallow again and cup his cheek. "I…I…"

"I know," he says, everything in his gaze softening. But what does he know? How I feel about him? Will it scare him or… "Come here." He stands and tugs me to my feet. I go up on shaky legs, and he slides his hands around my body, cups my ass and pulls me to him.

His lips find mine again, and one hand burrows into my tousled hair. I grow wet between my legs as his tongue delves deep, tasting all of me, savoring, exploring until I'm moaning and arching my back, wanting more…wanting everything.

I slip my hands under his T-shirt, and his muscles clench as I spread my fingers, unable to touch enough of him at once. His mouth is at my ear, and the hungry sounds curl around me, take me to a higher state of passion. I go higher and higher until I reach a place where I'm free-falling without a net. Will I fall or will he catch me?

"I fucking love the way you touch me," he says, and releases the button on my shorts. He inches back, and my hands fall to my sides, a whimper catching in my throat at the loss. But then his mouth is on me again, my grumbles turning to a moan, as he gently swipes the soft blade of his tongue over my hard nipple.

"Yes," I moan, and move against him.

His lips trail lower, and he drops to his knees as he slides my pants down my legs, his heated breath scorching my skin. My hands go to his hair, and I fist it to hold on as he buries his mouth between my legs and pleasures me with soft, gentle licks that vibrate through my entire body. If he weren't holding me, I'd drop to the floor, a quivering mass of need.

"Oh, yes." Sensations are pulling me under, making it harder and harder to think.

He glances up, his eyes the darkest shade of blue I've ever seen. "I love how wet you get for me."

"I love how hard you get for me."

He grunts and gestures to the mirror. "You've seen yourself, right?"

My heart squeezes. "You always make me feel beautiful, Will."

"You are beautiful, Khloe."

I look in the mirror. The sight of Will on his knees, loving every moment of what he's doing to me, nearly pushes me over the edge. My muscles tremble, and Will chuckles softly between my thighs. And somewhere in the back of my mind, I register that my phone is ringing, but then it stops. It's not like I was going to drop everything and answer it anyway, and I'm not even sure Will can hear it over his hungry moans.

My thoughts shut down, go completely blank as he slips a thick finger into me, to tease the sensitive bundle of nerves. My hips involuntarily jerk forward, my clit smashing against his face.

"Will!" I cry out as I come, shattering completely. His tongue continues circling my sensitive clit as he slowly swirls his finger inside me. I wobble on shaky legs, and he backs me up until I'm on the bed, his mouth still between my thighs, his fingers still buried deep.

"I want you inside me," I whisper.

His head lifts. "Now there's an invitation I can't refuse." He stands, and I admire all six feet of hard muscles.

I point my finger. "Naked. Now."

He grins. "You are a woman who knows what she wants."

I'm about to roll over, but he puts his hand on me to stop me. "Center of the bed, on your back."

I eye him. Is he seriously telling me he wants to do this missionary? But that position is boring and has never brought me to orgasm. I open my mouth to protest but he stops me. "Do it, Khloe."

I do as he says, and he sheds his clothes, grabs a condom from the nightstand, and quickly sheathes himself.

"Open your legs. Show me your sweet pussy."

My thighs widen, and I slide a hand in between. He grins. "You can remove your hand. Your pussy is all mine tonight." He kneels between my legs, grips them and bends my knees, opening me even more. His eyes drop, roam over me. With the lightest of touches, he pets my pussy.

"So pretty," he says. I turn my head to watch in the mirror. "Eyes on me, Khloe," he commands in a soft voice. My head jerks back to his as his gaze bores into me, like he can see into the depths of my damn soul. I pray what he sees doesn't scare him off.

He strokes himself, and balances on one arm as he lightly rubs his crown over my clit. A whimper catches in my throat.

"Right here," he says. "This is where I need to be." His hips power forward, and he fills me with one hard thrust.

"Will," I cry out, and slide my hands around his

back. His eyes never leave mine as he moves in and out of me, sliding easily into my slickness. An odd little lump settles into my throat as his lips find mine. His kisses are soft, wet, a deeper hunger, like he's seeking something more, something we've yet to share. My hands circle his back, and my knees brush his sides as he thrusts, stretching my walls and stimulating me all over again.

His mouth leaves mine, and he kisses my nose, my eyes, my cheeks and chin before he buries his face in the sensitive hollow of my throat. I turn toward the mirror to see his body moving over mine, and there is a part of me that can't believe this man—one with a kinky side—is taking me in the missionary position.

But it's unlike any missionary position I'm familiar with. No, the way he's taking me feels anything but vanilla. In fact, it's deeply profound, incredibly moving, and I can't help but wonder if we're... making love...with our hearts involved. Could Bevey be right? Could Will be the happiest he's ever been, because of me? The way he's kissing me, touching me, loving me... I've never experienced anything quite like it. Is it possible that I was wrong, that there is a man out there for me and I'm currently in bed with him? If so, does that mean when I tell him my findings, he won't run back to Naomi?

He inches back and places a hand on my cheek, and his heat seeps below my skin, wraps around my trembling heart. His hips rock, rotate, his pelvis stimulating my aching clit, his eyes moving over my face. But there is something in that gaze, something that I've never seen before.

"Will," I say as I hold on to him harder, afraid if I loosen my grip, I'll tumble into the unknown and never be able to find my way back…from loving him. My flesh ignites, pleasure pinpoints between my legs, and all the air leaves my lungs as the most powerful orgasm I've ever had tornadoes through me. I gasp, clench around him and scratch at his back. His mumbled curses whirl around me, the room fading to black. Wetness coats him as he continues pulsing in and out.

"I feel you," he murmurs. He pumps into me, slow movements that prolong the pleasure and bring on another orgasm. My inner walls quiver, pull him in deeper, until he's touching me on a whole different level.

"Oh my God!" I cry.

"Khloe, look at me."

I crack my lids open, and our eyes meet and lock. His nostrils flare, and with the utmost tenderness, he cups my face in his big warm palm. That's when I understand why he wanted this position. He wanted to see my face, my expression. He wanted to see me, and he wanted me to see him as we tumbled over the edge together. As I stare at him, I struggle to breathe, to understand the true depths of what is happening between us. He lets out a loud growl and pulsates inside me. My lids feel heavy, but I don't dare blink or close them. I want to remember this moment, to memorize every curve of his face. But a second later, the vision before me is gone, and he's collapsing over my boneless body.

I link my fingers together behind his back, and catching me by surprise, his mouth is on mine again. His kisses are so slow, so achingly tender tears prick my eyes, and I squeeze my lids together to fight them back.

"This…" he begins, and lifts his head, his eyes searching my face. "This was everything," he whispers.

"Yes," I say, and he's kissing me again. A long time later, he rolls off me and pulls me to him. I snuggle into his warmth, breathe in his familiar scent, never wanting to break this moment between us. I trace his nipple, and his body quivers. His hand closes over mine, and he brings my fingers to his mouth, kissing them one by one.

I close my eyes and bask in the euphoria of post-orgasm bliss. My heart slows and sleep pulls at me, until something Bevey said jumps to the forefront of my mind.

"Will," I say sleepily.

"Yeah." His voice is as groggy as mine.

"Do you make all your assistants wear French maid outfits?"

"What are you talking about?"

My head clears a little more as my heart beats faster. "I'm talking about all the outfits in the closet when I arrived."

"Khloe, baby. I have no idea what you're talking about."

My mind races back to my meeting with James. What the hell is going on? If Will doesn't make his assistants wear the sexy outfits, who does? Surely to God, a ninety-year-old man couldn't be behind this.

You're perfect for Will.

"You said you thought your grandfather set Tate and Summer up, right?" I ask.

"Yeah, I think so," he says, his voice fading. He shifts in the bed until we're facing each other, and from the strange way he's looking at me, it's easy to tell he has something other than James and Tate on his mind.

He cups my face. "Khloe…"

Just then my stupid phone rings, and Will stiffens.

"Ignore it," I say, dying to know what it was he was about to say to me.

"It's been going off for a while. Whoever is trying to get a hold of you is not going to stop anytime soon. We'll talk after you answer it."

Before I can stop him, he's out of the bed and fishing the phone from the back pocket of my shorts. His gaze lazily goes to the screen as he's about to hand it to me, but then he goes still…too still. His mellow expression changes, his features morphing from confusion to anger, and in that instant, my entire life comes crashing down around me.

CHAPTER SIXTEEN

Will

"WHAT THE FU—"

My gaze goes from *Starlight* written in bold letters on the screen to Khloe as she jumps from the bed and nearly falls on her face when her foot gets stuck in the tangled sheets. Her hair is a wild mess, and her eyes are huge as she reaches for the phone and snatches it from me like it's on fire. It might as well be, considering someone from the magazine from hell is calling.

"It's not what you think," she says quickly as she puts the phone behind her back to hide it from my view.

"Seriously, Khloe?" I shake my head and almost laugh—manically. "I can't unsee what I've already seen."

"It's not what you think," she repeats, a measure of panic in her voice as she blinks rapidly.

The room spins around me, and I scoop my pants

and shirt off the floor. As I tug them on, I say, "Tell me what I think."

"Will," she begins, and reaches for her own clothes. She holds them in front of her body like a shield. "You think I'm working for *Starlight*."

My nostrils flare as I suck in a fast breath. "Are you?"

"I…used to."

"You used to?" I rake my hands through my hair, trying to wrap my brain around this unexpected turn of events. Khloe worked for *Starlight*? Of all the… I sift through the information, and in a calm voice that belies the storm going on inside me, I ask, "You're a reporter, then?"

"I…" She stops speaking and jams her teeth into her bottom lip, answering me without words. And this time, I do laugh, like a goddamn crazy man. Hasn't *Starlight* screwed with me enough already?

"Yeah, okay. You're a reporter. I get it."

"Technically, I am," she finally says. "But you don't get it."

I gesture to her arm, the one still behind her back. "Who's calling?

"Ah, it's Benjamin Murray."

I stare at her, incredulous, and my head rears back. "The fucking owner of *Starlight*?"

She waves her hand. "But it's not what you think."

"So you keep saying." What the ever-loving fuck. I stare at her, hard. "What the hell have you done?"

"The story…the story Avery did on you," she says as she comes toward me.

I back up. I can't be close to her right now, not when all signs lead to one thing. Khloe is here to get a story on me. "What about it?"

"None of it was true." She tugs on her T-shirt and slips into her shorts as she says, "I talked to Avery this week. She said she set you up."

"What are you talking about?" So those were all the secret phone calls? To Avery? Then why the hell is the owner calling her? None of this really adds up.

"She set you up. She knew the dancer and had her slip something in your drink. You were drugged and tricked, all for a headline."

I take a deep breath, hold it for a second as I process, then let it out in a loud whoosh. "And you were going to tell me this when?"

"I wanted to tell you, I just—"

"Wanting to and telling me are two different things," I blurt out, cutting her off as rage rockets through me.

"Will, listen. Benjamin wanted me to do a follow-up story on you—"

"Fuck." Anger spikes my blood pressure, and a headache begins brewing at the base of my skull. The bedroom starts to close in on me, each breath getting harder and harder to take. I gulp but can't fill my lungs. "I need air."

I step from the room, hastily make my way down the hall and open the back patio door. Outside, I lean over the railing and work to sort things through as I glance at the pool and the stirred-up ocean beyond. The sight is fitting, really, matching the state of my stomach.

Khloe worked for *Starlight*?

Wait, how do I know she doesn't still work for them? I briefly close my eyes and go over everything that happened between us since the second she arrived on Granddad's plane, sick with the flu.

"Will…" Her soft, tentative voice has me spinning around. "I wanted to tell you, but—"

"Why should I believe anything you say? How do I know you're not just telling me that to get me to trust you?"

"I guess…" She stops and shrugs, like she's working hard to come up with an explanation that's believable. "Maybe because of the time we spent together."

"That's it? That's all you've got?" I stare at her, my gaze moving over her face. "Why did you go see Granddad? After all these years, why did you suddenly pay him a visit?" I can't ask Granddad myself since he's yet to call me back. My stomach coils, and my shoulders are so tight the strain goes up through my neck. Khloe moves toward me again, and I hold my hand up to stop her.

"I went to see James because my boss wanted me to do a story on you."

I pinch the bridge of my nose, the tumblers all falling into place. "And you needed to find out where I was and what I was doing. I keep my private life private, my whereabouts mostly unknown, but you used your connections to get the inside scoop. Wow, I didn't see that coming."

She winces. "I can see how you'd think—"

"It's common sense. It's two and two." I swallow past the knot in my throat. "I can't fucking believe this." I turn around and stare at the ocean.

"Do you really think I'd do that, Will?" she asks, her voice low...offended.

She's the one who's offended?

I spin around and glare at her. "How did you talk him into it?"

"Talk him into what?" Her hand is as shaky as her voice as she sinks into one of the chairs at the small café table. I laugh again, thinking about all the private conversations we had at that table. All the things we shared.

"How did you get Granddad to hire you?"

"He offered me the job. I didn't ask for it."

I spread my arms, grip the edges of the handrail and squeeze until my knuckles turn white. "How fucking convenient." I shake my head. How the fuck did Granddad not see this coming? Not see *her* for who she really is? Oh, maybe because she's such a great con artist and has no trouble lying or doing whatever it takes—even sleeping with me—to get the headline. Granddad is old and slipping, which is probably why he didn't recognize a con for a con. But what excuse do I have? Why didn't I see through it?

Because you were too busy having the best sex of your life and falling in love.

Fuck me.

My gaze leaves hers, goes to her journal on the table. I'd caught her writing in it earlier this morning when I joined her for coffee. A sound crawls out of my throat as I gesture with a nod.

"Have you been writing about me?"

Her face pales. "I… Will… I…" She swallows hard. "Yes, but it's not what you think."

"Of course not. Do you seriously take me for a fool?"

"I don't think you're a fool at all," she says.

I consider that for a moment. "Yeah, well, then you'd be wrong. I am a fool." I'm a goddamn dumbass who was duped by a reporter. Again. If she's telling the truth about Avery, that is. I shut my eyes, my thoughts going to Naomi. "My life was ruined because of that article."

"I guess you can go and get her back now." Her voice is low, pain edging her words.

My lids open slowly, and when I see Khloe gripping the journal—clearly not wanting me to see what's inside—my stomach plummets. "You should go."

"Go where?" she asks.

"Back home. You should go, Khloe. No, you *need* to go. I'll call for a car. It will take you to Granddad's jet, and I'll arrange to have you flown back to New York."

"So that's it? You're just sending me away?"

Anger coloring my words, I say, "What choice do I have?"

She goes quiet for a long time. "I guess you don't have any. You see what you want to see. You hear what you want to hear. I obviously can't change any of that." She turns and is about to walk back inside the villa.

"The journal stays," I say in a hard voice that stills her. "It's in the nondisclosure agreement you signed, remember?"

She spins, gives me a long, hard glare, but in the depths of her eyes there's a profound sadness. What? Is she sorry she's not going to get the headline? For a second, I think she's going to protest, but then she tosses the journal onto the table, and her face tightens. "Just so you know, Will. You're not a cheater. You see, there is no cheating gene, and you *do* have staying power. You were just screwed over. Go ahead and take that information to Naomi. I'll confirm it for her."

"How do I know you're telling the truth about that?"

"Spend a few minutes thinking about the events of that night," she says.

I blink, that night a blurry haze. "I don't remember much."

"How much did you have to drink?"

"It was my bachelor party. I drank a lot."

"Let me guess, you felt like hell the next morning."

"Yeah."

"Different than a regular hangover?"

"Much worse," I answer, and she opens her mouth, only to close it again. "Go ahead and say what you want."

"It's none of my business, but why didn't you look into it? Why did you so readily accept that you didn't have staying power?"

I scoff. "Because none of the men in my family do."

"What about Tate?" She arches a challenging brow. "What about your brother? What about James?"

I laugh at that. "James had numerous women in his life over the years."

"Before your grandmother passed away?"

I look down, search my memory. "Well, no, not that I remember."

She takes a big breath and lets it out slowly. "I think you need to spend some time asking yourself *why* you just accepted what the papers wrote about you."

I fold my arms, lean against the railing. "What are you trying to say, Khloe?"

Her chin nudges upward, her intense gaze locked on mine, unwavering, challenging. "Maybe you didn't really want to marry Naomi."

Before I can voice an argument, she steps into the house and disappears. I stare at the spot where she'd been standing, my blood draining to my toes. Jesus, could she be right? Yeah, sure, Granddad had been pressuring me into marriage, but I loved Naomi, didn't I?

Then why didn't you fight?

Doors slam inside, and my brain shifts direction. I pull my phone from my pocket and make a few calls to arrange for Khloe to be picked up and for the staff to be waiting for her on the plane. I'm about to shove my phone back into my pocket, but once again I'm thinking about Khloe's parting words. Naomi was deeply hurt by my actions and deserves to know I wasn't unfaithful. While this truth won't change things between us—do I even want it to?—I pull up my contacts and find her number.

I turn to face the ocean, my world a goddamn mess. I swallow as my phone vibrates against my ear. It rings three times before I hear her breathy voice. "Naomi," I say, and spin when a bang reaches my ear. I turn to find Khloe standing there, staring at me. "What?" I ask.

Glossy eyes meet mine. "Never mind," she says, and as she darts toward the front door, I have half a mind to go after her. But she's a reporter who went undercover to take me down, right? Why is it that I'm suddenly not sure of that now? Spending time with Khloe reminded me I hadn't been living, only surviving. I loved talking to her, doing things with her, taking her to my bed and making sweet love to her, and she'd blossomed under my touch. She'd been so honest and open with me, and the look on her face after working at the school had been pure bliss. No one can fake that. And putting herself out there was all about her, not me. She was volunteering and helping out from the kindness of her heart.

As that thought rings inside my brain, Naomi's voice pulls me back. "Will," she says. "It's been a long time. I'm glad you called."

"We need to talk." I drop down into the chair, and run my fingers over the leather binding of Khloe's journal. A warm breeze washes over my damp skin as I tell her everything. We spend the next hour talking, getting caught up, and I hear a new lightness in her voice. As we talk I learn she's engaged, and I'm genuinely happy for her. She asks me about my love life, but I gloss over it. The woman I'm in love with played me for a fool. After a long time, a ding alerts me that there is another call coming through. I glance at the screen to see that it's Granddad. About time.

"Naomi, there is a call coming in I have to take."

"It was good talking to you, Will."

"You, too."

"I hope you can come to the wedding."

"I wouldn't miss it."

"I'll look forward to an invitation to yours when it happens."

I laugh at that, end the call and switch over to Granddad.

"Granddad, finally."

"What's going on, Will? I got a call that my plane is on its way back."

"I sent Khloe home."

A moment of silence, and then, "Why is that?"

"Because she's a reporter. She was here to do a story on me."

Ice rattles in a glass and then, "I think you're mistaken, son."

"I have proof, Granddad." I push to my feet and fist my hair, the gorgeous view below doing little to calm the storm raging inside me.

"What kind of proof?"

I turn, lean against the rail and catch my unkempt reflection in the glass door. "She's been writing about me in a journal."

"Do you have the journal?"

"In my hand."

"Open it."

"I'm not opening it. I don't want to see the lies she's written in there." Restless, uneasy, I pace to the patio door and back to the rail. "How could you have hired her?" I ask, not wanting to make him feel old and senile but needing to get to the bottom of matters.

"Because she's perfect for you," he says smugly.

"Perfect for me?" As his words sink in, my mind takes me to our conversation about the French maid outfits. What was that she asked? If I made all my assistants wear them. My gut tightens. "Granddad, tell me you didn't…"

"Didn't what, son?"

I swallow. "Did you arrange for all those French maid outfits to be in Khloe's closet?"

A hoot of laughter follows my question, and then what sounds like him slapping his leg. "That was Summer's idea. She's a brilliant one."

Holy fuck.

"You were…matchmaking?"

"Of course I was."

"She's a reporter. Did you know that?"

"Yes, boy. I knew that."

I shake my head and try to wake myself up from this nightmare, but no, I'm not dreaming. This shit is really going down.

"Then why did she keep it a secret?" I ask.

"I asked her to. I know how you feel about reporters."

"Then why her, Granddad? Why hire her if you knew how I felt about reporters?"

"She came to me to warn me that her boss wanted her to do an exposé on you, but she was fired because she refused. Just as well she left *Starlight*. Her dream is to write for the *New Yorker*. That place was only holding her back. But she's too proud, too much like her father to let anyone give her a leg up, even though she's talented."

My fuzzy brain spins. Wait, what was that she'd said about being out of work?

My boss wanted me to do something, and when I refused, he canned me.

Christ. I'd thought it was about sex. But it was because she'd refused to do a story on me? I grip the journal harder, my world sinking around me.

"Open the journal, Will."

I slowly peel the cover back and begin to read. I skim the page and read faster. My heart leaps into my throat. "Jesus."

"What's that, boy?"

"It's…it's all about me, all about my kindness and the community services I do here on the island. She wrote a whole article on me."

The sound of Granddad slapping his knee again reverberates through the phone. "I knew it."

"But I don't like my business known. You know that."

"Who says she was even going to publish it?"

A knock on the door reaches my ears, and my heart leaps. Has she come back?

"Someone's at my door."

"Go check. Might be her."

I hurry down the hall, pull the door open and find Bevey standing there, a plateful of johnnycakes in her hands. "It's Bevey," I say.

"Hey, don't sound so disappointed," Bevey says.

Ice clinks in Granddad's glass again before he says, "Tell her I said hello."

"I'm not disappointed. Come in. Granddad says hi," I say, and turn back to my conversation with Granddad. Even though Bevey is listening, I say, "I…fucked up. I said cruel things. I sent her away, and I don't think she's coming back."

"Then go fix this."

"How?"

"You're a smart boy. You'll figure it out."

Bevey follows me into the kitchen as I resume pacing. "But what if…what if she doesn't feel the same way about me as I do about her?"

"Oh, she does," Bevey says with a big smile.

CHAPTER SEVENTEEN

Khloe

IT'S BEEN A WEEK since I've returned from Saint Thomas, seven whole days that have felt more like four hundred and twenty-seven days and a whole bunch of hours and minutes. I haven't been sleeping or eating very well since coming home, and forget about functioning properly. Only problem is, if I don't pull myself together, I'm going to lose this temporary gig that's going to keep me afloat until I can secure a permanent position. I refused to deposit the check that arrived at my apartment and refused to take James's calls. The man had no right sticking his nose into our business. *Around Town Magazine* isn't where I ultimately want to work, but I'll take anything thrown my way. And I'm just filling in while one of the reporters is off on maternity leave.

It's funny, Will said to me that by the time I left Saint Thomas I'd know what I wanted and what I loved. He was right. It's hard to believe how my priorities have shifted. I didn't know what I wanted in life until I spent time in Saint Thomas. I think it would surprise everyone, Will included. But now Will thinks I was out to sabotage him, and he's back with Naomi, which means my dreams will never be fulfilled. Not in this lifetime.

Stupid tears prick as the bell over the front door jingles. I swipe the moisture away and glance up from my desk to see Steph bouncing in, a smile on her face as she checks the rows of desks in search of me.

"Over here," I say with a wave, and she bounds over to my side of the room. I lower my voice, not wanting to disturb those working close by. "What are you doing here?"

"I wanted to check out your new workplace."

"Well, I'm only here temporarily, so don't get used to it."

"Look on the bright side, you're not a pod person anymore."

I stand and take in her fashionable attire as I give her a hug. "Look at you. All dressed for your new position at the *Cut*. It's always been your dream to write about fashion and trends. I'm so proud of you. I told you that, right?"

"Only a million times." She jabs her thumb into her chest. "And this girl with the fancy new clothes and office wants to go out to lunch with her best friend."

I crinkle my nose. "I can't really—"

She cuts me off. "It's on me, girlfriend. When you're rich and famous, you can buy."

I snort. "Like that's ever going to happen."

"Maybe sooner than you realize," she mumbles.

I eye her. "Have you come off your meds?"

She laughs out loud, and I close my laptop and reach for my purse. "I could eat. I think. One condition. We don't talk about *him*."

At the mention of *him*, her eyes travel the length of me. "Have you been taking care of yourself?"

"Yes, Mom," I lie.

"Okay, I'll shut up, but you're ordering one of everything." I link my arm with hers, and we step out into the sunshine. People bustle by, one man with his face buried in his phone nearly mowing me down.

"I sure miss Saint Thomas."

"I bet you do." She steals a glance at me. "Do you think you'd ever go back?"

I give her a look that suggests she's insane. "Not now. What reason would I have?"

"I don't know. You said you loved working with the kids." Her eyes light up. "Hey, maybe you could get a job here teaching."

"Since it doesn't look like I'll ever write for the *New Yorker*, maybe I should," I say, even though, strangely enough, the *New Yorker* isn't where my heart is anymore.

"Why can't you do both, part time?"

I stop walking and stare at Steph. "Who are you, and what have you done with my best friend?"

She laughs. "Come on, before lunch I have to make a quick stop."

I glance at my watch. "I don't have a long lunch hour."

"Yeah, well. I think it might be longer than you realize."

I grab her arm. "Oh my God, please don't tell me I'm getting fired again."

"Come with me," she says, and I once again go over the few bills left in my wallet. I ate the Mentos in the bottom of my purse, so there goes my backup.

We step into a bookstore, and I furrow my brow. "What are we doing here?"

"Oh, you'll see." She takes my hand and leads me to the stack of newspapers. "I wanted to check out the papers."

"Don't you get like every newspaper known to mankind already?"

"I do, but you don't."

I grimace. How's a girl supposed to write for the *New Yorker* when she had to cancel her subscription because she couldn't afford it? Heck, I can't even afford the cheaper digital version. A saleslady walks by me, a grin on her face. Okay, why is she looking at me like that? I turn to see her switch the sign on the door from Open to Closed.

I nudge Steph. "We need to go. She must be closing up for lunch."

"Hang on, I heard there was an article on Will Carson in today's paper."

Blood drains to my toes. "Oh, God, no. Who wrote it?" Did Avery find him after I called her? If so then I'm the one responsible for whatever is written about him. I swallow and lean against the stack of books as my legs weaken.

Steph blinks at me. "Khloe, you've gone white."

"What was written about him? Oh, Steph, please tell me it's nothing bad. He's a good guy. Yeah, okay, he was a jerk who accused me of some nasty things, but I can see how it all looked to him. He doesn't deserve any of this."

"A jerk, huh?" The familiar voice comes from behind, and I gasp as I spin around and nearly sink to the floor. My gaze rakes over Will, who is dressed in a perfectly tailored suit, looking as handsome as he did the first day I met him on the plane.

"Will, I didn't—"

"You're right, though. I don't deserve any of this," he says.

I point to the paper that Steph is riffling through. "I…I don't know…anything about it." Wait, why is Steph so calm, flipping pages without even acknowledging Will or my burst of panic. What is going on?

"Will, it's not what you think."

"You keep saying that to me, and I have to stop you because you need to know what I do think. But before I say anything, you should read the article."

Steph's grin is wider than I've ever seen it when she folds the paper and hands it to me. My eyes go big when I skim the article—my article. Oh no, these are *my* words.

"Will," I croak out. "I never meant for anyone to see this. I have no idea how my journal ended up in the wrong hands, but—"

"What I think is that I'm the world's biggest idiot." Feet shuffle behind him, and before I know it, there are numerous people lined up watching us— including James. I recognize Tate, Summer, Brianna, Luca, Alec and Megan from the tabloids. What the heck is this, a Carson family reunion?

"What…what's going on?"

Will laughs. "Family. They don't know when to mind their own business."

I grip the edge of the bookshelf, the room closing in on me. "Will—"

"I don't agree with my granddad's meddling, and for the record, Summer was the one responsible for the French maid outfits." I glance past him to see a pretty woman with long strands of honey-blond hair piled on the top of her head. She gives me a small wave and coy smile. "But how can I be mad?"

"Mad? What? The article… I didn't…"

Will steps up to me and takes my shaky hands in his. And the second he touches me, tears fill my eyes. I blink through the haze, take in his handsome face, the way he's looking at me with pure adoration.

"I know you're an independent woman who likes to do everything herself, and that's one of the things I admire most about you."

"Thank…you. But… I just can't understand—"

"I submitted the article, Khloe."

My jaw drops, and filling my lungs with air becomes an impossible task. "No, you're a private guy." I shake my head hard. "You don't want anyone knowing anything about you."

"But your dream was to write for the *New Yorker*. Granddad told me."

As understanding dawns, tears spill from my eyes. "Wait, you…you did this for me? You put yourself out there, let the world know your private life… for me?"

"Of course."

But Naomi. After he accused me of trying to sabotage him, I'd run back to the patio to fight for him, to tell him how wrong he was about me, but he'd been on the phone with Naomi. He'd called her the second he sent me packing. So why is he doing this? Maybe because I told him the truth, and he wanted to do something nice to thank me? Maybe that's all that's going on here.

"Naomi," I begin quietly. "Did you get back what you had with her?"

"I'll never get back what I had with Naomi."

"I'm sorry."

"Don't be. I don't want that."

"You don't?"

"No, because you were right about everything. I didn't really want to marry her, and something better did come along."

Steph shrieks beside me, and I catch the way she's holding her hands in front of her face like she's trying not to shout. I make eye contact with every person standing behind Will. My God, why is his entire family here?

"Will?"

"This time, this time, Khloe, I'm not going down without a fight. When I said I didn't deserve this, what I meant is I don't deserve you. Not after the way I treated you. But if you let me spend a lifetime making it up to you, I will."

He pulls something from his suit pocket and drops to one knee.

"Oh my God," I whisper.

"I love you, Khloe. I think I fell for you the minute you boarded Granddad's plane all flustered and beautiful, and…your independent, wild self. Will you marry me? Will you make me the happiest man in the world?"

Our gazes meet and hold, and my mind races with everything that's happened—how much I've changed, how much my wants have changed.

"It's not what I want anymore," I blurt out, and the room grows so quiet I can hear the clock behind the counter tick.

He swallows so hard it echoes in the room. "Khloe, I'm sorry about everything. I'm sorry I didn't trust you. I'm sorry I jumped to the wrong—"

"The article," I say, and drop the paper. "You shouldn't have done that."

"I might have sent it to a buddy of mine, but he wouldn't have printed it if it wasn't great, Khloe. You did this on your own merit. Isn't that what you always wanted?"

"No, you don't understand."

"Make me understand."

I drop to my knees. "What you've done, exposing the private side of yourself for me, that's just about the nicest thing anyone has ever done for me, but it wasn't necessary."

Confusion fills his features, and the muscles in his neck are so tight I'm sure they're going to snap. "Isn't it your dream to write for the *New Yorker*?"

I shrug. "Used to be, but things have changed."

As his eyes roam my face, so lost and vulnerable, the love I feel for him bubbles to the surface. "Do you remember telling me that when I left Saint Thomas I'd know what I wanted and what I loved?"

My eyes drop to his pulse hammering against his neck. "What do you want?" he asks.

"My dream used to be to write for the *New Yorker*, but now I want to be with the children in Saint Thomas." His eyes light up. "I want to go back. I want to help, to be a productive member of the Saint Thomas community." I shrug. "And you know what, if I want to write the odd article for the *New Yorker* I can do that, too. Maybe I can even write the book I've always wanted to write."

"Bevey and the kids will be happy to hear that."

I cup his face, and my heart crashes against my chest. "You also told me I'd know what I love."

"What do you love, Khloe?"

"I love you, Will Carson, and the answer is yes."

Cheers erupt behind us as a huge smile tugs at his mouth and lights up his eyes. He lets loose a breath. "You know you had me scared there for a moment."

I grin at him. "And maybe for a moment you deserved it."

"You might be right." He takes the ring from the box and slides it onto my finger. I examine the huge rock for a second and lift my gaze to his.

"I love you," I whisper.

"I love you, too," he says, giving me a kiss so full of warmth and adoration that my heart overflows with all the things I feel for this man. "I'm so happy you decided to take the job in Saint Thomas."

"I realize you can't always be there with me." I cast a quick look at James. "You need to be close to family."

James slams his cane onto the floor. "Don't you worry, child. I'm not going anywhere soon." He taps his head. "Still as sharp as a tack." Everyone nods in agreement. "You two go live your lives. You're only a flight away."

"He's right," Brianna says, putting her hand on Luca's chest. "We live in Italy, and I see Granddad more now than when I lived in New York."

I pull Steph to me. "Everyone, this is Steph, my

best friend. My sister." I hug her. "Clearly she was in on all this, too."

James glances at Steph, checks out her empty ring finger. "I was wondering if you could do me a favor—"

"Oh, God, James, no," I say. "Your matchmaking days are done!" As everyone laughs, I inch away from Will and glance at his family. "Speaking of matchmaking." I glare at the men and women watching me carefully. "Who was behind this?" I wave my finger back and forth between Will and me.

"Uh, well," James says, and the rest of them shift from one foot to the other, all of them looking around the room sheepishly. I point my finger. "Let me just say one thing." My gaze falls to Will, who has a worried look in his eyes. I wink at him, look back at his family and say, "Thank you."

Before I even realize what is happening, his family is hugging and kissing me and introducing themselves as I'm passed from arm to arm. They even include Steph, and for that I'm grateful. Once the hugs are done, Will comes to my rescue.

He pulls me into his arms, places a soul-stirring kiss on my mouth and says, "Did I mention I come with a big, crazy family?"

I laugh and hug him. "I wouldn't want it any other way."

* * * * *

COMING SOON!

LET'S TALK
Romance

For exclusive extracts, competitions and special offers, find us online:

MILLS & BOON

THE HEART OF ROMANCE

A ROMANCE FOR EVERY KIND OF READER

MODERN

Prepare to be swept off your feet by sophisticated, sexy and seductive heroes, in some of the world's most glamourous and romantic locations, where power and passion collide.
8 stories per month.

HISTORICAL

Escape with historical heroes from time gone by. Whether your passion is for wicked Regency Rakes, muscled Vikings or rugged Highlanders, awaken the romance of the past.
6 stories per month.

MEDICAL

Set your pulse racing with dedicated, delectable doctors in the high-pressure world of medicine, where emotions run high and passion, comfort and love are the best medicine.
6 stories per month.

True Love

Celebrate true love with tender stories of heartfelt romance, from the rush of falling in love to the joy a new baby can bring, and a focus on the emotional heart of a relationship.
8 stories per month.

Desire

Indulge in secrets and scandal, intense drama and plenty of sizzling hot action with powerful and passionate heroes who have it all: wealth, status, good looks…everything but the right woman.
6 stories per month.

HEROES

Experience all the excitement of a gripping thriller, with an intense romance at its heart. Resourceful, true-to-life women and strong, fearless men face danger and desire - a killer combination!
8 stories per month.

DARE

Sensual love stories featuring smart, sassy heroines you'd want as a best friend, and compelling intense heroes who are worthy of them.
4 stories per month.

To see which titles are coming soon, please visit

millsandboon.co.uk/nextmonth

JOIN US ON SOCIAL MEDIA!

Stay up to date with our latest releases, author news and gossip, special offers and discounts, and all the behind-the-scenes action from Mills & Boon...

 millsandboon

 millsandboonuk

 millsandboon

It might just be true love...